Joyce Collin-Smith

OF FIRE AND MUSIC

km

Kempton
MARKS

www.kemptonmarks.com

A Kempton Marks Book

An Authors On Line Ltd. imprint

Copyright © Joyce Collin-Smith

Cover design by Karl Phillips ©

ISBN 0 7552 0504 9

Kempton Marks
19 The Cinques
Gamlingay, Sandy
Bedfordshire SG19 3NU
England

This book is also available in e-book format, details of which are available at www.authorsonline.co.uk

In Affectionate Memory of

Dame Flora MacLeod of MacLeod

Twenty Eighth Chief

and for her Grandson

John MacLeod of MacLeod,

Twenty ninth chief of

MacLeod of Dunvegan.

'High on mountain brows be thy stag-tryst."

BY THE SAME AUTHOR

Locusts and Wild Honey, James Barrie 1953 and Little, Brown and Co USA 1954.

The Scorpion on the Stone, James Barrie 1954.

Jeremy Craven, Hodder and Stoughton 1858 and Houghton Mifflin USA 1959.

The Wreath of Chains, W H Allen 1960.

Call No Man Master, Gateway Books 1988 and Editoria Siciliano, Brazil (in Portuguese) 1993.

Call No Man Master – Second Edition, Authors On Line 2004.

The Pathless Land, Authors On Line 2004.

CONTENTS

Chapter   **Page**

1	THE BOND OF MANRENT	1
2	ALASDAIR THE HUNCHBACK	14
3	THE LURE OF RODEL	30
4	BORRERAIG AND FIRST BLOOD AT DUNTULM	42
5	THE TOUCH OF THE FLAG	59
6	SUMMONS TO THE KING	69
7	THE FRANKISH MINSTREL	81
8	THE GENERAL BAND	93
9	THE PRISONER UNDER THE HILL	108
10	TORQUIL THE BLACK-HAIRED	121
11	THE LONG SWORD	135
12	THE OUTLAW	140
13	THE BASTARD CLAIMANT	152
14	THE WAR OF THE ONE-EYED WOMAN.	176
15	THE SOJOURN IN IONA	197
16	RETURN TO DUNVEGAN	211
17	THE ROYAL COMMISSIONERS	219
18	THE VENTURE TO LONDON	232
19	THE KING'S BOUNTY	246
20	THE FIRE AND THE MUSIC	252
21	THE UNCHARTED SEA	267
	HISTORICAL NOTES	280
	BIBLIOGRAPHY	284

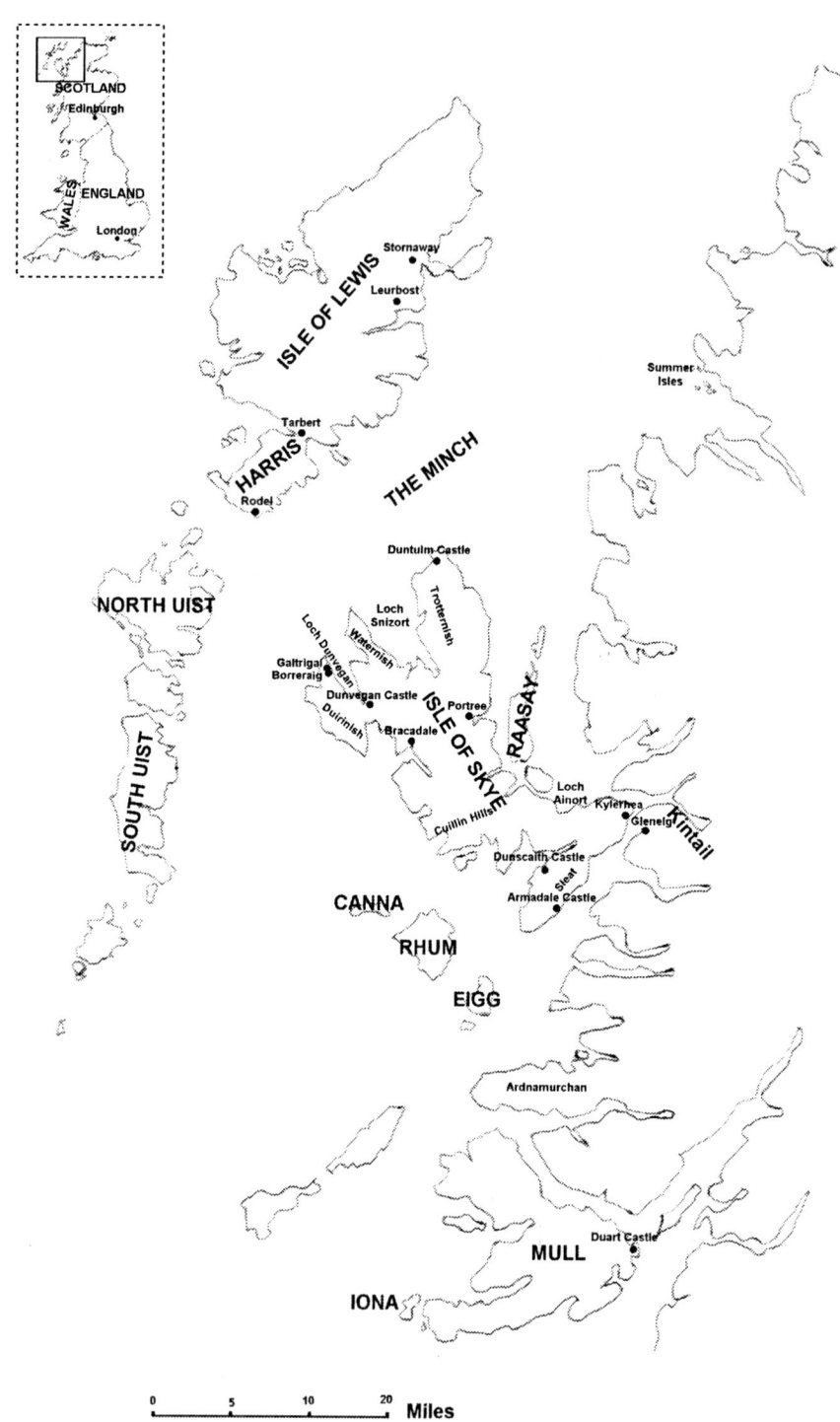

Chapter One

THE BOND OF MANRENT

The castle grew from the rock. It was rooted and grounded in the rock, living and breathing from the rock itself, seeming ancient as the seas that lashed about its bed, its walls rearing upwards to the eternal skies. Mist swirled about those walls, eddying in gullies within the courtyard and uncovered passageways, moist and cold, clinging subtly to the rocky faces and the granite slabs. In rock it had its being. The rock lapped up warmth by day and in steady summer heat and held it until the night came down. Rock was its nature and its heart was very old.

Iain MacIain lay face down, splay-legged across the rock within the curtain wall, heavy with the weight of his own exhaustion, in deep sleep. The ragged remnants of an old plaid were up round his back and his scarred legs and skinny buttocks were completely bare. He had once had a saffron shirt to wear beneath his plaid, but that had gone long since. His long-limbed frame was bony and hard, carrying not a mite of surplus flesh. His thick hair fell in unkempt wads across his shoulders, matted with dirt and blood.

MacAskill stood arms akimbo, grinning at the sight of the young stranger, nakedly, defencelessly displayed. He kicked him and turned him over, yelling

"Sorner!"

Iain MacIain drew up his legs, scrambled and stumbled to his feet, awake and shaking, eyes huge and dark with sleep. Sorner? I am no *sorner*, no sojourner of ill-repute to be kicked at and shouted at and mocked. He doubled his fists. But MacAskill laughed, flung an arm round his shoulders and called him by his proper name.

"I'm away to wash myself. You would do well to come with me, in case the Chief MacLeod sends for you later and finds you in this state."

Iain pulled his torn plaid down, groped for his rawhide belt and fastened it and in silence went after the young man.

The way was down a long narrow flight of steps cut deep into the face of the rock, past a well which supplied drinking water from a strong clear spring, inside the rock itself, and down to the guarded sea gate that opened straight onto the boulders below the castle.

Waves beat high here in winter and great seas would pound immediately beyond the door. There was no other entrance to Dunvegan Castle, and because of the narrow and tortuous stairs within, it was said that a single armed man could defend the island stronghold against all comers.

There was a clansman on duty as cockman at the sea gate. He and MacAskill buffeted one another in seeming anger before he would allow the heavy bolts to be drawn back, for it was the Chief's rule that the gates were not opened before sunrise.

In these days when King James' men might descend at any time on the island castles in the Hebrides, and drag off a young chieftain, or a gentleman and his sons, or a few fighting men to be held hostage as an indication of the strength of the crown of Scotland, it was never safe to be without an armed watch on duty day and night.

"His Grace the King may *say* he is only patrolling the Isles to keep the Island clans from fighting one another," MacLeod had said after one of these sorties. "But it seems to me it is no less than the spirit of the clans that he is really trying to tackle." A man o' war had run right up into the mouth of Loch Dunvegan and stayed there for a day, swinging at anchor menacingly across the fairway, so that all the household were on tenterhooks throughout the hours until she sailed away. "The King fears our independence. He hates our sovereign rights."

"Or our wilfulness," his son William answered, laughing with relief now the ship had gone. "He knows we shall have our own way in our lives, no matter what he wishes...if we can. He will have a mighty task to subdue *us*, I'm thinking. How many years now since they declared the Hebrides to be part of the state of Scotland? I'm thinking it's a long, long time since King James IV called the Lordship of the Isles forfeit to the Crown, in great-grandfather's day. Yet here comes King James the sixth of his line still trying to bring us to heel like whipped puppies."

"And still feeling our teeth in his backside once in a while, too!" William's young brother Rory interjected cheerfully.

Tormod MacLeod chided his two sons for their levity. The matter was too serious. Too much blood had flowed, and would flow yet and too many lives be forfeit in this struggle. They are young and think with their hearts and not with their heads, as all youths do. As I did at their age. Time enough later for them to think with their heads as well,

2

he supposed, dismissing them. He turned to his clerk, and made his mark on a document where the pointing finger indicated.

The mist was lifting and the lightening sky outlined the hills and the distant Cuillin mountain peaks, as MacAskill and MacIain ran barefoot over the boulders and the shingle to the water's edge. In the foreground MacLeod's Tables, two heather-crowned and flat-topped hills, loomed up across the width of the loch and the boggy pasture beyond. It was said that the old Chief, Alasdair the Hunchback, had once taken King James V up to the top of the higher one, to dine by the light of flaming torches held by tall clansmen, under the stars, to fulfil a rash boast made at Edinburgh that he had a finer table and bigger candlesticks than any at Holyrood.

Iain glanced down the curved length of the sea loch, with its scattered rocky islands, light-touched and empty, where only sea birds lived…and in Summer months, the grey seals which came south from the Arctic regions with the changing of the seasons, and settled within the mouth of the loch and within reach of the Western Sea.

An oyster catcher - the Page of St Bride, as the islanders called it - swooped and touched the rippling surface of the water, its long red beak extended, and rose with its shrill call that echoed in the morning silence back and forth from the end of the rocky inlet to the turfy cliffs and against the castle walls.

On windy days, up this long neck of water, under the high cliffs of Galtrigal and Borreraig, would come the galleys and the birlinns that bore the men of the Hebrides about their business in peace and war. But now in this early Spring morning, only a single small *curragh* of stretched hides, with two men in it, was visible far up the loch, turning quietly three times sun-wise, in accordance with custom, to bring the blessings of the day on the fishing.

The wet stones felt cold to the feet at this early hour, and the sharp tang of the morning caught at Iain's lungs and made him sneeze. He leapt downward to the tide's edge, and hesitated a moment at the thought of the shock of the water on thin limbs.

MacAskill took his plunge from a rocky ledge, yelling and spluttering with excitement and delight as the cold engulfed his well-fleshed body. "Come down with you! Come in! It's fine."

MacAskill's father was Constable of the castle, and for generations his clan had held a position of some trust and privilege with the clan MacLeod of Dunvegan and Harris, serving him and his line here in Skye and throughout the island territories. *He* had not known, as Iain had, what it was to go hungry and homeless, cast adrift, his own clan broken in warfare, a known "broken man", who must of necessity take shelter with one of the stronger clans for the sake of earning his bread and meat and a place to sleep at nights. The MacIains had lost their stronghold at Ardnamurchan on the mainland long since, and the ragged remnants of their tribe had been growing less year by year. Sorner, indeed! All manner of renegades, ruffians, outlaws were known by that title of "sojourner."

But I have no regret for entering into a bond of manrent with MacLeod, thought Iain MacIain. No regret yet. I shall eat well, and if I defend myself as I did in the rough and tumble after last night's feasting, I shall survive. Doubtless I shall survive.

He unfastened his belt and pulled off the worn and tattered *breacan feile* - the plaid - and waded naked into the water.

He was a tall, well-built, fair-skinned young man, with the blood of the Norsemen in him and the blue eyes and high cheekbones that declared his ancestry. But, his features were bony and angular, his mouth and chin mature and firm in their expression. His hair curled low on his neck and on his temples.

He would hack the long strands off with a dirk later, for they had grown long enough to be irksome, and trim his growing beard. The water struck chill to his bones, but he drew in his breath and took pleasure in the morning, striking out with a long dog-paddle stroke, then turning and kicking and splashing back into the shallows.

He stood up in water reaching to his thighs, and washed his face and body and unruly hair. There was blood on his temple and a long weal down one cheek where a gang of young toughs had set upon him outside MacLeod's great hall last evening, when everyone was boisterous with wine or home-brewed bland, a potent drink made from long-fermented whey. The salt stung the wound, but hard-schooled to discomfort, he thought nothing of it, as he washed the dried blood away and kneaded his scalp to clean his head.

The sun rose above the distant uplands and touched his naked flesh with the benison of its rays as he stood dripping, drying, his wet hair curling and pulling, gilded with the weight of light-filled water drops.

MacAskill was pulling on his tunic over his yellow shirt. He called to MacIain that he was going off behind the boulders for a few minutes, and disappeared from view. Iain MacIain waded out. Ankle deep, with the water rippling across the stones, instinct made him pause and look about him sharply. A sound, a movement among the rocks, and someone appeared close at hand, stooping low, moving and gathering something at the tide's edge. A girl from the castle. A young lady.

Getting a handful of *carrageen* seaweed here and there, pulling it up wetly and dumping it in the basket she held in the crook of her arm. Carrageen for gruel for the chief's children, he supposed.

Defenceless, his retreat cut off, he stood in the water agitatedly. She lifted her skirts, intent on her task, showing her bare thin legs. Her hair blew outwards in the wind, not held neatly in a maidenly snood, but wild, unkempt and free. Then when she stood up she saw his naked body. She stood still, expressionless. She raised her eyes to his, then looked away, and back again, and saw him cover himself with his hands, with an anxious look. Immediately she laughed, full and frankly, showing her teeth and tossing back her hair. Then gathering up her skirts she ran and leapt away from him towards the sea gate and the safety of the castle.

MacAskill, reappearing, forestalled her, making a grab at her hand and her waist and whirling her round towards him with a whoop and a smacking kiss as she tried to duck away.

She hit out at him with her basket, wrenching herself from his grasp with a sharp anger.

"Away with you, Master MacAskill! Let me go."

"Well, lady, you do ask to be attacked. Look at you now, outside the curtain wall at dawn, alone, unshod, your hair undone, your laces all awry." He pulled at her bodice with his fingers, loosening it. "What can MacLeod be thinking of to let his prettiest daughter run so free? And with the likes of me around, for you to deal with all unaided." As he spoke he manoeuvred himself between her and young Iain, who seized his garment and pulled it round his damp limbs. "And a naked stranger making the very water boil with his own heat at the sight of you," he said over his shoulder.

Iain burned with annoyance and shame as he fastened his belt, at the mocking note in MacAskill's laughter and turned, then came back slowly over the rocks, watching his feet as though minding where he trod, and went to pass them by.

The girl looked after him curiously. Then called to him "You are the sorner who took the bond of manrent with my father?"

He stopped and nodded, looking at the ground.

"What brings you to Dunvegan, Sorner?"

He raised his eyes, hostile and proud.

"I must eat. I must earn my bread."

She looked at him straightly, eyeing him up and down. "But why to Dunvegan? You come from a mainland clan? You are not an islander?"

"Since Sir Donald of MacAlsh sacked my father's stronghold at Ardnamurchan and destroyed us, we MacIains must live as best we can," he said. "I found myself in Skye, and so…"

"Your clan was always meddling in affairs too big for you," she said quickly. Her face was thin and pointed and her wild hair blew across her cheek. She flicked it back. She had no great beauty of features, but such life, such colour in her cheeks, and her eyes were so deep a blue that one thought the waters of the loch on a May day had been poured in them. What mattered any imperfections, with such eyes as those, he thought, bewitched by her. "It was in the fighting when the Lewis rose, that your clan was broken, wasn't it?" she asked. "I learn my history from the *seanachie* and the children's old nurse," she said. "The men of the Lewis fought for Donald Dubh, the Pretender to the Lordship of the Isles, didn't they? And the Earl of Argyll called your kinsmen out for the King. And Sir Donald of MacAlsh attacked and well nigh killed every man of you and destroyed your house."

"The *seanachie* and the children's nurse teach well. But it is an old tale now," MacIain said. "I can't remember the house of my family… what there is left of it, and I don't expect I shall ever see it again. It all happened in my father's young manhood."

"There seems to have been more trouble over the Lordship of the Isles than over any matter in all history," she said. "Now there is no Lord of the Isles, why can't men let it be, and obey King James, and live in peace?"

MacAskill snorted.

"How like a girl, to put all history in the shell of a nut, and dismiss all matters of honour and chivalry and pride of clan and ownership of land and property…"

"Men will be always fighting. Men should not fight," she answered seriously, "but live in peace as brothers as our Lord and Saviour bids…"

That is fine for you madam, MacIain thought. Your father's house is safe enough. Here in Skye the strong clans were the MacDonalds of Duntulm, who held all the lands to the north by force of arms, and Sleat in the south by charter of the King. And MacLeod of Dunvegan and Harris, whose family had lived in the castle on the rock since their ancestor Leod the Norseman had landed there three hundred years before, and taken a Celtic bride, and made her lands his own.

You might think differently if you were such as I, he thought, sheltering wherever the day's ending may happen to find you, in rocky corry or cave or ruined cottage or castle, knowing no softer bed than boggy turf, or at best the heather uplands. He had no memory of a better bed than the heather, and often in discomfort or cold, he had thought of warmer nights, plaid-wrapped, upheld among the springy stalks but always sleeping lightly with knife at hand in case of sudden danger. There were many lawless gangs and renegades roving the Highlands in these unsettled times, and there was no safety outside castle walls.

"So you have bound yourself in fealty to MacLeod?" the girl said, as they all three started upwards. "You are not a serving man, though, are you?"

"My father told me to take a bond of manrent with MacLeod or MacDonald. He said it before he died. He died of cold and lack of food and a knife wound in his foot that went bad last winter down in Strath. I promised him. He thought it for the best, and it eased his mind at the last, to make me swear to do it."

"If all men listened to their fathers and all girls to their mothers, there would be little courage shown and few chances for adventuring," MacAskill said.

"And the peats would never be cut, for warnings of wet weather, and the galleys never put to sea for fear of storms," said the girl.

"And all good men would die safe in their beds, with the blessing of the priests…and at peace, as men should, madam," MacIain answered. And added: "If they had beds to die in."

"And why did you choose MacLeod?"

"Well, MacKinnon of Strath has little strength. And Duntulm has a black reputation, so men say. I was not drawn to MacDonald of Clanranald. A young man *must* fight to prove his strength and manhood," he told her earnestly, "and if I must die in battle for another man's causes, I would as soon it be MacLeod. There are strange tales told of MacLeod of Dunvegan and Harris. They say fairy blood flows in your veins and there is nobility and greatness in you. They say you are the clan of fire and music. They say you have a fairy banner that will save your clan in battle if the day goes against you. They say it was waved at Trumpan in the old chief's time, and earlier at the battle of Bloody Bay. They say fairy forces came to your aid and drove the MacDonalds back into the sea."

He glanced sideways at her to see how she looked as he spoke of the fairy flag and the tales he had heard told around the peats at night. But she made no answer to him. "Even if it's not true…I would as soon serve MacLeod of Dunvegan and Harris as serve any man," he said.

As they went up the sea stairs a head appeared over the battlements and a voice called "Roddy MacAskill! Your father wants you up in the hall. The Chief has orders for you. The boats are to be got ready. We're away to Rodel."

"God save us, what for?" MacAskill said, and ran up with all speed. The girl went up after him, the basket of carrageen swinging from her hand and dripping water across the courtyard as she went.

Iain's stomach was empty and he looked about him to see if anyone was eating. He supposed the fighting men and the castle servants did not normally eat with the chief and his family, though they had done so last night. There was a bearded, shaggy-headed little man sitting on a stone seat in the sun, and thinking he looked harmless, he went and stood near him.

"You'll be wanting your victuals, then?" the little man said, not raising his eyes from the task which occupied his hands. An old pair of hand-made *brogues* lay beside him on the seat, the soles coming away from the uppers and holes where the big toe should be. He stuck out his tongue as he struggled to thread a long thin leather thong into the eye of a bone needle. "Oh-aah. There," he said squinting at it, and getting it through at last. He took up one of the roughly-made shoes and turned it and looked at it. "You'll be hungry," he said.

"I am that."

"The cook will call out when the food is ready. Sit you down."

The young stranger sat and looked about him. "Who was that girl?" he asked at last, wanting to talk about her.

"What girl?"

"Why, the one who came in with the *carrageen*."

"Mistress Christiana. Don't be losing your heart to *her*, young man. She is not for you."

"I only wondered."

The little man turned his head and looked at Iain, screwing up his eyes as he had screwed them up to thread the needle. "She will wed another man," he said.

"How do you know? Is she betrothed, or given in handfasting?"

He gave a chortling cackle, shaking his shaggy head, and bent again to his task. Inexpertly, with difficulty, he thrust the needle into the soft shoe. The rawhide was sewn with the hair outward, and he fiddled ineffectually to find the needle's point and pulled it through and pushed it in again in another place. "Och ay, well. That will have to do, I reckon. At least they'll keep the cold from my feet a while longer."

He looked at his handiwork glumly.

"I'll do it if you like," Iain offered. He had made himself shoes this way, in his father's days, but since then he had not bothered but had gone barefoot like many young men and boys. He took the shoe, thrust the needle back and forth strongly, and with big, cobbling stitches pulled it tight where sole and upper had parted and over the holes in the toes. He handed it back.

"Thank you," the little fellow said. He pulled the one shoe back on to his horny foot, and sat with the other foot bare, gazing in front of him.

"Does the other one need doing?"

"Ah." He handed it to Iain, and sat with hands on splayed knees, seeming lost in thought. "It's a sad day," he said, sighing and shaking his head. "A sad day when he who unfurled the fairy standard sees no longer the silken folds stream outwards on the hilltop, in the wind from the sea. Now he sees only the pit. Only the deep, dark pit where the bones of dead men lie. "Ah me, a sad, sad day."

Iain stared at him. The little man seemed to be rambling, as MacIain's father had done with the fever, when his wounded foot swelled up and turned purple and went bad. Before he fell asleep, and died. But as the young man looked wonderingly, the little fellow seemed to come back as though from a far place. He drew himself up, took the finished shoe and pulled it on and stamped his feet appreciatively.

"Thank you, lad. You've done me a good turn." He looked at the mended brogues with pleasure. "They'll bear me to the grave, he said.

As the serving wench was pouring porridge into the bowls on the long, rough table, word went round from one to another that Vic Mhurichie, the standard bearer to the clan, had died two days ago. Macleod had had news from Bracadale, where he had lived.

The chief and his family would all be going over to Harris for the burial in the monastery at Rodel which Macleod's father, Alasdair the Hunchback, had built. And where he lived still in semi-retirement as self-appointed Abbot.

"That will be an outing worth going on," Morag the round-faced serving maid said. "I wish I could go, but they won't take us, I reckon."

"I've never been to the Outer Isles," said Iain "I've only seen Harris and the Lewis from the hilltops on a clear day."

"Well, *you* might manage to go," she said, giving him a thump on the back with her forearm, as she passed behind, handing out hunks of meat and small round loaves. "If you are quick and willing, and get down to the quay and help launch the boats, you never know. Have you heard of poor old Vic Mhurichie, then? And how he unfurled the standard down at Trumpan?"

"Why someone out in the yard spoke of it only this morning. A little man whose shoes I helped to mend."

"That'll be Dun Kenneth!" she laughed. "He told you, did he? He knows things before they happen, that one. He has the second sight. He carries a black stone the fairies gave his mother for him, and with it he sees the future."

"He is often right," said the cook, wheezing as he sat down. "Why no one had heard the news this morning…only that MacLeod was going to Rodel. We did not hear why till this few minutes ago."

"Does MacLeod really have a fairy flag?" Iain asked doubtfully. "And Dun Kenneth a fairy stone? On the mainland people think such tales are just the foolish chatter of ignorant men who know no better."

"Do you say so?" roared a huge clansman, with a rough plaid of natural homespun over his shoulders. He leaned forward over the board, breathing noisily. "'Is that *so*?' Do you *say so* indeed?" he looked fierce and strong, with beetle brows, though he was clearly aged.

"Now Big Finlay, eat up and don't go picking a quarrel with a young stranger who does not know any better," the serving girl said to him. "Here's your brochan, now. Eat it, since you have no teeth left and can't eat the meat."

Big Finlay of the White Plaid took up his bowl and supped from it noisily, then banged it down on the table and ran the side of his fist across his mouth. "Well, I was there, boy, see? The Battle of the Broken Wall, men call it now. For at the end of the day we hurled MacDonald and his men along below the dyke at Trumpan and tumbled the stones from the wall down on top of them where they lay. Aye, we left them there to rot. We left their carcases to the ravens and the wind."

Several men groaned and coughed and told the big chap to hold his tongue, for they had heard the story a thousand times before, growing better with the years. It was a long, long time ago, in the old chief's time…when he was a warrior still, and before he became hunchbacked from a battle-axe wound between his shoulder blades. And before he took to living like a monk at Rodel.

"It was I who gave the warning that MacDonald was coming," Big Finlay persisted. "I was right young then, a young, hearty lad with a fine pair of lungs in my chest. I was out fishing in my curragh, off Dunvegan Head when I spotted them coming out of the morning mist.

10

A great fleet of galleys, with their sails flapping against the masts, and men rowing to give more speed until the wind should rise. I got ashore as quick as I could, and climbed the great cliff at Galtrigal and ran along the headland calling the chief. 'MacLeod!' I called. 'MacLeod! MacDonald of Clanranald and all his men are coming to kill you sir!' Aye, I shouted right enough. I called so loud they heard me a full seven miles away, so men said."

There was a commotion on the stairs, and voices shouting orders and bare feet running down. Everyone got up from the table save Finlay White Plaid, too engrossed in his reminiscences of long ago to respond to any new adventures that the years might bring. "And when the day went against us, the chief ordered the flag to be brought. It could only be unfurled thrice in battle before it would lose its power, so they said. It had been unfurled once before, at the Battle of the Bloody Bay, and since then we'd had it afore us many a time, but always folded and furled with silken cords and kept safe by Vic Mhurichie and his family between whiles. It was their duty, see. Always had been. All that family were always the standard bearers for MacLeod and his line, just as MacCrimmon and his family are always the pipers. Well, no man ever thought to see it opened out, not in our time. But on that day…"

"Did it bring fairy help?" Iain asked.

"It brought help. It brought help right enough, as we knew it would," he said. He nodded solemnly.

"Away with you, Sorner, if you want a chance to see the galleys sail at least," said young Morag the serving wench, thumping him again and laughing. "Never mind old Finlay. Time enough to hear his stories when there's nothing better to do. He's always here, and always talking, aren't you, Grandad?"

Iain jumped up, and ran down the steps. It was an exciting sight down at the water's edge, where two galleys and a birlinn tossed at the little quay, moving like restless horses on the rising tide. The men were settling at their oars, others scrambling in and out, tossing in bales and baggage, unfastening ropes, unfurling great speckled hempen sails and running them up against the masts, holding them fast there with shouts and cries, lest the wind bear them off before all was ready. There was a stiff breeze now, and the slap-slap of water against the boards. Much noise and bustle and confusion as though it were a festive day instead of a day of mourning.

Iain lent a hand, loading the foremost vessel with clothing for the chief's family and food for all, for there would be little to be had in the monastery and the arid countryside surrounding Rodel. Crops did not grow well in the rocky soil at the southern tip of Harris. There would be little bread and meat to spare at the monastery.

When everything was ready, there was a pause and everyone looked back and up towards the castle, and down along the loch by turns, falling silent, waiting.

"The chief will not come down until the funeral vessel from Bracadale is sighted," someone said. "It could be a while yet."

"The messenger who came overland said she sailed on last night's tide. We'll see her soon, for sure." The boatman shaded his eyes and looked again.

Because the Isle of Skye consists of long wings of land each jutting out into the sea in different directions, no part of its fifty miles in length is more than three or four miles from a long inlet of sea or the open coast. For some journeys the sea would be the quickest highway, while for others, a messenger in haste would do best to take one of the sturdy island ponies that went unshod through the heather and the corries, and ride overland. From Bracadale was a long way round by sea.

Suddenly the clear note of the bagpipes played by MacCrimmon sounded up above. All talking stopped and everyone was silent. From there on the battlements, the funeral boat had been sighted, and soon those down at the water's edge saw it coming round Sheep Island and into the fairway and under the lea of the castle.

The sail was run down, and two pairs of oars alone were enough to bring the slender vessel into rest. Crowding round, the men of MacLeod, MacAskill and MacCrimmon, MacSweyn the warden's wife and children and a few women and boys, all jostled and breathed heavily in silence, trying to look down into the open boat. Lying among rough heather-filled cushions on a simple bier, they saw the thin, tired, frail face of the man who had unfurled the fairy flag, his hands folded, his eyes closed, never to open again and look upon the well-loved island hills.

The women in the boat were keening softly. A child on the quayside gave a frightened sob, and one or two of the men rubbed their fists across their eyes and their noses, ashamed of tears that sprang up at the sight of the familiar face grown as yellow-white as the homespun shroud in which his form was wrapped.

Tormod, eleventh chief of the Clan MacLeod, was a big, heavily-built man with a shrewd eye and a confident dignity in his slow gait. There was a rustle of skirts and a clink of ceremonial swords as the mourning party came slowly down the steps. Men pressed back away from the boat to give him room. As he approached the water's edge a light wind touched the funeral boat so that Vic Mhurichie rocked gently on his bier like a baby in its cradle. MacLeod looked down at him gravely, then crossed himself. Looking about him, he raised his hand in blessing to the women and the men of Vic Mhurichie's family who huddled with upturned faces at either end of the bier.

Turning away slowly, he stepped across the boards into his own galley and settled down. His lady and the young chieftains William, Rory and little Alexander, the girls Margaret and Christiana, and MacSweyn the warden got into the boats, together with a number of others close to the chief by blood ties or by custom.

Men took the oars and made ready to pull away. Iain helped to loose the ropes. Almost at the last moment, the head boatman shouted "Where's Pock-faced Tam then? We're one man short." Looking round for a likely substitute, he spotted Iain heaving away willingly on a rope, caught him by the arm and pointed "Jump in and take that oar there, lad. Look sharp now. Never mind arguing. If you don't know how, pull away with the others and you'll learn right enough."

"Or take the skin off your hands finding out," his partner at the oar muttered, giving him a grin and moving up.

With a shouted order, the sails were loosed and ballooned out vigorously in the wind. Those ashore still, pushed the vessels off one by one and the oarsmen took up the rhythm from the bagpipes that sounded loud and clear from the battlements.

The great galleys and the birlinn, like the Viking vessels that the islanders' Norse ancestors had built, seemed large and high beside the slender funeral boat and the high prows rose and dipped gracefully into the cresting waves. They each had twenty-four or twenty-eight oarsmen, two to each heavy oar. The *Song of Ossian* and the *Pride of Lochlann*, guarding the slender *Water Lily* in which the dead man lay, moved outwards to the piper's lament and headed towards the open Western sea.

Chapter Two

ALASDAIR THE HUNCHBACK

Iain pulled on the heavy oar keeping his eyes for a while on the grey hulk of the castle, standing high on its rock at the far end of Loch Dunvegan. Then, turning his head, he searched for Christiana and spotted her in the other galley, facing forward into the wind. High on the battlements of the castle, three pipers from Borreraig college of piping, which the Clan MacCrimmon had founded and MacLeod supported and maintained, stood with their coloured tartans blowing in the wind as they played the galleys out. The rise and fall of the bagpipes' note became fainter, distorted by the sound of the wind and water and the creaking of the timbers and the oars, until it faded away at length and was heard no more.

The long land wings of Duirinish and Waternish could be seen on left and right, with their rocky coasts, their heather uplands and their scattering of turf-roofed cottages along the water's edge. The ruined church of Trumpan, which the MacDonalds had set fire to while the Mass was on, on the dreadful day that ended with the broken wall, lay blackened and gaping on the headland. No man went near it now, for it was said that on some nights the ghosts of those long-dead warriors rose from their rocky graves and fought out the battle once again with eerie, horrific cries.

The high cliffs of Galtrigal and the grey walls of the piping college on the hill at Borreraig, had fallen behind and even the tall, straight cliffs of Dunvegan Head itself seemed to grow small and low on the skyline after a while.

The boats rose and fell, pitching and tossing in the increasing swell once out in the Minch. Gradually, Iain's full stomach began to heave. He leaned on his oar and groaned. And then, to his own horror, suddenly vomited without warning where he sat.

"God save us! I'd forgotten the lad was a landsman," the boatswain cried. He cuffed Iain aside with the back of his hand and told him to get out of the way and he himself would take the oar. Reeling and scarcely conscious of what he was doing, Iain stumbled and tumbled over people's feet, got to the heaving side and hung there while the bread and meat and homely Morag's porridge took to the waves. Eyes closed, he lent his forehead on the gunwale, gritting his teeth and trying not to moan and groan aloud. He had never felt so ill in all his life.

A hand touched his arm and he was pulled slowly and firmly upright.

"You'll be better amidships, Sorner. Come away from the side and sit by me."

He looked blearily into the face of young Rory, MacLeod's second son, who had been pointed out to him at last night's feasting. The boy made room for him on the boards at his feet and looked down at him, grinning.

"Och, don't be so shamed, now. I was sick myself the first time they took me to Rodel," he said. "There's often a mighty swell between the Inner and the Outer Isles of the Hebrides, and you landsmen are not used to it."

Young Rory was right. There was less movement here in the centre of the vessel and presently his empty stomach settled down somewhat and he began to look about him again.

Pipe music had started up close at hand, and he saw a tall piper away ahead in the chief's galley, standing forward, facing into the wind, his plaid blowing out behind him and the ribbons on his bagpipes tossing. The long, slow repetitive phrases of a lament were borne across the water from one vessel to the other.

"It's Donald Mor MacCrimmon," Rory said, following the direction of his eyes. "He is the Master up at the college. He composes the finest and greatest bagpipe music in all Scotland. Men will come far to hear the *ceol mor* played by the Master. Listen now, it is a sweet sound. A sweet, true note he plays."

Iain listened and the great throbbing notes touched his sensibilities, bringing a smile to his lips and a sense of dignity and courage and of purpose to the day. His spirits rose. He looked up into the keen, dark, aquiline young features turned downward toward his own.

"Ah, that turns your mind to better things than your belly, that I'll warrant," Rory said.

He was a good-looking boy, younger than MacIain, much darker than his brothers William and little Alexander. The blood of the Norsemen and the Celts, and some remnants even from the early Picts who had inhabited these islands before history, was mixed together in the veins of the clan, so that fair and dark were in equal number, tall and short equally common and their eyes were every hue from the brilliant blue of their seagoing ancestors to the deep and secretive black of the earliest inhabitants of the Hebrides.

Rory was not very tall, but his shoulders were broad and strong. His eyes shone with a brilliant life, intelligence and laughter. His hair curled, quite short, blue-black, falling in waves and tendrils on his cheek and forehead. No beard had yet begun to grow on his young face.

"The Master *is* a mighty sweet piper," MacIain said.

"Donald Mor says it takes 'seven years of a man's own time and seven generations before' to make a piper of his calibre," Rory said. "I go to the college for my lessons with him. But I'm afraid I'll never be as good as the MacCrimmons, though I do love the *piobroch* and the laments and the lively strathspeys that they have composed. They say they brought their ideas from the Orient. No man knows where the MacCrimmons came from. They are not true Scots born and bred from way back. When my grandfather founded the college for them, they had some foreigners there with them, but they are all dead now and MacCrimmon wears the tartan and the *breacan feile* like the rest of us."

"Seven years of a man's own time and seven generations before?" Iain said, puzzled. "What does that mean?"

"Well, it could mean, if your forbears were not pipers you will not be. Or it could mean, maybe we have lived before."

"Could it?"

"Does that seem possible to you?"

"Yes," said Iain. "Yes, it does." He looked at the young chieftain with interest. "I sometimes have a great feeling that I have done a thing before, and that it is all familiar and happening again. Like coming to Dunvegan. It seemed when I heard tell of the fairy flag, I knew of it already. When I first saw the castle on the rock it seemed to me I had already lived here, in the long ago."

Rory looked down at him darkly and silently. "Yes," he said softly. "This too I know…this feeling of the familiarity of many things, and people, and places. The Hebrides are very ancient lands, very ancient parts of the great world. Sometimes I feel that I am ancient too. My soul is old. Ah, we have had this conversation before, don't you think so, Sorner?"

"I am not…" began Iain.

"…a sorner," Rory finished for him. "Well, I knew you were going to say that, friend! What are you then?"

"A servant of MacLeod," Iain answered seriously.

"Well, you shall wait on me, if you will, since we seem to understand each other well enough. Would you like that?"

"Sir," he answered, and lifted his chin with willing acceptance of this new and yet familiar-seeming bondage.

Away in the distance the Outer Hebrides lay like hump-backed monsters of the deep, now visible, now lost again in scurries of ever-moving mist and light spring rain. Throughout the journey the piping continued, taken up by young Padruig, Donald's elder son, in the galley in which Iain and Rory travelled and then again by the Master himself in MacLeod's own boat. The little fleet forged its way onwards, pitching and tossing through the grey-green seas, with a straining of the rounded, speckled hempen sails in the wind, and the oarsmen pulling rhythmically and strongly for a greater speed of passage, as was always the custom. The bigger boat, with twenty eight oarsmen, two to each oar, pulled ahead of the others.

Slowly the wide expanse of the Minch with its sharks and whales gave way to the small ships.

Behind them, the great Isle of Skye, with the dark, sharp range of the Black Cuillins, cloud-tipped against the Western Highlands of Scotland, dropped lower and lower on the horizon until it sank into greyness, indefinite and lifeless and far. Then the skerries of Harris and the Lewis grew large in the foreground, with the arid and watery landscape on either side of the little rounded harbour of Rodel, and the tower of the monastery rising among the rocky hills just inland from the shore.

In the old days it had been customary for the island chiefs and their families to be buried in the holy island of Iona where St. Columba and his followers had landed first in a curragh from Ireland in the sixth century, and begun their ministry of the Western Isles. The old chief had broken with this custom, and now the graveyard known as the *Reilig Odhrain,* where the bones of St Oran lay beneath the foundations of the old monastery and many kings and chiefs beside him, would hold no further bones of the MacLeods of Dunvegan and Harris.

MacLeod of MacLeod and his near kin, and all the bearers of the sacred standard, were to be taken to Rodel when they died, and laid in turn on an iron grid within an open pit, until their bodies fell away to dust and descended into the dark depths. Such was the custom. It was much nearer than the long sea journey down the Western coast of Scotland to the holy isle.

A solitary fisher monk, drawing up lobster baskets just outside the harbour wall, saw the vessels a great way off, and the familiar pennant flying from the foremost one, and pulled back quickly to the little quay to tell those who lived in the religious community. By the time the boats were close inshore, a little group of monks were standing together by the quay, their white homespun habits blowing about their ankles in the wind.

When MacLeod had landed and been greeted by the older members of his father's community, he walked slowly ahead of the two elder monks, up the winding pathway to the church.

Like all the earlier monastic communities of the Isles, Alasdair the Hunchback's monastery was not enclosed within high walls. None of the religious houses of the mainland could compare with it in construction, for it was small and exposed, with a little towered church at its core and heart and a simple range of single-storeyed buildings running down the hillside, finding foothold on the sloping rocky outcrops, wherever there was space. Here the brothers ate together and in the church they gathered together for worship. But for the most part of their days, they occupied separate beehive cells – *Culdee cells* - that lodged around the site of the church on the uneven hillside, each a little way from the next, to give privacy and solitude for contemplation and prayer.

In this, Alasdair the Hunchback had followed the custom of St Columba and the early Celtic saints in Ireland, who had never formed large communities, but had lived out their simple existence in a loose-knit brotherhood, tilling the land and celebrating the Holy Communion on an out-door altar beneath open skies.

The old chief himself, as Abbot of his little community, lived in the tower rooms of his church, as was sometimes the custom.

The ground-floor room had for one wall the sheer face of rock against which the church had been built and which had been hewn away to hold it, for there was so little flat and open ground hereabout that a rock face might often serve as a wall of a house, and rocks served always as foundation beneath the shallow soil.

In this lower room, which gave access to the hillside by an outer door and narrow window and to the interior of the church by steps leading downward with the contour of the hill, the old man had in the early days received his monks and his occasional guests, and conducted the small business of the community.

But this time, he remained upstairs in the highest of the three rooms of the tower, which could be reached only by a ladder stairway, and sent word for his son Tormod and his grandsons to go up there to him.

"He never comes down now," the old sacristan told MacLeod.

"Does my father keep to his bed then?" MacLeod asked. "He is a great age."

"No, he still gets up at sunrise and prays for two hours as he has always been accustomed to do. And in the hours of daylight, he works at his translations of the psalms."

The chief and his family and attendants entered the square, stone-walled lower room, where bread and cheese and fish and home-brewed ale were being laid out for them. Because the windows were no more than slits, the room was almost dark, but a branch of home-made candles was brought and placed on the long table, and a fire kindled in a brazier to warm and cheer it for the visitors, after the long sea journey.

Leaving the ladies and their attendant warriors below, MacLeod and his two elder sons went on at once up the few stone steps in the wall and ascended the ladder stair, to the room above. This room was used for craft-work of many kinds. There was a table and stool and a heavy leather-seated chair, and a closet for robes and the monks' winter cloaks and a kist wherein books and parchments and the Abbot's few personal possessions were kept. There were the parchments and the vellums and the pots of inks and dyes used by the scribes, and the leather workers; a highland harp in the process of restringing; an astrolabe upon the window ledge, and manuscript music lying in the corner. And on the table, designs for a tall silver communion cup which the silversmith had left for the Abbot's approval. Against one wall a heather-filled pallet served as a bed for the old chief's attendant, a young gentleman from Bernera, a kinsman who had taken the habit and was employed now as chief scribe, and slept within call in case he should be needed.

From this room also a ladder staircase led. MacLeod clicked his tongue in annoyance for he was a heavy man and this climbing of ladders was not at all to his liking. His father had done it four times daily, to a great age, for the services in the church, but Tormod was no monk, and had long lost his agility with much red meat and wine and comfort at Dunvegan.

He unfastened the bodkin of the heavy plaid be had worn about him at sea, and laid it aside; unbuckled his sword, which had encumbered him enough up the first stairway and put it on the table. And began slowly to haul himself upward, with William and Rory clambering behind.

The Abbot was seated in the embrasure of the window of the upper room on the low, wide sill, from whence he could look out on to the hillside and see something of the sea, and watch his monks about their duties as they cultivated the infertile land, or carried in the products of the day's fishing, or passed back and forth between their little cells, and the thatched-roof communal frater and the church.

Sometimes he would sit for an hour or two, watching them there below, pondering on the lives of these men of the Isles who had given themselves into the hands of God, and wondering what would become of them after his near-approaching death.

Long years ago, even before he had first conceived the idea of this community, he had set himself a lengthy task. He intended to translate the whole of the psalms into the mother tongue, the Gaelic that the islemen spoke, so that all his kindred and his people could hear in their own language the words they had been accustomed to chant, with little comprehension, in Latin.

Seated on the low stone sill in his church tower, he recalled often how he had first conceived this notion nearly three decades ago. And how he had gone down from Dunvegan to Iona, the sacred isle, and spoken there with the Abbot, and explained that he wanted to do this long work of translation as a penance for a sin that sat heavily on his conscience.

His guilt concerned an event that was told now by the bards and the *seanachies* at many a *ceilidh* on a winter evening, when tales of war and valour were remembered and repeated. In the continual violent struggles and acts of revenge between MacLeod and MacDonald, young MacAskill's grandfather and his brother had fallen into enemy hands in the Isle of Eigg. Donald MacDonald had ordered them stripped, and with his broad knife in one hand, had seized their sex organs, and hacked them off. He had them carried screaming and pouring blood, down to an oarless boat, to be thrown in and left to drift on the current back to Skye. When the boat had been found, jostling against the rocks in a snow storm, filled with blood-stained ice, the older man was dead, the younger dying.

Such was Alasdair's rage that he had launched his galleys, set off for Eigg, and there had the small population herded together and driven into a cave. His men had lit a huge fire on his orders and roasted them to death.

The shouts and cries of the old men, the pleading of the women, the terrified screaming of the children, went on for a long, long time; before it lessened and faded and ceased and the fire stopped cracking, and the only sound was the seabirds calls and the washing of the waves upon the rocks. In the ears of Alasdair *Crottach*, the Hunchback, the cries had echoed and re-echoed down the years.

20

Often he had sat silent in his room at Dunvegan, sometimes holding the silken folds of the fairy flag in his hands as though its touch might absolve him; sometimes setting it aside as though he feared to sully it with unclean hands. At last he had summoned a boat and gone down to the small Isle of Tiree, St Columba's penance place, and fasted there for a week, and then on to make his confession at Iona.

The conversation with the Abbot of Iona had been a most unhappy one. Afterwards, Alasdair Crottach had risen and walked out of the richly-furnished chamber of the Abbot, walked inward from the shore of Iona, above and past the *Reilig Odhrain* where the chiefs of his clan lay buried beneath the Celtic grave stones half hidden in the turf.

In a hollow of the hills, hidden from view, out of sight and sound of the sea, was a ruined hermit cell, built of the warm red stone of Mull, from which the Abbey itself was built. By tradition, St. Columba himself had lived there nearly a thousand years before, in the sixth century.

Alasdair Crottach remembered still with great clarity the day he had set foot in the hermit cell, comparing this dwelling, typical of the Celtic saints of old, with the great glory and luxury of the Abbey in the days now, when it acknowledged the Roman papacy.

Because the teaching of Rome had been superimposed after the eleventh century, upon the teaching of the churches that had stemmed from St John, the religious communities of the mainland of Britain had long ago severed the link that had existed in early days with Ephesus and Smyrna, and the churches of Asia Minor. Now, for many generations, they had come under the authority of Rome. But he felt in his bones that the churches of Ireland and Wales and Western England and Brittany, which had stemmed from the wandering hermit saints – the Culdee saints - had had secrets that were never known to Rome – secrets that had been treasured in the monasteries of old Egypt and known to the Desert Fathers.

Alasdair Crottach had chief's blood and King's blood in him. He had gone into the Abbot's chamber in humility, and spoken quietly and reverently as was fitting, and knelt for a blessing before he left, but he felt his own innate authority rise in him with vigour as he pondered the Abbot's words.

He burned still as he recollected how the Abbot had forbidden him to translate Holy writ into the common tongue: as though his very coming there – a layman, and a warrior – with a request to deal with matters that concerned the clergy and the monks in their enclosed communities, was in some way an affront to God himself.

"Why do you wish to do this work? As a penance? No, For your own glory, so that all men may know you for your scholarship."

"No, for the glory of God, Holy Father," the chief had answered.

"The glory of His Divine Majesty is far above the understanding of the common man," the Abbot had replied. "His Holiness the Pope protects his children from their own foolishness and folly by decreeing in clear terms what is fit matter for their minds to digest. If it were considered necessary for the psalms to be made free in the common tongue, such work would be carried out under my supervision, within these walls – and here in the sacred Isle to which men look for guidance. Put such thoughts away from you, and accept what penance may be set you by your own confessor, as other men do."

When he had left, the door of the Abbot's chamber closed behind him, and it seemed to Alasdair that a door closed in his own mind also.

St Peter of the Keys, he thought, began to open many doors. But the janitors who came after are locking them again.

St John of the mountain top, with his vision and his ecstasy of emotion and love, had fathered a church of no doors, no keys save the one great key of Love. From his reading of the Irish manuscripts the chief knew how some of St John's followers had crossed from Asia Minor into Gaul in the second century after Christ, and thence had filtered Northwards, across from Gaul to Cornwall, up through Wales and Ireland and the Western Isles. Some men believed the legend that St Joseph of Arimathea was the first to come and bring the teaching of St James and St John into the west, or even that Jesus Himself as a boy had travelled there and walked the hills of the west country of England, with his saintly uncle. But however that might be, the western churches had adhered to Smyrna and Ephesus, when the great split came in the third century, and had held to the Eastern tonsure and the Eastern date of Easter as the outward signs of their non-conformity with Rome.

But bit by bit, over the centuries, the inner teaching of the Celtic church had become confused and feeble, separated as it was from its Middle Eastern heritage, and the secret knowledge had been locked away at length in the hearts of the Welsh harpists and the Irish bards and the singers and the women of the Western Isles. And all the Celtic monasteries were brought under Rome.

But on this day, the lined-faced Island chief, whose crime of violence in the past sat more heavily on his back than the hump that MacDonald had given him when his battle axe thrust severed the tendons of his shoulders, stood in the ruined cell of a Celtic monk and thought of the distant past.

St Martin of Tours, St Ninian, St Columba of Iona and St David of Wales moved in his thoughts, and with them the lesser saints whose names are little known beyond the west: St Iltyd of Caldey Island who taught Gildas the Historian, and St Adamnan who went to Skye and who wrote the life of St Columba; and the hermits like Turog, and St Maelrhuba in MacLeod's own mainland place at Applecross, and many others who lived in solitude among the island hills.

And suddenly he thought, with a great uplifting of the heart "As my penance, I will build a monastery of the old order, and the old ways, and all men who think more with the heart than with the head shall be free of it. And we will sing the songs of St Patrick and read the poem-prayers of St Columba. And men shall play on the harp as the Celtic saints did always, and sing the psalms antiphonally with all the old responses and parts that the people joined in, as St Gildas wrote of it.

And we will make the teaching of St John live anew – not within cloistered walks, but in the hills and under the stars and the great skies of the Isles. And when I have done all that I may do for those who come to join me there, I shall sit by myself by the cruisie light, in a small room at night, and shall translate the psalms into the common tongue, as I intended."

Though Alasdair Crottach had known nothing of it at the time, the days of the Abbey of Iona were numbered. In England the Reformation had already struck at the rich monasteries and nunneries, and those not dissolved by Henry VIII for his own purposes, and to fill his own coffers, had succumbed one by one in late years to the revulsion against the wealth and corruption that had set in, in once austere communities. In Scotland the old houses had been fostered still by Mary, Queen of Scots, but within the next era they too were going as the wind of the Reformation blew upward from the South, and old ways gave place to new.

Alasdair MacLeod, single-minded and purposeful now that his own future was clear to him, had travelled to Harris and walked the hills he had known as a boy; and looked for a place to build and found his new community. What he discovered at length was the ruin of an ancient and long abandoned place of worship. Men said it had been built by the Druids, even before the Christians came. It was at the very southern-most tip of the long island of Harris and The Lewis. This became the basis of his new church and monastery.

While he had been hewing into the rocky land for his church at Rodel and a few of his kin and friends were setting forth from the other isles to join him there, the foundations of the old churches had cracked and broken throughout Scotland, as they had in England in the preceding era. The mainland churches everywhere were now too torn by their internal problems to take notice of the distant activities of MacLeod of MacLeod in his own land of Harris. Though he might well have been outlawed and declared a heretic a few years back, he managed now to go on undisturbed.

So the walls rose, and the few men took the natural coloured homespun robe of the early Celts, instead of the black robes of St Benedict worn at Iona in the latter days, and the small monastery made itself self-supporting.

*****

When the old chief saw his son's head emerging from the ladder stair that came up through the floor, he rose from his seat on the window sill and went to greet him.

Tormod clambered up, breathless, and displeased that it should be seen he was less fit and agile than his father had been.

"I almost thought we would find you in the belfry among the owls and the bats," he said, when they embraced one another briefly. "Why do you live up here under the roof instead of two floors down, as you used to do?"

"So that my heart may be nearer heaven," the old chief answered, with a twinkle in the dark eyes that had once been black and fierce, but now seemed gentle. "Be seated, my son. And my grandsons too."

Tormod seated himself in the only chair, and William, having stooped over his grandfather's hand and kissed it, retreated to a bench against the wall and settled there.

When Rory emerged from the ladder, just behind his elder brother, he crossed the floor eagerly as though to embrace his grandfather warmly as he had done in his earlier boyhood. But the sudden shyness of increasing years brought him up short, so that he hesitated, seized the thin old hand and kissed it, and then with an embarrassed laugh, laid his hands on the arms that were extended to him and kissed the old man's cheek.

Because of his humped back, Alasdair had not stood tall since his youth, and Rory was now the same height as he and a little more.

They looked into one another's eyes for a long moment. At last the old chief said

"My Rory, grown a man – so soon?"

"Alas, not yet, grandfather!" the boy answered. "Though it is not a short time, but an age since I was here with you last, and learned the scriptures at your knee. I remember this room well," he added, laughing again, with pleasure, as he glanced at his surroundings. "There's where my small truckle bed stood, and there is the table where I learned my letters and my figures. And there the prie-dieu. But it is all grown smaller since I lived with you, I do believe!"

The old man leaned a moment on the boy's shoulder, drawing him to a stool that stood near the window, with a parchment manuscript and a couple of hide-bound books laid upon it near his hand as he had sat on the stone window seat. He took them up and laid them aside, and motioned to Rory to seat himself on the stool.

"There – as you used to do."

"Yes, but then I looked up into your face," Rory laughed, "and my feet dangled and you had to tell me to keep them still and not to fidget so. And now…" He sat with his legs bent and elbows on his knees and said: "I have waited a long time for this day, to be with you again."

"You know why we are here Father?" Tormod asked the Abbot, interrupting these affectionate exchanges.

"Yes, my son. It is sad news to me. I had not thought to bury another standard bearer in my own lifetime. Vic Mhurichie's father was the first man to lie at rest in my new church. And who will you appoint to succeed him? He has no sons, I think?"

"His nephew. It is arranged. We shall not lack a standard bearer."

"It is well that the line is unbroken," Alasdair responded. "Well, we will have the tomb re-opened, and the dust of the father shall be shaken through the grid this very night in readiness so that Vic Mhuirichie may lie upon the bars as long as his body remains whole. Alas, it was so recently that the tomb was constructed here for the standard bearers to lie beside MacLeod of MacLeod – and two men's bones will be within it before a chief lies down beside them."

"Well, you *would* have them here," Tormod said almost tartly, "instead of in Iona where MacLeods without number lie in the sacred soil."

The Abbot glanced at his son, but Tormod sat looking about him, unconcerned. "At least the journey is shorter," he threw out as an afterthought. "If you are speedy with your Mass and your requiems for the dead these next days, we may set sail again by noon three days hence and be at home before the Sabbath. And that I shall be glad of, for I have affairs with Lord Lovat over Glenelg. The rascal claims our land there as his own, though it has been ours since before men can remember. He has been turning our cottagers out. It seems my wife's father, our overlord the Earl of Argyll, is supporting this unjust claim. It is a veriest hornet's nest, and I must sort it out."

"You will be going so soon?" The old Abbot asked. He seemed scarcely surprised, for there was little in the monastery life that could hold his son's attention. But his eyes turned a moment wistfully to his grandson's, and Rory met his look with an expression of affection and regret.

"Will you come down to the church for the burial and the Requiem Grandfather?" William enquired. "They say you don't come below stairs now, but you are not bedridden – though I suppose it is a long way down for you."

"I had not thought to go down those stairs again until I am carried down them to my tomb," Alasdair Crottach answered with a gentle smile. "But I will descend, if I can get my old bones down there, and see Vic Mhuirichie safely into his grave." He moved a little on the thin pallet of homespun stuffed with heather which was all the cushion he had between himself and the cold stone sill, and went on in his slow, deliberate voice, that had quite lost the ring of authority his men had known in old days on the battlefield: "You shall admire the tomb I have had built for myself, in readiness. I have an Iona stonemason here. He has done some most fine carving upon it, at my request – and added, of his mind, enough figures of saints and angels to keep him busy this whole last year – lest when he finished I might pay him off and send him away I suppose."

"Would you do that?" Rory asked.

His grandfather looked at him with a twinkle of laughter. "No, we will find other work for him, if he wants to stay. I have a mind to set him to carving figures for the outside of the tower to keep him occupied and useful. He has a pretty fancy. They tell me now he has an angel and a devil weighing my sins in the scales, all carved in a fine bas-relief upon the canopy." And turning to Rory, he said: "When my scribe told me of it, I asked which scale the mason showed to weigh the heavier – the virtues or the sins. And he, who is ever truthful, looked as though he did not wish to answer. But I pressed him and he answered me that the devil's end would win the day, but that the sculptor showed the angel had the tip of his wing a little in the scales to tilt them on the side of heaven. He has a gentle humour. I liked well to hear of it."

"You liked such a thought?" Tormod answered incredulously. "I'd have had the fellow whipped for such impertinence! Did you not order its removal? You will not shame MacLeod by leaving such a foolish and ignoble token of yourself as founder of this monastery?"

"Oh, yes, I have left it," the old man answered easily. "And why not? It may be true. At least, I pray it is, but I do not presume it. If there were no wing within the scale it would surely be tipped the other way," he added. "I am glad enough he did not show it so. That comforts me," he finished with a smile.

"Well, I think little of that as a thing for all posterity to see," Tormod remarked with annoyance, but after a moment he shrugged his shoulders over it, seeing that his father was unperturbed and obstinate too. "We will go down and refresh ourselves." He said, rising to his feet. "They have set a table in readiness down below."

The old man nodded. "I will have Brother Robert of Carinish up here presently, and make with him the arrangements for tomorrow, and he shall tell you later what we have decided and all details. And now do go down and refresh yourselves. Our cousin, Brother Allan of Bernera – my scribe who sleeps below – is already seeing about pallets and quilts for your bedding and he will show you where to sleep – in warmth, if not in the same comfort as at home.

Tormod thanked him and began to descend the ladder. The Abbot turned to Rory, and putting a hand on his shoulder said

"Go into the church and see my tomb when you have supped, Rory. Then come up here again and tell me what you think of it."

"Yes, I will."

In the downstairs room the ladies were being waited on by the monks, who were all in a flutter at the strangeness of their advent in this masculine community. There was no rule against their presence, for Alasdair had held that here at Rodel, as in Ireland and Wales in the early Celtic church, women whose business brought them to the monastery should be admitted freely and as a matter of course. In the old days Celtic monasteries and nunneries had often been built adjoining one another and men and women had worked and worshipped side by side. But the strict segregation that the Church of Rome had later imposed had changed the old ways.

However, Alasdair had shrugged off the things of Rome, and at Rodel women were employed where was need for them, at harvest time, or with the weaving and the spinning, or in the kitchen work. These were peasant women of Harris with their sleeves rolled up above plump forearms, and bare feet below black skirts and shawls over their heads against the stormy sea winds. It was a different and unusual matter to have ladies from the castle within these austere walls.

When Tormod and his sons were seated, Brother Gundred, the cook, served up a pottage of leeks, that he had had to spin out with water to make a little go a long way, and there were barley loaves, and soused herrings and a cheese made of skimmed milk and a little home-brewed ale, for the gentlemen. The provision from the boats had not yet been brought up to the kitchens.

MacLeod ate without much pleasure, talking with his wife Janet of matters at home, for he had little to say by way of conversation with the monks, and she, though courteous, was shy with them.

But Christiana further down the table with her elbows on the board, leaned forward into the candlelight with her face eager and alive and talked with Brother Allan of Bernera, who had served her. He seated himself on the bench opposite at her request, and began to answer her questions as though they were old friends. And then he, being young and serious, began to tell her how he had come by a copy of the Book of Kells, which was very old and had been first written by the monks at Kells in Ireland a thousand years ago, before St Patrick's day, and how he was studying it, and would copy it again, with the Abbot's permission, using the fine illuminated lettering of the Welsh and Irish manuscripts that he had seen and handled in the library at Iona as a boy.

"But now they will all be scattered and gone, I fear," he said. They say the Abbey is to be discontinued, and the lady Janet's father the Earl of Argyll has taken control of all the land of it, so it is well that those who can should remember, or copy, whatever they have seen there in the good days for it was the work of several artist-craftsmen and scribes working together. There are whole leaves finely painted to illustrate the text. I shall perhaps give myself the pleasure of making great P's and G's with interlacing and serpent heads. And at the end of each part I have thought to draw the symbol of the Triune, as they used to do – thus:"

He drew with his finger the Celtic design of the Trinity that he had found on tombstones in the *Reilig Odhrain*

She watched his finger moving on the linen cloth, and then said:

"It has no beginning and no end."

"That is as it should be, Madam," he responded.

"And it is simple and complete – one whole and three in one. I would like to remember how it is drawn. Please show me once again."

Iain MacIain had been serving at the top of the table, but Tormod motioned him away when he himself had eaten sufficient. For a few moments he stood against the wall, hungry, but not expecting to eat until the more important guests had finished. Rory noticed him suddenly, and moved a little along the bench to make a space, and beckoned to Iain to seat himself beside him, and eat – as though he were not a servant, in this place, but an equal with all other men who came there.

As he stretched his hand for the bread and took a piece of fish from the great wooden platter and laid it on the bread and began to eat, he looked across through the branch of the candlestick into Christiana's face, and heard her ask for the Celtic symbol to be drawn again. This time, the young monk marked it deep into the linen cloth with his finger nail, and Christiana and Rory and MacIain all looked down at it.

"It's very simple and pleasing," Rory said. "Like…like…"

"Like the old songs and the old music and poems before they grew all mazed and complex," Christiana interrupted.

"Like the new music that Donald Mor MacCrimmon plays on the pipes," her shy sister, Margaret, put in. "It says the same thing, over and over and yet gets deeper and better every time."

"Can one really make again such simplicity, or come anew to it?" Rory asked. "Are we not grown beyond such simple, childlike things?"

"We try to do so here," the young monk answered. "I have heard the Abbot say often that we must make anew, and consciously, the things that St Columba and the Celtic saints knew in their bones, and followed in ancient times. And that Rome forgot – or never knew perhaps. That we must simplify all that we understand of life, and of God."

"In the things of the Spirit. But I think it is the heart that is the fount of knowledge," Christiana said softly, looking about her round the square, barely-furnished room, and at the simple fare upon the table.

"But madam, is it not the same, the Spirit and the heart?" MacIain asked.

Immediately he had spoken, he felt he knew the answer to his question, and drew in breath to speak – and then saw Rory and Christiana each draw in likewise. But while the young monk watched them, all three let out their breath again and stared into the candlelight and answered nothing.

Chapter Three

THE LURE OF RODEL

When the meal was over, Rory went as he had promised his grandfather, into the church, to look at the tomb, taking MacIain with him to bear the rush-light that would enable him to see it.

They descended the few stone steps from the tower room and entered the main part of the church. The voices of four monks could be heard chanting in unison the Lorica of Gildas, which St Aldhem used, with its recurrent refrain:

> *'Help O Oneness of Trinity,*
> *Have pity O Threeness of Unity.'*

Beyond the group of monks, the sacristan and two of the lay brothers were by the standard bearers' tomb, and had opened it in readiness for the morrow. The body of Vic Mhuirichie lay covered by a woollen shroud before the altar. The bare-headed monks quietly shifted what remained of the bones and dust of the dead man's father, so that all descended through the iron grid into the empty vault beneath.

When Rory saw what they were about he hesitated, and looked at them in silence. Iain stood close behind, with the rush-light held high, so that the light of it ran up the bare walls of gneiss and trap from which the church was built, and caught the glittering fragments of quartz that had been used as dressing so that they shone like diamonds, every speck magnified with light.

The church was not large, and nave and chancel were in one, with no elevation between them. Two brief, unfurnished transepts made of its form the shape of the short-armed Celtic cross. And at the far end, an altar of green marble from Iona proclaimed the love the monks had still in their hearts for the Sacred Isle.

When they had completed their task and made all ready for the morrow, they turned to leave, on silent, bare feet. Seeing the young chieftain standing there behind them, each inclined his head to him a little, and looked into his face as though to ask of themselves whether he – the second son of MacLeod, who would never need to rule at Dunvegan, might be the one who would succeed his grandfather as Abbot of this place. For they remembered his early boyhood training here, and how the old man had loved and cherished him.

He smiled at them and let them go, taking their one candle with them, and then beckoned to MacIain to bring the rush-light hither.

He approached, and at Rory's command, held the light forward so that he could look downwards through the cleared grid into the darkness of the vault.

"In such a pit – in such a pit as this will my bones also lie?" he said as though to himself, and looked sombrely at the place where Vic Mhurichie's body would be placed on the morrow.

He shivered suddenly, and looked up and across at Iain, his eyes dark and seeming full of questions. But he said nothing. And then, after a moment:

"Where is the tomb my grandfather has built? Raise the light again. Ah, against the south wall, over there."

They moved towards it, and looked together at the carving of it, intricate and precise beneath its arched canopy, as Alasdair Crottach had described it to them.

Hunting scenes, a galley, and the castle of Dunvegan, all were portrayed in clear detail. And then a row of saints and the Evangelists, all with the Roman copes and mitres that the Iona-trained craftsman had carved because he was used to this manner of depicting the saints and not thought to show them differently. But it was the centre-piece that caught MacIain's eye, and he looked at in silence, and then said slowly:

"Sir, look at the strange order of the figures. Above, the Father lifting the crucified Son up in His arms. And under this, the sun, with twelve great rays. And under, still, the Madonna and the Child."

"And down below, the weighing of the sins and the virtues, as my grandfather described it," Rory remarked with pleasure. "See there the wing tip in the scales that he told us of!"

"And the hunting of the hart at the bottom too," Iain murmured, almost to himself, for he saw that Rory was absorbed in the detail and did not see the whole. "And the castle, and the ship are also on that level."

"Yes, see the sail, and the oars, and the shields of the oarsmen!" Rory whispered delightedly. "It is a very good likeness. And Dunvegan has its turrets all correct. It is a tomb fit for an Abbot – or a chief. It pleases me. Let's go up and tell him what we think of it."

Iain went with him slowly, holding the rush-light high so that they could see their way up the stone steps, and then up the ladder stairways into the upper room. But when he entered the topmost room behind his young master, and saw the old Abbot seated there at the plain oak table, in his white habit, with his old, thin, lined face lighted and shadowed by the little flame of a pewter cruisie lamp that stood by his book, and his eyes black and piercing, Iain stopped suddenly, as though in fright, with his legs still on the ladder and did not advance.

The Abbot greeted Rory and motioned him to a stool which he could bring forward and place beside the table. Then the old man turned to Iain with a smiling look, and said

"And who is this who bears a light for you?"

"My man," Rory replied, seating himself and beginning at once to look at the manuscript upon the table inquisitively. Then "My friend, Iain MacIain," he added on a sudden, turning with a smile and beckoning him forward. "He is in willing bondage to my father."

MacIain approached, looking so grave and reverent in the Abbot's presence that Rory said, teasingly:

"Put the rush-light in the bracket over there before you drop it, in your awe at seeing my Grandfather. And then come nearer – for it is not every day a serving man can look at a Holy Abbot so close!"

With a trembling hand, Iain placed the light in the bracket. But the old man, watching him, said:

"Extinguish it, my son. Do not waste it. We have light enough with the cruisie, and you can kindle it again when it is time to leave."

Iain blew it out, and turned and crossed the room. And then before he reached the table, he went down suddenly on his knees and bowed his head.

Rory, leaning with both elbows on the table looked at him in surprise and then glanced at his grandfather, but said nothing.

"Iain MacIain," the Abbot said looking at him kindly. And when he raised his head: "Come here. Bring a stool and sit with us."

When he had found a stool and brought it and was seated, Alasdair asked if both boys had seen the tomb, and what they thought of it.

Rory answered readily, praising the carving and the design of it. And then fell silent, because his thoughts had turned again to the black pit that stood open close by, and he realised, as he had not done before, that in a like place beneath the carved stone the body of his loved grandfather would soon be lying.

He looked at Alasdair and said "I have missed you greatly, Grandfather. I would come more often if I could."

The Abbot folded his thin and fine-boned hands together on the table, and turning to MacIain, asked:

"And what did you see? What took your eye?"

"The Christ is above the shining sun and the rays of it are half of them straight and the other half turn like a wheel. And the Madonna is below," he said, all in a breath, his head bent and his eyes lowered, and his hands to keep them from trembling pressed between his knees.

The Abbot looked at him in a long and tranquil silence.

"The rays turn like a wheel?" Rory asked, puzzled. "I didn't notice that. What does it signify? The wheel of the turning of the world? You are more observant than I, my friend, I saw none of these things in the way that you describe them."

Neither Iain nor the Abbot made a response to this remark. And suddenly Rory, who was already accustomed to command and see his own will done about the castle and the estate at home, and who had begun to feel in his bones that he saw further beyond the end of his nose than most men of his father's household, realised that he was outside the circle of understanding created by these two. He watched them, mystified.

"Is it true that you are under a bond of manrent? What would you wish to do if you were free?" The old man asked MacIain quietly. The boy hesitated.

"I am not sure. Once it seemed to me…" He knew that he had not thought deeply and often on this subject because it seemed he had never had a chance to do as he wished. "I wanted to run away from war and violence, Holy Father, when first I saw how the world is made and how men kill for profit," he said. "But I don't really want to leave the world. A young man must fight to prove his manhood, I suppose. I would rather do penance for my sins and then go forth again, as it is said the knights of King Arthur did in England and in Gaul in the days of chivalry."

The old man smiled at him. "Your sins?" he asked, and looked at the fair young face with its full indented upper lip and wide-set eyes and the up-curling tendrils of the hair that crowned him, as though he saw no sin in him, but only the cleanness of his youth.

"My father and I once took part in an attack on unarmed men," MacIain said suddenly. His voice shook for a moment, and he pressed his lips together and looked down at his hands. "My father was wounded in the foot, and when one of the men came at me with a burning brand, I drew my knife and stabbed him with it."

The old Abbot looked at him steadily, as though weighing him up and considering many things.

"Had you any choice?" he said at length.

"I thought I would have to kill or else see my father killed, and be killed myself Holy Father," Iain answered simply, looking up into his face. "We were desperate for food when we tried to steal. They surprised us at it. I don't think I killed the man. But Our Lord said it is the thought and the desire, and not the deed that counts as sin. So I have sinned."

"You had no choice," Alasdair said slowly, shaking his head. "As you are…as men are…there is no choice at such a moment. Even if the wit decided to refrain from commitment the hand would rise up and strike, in its own defence of your living body."

"Is it so?" Iain asked in a puzzled tone. "But yet, Holy Father, men say that after the burning of the people in the cave of Eigg you repented, and grieved over it for many years, and that you still do penance for those deaths. Do you say man has no choice?" he blurted out, forgetful of all respect in his desire to understand what bewildered him.

The Abbot put his hands inside the wide sleeves of his robe and sat with eyes downcast. He was silent for a while. Then

"Indeed, I thought I had a choice that day," he answered honestly. "For six long hours I prayed – or tried to pray – that I might know whether to take vengeance on the people as they perhaps deserved. Did they tell you of that? No, doubtless men have forgotten. I could not bring myself to destroy a people – and yet my power and my state demanded it, for such was always the custom with the Highland chiefs in war, and I am not a weakling, you know. So I prayed that God would help me to decide if I should slay them there or let them go. And as I heard no answer, Iain MacIain, I asked a sign. I asked that the wind should blow right strongly. And if it blew off the shore I told the Lord I would let the people go. And if it blew on the cave, such as would carry the smoke in and smother them if the fire were lit – then I would let them burn."

Rory interjected, knowing the story well, for it was often told "And in a little while the wind *did* blow, and my Uncle William – he is dead now – came to tell you how it blew directly on the cave; and so you let him light the fires."

"Yes, that is what I did."

"But you went away and sat in the galley facing out to sea and didn't watch. The men remember that," Rory remarked.

"Then God *did* give you a sign, and so you need not do penance," Iain put in, though doubtfully, for he saw that the old man's thoughts were working on a level far beyond his own.

"But can one make a pact with God, and bargain with Him, and say 'Do this, O Lord, and thus will I do'?" the Abbot said. "One may invoke the earth gods with their magic, as the Druids did. But now I seek the Holy Spirit and the risen Christ."

"To seek the Spirit – is it to follow the things of the heart?" MacIain asked as he had done at the supper table below. "If I followed my heart, I'd slay no man. Is the heart our true guide? Is it the Holy Spirit in man?"

"It may be one door to It. It may be one," the old man answered him. "Even now, I cannot answer with authority. I do not know, my son. But that man should be ruled by the heart, and not by the desires of the flesh and of the world of animals – that in itself is good. That I do know. Therefore seek the heart. Let us seek the heart."

"Grandfather," Rory said urgently, leaning forward upon the table into the lamplight. "Is it a new age – this age that is about to start? William thinks – we think – it seems to us the times are changing, but we don't know what it is that is happening to us. Is there beginning an age when men will pity their neighbours, and love them, as Our Lord instructed? Is it the age of the heart that we are entering?" He spoke with eagerness and stressed his words as though much depended on the answer.

"I cannot tell you," Alasdair Crottach replied, looking at the boy with his old countenance seeming simple and honest as a child – as though they were the three of them boys together, as ignorant and as groping. Then his expression changed, and he looked long into his grandson's face, and at last answered in a voice of greater authority:

"It is certain that new and strange things are happening everywhere. The power of the Established Church has crumbled, and there is Calvin's pupil, Master John Knox, on the mainland preaching a new doctrine of simple family worship and man's need to approach his Maker direct, and not through the mediation of the saints, or of the priests. And in the world of music and the arts, there is a casting off of the old complexities that have grown with the years, and a cry to simplify and go direct to the heart, as the troubadours of old used to do. There will be great changes and reforms in your life-time, Rory. Already men speak of it as the age of Reformation. In England and throughout Europe I am told this word is used in many fields of thought. In statesmanship also. Reforms, re-alignment of the nations. If

Queen Elizabeth of England dies unwed, as many think she will, and the throne of England comes to King James of Scotland, who is next of kin, there will be much reforming in politics and ways of government. The voice of London will be heard in Edinburgh, and Edinburgh in London. And where there are exchanges of thought and ideas, then often the heart is touched. But – an age of the heart? Ah, I do not know."

"Could it be…not the spirit of the age, but the spirit of MacLeod that we feel move in our bones?" MacIain said very slowly, in a diffident voice. "Is it possible – if there were a living spirit in a family, as the Druids said there was a living spirit in a tree, or a river, or a rock -?"

"Did the Druids say this?" Rory interjected. "I thought they were violent pagan men who practised human sacrifice."

"Their faith and teaching became corrupt, as all teachings do in the end," his grandfather said quietly. "Men remember the end, but do not remember the beginning, when there was no violence but a deep learning and knowledge of the nature of life and of the Universe. Yes, they did speak of the spirit in living things."

"Then – " Iain blurted out, "if there is a living spirit of the Clan MacLeod, could the unfurling of the Fairy Flag release it? Like when Moses struck the rock, and the water gushed forth…?"

"No," Rory said immediately, almost sharply. "You may not speak of the Flag."

And then at once he laughed and went on in a lighter note: "If we were not men of the Isles with a fairy heritage, we would not even think such thoughts and much less speak of them. It all leads to fantasy and moonshine."

"Moonshine or no, it was on such thoughts as these that Druidic teaching grew – and in these Isles. At their zenith the Druids awaited the coming of an expected teacher. They called Him 'Hesus, the Great Teacher', and prepared for Him," Alasdair Crottach made reply, looking from the younger boy to the older with a grave expression. "And you know well that where the Druid temples are and the sacred streams and woods and waterfalls, in these same places stand the cells of the Celtic saints and hermits who came after. Iona itself was *Innis nan Druinidh*, the Isle of Druids, when *Colum-cille* – St Columba of the Isles – first came. And where there is a Druid's altar under an oak tree, or a circle of stones where the ancients worshipped the sunrise, in those same places the Christian Fathers settled and blended the magic of the old teachings with the saving grace of the new. Throughout all the Islands, and in Wales and Ireland and the West Country of England

and in Brittany it was so. Do not despise our fairy heritage, or try to override all supernatural things. But seek the Holy Spirit by whatever doors may open to you."

"I think this also is a time of re-birth, Holy Father," Iain MacIain cried. It seemed to him that all his life he had awaited just such words as those, and to hear such ideas formulated in simple terms.

"A renaissance?" the Abbot echoed, almost to himself. "Perhaps. Perhaps a little like the Carolingian renaissance – I mean the days of the Frankish King, Charlemagne – when little that was new was formed, but old thought and old knowledge came to life again, cleansed and purified and made afresh."

"Is that why you live here in the way the Celtic monks of St Columba's day used to live?" Iain asked. "To try to make anew what once men understood in their hearts in olden days? I almost wish I might stay here with you, if that is so! But one day perhaps I should wish to be in the world again and perhaps to marry, and that would be forbidden if I were a monk."

"There was a married priesthood in those early days of the Celtic church," the Abbot replied, seeming to consider the boy's remarks. "The monks took vows of poverty and chastity, but Celtic priests were free to marry, until the church came under Rome, and she decreed celibacy for all the priesthood. And I myself was married, as you know – and happily, and was blessed with a big family. I have not presumed to call myself priest, or to seek ordination, like the old Bishop Abbots. We have Father O'Colgan from Ireland who is our priest and he alone may prepare the sacrament, and officiate at Mass. But my twelve monks take me as their Abbot and do not see my married years as an impediment. I do not know what the future holds, for everywhere the church is in great flux. But – if you wished to stay with us here, I do not think you would be bound to life-long seclusion and to celibacy, for our order is loose-knit, and men follow here the dictates of their hearts.

"Could I stay?" Iain asked.

But Rory took him up at once, saying:

"You are in bondage, Iain MacIain. My father would not let you go."

Iain's head swung round, and grave-eyed above the small flame of the cruisie lamp they stared at one another. At last: -

"Sir, if you would give me leave, MacLeod himself would scarcely be aware of my absence," Iain said.

"But no! You have agreed to be my servant, and I shall need you," Rory said, with a sudden arrogant tilt of his head. The Abbot shifted a little in his chair.

"Ah, my grandson," he murmured

"But Grandfather, I do need MacIain," Rory protested in his cracked, boyish voice. "He will be more than a servant to me. He will be a friend."

"And would you stand between your friend and God?" Alasdair Crottach asked.

Rory looked unhappy. After a moment, he shook his head.

"Then, if I may, I will stay here in Rodel and learn all that the Holy Abbot your grandfather and his fair company of monks can teach," Iain cried joyfully. "And later I will return to you at Dunvegan. Oh," he continued, as further possibilities struck him, "it may be that here I shall be taught to write, and to tell my numbers and to learn about the stars in their courses and other sciences. Oh, is that possible, Holy Father?"

The Abbot smiled at his eagerness.

"Such things, if MacLeod permits your sojourn here, you may be taught, my son, as far as in our power lies," he answered. "We ourselves are students and not masters. But with us you shall at least begin your schooling."

*****

On the morning of the second day, the old man made the difficult, labouring climb down the two ladders, saying to Brother Allan who assisted him:

"It is sometimes in my mind that the Lord Himself changes His plans…for I had not thought to enter my church again."

In the lower room he was helped out of the worn old robe that he wore habitually. Standing in his single white under-robe, with his arms stretched out for Brother Allan to place on him the fresh clean gown of natural homespun, with its pointed hood hanging at the back, he looked about him, at the books, the harp, the astrolabe on the window sill, and said:

"There is a boy here who would join this 'fair company of monks' and learn his letters with us. He used that expression, 'this fair company,' and it pleased me greatly to hear it, for surely we are children of that 'Order of the Fair Company' that our Father Saint Columba founded."

"It is surely so, the young monk responded, pulling the Abbot's robe straight, with the hood correct and neat across his humped shoulders. "And yet, if I remember rightly, *Colum-cille* called his own monks the

'Family of HY' because they dwelt on the Island of Iona. And was not the 'Order of the Fair Company' that much greater band that went forth throughout all the Isles and the mainland, to build churches and to teach?"

"Yes…yes… This boy…" the Abbot said, and stopped, pulling at his sleeves with an abstracted air, in thought. "He may stand close to my young grandson and thus close to the heart of MacLeod. I wish he were the elder brother's servant, for he will be chief. And this young man, well taught, may well become…" But again he did not finish.

From midnight onward there had been chanting down below in the little church, for though the small company of twelve monks and the few laymen who lived with them, was not sufficient to keep the unceasing singing round of praise that the older communities had rendered in relays all through every day and night, yet on special days they reverted to this practise of their early fathers.

The words of the Irish Lorica of St Patrick rose and fell:

> *"Christ with me, Christ before me,*
> *Christ behind me, Christ in me,*
> *Christ under me, Christ over me."*

The young Irish priest, Father O'Colgan, who had left Ireland from disagreement with the excessive pomp of Roman ways, and disliked also the starkness of the new Calvin teaching, stood ready in his embroidered robes, in the ground floor room to greet the Abbot on this rare occasion. Most of MacLeod's party and the relatives of the dead man were already on their knees in the church, but Tormod stood with his back to the brazier, warming himself, in no hurry to enter.

"I hear you are taking the sorner from Ardnamurchan off my hands," he said, when he had greeted his father briefly.

"The boy MacIain? If you will allow me."

"If you can teach him to be a scribe he may be of some use to me," MacLeod replied. He himself had never learned to write, having found it easier to achieve his purposes with the sword rather than the pen. But letters, and statutes and instruments of land tenure, now passed back and forth between the Privy Council and the island chiefs with increasing frequency, and must be read and understood…and sometimes at least, heeded. "My lady and the boys are in the church already. Shall I precede you there, or do you prefer to go in first?" MacLeod asked.

The priest led the way, and the three went down the steps in to the nave of the church, where narrow beams of sunlight streamed through small windows, splashing the paving stones with light and touching the glistening quartz of the wall dressings. The little building was filled to overflowing with the tartan-clad figures of the clansmen, the few ladies, and the cottagers and tacksmen - tenants of MacLeod's lands - from the surrounding countryside. They were all of the Clan MacLeod, and came in for the burying. The twelve white-robed, bare-foot monks stood about the bier. Their Eastern slave tonsures - the hair shaved from the front half of the head in a style which Iona had abandoned long ago in favour of the Roman tonsure - were visible, proclaiming them like *Colum-cille* long ago, to be 'the slaves of Christ.'

The long funeral Mass, the prayers and the chanting, continued for three hours or so. The body of Vic Mhurichie was moved at last from in front of the altar and laid on the gridded tomb. Then the tomb was closed with its stone slab over him.

After the funeral, MacLeod went up into the tower room behind his father and the priest, and others followed him. The rest of the people scattered, some going out of the church door into the sunlight on the hillside, to walk and talk a little there in twos and threes. Others of MacLeod's party dispersed towards the kitchen and the adjoining long, low hut of mud and thatch, where those who could not fit round the table in the lower room of the tower would eat their meal together.

MacLeod's lady was standing with a fine wool shawl – *an arisaid* - woven in squares of dark blue and green and a line of yellow and red, clutched round her form over the grey dress and veil she had worn in church. After her daughter Margaret had placed it on her shoulders, she drew it close, for she was again pregnant. It embarrassed her that the monks might notice it. Iain saw Christiana go to her, pulling the veil from her own hair so that it was free in the sudden warm sunlight. He crossed to where she stood, and waited until she turned and saw him.

"What is it?" she asked, seeing his grave expression.

"I am not returning to Skye," he said. "MacLeod has given me leave to stay in Rodel. I wanted you to know, Madam."

"To stay here?" she asked, surprised. She turned and walked with him, and together they began to go down the winding stony pathway that led to the harbour, where the curraghs lay, ready to take the visitors out to the galleys in the deep water beyond. "Why?" she said.

"To study, Miss Christiana. To learn. To be taught."

"To study which matters, Iain MacIain? Church matters? You don't want to become a monk, do you?"

"I can only read a little, and I can't write. I want to do both, as my father could. My father taught me as much as he was able, but there was not much opportunity, the way we had to live. I would like to learn all the sciences of the great Trivium and Quadrivium of the Druids. But that would take twelve years! I would like to learn all the arts, and all that men know of God…and the lives of the saints." He said.

She stood still on the pathway and looked at him with her enormous sea-blue eyes.

"Oh, if I had only been a man, I would have stayed at Rodel with you!" she declared. "But my father would laugh me to scorn if I suggested it. It is not easy for a woman to come by such schooling as a man may have. Will you teach me what you have learned, when you return to Dunvegan?"

"Indeed I will! I shall look forward eagerly to doing so."

She sighed and turned so that she looked towards the galleys, tipping and tossing in the channel down below.

"I look often at the sun rising behind the mountain and setting over the sea, and wonder what it is…that ball of fire. And I see how the stars lie, in the same patterns of light across the skies above the Isles each night…and yet the patterns are not always placed the same. There is one design of stars that the old nurse says is called the Belt of Orion, and I have seen it lie above Dunvegan at one season, and seaward to another. But who will teach me how it moves, and what it means? And the pull of the tides now in, now out. What causes it? Master O'Mhurgeason the bard, says that the moon causes it…but that explains nothing. If I could read in the books as monks do, I might find out. How I wish I might stay here with you!"

She clasped her hands together, looking at him eagerly, thinking of what she could do if she were a young man. But he saw her as all woman, and his young blood responded rapidly. In spite of the words Dun Kenneth said, she will be mine in time, he thought. "When I return to Dunvegan she will be mine."

In confidence and joy at all that these last days had brought him, he went into the church and fell on his knees to give God thanks.

The memory of the brief exchange of words with Christiana on the stony hillside remained with him, sustaining his mind and feeding his emotions, through all the days of study, and the nights interrupted by the single bell that called him to prayer with the brotherhood. The declaration of shared interests, the request for tuition and the willing answer he had given, ripened in his thoughts to an imagined exchange of loving looks, of words and vows and tender promises. The little incident grew larger than in life.

Chapter Four

BORRERAIG AND FIRST BLOOD AT DUNTULM

Bridie MacCrimmon leaned out of the small window of her low-ceilinged bedroom at Borreraig College, and listened.

Down below, the repetitive soft notes of a chanter, on which a young student piper was being instructed, could be heard rising and falling. In the distance from the Piper's Walk which ran along the cliff-top high above the sea, the sonorous great sound of the bagpipes played well and beautifully by a skilled musician at his daily practise, were borne back on the light summer air. Daily and hour by hour, the college pipers walked and played, rhythmically, precisely fitting the movements of their feet with the notes of the music. Pausing, turning, each step controlled and exact, they disciplined themselves to a perfection of accomplishment.

Bridie craned her head out further, listening to a familiar voice. On a bench against the wall, Rory was sitting with his master, discussing musical theory.

"I want you to think about the *urlar* and the *siubhall*, on which the *piobaireachd* is founded," Donald Mor was saying. "What are their subsidiary components?"

"The *crunlueth*?"

"And?"

"The *taobh-lueth*."

"Yes. Each has a rapid offset…"

"The *breabach*…"

"The *breabach*…, yes. Both begin rapidly…"

The lesson continued for over an hour. Then Rory went off down the hill towards the landing stage where he had left his small boat. He hummed to himself as he strode along, still thinking about the parts of the *piobroch*. Music was in Rory's bones, and ran through his thoughts and sounded in his mind continually. He practised with a will, walking even in high wind and rain, his kilted plaid beating back against his bare legs on the cliff-top. At the castle he could give a good performance on the *clarsach*, the small Highland harp. And now that his boy's treble voice had broken, a strong and true, deep singing voice was beginning to develop. He gave pleasure to the ladies in the hall when they had dined well, by singing the old songs of Ossian and the Irish Gaelic ballads.

Bridie MacCrimmon went softly down the steps and ran concealed between the bushes, her long green skirt bunched up in her hand. She went down lightly and quickly by a short way to the little shingle beach and the small landing stage. Stooping, she unloosed Rory's curragh and pushed it off into the still waters of the loch. Then she disappeared again into the bushes.

When the young chieftain reached the shore he clicked his tongue in annoyance to see his vessel floating far out, where the current would eventually bear it to Dunvegan without him. After watching it for a few moments, he turned onto the path along the loch side towards a fisherman's cottage where another boat could be had. As he walked along, Bridie appeared, coming slowly towards him as if by chance on this lonely path.

Both slowed their steps, halted, and faced each other. The music lesson flew out of the back doors of his mind as his full attention came towards the girl. He knew the dark eyes and the long fine dark hair looped up in a chignon, and the intensity of her expression. She was several years older than he, and she had knowledge to offer. He realised suddenly that their unsmiling, questioning glances at each other, at the college or the castle or in the woods and countryside for the past year or more, had presaged this moment. She had secrets to sell and she was a willing vendor.

He put out his hand slowly and touched her, enquiringly, uncertainly. Then suddenly, boldly and excitedly as she moved easily into his embrace. She was nearly his own height, but slight and vibrant in his arms. Her hand reached behind his neck and tangled into the thick hair and pressed his head forward and downward. Her lips were moist on his cheek. Her teeth nipped his ear. Her tongue explored the line of his jaw and felt its way towards his mouth. He held her hard against him, boyishly inexpert, eager and filled with pleasure. He drew her off the path and into the bushes. They fell to their knees among the curling fronds of the young bracken, and the sweet scent of the thyme was released by the pressure of their young bodies. The branches of the yellow broom curved low, concealing them, and the warm nutty smell of the gorse mingled with the scents of their own young limbs, blending in unison. Above them the larks sang.

Through the long hours of the afternoon, they explored one another deeply, eagerly, and with mounting confidence. At last they fell asleep, sated with love, her hair spread over him, and her green skirt covering their nakedness against the slight chill of the evening breeze.

At dusk, the sound of oars was heard below, and Roddy MacAskill's voice calling: "Master Rory? Master Rory, sir!" along the beaches and the paths. Rory stirred and turned his mouth to Bridie's. He did not open his eyes or make an answer.

By moonlight, they groped their way to the water's edge, and stood hand in hand watching it lapping gently on the shore.

"Ah, Love, I must go home, I suppose," he said at last.

"You have no boat." She smiled, clinging to his arm.

"I can get old Hector's from the cottage."

"He'll question you, where you have been these hours."

"It is no business of his to do that," he answered. "But maybe I will walk round the loch. I feel such energy in me, I could walk from here to Bracadale and never flag, tonight."

"I'll come with you, part of the way. My father will think I am with grandmother at Pooltiel, and she will believe I am at Borreraig. No-one will miss me before tomorrow noon."

They set out hand in hand, looking at each other, pausing to kiss and murmur in each other's ears.

Rory broke into a snatch of an old song, but she hushed him, lest the sound would be borne over the water. Across the loch the castle could be seen dimly outlined, backed by its belt of trees, dark, far away across the silvered loch. Its square tower where the Fairy Flag was kept stood out against the clear night sky. The hours of complete darkness were short in mid-Summer in these northern lands, for the sun did not sink until eleven in the evening and rose again at two or three by the dial on the wall.

It was a long, long walk round through the boggy pasture land by the head of the loch, and back towards the beaches near the castle. Thirsty, they stopped to drink from a peaty linn. They ate wild strawberries. Rory had a sleepy memory of hearing his name called some hours ago, and hoped there would not be a search party out for him.

"They will think the seal maidens have taken you to Lochlann," Bridie laughed.

All men knew that the seals were bewitched daughters of the King of Lochlann, land of legend from which the ancients came. It was said if you looked into their faces you could easily tell it, for they have royal eyes. "We shall see some of them soon. I have watched them play beneath those boulders along there."

At dawn they sat on a boulder at the tide's edge and watched the shining wet bodies of the seals slipping past them through the rippling water, making their strange cries to each other as they played.

"*Cha b'ann air na sgeirean a dh'ionnsaich na ròin an ceòl,*" Bridie said, echoing her grandmother and the cottage women. "It is not on the rocks that the seals learned their music."

High above them the great rocky cliffs rose, with the castle walls built into them. The seabirds stirred and quarrelled and began to call from their nests on the ledges and in the face of the cliff.

"I wish you would let me sing aloud," said Rory. "I want to sing to the dawn of the day!"

In his tumbled bed in the castle, *Coinneach Odhar*, Kenneth of the fairy dun, stirred and murmured, between sleep and waking. He had his black shiny stone in his closed fist, for he always slept with it clutched safely to him. "He shall be to minstrels as their homecoming..." he muttered in a whisper of a breath.

"I love Dunvegan," Rory said, his eyes alight with happiness, looking up at the ancient walls. It is a fairy place, like all the duns. Though I did not believe in fairies and magic things – but today I do."

"I love you," Bridie answered, watching him.

"If I were chief, I would fill the halls with bards and minstrels from all over the land," he said.

"I love to hear you play the pipes," said she.

"I would fill all the castle with music overflowing, like wine overflowing from the bowl! There would be great roaring fires in the hearths on winter evenings, and all men should sing and play, and no man should got to war again, not ever," he said.

He threw his arms out wide in boyish drama and exuberance.

In his half sleep, Dun Kenneth saw two arms outstretched and strong. Then the hands took hold of the great two-handed claymore of William of the Long Sword, that the early chief had wielded in battle, raised it on high, to come slashingly downwards in a whirring roar. Sword and hands dissolved away in the gushing stream of blood that seemed to flow like a torrent downward to the sea. Dun Kenneth whimpered, turning on his pallet. He pulled himself up and swung his short legs to the ground and sat in his brief shirt with his face screwed up, rubbing his eyes with his fist. He looked around him vaguely, blinking and scratching himself. Then he reached for his shoes and pulled them on.

"But since my brother William will be chief, and his sons after him, I shall travel through the Highlands and the Isles, playing my lute like a minstrel, and kindling the fires of love in all men's hearts," Rory said, tossing his head back, standing arms akimbo.

"Will you come to Borreraig again later today?"

"No, sweeting. Not today." For the moment he was surfeited with love-making. "I shall ride with the deerhounds today."

"Tomorrow, then?"

"I don't know. I will come soon. I will come. Or I will send for you."

He held her to him, but she was looking beyond him, not smiling. "There is a raven on the rock," she said.

He followed her gaze. The great bird was standing alone up there, preening its glossy feathers.

"There must be a pair," he answered. "Perhaps they have a nest."

"It is alone."

"Go, find your partner!" he called out laughingly.

"A lone raven brings misfortune," she said.

"Ah, that is superstition and moonshine," he answered lightly. He picked up a stone and tossed it, and watched the raven spread its great dark wings and launch itself into the morning. He turned and kissed Bridie's lips.

In the castle they were saying "Young Rory did not return, and MacLeod would have a search party go out if he is not back."

"Ah, leave him alone," Dun Kenneth said. "He has taken the wings of the morning. He will be back anon."

Trusting the old man, they did not launch the boats, and in an hour they heard him at the gate.

"Where were you?" the clansmen asked as they admitted him.

"That is my business," he told them, climbing the stone stairs through the rock. But playing chess in the Fairy Tower room with his brother William later that evening, he said: -

"I was in the bushes…with a girl," and laughed.

*****

Donald Gorme MacDonald of Clanranald, and MacKinnon of Strath, had sent the flower of their families to be taught English and have their minds broadened in Edinburgh and Glasgow. The King had had letters despatched, ordering the Island chiefs to send one of their sons each, to be schooled, and get a wider view of the world beyond the Hebrides.

46

Tormod felt he could not spare William, who was a steady, reliable young man and of use about the estate and in the household. He considered sending Rory instead.

"No, Father! No, I beg you, I learned with grandfather," his second son had answered and had set so stubborn a face against the idea, that the Chief laughed indulgently and dropped the matter. He was an unlettered man himself, and attached little importance to further education. Maybe young Alexander could go, when he was big enough, he thought, and there it rested.

Throughout the summer days, Rory went back and forth to Borreraig, acquiring greater skill in music under the master's tuition, and greater skill in love-making under the daughter's. Between whiles, mounting his sturdy island pony, and taking some of the young men of the castle with him, he rode throughout Duirinish and Minginish, exploring the outlying parts of the estates. And then, seeking fresh fields and growing bolder, he took the track between the hills to distant Sligachan and brought in hares and partridges and grouse for the pot. All that land grown familiar, he ventured with his party into MacDonald's Forest, and poached the red forest deer that grazed the wooded hills, trusting to luck that in the uninhabited hill ranges he might escape the notice of the Clanranald's foresters. Tormod laughed at his boldness, seeing him riding in, his dark eyes shining, his hair full of twigs and brushwood, and the young clansmen panting under the weight of the meat they carried.

Everyone ate and drank well at Dunvegan. "Twenty times a day we were drunken, at Dunvegan," the clansmen roared in their cups of an evening. There was boisterousness and simple pleasure in their merry-making.

Rory visited the Clan MacKinnon down in Strath, taking them a fallow deer that he had poached and he thought the venison would taste a little sweeter for being thus ill-gotten. He was received with courteous smiles and hospitality. Then he went on down through the wild hills into Sleat, the southernmost land wing of all, full of gardens and green pastureland, softer and pleasanter than at home. At dusk he scouted round Dunscaith Castle to see how it stood, atop its rock, impregnable by land and difficult of access even by sea. He sighed over it, because once it had been MacLeod's and now MacDonald had it, though Donald Gormson himself rarely visited it, preferring Duntulm Castle up in Trotternish.

All the time he kept out of serious trouble, involving himself only in boyish devilment in which no serious harm was done, and having a friendly word for everyone.

William made regular rounds of the Dunvegan lands on their father's behalf, watching the interests of the many clansmen who lived on the land, tilling the stony soil around their turf-thatched cottages, and catching the herring in their curraghs off the coast. But Rory, taking little interest in such homely matters, ranged the whole length and breadth of Skye. There was scarcely a hill, a corry or a mile of coastline he had not travelled and examined by the time he was twenty.

He knew the rocky Cuillins with their treacherous slopes, and mighty Blaaven topping all of them. The ancient battle sites of Glendale and of Trotternish; Castle Camus and the ruins of Castle Moil, where a Norse princess had lived in the long ago. And all the approaches up to Duntulm Castle that a man might take on foot or on horse-back, were familiar to him. After crossing the River Snizort, he ran the gauntlet of MacDonald's watchmen...but they looked more to seaward than landward for attack.

One morning in early autumn, riding down a wide glade between the wooded hills above Kilmuir, with young Roddy MacAskill and Murdo MacSweyn, and three or four other young men, with a fine stag being carried between them, upside-down with its four quarters secured to their staves, they ran into a group of MacDonald's own huntsmen. The men from Duntulm greeted them with shouts and oaths and set upon them vigorously. Out-numbered, they were soon over-powered and dragged unwillingly to MacDonald's stronghold as prisoners.

Duntulm was grander nowadays than Dunvegan, for what Tormod spent on wine and good-living, Donald Gormson had spent, before his recent death, on the upkeep of those pleasances that King James V had so admired on his royal progress in the chief's father's time. It was said soil from twelve counties had been brought to grace the flower gardens, and many strange plants grew inside the boundaries, protected by the high walls from the sharp sea wind. Apart from the greater size of the outer enclosure, Duntulm was much like Dunvegan and Dunscaith, which was to be expected, for the MacLeods themselves had built all three castles in the distant past before the Clanranald came to these parts. But it stood higher than the other two, on a sheer cliff-face, with a long climb up a green hillside to approach it from its landward side.

Before it was the small round Hill of Pleas, where such rough justice as MacDonald dispensed in his own lands, was meted out. And next to it, the Hill of the Round and Round. It was said that malefactors were rolled in a nail-studded barrel from top to bottom of it, to their tortured deaths.

With buffets and oaths, the young men from Dunvegan were propelled through the oaken door to the inner gardens, led across the courtyards, up stone stairs onto a battlemented walk above the sea, and into a small low-ceilinged chamber. Here James Gruamach, the Regent for the young chief who was still a minor, sat with his steward at a heavy table. Rory came instinctively to the front of the group and halted before him, feeling both foolish and angry to be standing thus.

"They had a young roebuck slung between them which would have sired a hundred more had he lived." The MacDonald huntsmen said indignantly.

"Your lands are well stocked with deer, sir," Rory said quickly, "In fact there are too many. The trees on the foreshore beyond Uig, where my father's tacksman MacTowll lives on land adjoining yours, are almost stripped of bark as far up as the deer can reach. You need to cull quite a few of them."

James Gruamach - the grim-faced - looked him up and down.

"You have a pretty freedom of tongue, young man," he said, "Are you telling me how to manage my ward's estates?"

"No, sir, but…"

"I will tell you this, sir. I shall give orders that if my men catch you again on our land, you are to be brought here with your men and soundly whipped, even though you are a son of MacLeod of MacLeod."

Rory flushed furiously, and opened his mouth to answer further. Grim-faced James waved him away impatiently.

"I have troubles enough without you. You may go your way."

He turned once again to the papers and documents on the table, but since he could not read, he merely shuffled them with his hands, waiting until he was alone with his steward and his scribe again. As Regent, he was harassed by the demands the newly-appointed Bishop of the Isles was making for large dues and arrears of teinds. He had come up from his home at Castle Camus down in Sleat to attend to matters for the boy chief. In his absence, he had heard, the Earl of Argyll had had men surveying Sleat, and he feared for his land and his home under those steely, covetous eyes. No man's land was wholly safe, for few of the island chiefs had deeds that covered their possession of their own properties, and in the past they had retained possession purely by force of arms. Argyll, however, had the King's blessing for setting matters on a more regular footing throughout the

Hebrides. James Gruamach was torn between his duties and his obligations here at Duntulm, and his wish to get off home and keep the King's men away from his own property with placatory words.

Rory was nonplussed by the Regent's lack of interest in the deer. In the past, the bones of many a clansman of MacLeod had mouldered in the dungeons of Duntulm and Dunscaith for such a matter as poaching on the Clanranald's lands. And MacDonald's men had been left to starve in the dungeon at Dunvegan for offences as trivial as he and his band of youngsters had committed. He did not know what to expect when he was led into this room, and now he was half-angry and half-laughing with relief. He burst out in impulsive boyish confidence:

"Are you not inviting us to sit and share your roebuck, then?"

Murdo MacSweyn gave a swift ejaculation of nervous fright. Anything could happen if the young chieftain should rouse James Graumach's wrath by further impertinence, he thought. But before the Regent raised his frowning face, an answer came from the big-boned youth who stood by the further door, leaning there with arms crossed on his chest.

"Why don't we do just that, Uncle?" he said. "I would like to make the further acquaintance of MacLeod, the younger of MacLeod, before I kill him in battle…as doubtless I shall before many more years are past."

Rory swivelled round and stared at young Donald Gorme. Named after his grandfather Donald Gorme, and his father Donald Gormson, he was known already as Donald Gorme Mor, not because he was a great man like Donald Mor MacCrimmon, but because he was physically big and strong. By comparison, Rory MacLeod did not seem tall, though he had dignity and confidence in the carriage of his head.

"I thank you for the honour," Rory said. "I think you mistake me for my brother, though. I will answer for him, if you challenge the honour of MacLeod. But I have no battles to fight with any man, and I trust I never shall."

Donald Gorme grinned. "Come, dine with us," he said. "Tammy, have the roebuck roasted on the spit and tell the cooks to bring other meats as well. Call all the men in to join us. We will make merry tonight! What do you say Uncle? Will you join in the fun?"

James Gruamach looked at him glumly.

"Feast if you wish," he said irritably after a moment. "Since you are only newly arrived home from Glasgow from your schooling, I suppose you have a right to have a feast. But I shall not dine with you. I must finish your affairs for you, and get off to Sleat in the morning."

50

"Oh, don't bother so about all that nonsense," Donald Gorme answered lightly. "Let's pay up what they ask, and forget about it. Come and make merry with us, Uncle! Hmm?"

He picked up a quill, flicked the goose feather with his finger, and with a smirk, stuck it in his uncle's hair. The clansman sniggered, clicking his tongue. The Regent pulled it out and laid it down, frowning.

"Well, since you know what we should do, perhaps you will give me the benefit of your advice on how to raise these sums that are demanded in cattle and sheep in goods," he said sarcastically.

"I know nothing about it, except that my father said 'support the Protestants, for the Romans are ousted everywhere save in Uist and in Eigg,'" young MacDonald replied. "What do you say about these taxes for the church, young MacLeod of Macleod?"

"My father paid the first dues," said Rory. "But he took no notice of the second dues demanded. Nothing has been done to get them from us. Nothing at all."

"Ha!" MacDonald cried. "You will be outlawed and put to the horn. You must move with the times."

"Well, we heard that the Privy Council had reported that the Hebrides are 'barbarous isles where His Majesty's officers dare not go for fear of their very lives'," Rory said. He grinned. "Maybe we should just keep quiet and do nothing. They may think it safe enough to send a man o' war to look us over from the sea-lochs. But little clerking men who are armed only with their quills and their scrolls might not find themselves so full of courage - so my father thinks."

Donald Gorme guffawed.

"It's as well the fortunes of your clan don't rest in your hands." James Gruamach remarked. "Away now and leave me to sort out this tangle without your chattering tongues giving advice to your elders and betters."

"Come on then. Let's go out and walk and talk for a while. The venison will be a long time roasting," Donald Gorme said. "Barbarians together, eh?"

"Well, we need not resort to fire and sword these days," Rory said cheerfully. "Those times are gone. We shall be friends and work together for our common good. Together we will outwit the King, if he fasces us too much. What do you say? I remember I used to think we should stick our teeth in his backside – but I have changed my mind. We are more civilized than our forebears were!"

They walked the battlement and the terraced garden. The ladies of the Clanranald and the clansmen in their MacDonald tartan looked curiously at the little group, clearly expecting at any moment to see dirks drawn, and the young hunters' bodies tossed over the high walls into the sea below.

As they dined, they raised their drinking horns to one another, and laughing, talking and eating well, warmth and hilarity stole over them and loosened their tongues yet further.

"It's a mighty fine beast you have given us," Donald Gorme cried, cutting thick slices off the roast meat with his broad short knife with its single sharp side and pointed end. "Your arrow shall shoot us another since you choose your mark so well."

"No...come to Dunvegan and try your bow-hand in our woods instead," Rory responded, flushed with excitement and wine.

Great log fires from the forest crackled and flamed in the open fire place, for the autumn evening was chill. They added their heat and dancing light to the torches in brackets all down the hall. Mutton and great sides of beef came in, borne on great dishes, and everyone ate hugely, using their hunting knives as table implements, and spearing the pieces of meat on their points. Pies and pasties and sweetmeats were handed the length of the table, piled high on wooden platters. The bone beakers were filled from jugs of home-brewed ale, and Spanish wine, from a ship Donald Gormson had plundered on the high seas.

"Where is the bard?" MacDonald cried at length.

A tall man with his little grey beard curled and coiffed, his small round cap set on his balding head, and his long straight gown that proclaimed his profession and his training at the Irish schools, came down the hall. His son, in a short tunic, carrying a Welsh harp, and other singers, trooped in behind and bowed to the young chiefs. They were greeted with shouts and cheers. Behind them came the *seanachie*, a little wizened bent-backed man with sharp-looking eyes, and a limping gait. Unlike the entertainers, he had not put on his best attire, but came in, in his usual homespun tunic reaching to his bony knees, and with his rolled parchments and a great hide book hitched beneath his arms. While the others were bowing and smiling to their audience, he dumped his books with scant ceremony on the table end, cleared his throat and waited to be told to begin the ceremonial re-telling of the battle sagas, as was always the custom on a night of feasting.

But Donald Gorme said: "No tales of war, with young MacLeod of MacLeod here tonight! I will not have my young friend hear how his forebears were attacked and soundly trounced by us. Eh? Ha!" he said and dug Rory in the ribs, "You would not want to hear those old tales tonight, Young Rory MacLeod, would you? I'll wager they know them too well back at Dunvegan any way. Let's have some songs instead."

They called for the ballad of Fionn and the White Hind; and the song of Fair Bragela in the Hall of Shells at Dunscaith Castle waiting for her lover who never came. A girl's voice began the sad lyric of Dierdre of the Sorrows; but the men shouted her down with a racy, rumbustuous hunting song, banging their drinking horns down on the table as they thumped out the words of the chorus.

"You have a singing voice yourself, young MacLeod of MacLeod, so your men here tell us," someone shouted. "Let's hear a song from you!"

Prodded and pushed Rory got to his feet, his brain muzzy with wine, his face flushed with the heat of the fire. He realised that Donald Gorme had refilled his drinking horn too quickly and bade him tip it back. Steadying himself with a foot on a stool, he broke into the Rune of Tir-nan-Og, which all men knew to be the Celtic Heaven, the Island of Eternal Youth, whence the soul of the Norseman comes and where it returns at death. It had many verses and began:

> *"There is a distant isle*
> *Around which sea horses glisten…"*

The MacDonalds fell quiet, listening to the fine quality of the young voice pouring out the familiar words with effortless power. They knew it so well that they could not forebear to sing too and soon everyone was joining in the ringing phrases:

> *"Golden chariots on the sea-plain,*
> *Rising with the tide to the Sun,*
> *Chariots of silver on the sports-plain,*
> *Chariots of unblemished bronze…"*

Many of the ballads and the tales were very old, belonging to the long ago before the Norsemen came to the Isles, when the Irish god Cuchullain walked the Cuillin Mountains of Skye and the Little People dwelt in the Pictish Duns, and Fionn the Mighty lived in Fingal's Cave in the Isle of Staffa. Together they blended their wealth of ancient wisdom that belonged to the long heritage of the mingled Norse and Celtic blood…the wisdom of an island race of sailors and swordsmen and singers.

"Well now, let us hear some tales of our common ancestor." Donald Gorme said at last to the old *seanachie*, who was sitting brooding with his head on his chest, seeming half asleep. He got slowly to his feet and cleared his throat. A little bent man plucked the strings of the clarsach and the *seanachie* taking up his scroll began to speak in the ancient Gaelic tongue:

"From the race of Eremon, through Conn of the Hundred Battles and through Coll the Noble are the Lords of the Isles: whose likeness was Cuchullain and he the sun arising: and to whom is the headship of the Gael, as it is but right to proclaim.

"Donald of the Isles, son of the Good John, son of Augus Og, son of Augus Mor, son of Donald, son of Ranald, son of Somerled the noble and renowned high chief of the Hebrides. He it was who received the sceptre from his brother Ranald at the cell of St Donnan, in the Isle of Eigg.

"And this is the manner in which a Lord of the Isles was crowned: There was a square stone, seven feet long, and the tract of a man's foot cut thereon upon which he stood, denoting that he should walk in the footsteps and uprightness of his fathers, and that he was installed by right in his possessions. He was clothed in a white habit, to show his innocence and integrity of heart, and that he would be a light to his people, and maintain the true religion. Then he was to receive a white rod in his hand, intimating that he had the power to rule, not with tyranny and partiality, but with discretion and sincerity. Then he received his forefathers' sword, signifying that his duty was to protect and defend his people from the incursions of their enemies, in peace or in war, as the obligations and customs of his fathers were.

"The ceremony being over, Mass was said after the blessing of the bishop and seven priests, the people pouring their prayer for the success and prosperity of the new created Lord. When they were dismissed, the Lord of the Isles feasted them for a week thereafter; and gave liberally to the monks, poets, bards and musicians.

"And this is the manner in which a Lord of the Isles would die: Monks and priests being over him, his fair body was brought to Iona of Colum-cille. And the abbot came forth to meet him, as it was the custom to meet the body of the King of the Isles; and his service and waking were honourably performed during eight days and eight nights; after which, his full noble body was laid in the same grave with his fathers in the Reilig Odhrain."

When the *seanachie's* voiced ceased, there was a hushed quiet among those who sat at head of the table.

At last, Rory said

"Though I knew your line stemmed from the great Somerled in the beginning, as we from Olave the Black, King of the Isle of Man, yet I did not know – I never knew these things."

"How could you know, since MacLeod is not of the line which held the Lordship of the Isles?" Donald MacDonald answered.

Rory began to realise he was drunk, and making great efforts to think clearly he said earnestly:

"I know we always disputed your claim to the Lordship before it was broken by the King – though my grandfather did once come out in your support, I remember. But that was for a principle, he said. For an old belief in the integrity of that over-lordship and the independence of the machinations of statesmen and courtiers at Edinburgh. However that may be..."

Donald Gorme refilled the drinking horn in spite of Rory's protest.

"Ah, it is all dead, anyway," he said. "And now Iona has lost her ancient power, and is become a place of politics instead of the church's heart from whence the life blood of her arteries is drawn. And Master John Knox, and now my Lord bishop of the Isles bid us believe there is no intercession of the Blessed Virgin or the saints and the Bread and Wine is but bread and wine, and all the great mysteries are reduced to the common-place. I do not know what to think."

"And yet you support the Protestants, or so you said?" Rory murmured.

"I shall do what is expedient, as my father did," MacDonald answered irritably, and changed the subject.

At the same table with Donald and Rory was one of Donald Gorme's sisters, red-headed Catriona. She caught and held Rory's eye with a bold look and a ready smile. He leaned across towards her, trying to see her clearly though his head was spinning. She was lively and full of opinions on everything and with plenty of coquettish talk. Seeing that the eyes of the other ladies also were upon him, he looked about with amusement and pleasure. MacLeods and MacDonalds had married often enough in the past, for being two of the three main clans in the island, they met one another often enough at peaceful MacKinnon's stronghold on social occasions; and in the houses of the tacksmen and the cadet branches of the families who entertained each other when they were not at war. But old hostility and quarrels over land ownership and ancient rights flared up again and again in these hot-blooded and impetuous men, and in spite of matrimonial entanglements they would be at daggers drawn again. It was said

'MacLeod and MacDonald are forever thrusting rings on each other's fingers and dirks in each others hearts.'"

"If I had my way I would shpend all my days listening to such music and songs like I heard tonight," Rory said "my daysh hunting, evenings making music, nights making love. There wouldn't be – wouldn't be time to make war."

"Your days hunting my deer, your evenings at my table? Your nights making love to my sister?" Donald winked at Catriona.

"We could make a bond for ever…I will marry your shister and you shall marry one of mine!" Rory shouted. His voice had become slurred with drink and he could no longer control it. "How'sh that for a fair offer, Friend?"

Donald Gorme laughed. "May be I will come to Dunvegan and look them over." He prodded Rory's bare forearm where it lay on the table, pressing gently with the point of his knife, seeming to tease, yet waiting to see him withdraw it when it hurt. His eyes looked suddenly less friendly. Stubbornly Rory kept his arm where it was, smiling broadly. "You are a trim little fighting cock, and will draw blood with your sword in spite of your fine words, I warrant," MacDonald said softly. "No, if I make a pact it will not be with you, young one. It will be with Big Brother William." He pressed the knife point just a little further, looking beady-eyed. Rory did not flinch, but he fell silent. The knife point prodded just a little more. Rory began to stiffen. His eyes widened and darkened. But he did not move his arm, for he could not seem cowardly. Suddenly the skin punctured under the increased pressure, the blood spurted up, and ran downward on to the table top, in a widening pool. Rory gasped. There was a groan and then an ominous silence from the clansmen. All eyes turned to the steadily flowing stream.

Rory drew his arm away. He stared at Donald Gorme, then jumped to his feet and put his hand to his dirk. Donald Gorme Mor lent back in his chair and roared with drunken laughter.

"He draws his own knife now, I see. I will make love, not war, he says, mark you! Make *war*, not *love*, I say…"

He too leapt up suddenly, his chair crashing back behind him and his knife at the ready. Ladies screamed and all men reached for their swords or their hunting knives. But at that moment there came a mighty roar of anger and authority from the open doorway and James Gruamach stood there, towering and glowering at them all.

"Sheath your swords!" he commanded. "For shame, sir!" he shouted at his ward. Then turning to Rory and his men:

"We bid you goodnight, young MacLeod of MacLeod," he said. "You may take your leave of us." He stood in silence, waiting.

Rory hesitated, knife in hand, looking from one to another of the red and staring faces turned to him. It seemed to him suddenly that there was a coarseness and a cruelty in them and that they were alien and strange. "For all their ancient lineage, it is not the Clanranald, but ourselves who are the finer clan. To us a gift was given," he thought, "for we hold the Fairy Flag." He thought with youthful confidence. "I am of finer stuff than they," and lifting his head fearlessly, he pressed his dirk back slowly into his leather belt and stood a long minute quiet and still, looking at the clansmen of MacDonald. Slowly the sword arms were lowered, the knives tucked back into belts or laid by the dishes on the tables. He gave a mocking bow, then passed in silence through their ranks towards the door. His men came after him.

They groped their way through unlit passages and found the entrance to the courtyard. Catriona, seeming overcome with a fit of coughing, pressing a kerchief to her face, left the hall also. Once outside, she picked up her skirts and ran down, caught Rory by the arm and said:

"Quickly! This way, I will bring you to your ponies before Uncle Grimface loses his hold on them and they come after you."

She conducted them with all speed to the outer courtyard. They untethered the ponies and she bound a kerchief hastily round Rory's bleeding arm after he had mounted. Rory leaned over, caught her round the waist, lifted her off her feet and gave her a lingering kiss and a laughing, tender word. She watched them clatter out over the cobble stones and trot off down the green hill, breaking into a long canter as they reached even ground.

Splashing through the shallow River Snizort, Roddy MacAskill said:

"We barely escaped with our lives, sir. MacLeod will send out an armed band when he hears of it."

"No," Rory said, "we will not tell him. It was my fault, Roddy. We are safe, so let it be."

His head was clearing, in the open air, and he found himself thinking how his grandfather at Rodel had counselled Iain MacIain, whose sword hand had also risen in self-defence, as Rory's had tonight. How quickly all in a minute, the situation and the whole tenor of life had changed, against his will, and beyond his power to control anything. He rode on through the woodland in the half darkness, thinking: "I will be glad to see Iain MacIain again, when he comes home. We seem to understand each other well."

Iain had written many long letters to Rory – addressed to Rory, but in words he intended for Christiana of whom he thought constantly. She had hoped for learning. He longed to teach her. Rory read them all and liked the tenor of his thoughts, though he never troubled himself to reply.

In spite of Rory's orders, word went round from one to another at Dunvegan that Donald Gorme Mor had drawn first blood from Rory, and that he would surely have his revenge in the days to come.

Chapter Five

THE TOUCH OF THE FLAG

William MacLeod of MacLeod raised the great two-handed claymore, and swore fealty to the clan, and that he would guard them as their father and their chief. Then he called for the sword of the previous chief and buckled it on.

The death of Tormod, his own father, had followed closely on the death of his grandfather at Rodel, and there had been a double burying.

William was a steady, slow-speaking man, more temperate than most of the island chiefs, and anxious that there should not be many changes at Dunvegan. He was happily married now to Janet MacIntosh, daughter of MacIntosh of Dunachton.

In the first flush of husbandly fervour, he had placed himself under a bond of manrent to his father-in-law, so that in all matters in which MacIntosh might be at variance with other clans or with the King, MacLeod should in future come to his aid. He had signed the document in his own hand, holding the quill carefully, his tongue protruding between his teeth as he formed the letters: "Wm. M'Lloyd of Dunvegane."

Tormod had disapproved of this bondage, and had pointed out that MacIntosh had made a contract with Donald Gorme the previous year and promised to aid him over certain land rights. William replied that he had made his bond out of friendship, to foster mutual trust and goodwill between the clans, and asked was this not a good enough purpose to uphold?

"If you know whom you can trust. If you trust a man because your eyes have looked steadily into his and they have not flinched, and your hands have clasped his and you have seen honesty of purpose there, lad. But if it is into the shining eyes of the daughter that you look as you sign your pact…may Colum Cille protect you from folly."

But William had been unperturbed by the warning. After Tormod's death, he was formally instated as chief.

The double funeral at Rodel distressed Rory, more, it seemed, than William. He had loved his grandfather deeply and held his father in great affection. Standing before the tomb, during the long Mass, tears ran down his cheeks, though he kept his chin raised and his back straight and did not allow himself the luxury of uncontrolled weeping.

Later he went to the hillside culdee cell where Iain MacIain lived, and looked into the eyes of the man who had once promised to be his servant, and then broken the contract even before it had begun. He had seen him only two or three times in the intervening years, and had always chided him lightly for his faithlessness, while thanking him for his letters. They came from time to time, whenever there was a vessel going over to Dunvegan. Each time they met they enjoyed one another's company and talked with ease together.

Iain was bearded now, and wore the simple brown habit of the lay brothers of the community. His face had filled out a little and he was no longer so painfully thin and bony, nor so nervously tense and anxious as he had been when he first came to the MacLeods. His direct and frank blue eyes had a serenity and stability in them.

"Will you come home with me now?" Rory asked, when they had talked about Tormod and the Abbot for a while. "You are a fine servant, who never served me at all!"

"I serve MacLeod," Iain answered easily, "by my prayers. In truth, I think there are many years ahead in which I shall do my duty to you, sir. But if you will give me leave, they do need me here for a while. Our Holy Father left instructions for the winding up of the monastery as soon as he was laid in the tomb, for we have had demands from the Bishop of the Isles which make it perilous to keep the community in its present footing. We think to make a more loose-knit body of itinerant monks, who come and go freely, and even lodge in the villages at times. There is much to see to. And beside, my studies…"

"You have an uncommon hunger for study," Rory said. "Well, come when you can, and write to me and tell me how all is going, and what you are thinking in your monkish heart!"

Before the galleys sailed again, Iain brought himself to ask: "Your sisters, sir, Christiana and Margaret. Are they well? They did not accompany you."

"They stayed to comfort our mother who was too prostrate with grief and poor health, to come with us. Write letters to us, Iain," Rory said again, looking back as they embarked. "Send them by any vessel that is coming our way."

Going about his duties in the monastery and the surrounding rocky countryside of Harris, Iain wrote many letters in his head, addressing them to Rory but thinking them in his mind as though they would be for Christiana's eyes. He had not seen her since he came to Rodel, and only had scant news of her from time to tome. It gave him happiness beyond measure to think of writing to Dunvegan, and he thought of all the wisdom and knowledge he would impart to her later, all the information he would pass on, all the thoughts, ideas and dreams he would express for her benefit.

One day the acting Abbot called him and instructed him to make the long walk to the little harbour town of Tarbert in South West Lewis, and enquire there for accommodation for one or two of the brothers if need be. It was a journey that took two days on foot. Iain had made it before, carrying a sack of lobsters and crabs as far as Tarbert, to barter in exchange for salt and other commodities that came down on the trading boat from Stornaway. He took a satchel with some raw oats in it for his supper, and the cook gave him a little crowdie cheese. As an afterthought, the cook handed him a flask of home-brewed ale, made from the heather tops, which the lay brothers drank, though the monks abstained. Iain smiled his thanks for this luxury.

He struck up through the woods of birch and hazel that backed the monastery on the landward side, stopping to cut himself a staff to aid him over the rough ground that came later. Within the wood, bluebells were in bud and the air was sweet with the scents of the trees and blossom and the flowering May. Though bleak and austere throughout the winter months, the island landscape had its brief flowering in Spring, when the winds and snows abated, and before the aridity of high summer robbed the infertile soil of its moisture.

While he cut his stick and sliced off its notches to make it comfortable to his grip, he thought of his next letter and what he might say in it. Then he plodded up along the path. Beyond the little wood were wild, heather-covered uplands where scant earth covered the rocks and there was too little surface soil to hold rain long enough for the growing of crops.

Where there were hollows or damp places among the rocks, there would be a cottage or two, built of turf or mud, low-roofed and thatched with heathcr, with a central hole for the chimney, and so low a door and windows that sunlight never entered the smoke-grimed interiors.

Barley and oats and a little flax had been sown in these green hollows, in small fields of narrow ridges, such as a cottager could till with the *cas chrom* - the Hebridean foot plough which was like a bent spade. Earth had been scooped up in the run-rig way, to get the maximum depth of soil in each ridge, and a narrow ditch left barren in between. A bent apple tree, leaning landwards from the salt winds that blew upwards from the sea, or a silver birch or two, or wild rowans, provided all the shade that could be cultivated here, and many cottages stood shadeless and unprotected from the wind, save by the rocky hills. The short, springy heather grew among boulders to their very doors. The cottagers raised their hands in greeting as he passed, and he called a cheerful, friendly word or two to them, still climbing upwards into wilder lands.

When he needed to pause and rest, he turned, leaning on his staff and breathing deeply, his old brown habit blown about his legs. The monastery could be seen, far behind and below, its church tower topping the belt of trees. Sunlight glistened on the sea and the little rocky skerries and many small islets. And far off, across the wide stretch of water, slate-blue and steep and fierce, were the bare, scree-covered slopes of the Cuillins of Skye, thrusting sharp peaks into the small white clouds that wreathed themselves like ghosts about their tips. The day being clear, from this height he could just see Dunvegan Head.

"Ah, Christiana, you who longed to be schooled: you for whose sake I glean all my knowledge from my books: you to whom I shall return, when God gives me leave to depart from Rodel for ever: you who dwell over there, where I am looking: I send my humble greeting."

Onward he went, down hill now, where a burn ran shining and cold over its rocky bed with the force of its fall from the highlands. There were salmon-trout in the rocky pools, and primroses hung bunched above the water, and long-stalked violets, seeking the moisture of the overhanging banks. Lower, came bog, and peat beds, where cottagers had cut deep into the richness of the strata, and taking advantage of the sunny spell, laid out their peats along the ground in rows above the seams to dry, to be ready for loading into creels and taking home. Later they would be stacked against the outer walls of the earth houses ready for use, for a peat fire was all the fuel for warmth and cooking they had, there being so little timber in the hills.

Down here, the greenness concealed treacherous bogs, and it was only a man who knew the way who could come safely through. Here was bog-myrtle, and the white carpets of bog beans in flower. And kingcups on every hand in a great mass of gold. Yellow irises lined every linn, and the silky flags of the tulse, the wild bog cotton were just beginning.

Iain strode on throughout the day, leaving all the habitations behind. When the sun sank low, he found himself a hollow underneath a rock, split by a bent and ancient rowan tree that grew outwards from its cleft. He kindled a fire with the flint and tinder he had in his habit, and sat by it to eat his supper. It was only *brochan*, made from dried oats moistened in water from a peaty pool, and stirred over the flame until it was warmed a little and half-cooked.

It was almost like the old days with his father, he thought…save that here he had food to eat without begging or stealing it, and he could light a fire and cook on it, instead of eating the *brochan* raw as fugitives did. And here he was in no danger, for anyone who might see his fire and come to investigate, would know the habit of the lay brothers from Rodel and bid him journey in peace, unmolested. He sat, gazing into the crackling fire, feeling light-hearted and free, in spite of the recent loss of the Abbot who had been his spiritual father. Now there would be changes and new developments in his life within the next twelve months. I shall go to Dunvegan soon, he thought, and let his thoughts yearn towards Christiana for a while. At last he roused himself, said his evening prayers, then wrapped himself in his habit and fell asleep.

In the morning, mist lay along the hilltops and the air was chill. He rose at dawn; drank from a small linn where the water tumbled in a little fall into a sudden, icy pool: then walked on steadily until he came in sight of the little harbour of Tarbert, where a narrow isthmus links Harris with the Lewis. He went his way downhill, pressing his staff downwards into the heather, and came at length to the little settlement at the water's edge.

He stayed a night with the village schoolmaster at Tarbert when his business was finished. He was on warm terms with him, for he too was a scholar and had taught Iain and other student monks at Rodel a little Greek, as well as giving them their extensive Latin learning. The matter of accommodation for the itinerant monks was discussed and settled satisfactorily.

The next morning, he borrowed parchment and quill from the schoolmaster, and a little powdered ink, for the pressure to compose a letter that Christiana could appreciate was so strong that he could not wait to get back to his cell to do it.

He struck up into the heather uplands again, and found a flat-topped rock on which the sun fell full and warm at noon. He dribbled the powdered ink into a little hollow in the rock that made a natural ink-well, and moistened it with a few drops of peaty water from the burn. And so began, in his careful, upright script the continuation of his many letters to Dunvegan. And after all, it was not a love-letter, or a screed of news, though both had run interminably through his mind on the outwards journey. But instead a kind of sermon from his heart:

"It seemeth that the Way of Man toward the Godhead is like the Way of the Salmon in the Rivers of the Isles," he wrote. "For the Way is very long and hard, and not many survive the Ardours of it without falling away in Dreams and Sleep and Spiritual Death. As the young Salmon Elvers drift slowly downwards, tasting the pleasures of the Waterfalls, the Joy of Eating well from the Summer growth under the Leafy Banks, the Delight of Sleeping and Basking in the Shallows, so does Man by his own Nature swim downward with the Tide of Easy Living and congenial Circumstances. So does Man lightly come to the Mouth of the great River and enter the great Sea of Unconsciousness, in which he will combine with all Living Creatures great and small to be carried to and fro upon the tide of the great Ocean, swaying back and forth in idleness beneath the silver Rays of the Moon. In such a Great Bowl many Fishes swim, with no knowledge of another Way of Living and they are lulled to Sleep in that great Lap. But the great Royal Fish, the Salmon never loses Memory of whence he came. At the Time of the rising of the Tides in Spring, he turns back again and seeks the River he once knew. He swims against the strong Current, he leaps upward from Waterfall to Waterfall, striving with all his might to reach again the great Spawning Place in which he first was born. So must Man awake to Himself and turn him back to God our Father, with great Effort and hunger for that Still Centre which is the Source of all our Being, whence Man issued forth at the Creation of the World.

Be like *Fintan* the Salmon, O Beloved, leaping joyfully, striking back even against the Tide of Circumstances, up toward the great Pool that lies ever silent under the Great Sun that is our Lord and Father."

Iain read his letter through and remembering who the addressee really was crossed out 'O Beloved', dusted it dry with a little sand from beside the burn, and rolled it up carefully. Then he stood with it in his hands, on the hillside, looking across towards Dunvegan Head. But the rocky Cuillins hid their faces in cloud.

Rory read Iain's missive with curiosity and attention. It struck a chord of reality in him and gave him pleasure. But it did not occur to him to read it to Christiana, and presently it rolled off the table where he had left it, and bounced away to a dusty corner of the Fairy Tower Room, and lay there till the mice came and chewed its corners.

All the same, he continued to think how man's life might be a struggle against his lower nature in some way.

He had been much distressed inwardly by the memory of the feast at Duntulm, though he never discussed it with anyone. He saw how he had been easily duped into a trusting and boyish acceptance of Donald Gorme MacDonald's hospitality, and how he and his men might have paid for it with their lives.

He felt a smouldering hatred of Donald Gorme Mor, whose reddened, drunken, grinning countenance and bloody knife troubled him in his dreams with a sense of heaviness and foreboding.

*****

Shortly after William's accession, MacDonald of Dunnyveg attacked MacLean of Duart, coming to the aid of Donald Gorme's rascally cousin Hugh MacGillespie, who was always falling out with someone new. Hearing of trouble down in Jura and Islay on this account, Donald Gorme summoned his own men to Duntulm, and went off by sea to join in the fray with his various cousins and his kinsmen from Dunnyveg. They sailed south and landed on the Isle of Mull, and there fought a running battle over MacLean's property. Soon blood lust was rampant, as so frequently in the past, and they were firing cottages and running landsmen through with the sword before they reached the ramparts of Duart Castle itself.

"Oh William, my poor uncle Hector MacLean and the family at Duart!" Lady Janet, Tormod's widow cried, when she heard the news. "We must surely go to their aid. And besides, your brother Alexander is with them there."

William ordered his men to arms, and sent word to LachLan MacKinnon to join him, if he would, in this just cause. Word came from Strath that they were on the way, and MacLeod's own two galleys and the birlinn were got ready for the fray.

"Master Rory will get his revenge, now," the clansmen said, looking at the young chieftain as he stood by his elder brother's side. "You'll challenge Donald Gorme Mor on the battlefield in earnest, will you not, sir? Our clan honour demands it of you, that is sure."

Rory looked from one to another of their expectant faces, and heard their voices eager and urgent, requiring him to do his duty by them. William had buckled on his sword, taken up his shield, and was ready to embark. The standard bearer brought the Fairy Flag from the Tower Room, carefully furled, and went down the steps to the quay. Rory took the sword that Murdo MacAskill had sharpened on the rocks by the Seagate and polished, pressed it into its sheath and fastened it to his belt, and accepted the shield held out to him. A man must fight, to prove his manhood, as Iain said, he told himself, as he followed William down the steps. At the bottom, Bridie MacCrimmon slipped from the shadows, twined her arms round his neck and said: "My love, don't go! Take off your sword. You cannot undo the deeds you will do this day!"

He untwined her arms, unsmiling and moved on, answering over his shoulder: "Honour requires it of me." He crossed the plank and entered the galley behind his brother and sat down with his back to the quay where the ladies stood. His love for Bridie had worn away to nothing and he had had other girls since he first lay in the heather with her. Now he had weightier matters on his mind.

On the battlements, Dun Kenneth rubbed his black stone against his *breacan feile* and cradled it in the warmth of his hands.

"What can you see, Kenneth Odhar?" asked the old men who had been left behind. "Shall we win this day?"

"He is not as great in stature as Donald Gorme Mor, but he too shall be called Mor in his time," the little man murmured.

"Who do you speak of? William MacLeod, our Chief?"

"Rory Mor, Rory Mor," he whispered following the small fleet with his failing eyes as they moved off down the sealoch.

Rory, who had learned swordsmanship as he had learned skill at the butts, under Torquil MacSweyn's tuition as a matter of normal schooling at the castle, first drew his sword in anger on the high seas, as MacLeod's fleet, with the wild pipes playing them into the kill, moved headlong into contact with the MacDonalds. Battle on the high seas was as commonplace as battle on land, and the vessels crashed and ground together, while men leapt from one to the other shouting and yelling their jeers and their contempt and their fury one with another. Rory struck out at a boarding man and saw his throat slit from ear to ear, and the foaming water turned red with living blood about the vessels' sides.

A man must fight: make war, not love: shrieks and screams of wounded men struggling together in the water as the galleys manoeuvred and turned and came together with crashing and splintering of timbers: the raucous war cries drowning the loud notes of the bagpipes playing men on to stab, to wound, to hack off limbs, to decapitate, to throw bodies to the sharks: the gaping mouths: the blood-soaked tartan: the torn and blood-spattered sails: the broken sword: the weapon seized from a dead man's hand: then the fierce pain of a blade through the flesh of his thigh: the throbbing, pulsing blood gushing out and pouring down his leg and being stemmed by a salt-wet rag: the wild face of Hugh MacGillespie: then Donald Gorme himself, laughing and leering at him over the prow; the sudden unexpected hail of flint-tipped arrows from MacDonald of Dunnyveg's birlinn as his vessel drifted seemingly helpless: then young Roddy MacAskill falling, lying propped against the mast, one of his eyes hanging out against the battered face. He stooped and grasped his shoulders calling "Roddy! Roddy!" and heard the faint voice from the bloody mouth answering "Sir, well done. We've had our revenge this day." And then the good eye rolling upward in the head and only the white of it showing in the bruised and battered face as he lay dead.

Macleod and MacKinnon together overran the MacDonalds of Dunnyveg and Duntulm, who drew off at last and made for home. So the MacLeods returned to Dunvegan, having saved their kinsmen's castle in Mull for the time being. And MacLean and MacLeod and MacKinnon and MacDonald counted the cost in men wounded and lives lost: and listened to the wailing of the women for their husbands and their sons and the crying of the children for their fathers, as they had always done before and would surely do again in the time to come.

When he had cleaned himself and his wound had been bandaged, Rory limped into the Fairy Tower Room.

On the table stood the iron kist – the box in which the standard bearer had replaced the carefully folded flag and closed the lid, until the chief himself should bring the key and lock it up again.

Rory lifted the lid and looked at the faded silken folds and fingered them gently. The blood lust and the violence of the two-day battle had taken its toll of him, and though he had slept in the galley on the long sail home, he was exhausted. He closed his eyes, standing with his hand on the flag, and the pictures and the sounds of battle and the smell of blood and all the horror of it pulsated through him in wave upon wave of knowledge and new experience.

Does this then prove one's manhood, as Iain said? Am I more man, now, than I am when I am on the Piper's Walk with the sound of the *Ceol Mor* beating in my heart and moving through my veins and the very marrow of my bones? Am I more man than when I lay in the heather with Bridie, in those first good days of love? He raised his eyes and looked round the Tower Room and his expression had lost the last vestige of the boyish innocence and trust that had shone from him on that Autumn morning riding through the woods towards Duntulm. Roddy, oh my friend Roddy. He saw him lying against the mast with one eye out of its socket and hanging against his cheek. He drooped forward over the kist and saw a tear slip downward onto the folded silk. He had lost much blood and in his fatigue he seemed to have no control. He slid to his knees, groaning with the pain that this movement brought to his wounded leg, and half-fainting dragged the silken folds out in his closed fist, without purpose or intention in the act. Finding himself holding it, he stayed on his knees and pressed it to his face. Help us in the name of Colum Cille, to make music and make love and not make war. Help us to create and not destroy.

The legends said the Fairy Flag had been given to his forebears by the fairy wife of one of his ancestors. But Alasdair Crottach had told him that the flag was surely the Land Ravager of their distant compatriot Harald Haardraader, which history recorded the Norsemen bore before them in their battle with King Harold of England.

"It has always been used in war as long as men remember. But it is Eastern silk, I think, and maybe it was first a garment of a Holy man, brought back from the Crusades, by some good Christian knight," the Abbot said. "Let us use it for good purposes if we can."

With eyes closed and bowed head Rory uttered a plea to whoever stood behind the power of the flag. Let the power and the purpose of the clan be clean.

He slipped to the floor, and the silk tumbled all about his head as he slept. And all about him little voices seemed to whisper strange, half-audible, half-comprehensible words, of comfort, explanation and command.

Chapter Six

SUMMONS TO THE KING

At Stirling Castle, King James VI had just laid his eyes for the first time on a treasonous document that Donald Gorme Mor had sent by messenger to Queen Elizabeth of England, telling her, with protestations of friendship and goodwill, that if she would support such a venture with men and arms, he…as direct claimant of the Lordship of the Isles…would gladly raise an army of men of the Isles and send them off "to fasche King James." The horseman taking the document to London had been waylaid at Kylerhea by Argyll's men and his satchel removed and searched.

The king sat with the document in one hand, tapping the ringed fingers of the other on the arm of the chair, while the Earl of Argyll talked at great length about it.

There was little danger of large scale rebellion among the Island chiefs these days, for so frequently and ruthlessly had the Royal hand descended, directly or through the Clan Campbell of which the Earl of Argyll was hereditary chief, that many clans had been broken in strength and their estates forfeited long since. It was even doubtful if young Donald Gorme MacDonald could get the useful following he professed to be able to command. Probably only youthful exuberance was behind the boastful claim.

Argyll professed to see in this attempt by the young chief of the Clanranald to attract the Queen of England's eye, a greater and more serious threat to peace than the King thought existed. The Earl did not miss the nervous, irritable tapping of the Royal fingers, and the chilliness of the King's eyes, but they served only to increase his anxiety to make his point.

"In truth, sir, if this young man is not summoned and tried for treachery, I do not feel sure that we may not have our troublesome subjects in the Hebrides out in strength again, in spite of your Grace's past wisdom in dealing with the islanders," he declared.

The possessive pronoun did not escape the notice of the king, but he let it by. He permitted the Earl to run on unchecked until he had had his say, and then dismissed him. When Argyll had kissed his sovereign's hand and bowed his way out, the King got up from his chair and walked the length of the great chamber a couple of times, with his difficult, rickety gait that seemed more pronounced when he was troubled in mind.

He had thought before – and this recent audience seemed to confirm his thought – that the powerful family of Argyll, so long relied on to act as both mediators and guardians between the Western Highlands and Isles and the crown, were coming to regard their stewardship in a somewhat dangerous light.

The Earl had begun by offering to raise an army and cross to Skye at once and suppress any threatened rebellion by force, as his father had done on behalf of the Regent. He did not like it that the King saw no need for the raising of any army; and indeed he had looked affronted and disappointed by the Royal refusal to permit it.

Coming back to the great leather chair by the table, the King commanded to have brought to him those papers and documents relevant to the state of affairs in the last decade in the Western Highlands and Isles, and sat for some while listening, while they were read over to him. Then he took them into his own hands and studied them.

He looked up at length, and from the faces of the councillors gathered about him, selected the steady eyes of the Earl of Huntley, whose own stakes in the Western Isles were strong, and asked him abruptly: -

"How do the Islemen think of my Lord of Argyll? Has he their regard?"

"He has their respect, sir," Huntley answered, after a moment's cautious thought.

"Their liking? Or their fear?"

The pause was appreciably longer, and this time the King did not wait, but cut across the silence with: -

"My grandfather put down the Overlordship, and I would not have it revived again, either in the old way or in another form. I almost think Argyll would like to go off to the Isle of Eigg and get his own feet into that great stone where it is said the Lords of the Isles were anciently instated."

There was discreet laughter among the councillors, but Huntley's face remained impassive. If Argyll were out of favour in these matters, Huntley, if he bided his time, might well be in again, as he had been before, for there had been rivalry between these two for many years, and with the increasing bickering between the Catholic and the Protestant lords, old bitterness had flared up again. If Huntley were back in the sovereign's grace, he would form, with the Earls of Angus and Erroll, and the Lord Chancellor himself, a strong pocket of opinion that the old ways were best, against Argyll and his upstart Presbyterians.

"Study these, my Lord, and bring me tomorrow your considered thoughts about our Island territories," the King requested. "You will see that in spite of my Lord of Argyll's vigilance, there is unrest in many quarters again. Donald Gorme MacDonald of Skye, has his hands full already, for he is embroiled with MacLean of Duart over some trouble his cousin started in Jura or Isle Islay – it is a confused story. William MacLeod, the chief of Dunvegan and Harris, and the clan MacKinnon have been out in force against MacDonald of Dunnyveg – himself kin to those of that name in Skye – all on this same matter. And now Robert MacKenzie who holds Kintail on the mainland, has a quarrel with MacLeod of the Lewis – who is, I do not doubt, kin to MacLeod of Dunvegan as well.

"Acquaint yourself with it all, sir, and unravel its meshes. These Islanders' politics resemble the squabbles of a Persian harem. Ah, and consider also this other matter," the King continued, as his eyes lighted on two letters that had been attached to these rambling communications. The top one was from one Thomas Inglis, a merchant burgess of Edinburgh, stating that Hugh MacGillespie MacDonald, clerk, had boarded one of his ships in Loch Shiel in the Lewis, and "wrongously, violently and masterfully, against all order of law or justice, reft, spuilzeit, intromettit with, and away took the said ship, with the whole merchandise, goods and gear."

Fastened with it, was a letter of complaint written in High Dutch, with a translation into English pinned below, and couched in bitter terms. It dealt with the fishing rights off the coast of Scotland, which his Grace had so lightly conceded to the Flemish fishing fleet, but which could rarely be taken up without fear of reprisals from the islanders. Baiting the Dutch fishermen and stealing their catch had been an island sport for several years.

At the bottom of the document, some official had written the words: "Donald Gorme MacDonald of the Clanranald, William MacLeod of Dunvegan and Harris, and one Lachlan MacKinnon, the heir of Strathordell, with a goodly force attacked the Dutch Fleet off N. Uist and caused havoc and damage and did steal away the catal and herrings and mackerel and fired one of their boats."

Huntley read the latter comment aloud, one eyebrow raised sardonically, and looked towards his liege for guidance on his attitude.

"MacLeod and MacDonald at war on a Friday, and rubbing shoulders on some joint devilry on Saturday – as ever, like squabblesome children," remarked the Lord Chancellor Thirlestone irritably.

Huntley said smoothly, his eyebrow jerking up again: -

"Two dogs and one bone will always squabble, but let a bitch come in sight and the two will run together in pursuit."

There was a ripple of laughter, light and disdainful and superior. Looking the length of the table at courtier and councillor alike – all city men, breeched and coated in the latest fashion, the King said: -

"We have neither a bone nor yet a bitch to spare, my Lord of Huntley. But a lick of the whip will do as well. If they will not run together in peace, I would as soon have them lie together and howl."

Huntley took his cue willingly enough from the King's words.

There went out from Stirling on the following day messengers on behalf of the King's Grace to the principal chieftains of the Isles, bidding them come and present themselves at Edinburgh within one month.

To make assurance doubly sure – for he could not tell whether the King would still be angry, by the time the Islanders came, and he thought it would be a pity if they were only sent off with a flea in the ear, and came home cocky as ever, Huntley sent in, by a Secretary, for the royal attention, a copy of Master John Colvin's 'History of the Times', with a line of ink marking his survey of the Western Isles and their Inhabitants:

"True it is that the islandish men are of nature very proud, suspicious, avaricious, full of deceit and evil invention, each against his neighbour by what way so ever he may circumvent him. Beside all this they are so cruel in taking of revenge that neither have they regard to person, age, time or cause, so are they all addicted to their own tyrannical opinions that in all respects they exceed in cruelty the most barbarous people that has been since the beginning of the world."

If King James digested that with his supper, there would seem sufficient reason for the strong action that the sovereign's temporary irritability had initiated – and Huntley would be happy enough to be given something to do at this now opportune moment when his old rival, Argyll, was clearly out of favour.

At Dunvegan, William had assembled almost all the men of Skye and the neighbouring isles for a day of feasting and tourneys to celebrate the fifth birthday of little John, his son and heir.

There had been little merriment of late, but all fighting and bickering between one and another, and being by nature a peaceable man, William MacLeod thought to revive something of the hospitality his father had always meted out with a generous hand.

When Rory saw that Donald Gorme MacDonald was invited like everyone else, he protested angrily. But William got on well enough with everyone, and saw nothing odd about patching up old relationships in times of peace, as the islanders had always done. The continual warfare in the islands was much like the battleground that a large family may make within its own ranks, roaring with fury over slights, the stronger attacking the weaker, the elders defending the younger, and yet in the last resort all of them being bound together by bonds of blood and a continual love-hate relationship.

"Well, he is quite a good fellow, and our father entertained his father, Rory. So I will entertain him too," the chief replied.

"We cannot feast without inviting Duntulm, dearest," Lady Janet put in gently. "They would be mightily offended."

"Well, we shall need eyes in the backs of our heads to watch him, then," Rory grumbled.

The weather had turned fine again, and the households from Duntulm and Dunscaith, and Castle Camus down in Sleat, as well as Lachlan MacKinnon and his young family, gathered together with as many of their clansmen as could crowd into the castle courtyard and the cultivated ground outside the curtain wall.

As the clans competed at archery down at the butts, other teams were matched off to fence, and some were leaping the long jump, and others still playing the pipes and vying with the MacCrimmons in their art. There was noise and jostling and gaiety, with the music and the singing, and all manner of good things to eat as well.

William and his wife were sitting on benches on the grassy top of the mound called the Hill of Justice, just outside the castle, where he held court from time to time and settled the disputes that arose among the clansmen. All down the hillside, young men and girls sat in groups on the grass, watching the proceedings, and everyone was in high good humour. The chief leaned back, benevolent and placid, holding the hand of his young wife and with his little son on his other side.

The lively notes of a strathspey and the repetitive thwack, thwack of arrow on target, floated up from the clearing near the shore. In the foreground, two mighty clansmen struggled together astride a greasy pole, knocking each other with sticks, while the crowd roared their approval at their efforts to dislodge each other.

Suddenly Torquil MacSweyn appeared from the direction of the quay, which was invisible from where they sat, and came panting rapidly up the hill.

"MacLeod sir, a messenger with letters from the King."

William stopped laughing and rose slowly to his feet. He looked down the grassy slope and watched a lowland gentleman, looking green from the seasickness, begin to climb up towards him. "Was there no watch on duty at the gate? Did no-one see an unknown vessel approach?"

"Sir, we were all at the games," they answered, like children who forget their duties when at play.

"We might have been attacked," he said.

From where he sat, Rory could see William 's brown hands breaking the seal on the parchment. He ran his eye down the writing with a studious look, while the gentleman from the Court stood nervously looking round him at the bearded islanders, in their various coloured tartans, with their bare and brawny arms and legs exposed. Christiana giggled. William could barely read, since he had always declared reading and writing to be best suited to monks and clerks and had not applied his mind to it beyond learning how to sign his own name on a document. He was clearly in difficulty. But he handled the moment with ease, looking gravely and seriously at the long document, line by line, and then lifting his eyes to say:

"We had better have this letter read aloud, I think, since the King honours us with his attention once again."

Rory did not bat an eyelid as he summoned young O'Mhuirgeason with a gesture of his hand, and such dignity was maintained that the King's messenger saw nothing of the ruse, and was deprived of the pleasure of telling his colleagues in Edinburgh and Stirling that the chief was indeed barbarous and could not read his own letters.

Master O'Mhuirgeason the bard and scribe, who was schooled in Glasgow, read the English words rapidly and turned them with almost equal speed into the Gaelic tongue.

In the King's name, the Earl of Huntley summoned and ordered all the principal chiefs of the Isles to present themselves at Edinburgh within one month by the season of Beltane, to "account for divers deeds of treachery, insubordination, non-payment of dues and other wrongful acts."

There was a long silence when the reading had finished.

"Well," William said at last, speaking slowly and carefully, "MacDonald and MacKinnon, I suppose you must go home and receive the King's orders in person in your own houses. But let us first speak a while in private, before you leave."

He led the way down the hill, while the messenger, shifting nervously from one foot to the other, was obviously relieved to be offered a goblet of ale and a hot pasty by William's wife and told to sit and rest.

"I cannot eat, Ma'am, I am too sick," he said, "but I am grateful for the hospitality." He subsided on to the bench, thankful, it seemed, that no-one had offered to run him through with a sword.

Inside the great hall, Rory's tongue ran away with him, and before his brother spoke he said to Donald Gorme:

"Doubtless it is you we must thank for this summons. But for your hothead plans to involve the Queen of England in our affairs, this message would never have been sent. Do you think MacLeod has nothing better to do than go dancing off to Edinburgh to King James, when our kinsman of Dunnyveg is holding a portion of our men still, in Islay, and my young brother Alexander is held hostage for MacLean, and Lord Lovat plaguing us with his claim to our property in Glenelg? Why could you not hold your foolish tongue? No-one supports the old lordship now...it is dead a generation since, and even if Queen Elizabeth supported you, we would not support you."

"By Colum Cille!" MacDonald roared, banging his great fist on the table so that a pewter tankard overturned and spilled its contents, "I'd ask no help of you, young Rory, even if I were helpless...which I am not, for all the islanders save MacLeod would rise if I rose."

"That they would not," Lachlan MacKinnon said. He was a tall, thin man with a shrewd eye, and he knew well when a cause was worth supporting and when it must be accounted dead.

"You can't tell who would hold with you, Donald Gorme Mor, since you have not asked us," MacLean of Duart interjected sharply. "But it is certain we would not, after your recent forays into our lands. If you have the good of the Isles at heart, you will not name the names of any supporters you may have, in Edinburgh."

"If I go there," MacDonald said sulkily. "What do you say, MacLeod? Are we going? Must we?"

"It will not pay to disobey, that is a certain thing," William said. He shook his head, considering. He was a slow thinker, and did not like to have to make sudden decisions until he felt sure he understood what the outcome would be. "It will be difficult for me to leave just now," he added.

"Let me go for you, William," Rory offered. "I expect I would be acceptable, as I am your next of kin."

"Well, you are not my next of kin now that I have a son," William considered slowly. " But if you want to go…It is true I am not summoned by name. This summons has clearly gone to a great many chiefs of clans and it is certain they will not all attend in person."

"I shall go myself," MacLean of Duart said stoutly, "it's a journey a man should make once in his lifetime, to see the finery at Holyrood and eye the dandies at Court. It won't inconvenience me much to go by Beltane. And you, Dunachton: shall we travel together?"

MacIntosh of Dunachton ran a hoary hand through his great bush of hair and said dubiously:

"Since I am not an islander, it may be I am not summoned. I shan't know till I get home. Huntley has no cause to love me…I have picked bones with him before, because his estates adjoin mine. Or what he calls his estates." He sighed. "I would as soon stay home and face the King's wrath at a distance."

"No, father-in-law," William said, laying an affectionate hand on his shoulder, "It would be foolish to refuse, for my Lord of Huntley would be at your gates in no time to know the reason why. Besides, if I send my nimble-tongued young brother, I would like to know that you are there to watch his tongue and keep him in check."

All the chiefs were finally in agreement on the necessity of obeying the King's summons, either in person or by a prominent clansman who could represent them. They did not want further visits by an armed naval vessel. The only dissentient was Torquil Dubh of the Lewis, who sat sideways on the table, swinging one long bare leg, tossing and catching a broken arrow tip in his hand as he listened.

"Well, I'll not go," he said at length. "Nor, I am sure, will my old father."

"You are not likely to be summoned," Donald Gorme said, grinning. "It's your brother the King recognises as claimant to the Lewis, surely? The one they call *Conanach*…the Stranger?"

This was so sore a matter that it was best not touched upon among these fiery tempered men, for they were rarely quiet and in amity for long. Torquil Dubh rose to the bait at once:

"My stepmother's firstborn son Torquil *Conanach* is a bastard," he said hotly. "Everyone knows that. My father was very bitter about it, and rightly so. that's why he sent young Torquil away to be fostered in

76

Kintail by my stepmother's own clan. As for her, she does not dare set foot in Stornaway. Why, Torquil Conanach is almost a MacKenzie by upbringing, as well as being the son of…well, not my father Ruari MacLeod of the Lewis. If my father had not been sure about this, do you think he would have had me named Torquil too? Of course he wouldn't! It was always his wish that his true heir should bear this name, because it is the most ancient name of our line. We come from Torquil, son of Leod the Norseman, as Dunvegan here comes from Tormod the other son of Leod. That is why we go on perpetuating the same names throughout clan history…"

"Torquil Conanach is very like old Hutcheon, the Breve – your judge in Stornaway," a young chieftain said. "Did you not notice it yourself, at Portree Fair last year, Torquil Dubh? I remember your bastard brother was speaking most confidently of how he would inherit the Lewis, though!"

"Hush, hold your tongues, do," William cried, seeing that in the wrangling over who would inherit the Lewis, the chiefs would soon be at one another's throats and nothing of this more urgent matter decided. "Away now on your own affairs, Black Torquil. At least you are surely not summoned in person while your father lives."

The long-legged, black-haired young man looked mutinous for a moment, then ambled off through the open door, tossing the broken arrow head away from him across the battlements as he passed.

Outside, William and Rory's two sisters were sitting together on the low wall, waiting with interest and curiosity to hear the outcome of the conversation between the chiefs. Shy Margaret was scared by the raised voices, for she was easily alarmed, and Christiana took her hand and held it, laughing down at her anxious-looking face. Torquil strolled across towards them, smiling.

"Well, pretty ones, have you left the games? They are surely not all finished?"

"Oh sir," Margaret cried, clasping her hands and looking up at him, "what is happening inside?"

"The chiefs plan to go in force to Edinburgh with a mighty army to put out the King's eyes," he said.

Margaret screamed and clapped her hands to her mouth. "Oh, sir! Oh, no! What madness."

"But I shall protect you both, when the Royal troops come in revenge," he said, putting an arm round the shoulders of both girls and turning them to walk with him along the battlements.

"You are joking," Christiana said. "MacLeod would never be so foolish."

He laughed, hugged her to him, releasing Margaret, and said "You are right. I am only teasing." But Margaret was still not reassured and cried, "My lord of the Lewis, are you truly sure?" She clung to his arm, and was still hanging there, looking up at him with her nearsighted blue eyes wide, when the chiefs emerged from their conference together.

At once Donald Gorme came across and with an indignant look took Margaret from Torquil's arm, and with a proprietary air, led her off. She tripped obediently beside him, looking up at the heavily-built man with the same wide-eyed look she had given Torquil.

"Let me walk the other side. I can't see you well with this eye," she said.

"You could see Torquil Dubh well enough, it seems."

"No, really, I see little with this eye, and it troubles me rather. Dr. Beaton has tried everything he can think of, but nothing seems to work." He turned her towards him and looked at her. One of the mild blue eyes was almost clouded over and opaque.

"Well, lets hope he can cure you," he said with grumbling affection, "for I don't want a one-eyed bride."

She stared at him in silence.

"We are to be married?" she asked at last.

"MacLeod has given permission. It will be a good alliance. Our children will have the good of both clans at heart."

"He has not told me," she said doubtfully.

"He would have done so this evening, but now our plans are all upset by the King's summons, and I must away to Duntulm without a betrothal feast. Come, kiss me and say you are willing, little one."

"I am willing," she answered him obediently, and raised her closed lips, pushed out in a little pout. "I can't imagine why you want me, though," she added in a minute. "Would you not rather marry Christiana? She is much prettier than I, and *her* eyes are beautiful."

He gave a short laugh. "I have more important things to do than tame a girl like her into obedience. A wife should be pliable and willing. I have enough troubles without domestic ones."

At the other end of the battlement Torquil Dubh held Christiana to him, and laughingly kissed her upturned nose.

"I can't see why Donald MacDonald took your sister from me with such vigour," he said after a moment. "I never set eyes in the direction of any girl but you."

"You are lying," she answered laughing. "Your eyes run up and down any girl who comes within sight…you know they do."

"Well, when you are out of the nursery…"

"You know I have been long out of my nurse's charge…"

"Well, when MacLeod wishes, and if he agrees, and if I get my inheritance which I shall surely do, I shall come again and ask you to marry me. Will you do that? Will you marry me?"

She gave him a long and steady, considering look.

"I might," she said.

"You are a minx." He put his hand to her waist and raised it slowly and gently till it cupped her breast. He leaned over her, his breath on her cheek. "I shall woo you with such ardour you will faint for love of me," he said, his voice rich and warm and deep. She laughed, but her eyes widened and colour rose to her cheeks. His handsome face grown serious, he whispered: "Will you have me?" into her windblown hair.

"Yes," she answered. "Yes, I think so. Yes."

When he had gone, Christiana went leaping and striding down the steps, her skirt bunched in her hand for speed of progress, and out of the castle by the sea gate. She ran round into the woods behind the castle, went a little way up the path and then took off her slippers and thrust them into a fox's hole to await her, and went on barefoot.

Several cuckoos called among the trees, and she stood and listened to them, looking upward into the leafy branches. The woods had been silent in the spring. The legends said that the cuckoos leave Dunvegan when the chief dies and go to the Isle of St Kilda for a while. The cottagers and fishermen of that remote isle had been found standing on the beach when the birlinn came with news of the double deaths of Tormod and Alasdair Crottach within a few weeks, and all the women were keening over the peats.

"We knew MacLeod was dead," an old shawled woman said. The cuckoos came last week."

When William had told him what the boatmen had said, Rory had answered: "That can't be a true tale, surely?"

"Why not? Dun Kenneth knows things that no-one tells him, and young Bridie MacCrimmon foretells events through the flight of birds or the growth of the flax and the linseed, or the way the fish rise in the morning. There are more things in these Isles than lowlanders dream of."

"You will be saying like the old man in Iona our grandfather told us of: 'Iona is a verra thin place. There's no' much between Iona and the Lord.'" He mimicked the cottager's accent in island Gaelic. "All the same, the woods *are* strangely silent, " Rory had admitted after a moment, standing at the casement and looking out.

But now a new year had brought the cuckoos back, and Christiana went barefoot through the woods whistling like a boy, and thinking of the darkly handsome face of Torquil Dubh of the Lewis, and his hand upon her breast and his breath upon her mouth.

Chapter Seven

THE FRANKISH MINSTREL

When Rory heard that William had given his consent to a betrothal between his sister Margaret and Donald Gorme he was incensed.

"You can't permit this, William! He is an intemperate, violent man, and Margaret is so gentle."

"She is quite happy about it, Rory, and he seems fond of her. Besides, it will be a good alliance for both clans. Why do you dislike Donald Gorme so much? Is it that episode at Duntulm that still rankles with you the day you poached the deer? Yes, poor Roddy MacAskill told me about it. It was mere boyish devilment no doubt."

"No, it was more than that..." But he realised protest was useless, for the chief had made up his mind, and anyway nobody objected except himself. Lady Janet seemed to feel it was a good match for Margaret, who had none of Christiana's sparkle and good looks.

"I am more troubled about Alexander than about Margaret," William remarked. "It's time our brother came home, but I cannot get Dunnyveg to see reason over it. He holds him to no purpose, that I can see."

"Well, his letter was cheerful enough. He isn't ill treated."

The youngest of the three brothers had been sent to MacLean's household to be fostered as a young boy - this was an old custom among the chiefs' families, its purpose being to encourage mutual family interests and bonds of friendship. He had been happily brought up there, and had come home to Dunvegan so rarely that William and Rory scarcely knew their brother. A few months back he had sent letters telling of his betrothal to a kinswoman at Duart Castle. The news that Hector MacLean had handed him over to MacDonald of Dunnyveg after the recent disturbances, as a sop to Dunnyveg, had caused sharp words between William and his uncle. Hostages were frequently held for a while, usually in comparative comfort, even though dire threats were sometimes held over their heads. But it seemed hard that Alexander should be deprived of his freedom by his own foster father's action, especially when he wanted to marry and settle down.

William and Rory and their mother were all content to hear of Torquil Dubh's intention to marry Christiana later on. They celebrated it discreetly, since it was not yet an open betrothal, or yet a handfasting.

*****

"Who will you take with you to Edinburgh?" William asked Rory a few days later. "Roddy's young brother Norman would look after you well, I think."

"Iain MacIain," Rory answered, speaking with sudden conviction that he would come. "He is a scholar and he speaks the lowland tongue, and it is past time we called him home. His last letter said the monastery is all but disbanded and the monks settled in their new and independent way of life."

"Ah, his letters," William laughed. "His sermons, more like. He has a very spiritual turn of mind, hasn't he?"

"He is none the worse for that. He has a certain wisdom in him, and he may keep my tongue from running away with me at Edinburgh…as it sometimes does."

"Yes. Guard your tongue well, Rory. Consider your words and don't speak impulsively. Much may depend on how you bear yourself, and what you say to my Lord of Huntley, and indeed to the King himself if he receives you. I wonder if I am wise to let you go, and not to go myself?"

"I hope to do well for us," Rory answered.

When Iain received the summons from Dunvegan, his heart lifted and he knew in his bones that this was the time to take leave of Rodel. He packed the few books and scrolls the Abbot had bequeathed to him. The brothers gave him the hand-wrought silver communion cup that Brother Robert the silver-smith had made for use at the monastery, and which they felt should go now to Dunvegan to be used in the new church that was being built at Duirinish nearby.

He embarked in MacLeod's birlinn, and smiled and bowed farewell to the small group of monks who stood on the shore waiting to see their lay brother depart. Then he turned his face eagerly towards Dunvegan.

Almost the first news he was told when he set foot ashore and began to climb the long steps up through the rock was that both the young ladies of MacLeod were to be married and there would be feasting soon to celebrate it.

He stopped abruptly on the steps.

"Both of them?" he asked, seeming bewildered.

82

"Yes, Mistress Christiana and Mistress Margaret. Do you not remember them, then?"

"Yes," he said very slowly. "Yes, I remember…I understand…I see…Who are they to wed, then?"

The clansmen told him, wondering at the way he looked at them, piercingly, and yet with his face working as though he had the salt wind in his eyes and bringing tears to them. "She is happy, then?" he said.

"Which one of them do you mean?"

"Why both of them! Well, well. A double wedding, then?" he said, looking about him at the courtyard he had not seen for so long, and seeming agitated and distraught as though he did not know whether to walk on, or turn back to the quay and go away again. He cleared his throat standing with head bent and hands thrust into the wide sleeves of his brown robe. Then in command of himself again, he said in a firm voice: "Well lead on, friend, and show me where I am to lay my head this night."

They took him to the chamber he was to occupy. He thanked them, and began to place his books on the table, carefully, one by one. Then he unwrapped the silver communion cup which he had imagined placing reverently in Christiana's hands, to watch her eyes feast on the fine moulding of the figures of Our Lord and the Disciples. He studied it minutely, trying to hold his mind on a steady course, to still the violence which rose and fell in him like the crashing of mountainous waves against the rocks in a winter storm.

He raised his eyes and looked from the window, and saw away in the distance across the sea the low grey hump of Harris and of Rodel. It occurred to him for the first time that Christiana had promised him nothing. Rory had promised him nothing. God had promised him nothing. He seemed to be alone with the remnants of a dream of his own making.

He steeled himself - and later when they met and she ran up laughing to greet him with a kiss on the cheek, he turned his face sternly away from her. She drew back, thinking it to be merely due to his new, monkish ways.

*****

The chiefs travelled up to Edinburgh at their leisure, for there was still almost a fortnight to the May Day festival of Beltane, with its once Druidic rites of purification that had become corrupted into merriment and bonfires long since.

Those chiefs who were by time and nature allied, travelled together, or in groups with their men for safety, in the wild lands where they were not known. But there had been so much bloodshed and bitterness this last decade, that several who would have done better to seek company, travelled unguarded and alone, fearing their own kin as much as the outlaw bands that roamed the Western Highlands.

The King was at Holyrood House, but the chiefs had instructions that they would not be lodged at the Palace, but at the castle on the hilltop a mile away. They trickled in, in little bands over the space of several days, looking strange wild tall men in their swinging kilted plaids, so that the citizens of Edinburgh stared at them and said "they look like gods…or devils."

"It's said they are of Viking blood, these islanders."

"Or born of fairy stock like the old Celts who came from Ireland."

"Whoever they are, they can't go before the King unbreeched, in these days." The Warden of the castle remarked sourly, looking at the scarred and hairy legs with distaste. "We'd best have a tailor up here in the morning."

But on this the chiefs had divided ideas. While Hector MacLean of Duart grumblingly allowed himself to be measured for breeches and a coat of broadcloth, MacNeil of Barra swore at the tailor when he began his task, and knocked his hand away and called him an impudent fellow as he tried to measure him for breeches. MacDonald of Islay produced with a sheepish grin a suit of clothes his father had worn at Court once years ago and said they would serve him well enough, though they were a poor fit and out of fashion. MacKenzie of Kintail was measured in a way, though he would not stand still, so impatient was he of such foppish ideas. Donald Gorme sulkily acquiesced when he saw Rory MacLeod had made no objections.

When they came at last into the King's presence, they were barbered and neatly garbed as any city gentleman. Young MacKinnon even had scented pomade on his hair. In the ante-chamber his kindred told him he smelt like a girl and he fluttered his lashes, grinning, while Dunnyveg shook out a lacy kerchief such as his warrior's hand had never held before, and gestured with it, chortling like a schoolboy.

But when the great double doors to the presence chamber opened, their antics ceased at once and they straightened their faces, and went with dignity to offer their humble duty to the King.

Iain MacIain was free that morning to do as he chose, for Rory felt it would not be suitable for him to go uninvited to Holyrood. He had helped Rory to dress, served him his meat and bread, and waited on him until the time of departure. As they left, he looked into Rory's face and said: "Sir?"

"Yes?"

"MacLeod bade me say to you last thing 'guard your tongue well', sir."

Rory laughed. He laid a hand on MacIain's shoulder and said: "I will, my friend," and went to join the others.

When the bustle and noise of their departure was over, Iain went softly out, and down the long steep street from the castle, in the morning sunshine, looking at the great houses and little groups of dwellings round the cluttered courtyards, and the faces of the people passing up and down on their peaceable affairs. A few heads turned to look at him as he passed – a tall slim bearded man with an easy swinging gait, clad in a long brown habit and with his shock of brown hair shaved across the front and curling low on his neck at the back in a way no townsman would wear it – but he went on oblivious of their curious glances.

Down below at the end of Canongate, he could see the dark mass of Holyrood House, with the green rounded hill of King Arthur's Seat hunched like a shoulder beside it. In there the chiefs were waiting on their King. He paused, and looked down at it.

Then turning his head he saw the Collegiate Church of St Giles rising beside him, and crossed the street and looked through the open door.

After a moment, he stepped over the threshold and in the dim interior, crossed himself and went down on his knees in the aisle, his head bent. He began to repeat the prayers of St Columba.

Suddenly a firm hand took him by the shoulder and a voice ordered him in a loud whisper not to kneel there. He opened his eyes and found a little wiry black-eyed fellow in a plain gown and high collar staring at him with annoyance. "Be off with you. We want no Popish strangers here," he said, jerking his head towards the door.

Iain looked at him in astonishment. "What do you mean, sir? I only crossed myself and knelt to pray. Is this not a church of God, and free for all men?" he whispered back.

"It is a church of the new Protestant faith, which our sovereign lord the King supports with his blessing," the small man said in a pompous manner.

Iain began to get to his feet. "Well, the King's mother Queen Mary and all her forebears were of the Roman faith, and it's said King James himself only tolerates the reformers, so I don't see there is any need to berate me for following the old customs." He said softly. He smiled down amiably at the small official from his great height.

"We don't kneel. We don't cross ourselves. We've got rid of superstitious ways. In this church a man should have the dignity to stand on his feet to face his Maker."

"You have got rid of a good deal more besides…including loving kindness to your neighbour," Iain said. He spoke in mild tones, but the little sacristan answered sharply in a louder voice:

"Away with you and don't dare argue with me!"

In spite of him, Iain faced the altar table and genuflected before he turned to leave. The church had seemed empty, but as he moved away he came face to face with a gentleman, dressed in the fashion of the Court, who laid a hand on his arm to detain him.

"Come, friend," he said, "we are not all so inhospitable as Master Rigby. I do not think the Presbyters have ever bade you speak to a stranger in such a manner," he said to the sacristan in a low voice. "Or to raise your voice in anger on this holy ground."

"Master de Lérins, the Presbyters have given instruction…it is not part of my duty to put up with impertinence from…" The newcomer waved him away with an authoritative gesture.

"Come, say your prayers in peace, friend. I will stand guard over you."

Iain shook his head. "Thank you sir, but I will leave as I am bidden."

The stranger bowed with a cool grace, then followed him down the aisle and out into the porch. There they looked at one another and he bowed again.

"Hugh Whitby de Lérins at your service."

Unaccustomed to city manners, Iain answered awkwardly:

"I am Iain MacIain who lodges with MacLeod of Dunvegan and Harris."

"Sir." Lérins made a courteous inclination of his head. Then "It is enough to make Murray turn in his tomb," he said with a cheerful smile. Iain looked puzzled.

"You did not see the great tomb of the Regent, the Earl of Murray? The Earl of Huntley dispatched him ten years ago…or so men believe."

"My Lord of Huntley? Is he not the King's new favourite?"

"Well, so he may be, now. But great plots lay behind the Regent's sudden death…they say. Yet it all came to nothing, for our young King proved well able to take the reins in his own hands, and when it was seen he favoured the Protestants…my Lord of Huntley and his fellow

Roman Catholic earls were like galleys with no wind in their sails, idly flapping and not able to advance towards their chosen destination."

"Do you mean he intended to unseat the King? How then can he be back in favour?"

"Well, memories are short, when it is expedient to forget. But there are certain noblemen who ought to be on their guard, that is clear enough."

"The Earl of Argyll, do you mean? My master, MacLeod of MacLeod is in bond to him for some ancient privileges. What will the outcome be?"

"We are strangers, and we are talking too freely," de Lérins said, glancing round him nervously. "My tongue runs away with me at times."

"As my young Master's does! He is at court today and I am hot and cold by turns, with anxiety for him."

"Come to my lodging and drink with me," de Lérins suggested. "I live near, by the Canongate."

"I shall be glad to."

"So you come from the Western Isles?" he asked, as they entered an old house and climbed a dark stairway. "I have never been there, for I am not a good sailor, and they say the Western sea is very fierce."

"Well, you could cross to Skye easily enough…it is not so far from the mainland."

"If the King released me from obligations to him, I may come yet."

"Are you a Courtier, sir?"

He laughed. "You could say so. I am a traveller with no fixed residence. I am a minstrel."

They entered a richly furnished room where silks and brocades draped the walls and chairs and a wide couch was piled high with silken cushions. Iain looked about him with astonishment.

"By Colum Cille, what a Palace!"

De Lérins laughed easily and naturally about everything. He was a thin and slightly-built man in his middle thirties, supple and agile in his movements, with white hands like a girl and a great ring on his middle finger in which a green stone glinted. His eyes were large and brilliant in his small face. His hair seemed burnished, shining, upswept from his wide brow. His features were mobile and changeable, now falling into lines of gravity, now upturned in mirth, and then in a moment, falling into a look of grief and sadness. Iain looked at him with curiosity and fascination. He had never seen such a strange person in his life.

"I have good wine from Beaune in France. Taste it with me," de Lérins said. He poured the ruby liquid into crystal goblets and handed one to Iain. "The King," he said, "God bless him." He reached forward and touched his glass to Iain's, looking up at him.

Feeling awkward, half amused, half uneasy, Iain followed de Lérins actions. He sat down as invited, on the edge of the great couch. The minstrel took a lute from which coloured ribbons fluttered, and perching himself on a stool began to play and sing:

> *"Even so my sun one early morn did shine*
> *With all triumphant splendour on my brow:*
> *But, out, alack! he was but one hour mine,*
> *The region cloud hath maskt him from me now…"*

He had a sweet, light voice, very different from Rory's deep base, but pleasant to the ear.

"Do you earn your bread by your songs, then?" Iain asked.

"Oh, I am an idle wastrel…I earn one way and another as the fancy takes me. If there is no one who will feed and clothe me for the pleasure of my company, I find some other way. I used to play the great organ in the church, but the Presbyters have done away with music. I please the King with my lute, from time to time, and he can be counted on to toss me a purse of gold, if I take him at the right tide."

"My young Master Rory McLeod of Macleod would be glad to hear you sing. He loves all music."

"So you are from that party of foolish rebel chiefs whom the King has sent for to chastise?" de Lérins said. He sat on the table, leaning back on one hand and raised the wine glass to his lips with an elegant gesture.

"Yes."

"A barbarian, eh?"

"I would not say so," Iain said, but he looked about him at the elegant luxury of the room, so unlike anything he had seen in the houses and castles of the Isles.

"Let me fill your glass again."

He came forward, leaning over Iain, almost touching him, smiling into his face.

Suddenly uncomfortable, Iain made to rise.

"I think my master may be waiting for me by now."

"Not he! They are probably still in the ante-chamber. The King will probably only have them in when he thinks they have been waiting long enough to be subdued and quiet."

"Master Rory is rarely subdued and quiet. I can't recall ever seeing him so for long... though they do say he was quiet for a few days after he slept with his head on the Fairy Flag."

He regretted the words about the Flag as soon as they were out of his mouth. He could not think why he had uttered them."

"What is that, the Fairy Flag?"

Iain was silent. After a moment he began uncomfortably to describe the Flag and its tradition, in the way in which one would speak of something precious when questioned by a stranger: both diffident and proud.

When he had finished the reluctant story, he raised his eyes which had been downcast and saw de Lérins' face unmasked and open as it had been when he had bent over him on the couch.

"Master MacIain," he said, "I am sorry I mocked at you. I know well you are not a ruffian from the hills, for I heard you speak with Rigby in the church. You are schooled and though you call yourself a servant and are not familiar with the city, I am sure you are of gentler birth. If you permit me to ask...where were you taught?"

"At the monastery of Rodel in Harris."

"Has it not been suppressed? I thought the Episcopalians ruled throughout the isles these days save where our friends the Presbyters have ousted them, in their dislike of Bishops and the old forms of ecclesiastical government?"

"Some isles still hold to Rome...Rum and Eigg do so, and the new teaching spreads very slowly. Men do not understand what it means, to have the whole Marian doctrine torn away. Where they may not worship in the old custom, they often stay at home and don't worship at all nowadays. The difference between Episcopacy and the Presbyterian faith is too confusing for them. They know only that the church of Rome is forbidden to them, and the new faith is not yet fully understood. But Rodel was beyond the bounds of all these things, for the Abbot adhered to the old ways of long ago, and that which lived there was beyond time and place, it seemed to me."

"What old ways?" the musician said, after a silence.

"The way of teaching of the Celtic saints, who taught in the Isles long before St Augustine came to Britain, and built their churches there before the influence of the church of Rome was felt in the far West at all."

"Does a school tradition live there, then?"

"Yes. But the Abbot died this winter past."

"What did he teach you?"

"All Christian matters and doctrine. He also studied ancient knowledge of the Druids' tradition - from before the time of our Lord.

"And with such knowledge at your command, you came back willing to be a servant still?"

"Well, sir, I am bound to MacLeod by my father's wish, and but for the goodness of MacLeod of MacLeod I should have gone untaught all my days," Iain answered. "Besides, my learning is little. The Abbot told me it used to take twenty years to master the complete cycle of Druidic thought. The Trivium and Quadrivium alone took seven long years, and on top of all the study of the natural sciences and philosophy and the arts that they had, there has come all Christian theory and practice. I am only a student still and willing to serve in my master's house. Besides, my heart dwells at Dunvegan," he added with a sad and secret smile.

"With the Fairy Flag?" de Lérins asked. He had meant, with Christiana, but he nodded all the same, seeing it was at least half true.

De Lérins refilled the wine glasses.

"You learned the history of the Celtic church, then?" he said after they had been silent for a while. "From the journey of Irenaeus, pupil of Polycarp, pupil of St John from Asia Minor into Gaul?"

Iain looked up eagerly. "I believe I have heard of this. Yes, and the foundation of the church of Gaul. And how Charlemagne, the Frankish emperor filled his court with men who had been taught according to the doctrine of St John…"

"And of St Martin of Tours?"

"Who came at length up through Gaul to Brittany…"

"And of the great foundation at Glastonbury in England…"

"And the wandering saints who went onwards into Wales and Ireland and upwards thence to Iona…"

"Do you know whence their strength came?" de Lérins asked, a tremor of emotion in his voice.

"Why, from God," Iain answered simply.

"I mean, their earthly strength…the place of the central radius in Gaul?"

"No," Iain answered slowly.

"Some men say it was the isle of Lérins off the south coast of France."

"Where *you* come from, sir?" Iain asked softly, his eyes wide.

"It is so."

"The Abbot might have known of the island," Iain said confidently.

"Indeed, from what you say of him, he might have indeed. Shall I come to Dunvegan and visit you there?" he asked after a moment, on a different note. His mobile face lit up with sudden merriment. "Should I find a niche in your island life? I have a tongue like a courtier, but that will suit me ill in Skye, where I am sure all men speak their minds directly and simply. My mind is stocked with as much nonsense as a popinjay, and as much knowledge as a monk at Rodel, and that will seem a strange thing in a man from Gaul. I can play the viol, to boot, and my ribboned lute pleases the ladies. I cannot speak the island Gaelic, but I have merry songs in French, which I can put into the common tongue – though that is best done when the ladies are *not* present. I have a sweet medley for all folk, in a voice of right good quality, good sir!"

He picked up the lute, played a few notes, swept a low bow and turned his laughing face to Iain once again.

"Well, they are fond enough of music at Dunvegan," Iain said, though doubtfully. He could not imagine the minstrel at MacLeod's board on a day of feasting, though. To the great ravens, a bright small bird of paradise, he thought. They would surely take a peck at him.

"I shall feel like Talliessin come at last to the Court of King Arthur at Glastonbury, after all his wanderings," de Lérins said, half gaily but with serious eyes again.

"He was a Druid, wasn't he? I read about him in the old Welsh Triads."

"Yes. A Druid, a minstrel and a prince. He came to the Christian court of chivalry at Glastonbury where the Holy Grail had been, and found it was the home of all his dreams and imaginings. And there he sang his greatest songs and played his last sweet music by the Holy Chalice Spring, where the legend says St Joseph of Arimathea hid the Holy Dish. And when he was dying he said…"

"He said 'Christ Himself was our Teacher, and we never lost his teaching,'" Iain said soberly.

They looked at one another again, deeply and in silence.

"These are Holy, secret things," de Lérins said at length. "Save my own family, I never met a man who knew of them before. It is all dead at Lérins now."

"My teacher the Abbot knew many things," Iain replied at once. I only begin to push open the door of knowledge that his hand guided me to."

"I will teach you more, Master MacIain. The Druids, at their height were learned in many subjects men do not much study now in Christian times. Natural philosophy, astronomy, mathematics, geometry, medicine, rhetoric, music, poetry, grammar, logic and jurisprudence."

"Those together then, must be the subjects of the Trivium and the Quadrivium," Iain leapt to his feet. "You can teach me of all such matters?"

"Alas, by no means all. But get me to Skye that I may bow to the Flag and I will impart to you such knowledge as I may. I long to speak of great things again. And you seem to be an eager student."

Chapter Eight

THE GENERAL BAND

In the evening, when Iain returned to the castle, he found the assembled chiefs there full of talk and indignation about their reception at Holyrood.

MacLean of Duart, in Mull, whose hands had been bloodied often enough in the past in defence of his land rights in Isle Islay, seemed beside himself, and was shouting, red-faced, when MacIain entered:

"We shouldn't be able to hold on to our estates at all, if we agreed to this monstrous bondage that he wants to impose on us! I could hardly believe my ears when he said we must never call our men to arms without the King's personal and direct permission. Did you ever hear such impudence, now? If a clan chief may not call his own men out in defence of his own property…"

"Now Hector MacLean, you know well enough, if you call out your own men in full strength, it is not so often in defence of what you rightly hold by charter, as to get what you have set your covetous eyes on elsewhere," MacNeil of Barra interrupted. "But all the same," he added turning to the others, "this General Band as the King calls it, is quite unreasonable and absurd. He *can't* make Chiefs account to the Privy Council for the misdemeanours of everyone under their roofs or say the Chiefs are responsible for the debts of anyone they have living in their houses. It's impossible to…"

"By the Rood, I'll not have you calling me a thief of my neighbour's property," MacLean interrupted. "I've seen you draw a sword and strike a man down for a farm you coveted, and your son holds land I warrant you have no charter for! And if it's the debts of your household that trouble you most, you would do well to rid yourself of the sorners and ne'er-do-wells and vagabonds that fill your houses."

"It's not the sorners who will be giving us trouble." Kintail put in, "They are easily disposed of since they have no rights anyway. But the wording of the Band - if I remember rightly the words of the clerk who read it to us…says that we chiefs of clans shall be made to compensate all those whom our *vassals* shall have injured in property or person.

Our *vassals* mark you. That can mean anyone who says he is subject to us, and the debts that can be laid at our door by rascally fellows could easily be far beyond our means to pay."

"Yes, that'll cut your wings a bit, Robert MacKenzie," another fellow laughed. "If Torquil Conanach is your vassal, and I don't doubt he will count as one, you will need have a care how you support his machinations to get his hands on the Lewis. You know his father will have nothing to do with him."

"The King sent word a year back that Ruari MacLeod of the Lewis must acknowledge him and give him his rightful inheritance. His Grace will not hold me accountable if arms are needed to enforce those rights. That would be most unjust."

"Won't he now? The royal mind changes as often as the winds change round the Isles." Donald Gorme said. He had reason enough to feel bitter, for the charter he coveted for Trotternish had still not been signed by the King, and he suspected Argyll's hand was playing him and MacLeod of Dunvegan off against each other on this matter – discreetly behind the scenes. And now the dispute over the heritage of the Lewis would add the problem of the ownership of Waternish to his other difficulties with his neighbours.

Rory was sitting in the window embrasure looking down onto the clustered, ancient roofs of the houses that straggled down the hillside. He had been quiet in the King's presence that morning, but he had done some rapid thinking during the proceedings.

We *had* ancient sovereign rights, and they are being whittled away bit by bit. But we have got to look widely and see what is the purpose behind all this. What is the end that the King has in view? Is it to torment us, as my fellows seem to think, and as I myself believed when I was younger. Well, the King wants to unite us all for the good of Scotland, I suppose. He thinks it is for the benefit of the kingdom. The real purpose is the imposition of order, where once was chaos. That cannot be wrong…though the means to it are eating into our hearts, and gnawing at us as a rat gnaws at a garment until it is all destroyed and a new one must be made.

He looked glumly down at the wet tiles from which the light rain was running into the gulleys and away into the street gutters: and down again to the river's edge to mingle there with the tidal flow to the sea. The salmon leap up the river against the downward pull of all nature, so Iain said. Suddenly it seemed to Rory that the whole of nature was like a great two-way ladder, on which the downward pull was one of blind, unconscious merging into the ocean of eternity, and the upward pull a conscious striving movement towards something very simple at the summit. It is the movement up and down Jacob's ladder, like it says in the Scriptures I read at Rodel, he thought. The chiefs, arguing out of anger and pride will go blindly downwards…not because they are any worse than the rest of the world, but because the conscience of the King cannot tolerate them. Our multiplicity of purposes must give way before a simpler purpose…the union of Scotland under the crown. And presently the interests of Scotland and England will also merge as one, if the King gets the English crown, as men suppose he will. That is what a crowned head is for, he thought, with a sense of sudden revelation. He has to subdue us, because it is the nature of kings to simplify their subjects' purposes and unite them into one purpose. To subject ourselves to his will against our own many personal wills, is to look upward towards the Godhead that he stands for, I suppose. Though it is hard to see it that way if the King is a bad king, and wilful or cruel instead of good and wise.

Immersed in his thoughts, Rory stared from the window, paying no attention to the noisy conversation in the room behind him. He began to glimpse a confused picture…a vision…in which it seemed to him that the little figures of the island chiefs moved and struggled and tumbled downwards into the depths of an inferno where blood-red fires seemed to roar and rage and the sounds they made were like the screams and shouts and cries of the warriors falling into the blood-stained seas as he remembered them in the battle off Isle Islay. In his vision the very sea was afire like a red and bubbling cauldron full of bloody limbs. He felt himself descending into the cauldron, and with a mighty inward effort pulling outwards into the air and light. Above him was the sun, and this too was fire, but golden fire and light around which sounded the sweet harmonious music of the spheres. And at the heart was stillness, peace and silence.

"Young Rory hasn't said a word on this. Are you asleep, MacLeod of MacLeod?" MacKinnon called across the room.

Rory heard his voice from far off. He realised that his head had been pillowed on his arms on the window sill and he had indeed been asleep. He struggled back to consciousness of his surroundings, bemused still by his curious vision of the world. He cleared his throat and rubbed his face and looked about him.

"Sirs, we must understand fully what is at stake," he said. "We have been bickering like the seabirds on their rocky ledges, quarrelling for space." He got to his feet and raising his voice said to the room at large: "I am not convinced that the General Band has any evil purpose or malevolent intent at all. We must do our best to understand it. The King's men see us as being like the wild hill ponies…no use until they are broken to the bit and can pull a cart or bear a man with a will. We may need to submit ourselves to the new laws with dignity…for if we do not, we shall be destroyed."

"For shame, young Rory! Have you no spirit? And you your father's son!" the chiefs said angrily and contemptuously.

They will pay no heed, he thought. But maybe they will heed me later, he told himself. I will not waste time arguing with them now, he thought, for my will and my understanding does not accord with theirs at present. But theirs will accord with mine, in time to come.

Seeing he had nothing further to say, and had shut his lips obstinately, the chiefs lost interest in him and turned again to discussing ways in which they could evade the King's new laws.

Rory left the chamber and went onto the terrace. The rain had ceased and a low-lying sun shone fitfully between banks of cloud on the Western horizon. He stood and looked at it, his thoughts turning to Dunvegan and his island heritage, and love and yearning filled his heart, and fear for the future of his people there.

Iain MacIain came towards him, and a stranger walking a step or two behind.

"Iain, is the King representative of God on earth, do you think?" he asked, speaking out of the depths of his vision. "I suppose most men would think that a foolish thought, since we have certainly had no cause to love the kings of Scotland and they have often been monstrously unjust in their treatment of their subjects."

"I have been taught to believe in a hierarchy of beings," MacIain answered, pushing his hands into the sleeves of his brown robe in monkish fashion, as he always did when questioned on ecclesiastical things. "In this sense, surely the King represents God…and that is why all kings wear crowns of gold, with points that are studded with jewels. They represent the halos of light which it is said the saints had round their heads, and our Lord Himself. And these halos are themselves a faint reflection of the rays of the sun."

"*Is* that why kings wear crowns?" Rory exclaimed. "To help them be more godlike?" He felt pleased with the thought.

He looked beyond Iain where de Lérins stood, and acknowledged the stranger, who bowed and said his name. But having his mind full of other matters he took no further notice of the minstrel. He moved to the terrace wall, found a break in it onto a little sloping greensward and went through and sat down on a wooden bench outside the wall. He clasped his hands round one knee and looked down at the little twinkling lights that were beginning to spring up in the city below, as the citizens lit their many lamps and candles. Iain came and sat beside him in easy companionship.

De Lérins seated himself on the broken wall with one leg up on it and the other dangling down, unstrung his lute and played a few notes, looking at the top of Rory's head as though considering. Then he began to sing a madrigal of William Dunbar's composing, his voice light and clear as the little wind that moved round the turrets and across the greensward in the gathering darkness.

> " I fear not henceforth death,
> Sith after this departure yet I breathe:
> Let rocks and seas and wind
> Their highest treasons show:
> Let sky and earth combined
> Strive if they can to end my life and woe:
> Sith grief can not, me nothing can o'erthrow:
> Or if that aught can cause my fatal lot,
> It will be when I hear I am forgot."

Rory leaned back slowly against the wall, his shoulders relaxing, his face uptilted towards the first faint stars.

"Sing on, friend," he said. "No minstrel will ever be forgot while MacLeod lives."

De Lérins played old songs of the wandering jongleurs and troubadours, singing sometimes in old Norman French, sometimes in the Florentine tongue, with equal ease. In the background, doors opened and closed, the island chiefs' voices were heard in laughter and talk, footsteps came and went. At last Rory sighed and rose. He had been thinking how he had always declared he would support the independence of the isles. And yet now he saw the matter very differently. His face looked strained and not as young as his years. He felt for his purse and brought out a few coins.

"I thank you," he said "It was a delight to hear you. You are a court musician?"

De Lérins hesitated, before taking the coins with a bow and his wide smile. A flaring torch in a bracket had now been lit on the paved terrace and by its dancing flame, Rory looked at him and considered his strange, mobile features, the shining upswept hair, the great emerald ring on his finger. He saw that some motive other than money lay behind his performance.

"I play at the Court, but I am bound to no man," he said. "The King will let me go, when I ask my freedom."

"What do you want of me?"

"To come with you to Skye."

"For what reason?"

"To make music for you, sir," de Lérins said.

Rory looked at the great eyes and the wide-lipped mouth, considered the peacock clothes, and like Iain, saw that he would not be welcomed by the clansmen at Dunvegan. "Now is not the time to ask," he said. "My mind is full of other things. But if you have set your heart on it, and you come there, ask for me and I will welcome you."

In spite of the scant encouragement to persist, de Lérins did not leave him, but walked the length of the terrace behind him to the chamber where Rory slept. As Iain opened the door, a mouse ran across the floor, paused and stood upright – in fright, then scurried into a hole in the wainscot.

"To him, *you* are God, sir," the minstrel said indicating the mouse's hole, "for you are the greatest thing that he can imagine and you have all power…to feed, to cherish, to kill or to let him be. So is the King to you. So are the saints, to his Grace the King…and because he knows this in his heart of hearts, he only brings himself to tolerate the new faith which will have nothing to do with the great hierarchy of beings and thinks there is nothing between man and God."

"What is there between man and God?"

"Angels and archangels."

"But we can speak to God direct…and He will hear us."

"Indeed, it is a paradox, and both the old and the new teaching are true, do you not think so, sir?"

"Well, you should ask my friend MacIain. He knows more than I do of these matters," Rory said. He began to take off his doublet, but de Lérins lingered still in the open doorway, looking into the dimly lighted room. MacIain lit a second candle and placed it by the bed, took Rory's doublet and folded it, then knelt to pull off his new buckled shoes, as he sat down and held out his foot.

"I like this idea that all life is a hierarchy of beings, and to every level, God is the level just above," said Rory. "It makes good sense, and explains why men need a chief to lead them. He is a kind of god to them – though they know enough, in these enlightened days, to realise he is not really godlike, and makes mistakes like the rest of them, of course. It is like a ladder upwards. But is there not also a ladder that goes downward? I thought there was something awful down below. The fires of Hell. 'The Pit'." He thought of the grave he had looked into in the monastery at Rodel.

"The way up is the same as the way down. It leads through the fires." De Lérins said. With the toe of his shoe he drew in the dust that had blown in through the half open doorway to the terrace, a large six-pointed star, made from the intersection of two triangles.

"It is all the same, which ever way you look at it," he said. The Trinity: or the Trinity reversed." He gave his smiling bow, and went out silently, closing the door behind him.

*****

A few days later, in the great Council chamber of Holyrood, all those chiefs of the Islands and Western Highlands who had obeyed the King's summons, put their hands, willingly or unwillingly to the document of the General Band, and swore themselves into a state of greater servitude to King James VI. For the most part, they had argued themselves out of their initial wrath and persuaded one another that the matter was of little real importance and that they would still have their freedom, once away from the King's eyes and the Earl of Huntley's vigilance, in their island strongholds.

But Rory signed with sincerity, for he had decided as he lay awake in his chamber at the castle, that the King was honest and open in his intentions towards the whole of his realm, and could be trusted. Retaining something of his vision, he convinced himself that to obey the King was in a deep sense to obey the true law, as a good Christian should.

"Well, we have not done so badly after all," MacNeil of Barra said as they returned to Holyrood for the last time, to take their leave. "We have not lost our honour, we got a few concessions, and the King understands our natures better. Things will go on much as before."

"I thought young Rory MacLeod was our best spokesman," MacKinnon of Strath said. "I liked the way he said 'we would have your Grace comprehend we are not barbarians, but civilized folk like men in Stirling and Edinburgh'."

"He has a ready tongue, young MacLeod."

"Yes, he would make a good courtier," old Barra answered sourly, "so quick of wit and ready with an answer, before we greybeards had pondered on the points we could have made."

"He seeks to curry favour with the King," Donald Gorme MacDonald interjected. "I saw it in his eye." And he laughed sharply and gave Rory a jeering look, with malice in it.

"You have nothing to lose and somewhat to gain by keeping in with the nobles and the King," MacKenzie of Kintail remarked, contemptuously, looking at Rory who stood, frowningly, in silence. "All men know the little heiress to Dunvegan, your uncle's daughter, was kept a lady-in-waiting at Court at my Lord Huntley's behest so she would not inherit her rights, and later when Argyll had her in his house and married her off so profitably to a Campbell, why, who became chief in her stead? Your father, sir. If I mistake not. You did well to speak smooth words at Court for, but for the interest of those noble earls, you would not now stand here on behalf of the clan MacLeod signing your name with such a flourish."

"Indeed, sir, I did speak my mind in honesty and not from the thought of profit," Rory protested. He felt irritability rising up in him, for though the chiefs had done their best to co-operate with one another for their common good these last few days, old quarrels were already beginning to spring to the surface again, now that the purpose of their meeting was finished. "It is a web of half-truths that you told, my Lord of Kintail, for my father inherited with every right and ruled most wisely."

"Having first licked his overlord's buckled shoe and then despatched all rivals, he could afford to sit back in good comfort and rule most wisely!"

"Have a care, sir," Rory cried, his temper rising. "My father did what he could for the good of the clan. Is your sword-hand then bloodless?"

"More so than your father's, MacLeod, for I am an honest man and support the right against the wrong."

"What right, what right? You support a bastard's claim to my cousin's land of the Lewis and there is no right there, but only personal profit and thoughts of gain. It is common knowledge that Torquil Conanach was sired by Hutcheon the Breve of the Lewis and not by my kinsman who has disinherited him."

No sooner had Rory spoken, letting the words come out of him in a rush of anger and indignation, that he saw the folly of his action. Each day throughout the long and wearisome sessions at the castle and at the palace he had controlled his tongue, mindful of William's words, but now, when the matter was all but finished, the need for a guard on his speech all but past, in a flash of time, like a mindless boy, he had spoken such words as Kintail would likely never forgive him, for Torquil Conanach's mother was not only MacKenzie by birth, but as near to the heart of the clan MacKenzie as Kintail's own family.

"May the saints protect you, sir, for you will have need of protection if you say my kinswoman has borne a bastard son," MacKenzie said with dangerous quiet in his voice. He rose from his chair with a slow movement, controlled and venomous. His eyes, in the sharp-featured face, moving from Rory's upright figure to the faces of the chiefs and of the officials of the Court who were standing in conversation awaiting the King's summons for the Islanders' departure.

"Withdraw your words, young Rory," old MacLean advised, laying a hand on Rory's shoulder from behind. "That is a foolhardy thing to say for no-one can prove it."

"Can they not? MacLeod, my brother, has a letter – " Rory blurted out, "which says plainly that Hutcheon, the Breve had carnal knowledge of my Lord Kintail's kinswoman – and much more else besides" he plunged on, conscious in a wild and inward panic of his folly, and unable to withdraw from very pride in his own truthfulness.

"You are at fault whatever your reasons. For we know His Grace has given Torquil Conanach rights over his brother and does support his claim to the Lewis," MacLean whispered urgently.

But even if all the chiefs together had cried "Withdraw" at this stage, Rory could not have brought himself to do so. He stepped away from Duart's restraining arm and came up to MacKenzie who stood with a hand on his sword-hip, looking down meditatively from his superior height.

"I stand by my words for I am an honest man who speaks the truth for the truth's own sake without thought of personal gain."

"If this is so, you are not old Tormod's son," said Kintail.

"By St Clement – "

"Yes, by St Clement!" Kintail laughed contemptuously. "I have noticed how MacLeod always calls upon the patron saint of Dunvegan and the monastery, as though by doing so he can have special rights and be as impertinent as he chooses."

Suddenly, the full fire of Rory's temper was unleashed. He closed his right hand into a fist and struck MacKenzie, with all the weight of his fury behind the blow, so that the older man reeled back, knocking over a small table on which was a great porcelain bowl, which clattered off and broke to fragments on the floor.

At once an uproar of angry shouts and cheers and jeers rent the room. Forgetful where they were, the chiefs instinctively took sides for

MacLeod or for MacKenzie, according to their old allegiances, as both men drew their swords. At the same moment, the double doors to the Presence Chamber opened on the cry of "Here comes the King" – unheeded by the disorderly rabble.

King James advanced into the ante-room, with his few Councillors about him and paused and looked about him with amazement at the sight that met his eyes. On all sides courtiers and officials struggled in vain to gain control and quieten the noise while two or three attempted to intervene between the combatants. But, heeding nothing save their own outrage with one another, MacKenzie of Kintail and Rory MacLeod of MacLeod parried and leapt upon one another with their swords and moved back and forth in the open space the chiefs had made about them. The hot blood of the Islands ran in their veins and nothing now would deflect them from their purpose.

From amazement the King's expression changed to a sardonic look of humour. He stood watching, toying with the great ruby on his finger, unmindful of the agitation of his councillors at such behaviour in the royal presence.

"No, leave them, leave them, let them have it out," he said, and then after a moment: "Is that not young MacLeod who would have me believe a few hours ago that he and his fellows were not barbarians but civilised men?" And then, after a few moments longer, in which he saw Rory draw blood from MacKenzie's arm and have his own arm badly cut, the King's amusement died and he instructed abruptly: "Seize these fellows. We will not have this brawling in our presence. Enough, enough."

Two or three stalwarts of the Court succeeded in laying hands upon Kintail and restraining him, but Rory thrust out so wildly with the sword-arm that he could not at first be held. Noticing the King's presence at last and coming to themselves again, the chiefs' voices died away into an uneasy silence. In the sudden quiet, Rory came to himself and, seeing his opponent helpless, let his sword drop in his hand and turned his head and looked the length of the room towards the King. Seeing the resistance going out of him, the King's men laid their hands on his shoulders, but at their touch and at the realisation of where he was and of what he had done in the folly of his temper, Rory felt panic mount in him. However powerful the chiefs might be at home, here in the Court, the King could make short work of any one of them who displeased him. For such an insult to His Majesty a man might be despatched with great speed to a dungeon cell. He turned his head again and in a moment, before reasoned thought had run its full length, he found himself leaping upon a long table and jumping to the ground beyond it where no-one stood to prevent his passage, and then at top speed making for the door and out into another chamber and into the corridor beyond.

Not knowing his way about the Palace, he looked bewilderedly from left to right and, hearing pursuers coming shouting after him, he ran up a flight of stone steps, found himself in another corridor, and raced full pelt along it. The speed of his youthful limbs served him well for he outstripped the men who followed, though he heard their voices still below, and their feet clattering on the stairs. He mounted a further flight and, seeing at the end of a narrow passage two steps leading up to a door that stood ajar, he ran towards it. Through the opening he could see a casement window with a parapet outside and, thinking confusedly that he might make his way across the roofs and descend somehow into the courtyard below, he entered the room and started to run across it. Suddenly, a movement near the fireplace caught his eye and he turned, with his hand on his sword, which he had just sheathed, and looked into the fact of Hugh Whitby de Lérins.

The minstrel was seated cross-legged by a fire of coals, a manuscript of music on his knee, a quill in his hand. He looked at Rory with his face expressionless.

"Are you, the King's guest, become a fugitive overnight?" he asked with a touch of irony in his voice. Rory drew in his breath. The contrast between their last meeting, when he had so patronisingly given de Lérins a few coins for his pains, and this present one, struck him forcibly, even in the confusion of the moment.

"If you are a friend, conceal me," he begged urgently. "They pursue me for a misdemeanour." Not waiting for de Lérins' answer, he moved to the window and looked out.

"No, sir, there is no way of escape out there," the Frenchman said, not rising from his seat.

Seeing no other hiding place, Rory pushed out the window and thrust his head into the open air. A narrow parapet ran along outside and turned a corner and disappeared. At the corner a great stone heraldic beast, which had adorned the old monastic tower, dating from the days when Holyrood had been the Monastery of the Holy Rood, stretched its neck forward at this corner. He could not see beyond it. Drawing his head in again, he listened. Voices of those who came after were close behind, one crying:

"I think he went this way."

And another: "No, I think he is below."

In a moment, he thought, they would enter this room. With a last look at de Lérins, praying that he would at least hold his tongue, Rory flung his leg over the window sill and began to ease his way along the parapet. When he reached the corner and laid his hand on the great stone ear of the mythical beast, he saw with thankfulness that just beyond, where the creature's tail curled upwards there was a small space, big enough to hold him and not visible from the room he had just left. He eased himself down into it, breathing rapidly, his hands clutching the cold stone.

After a moment he heard voices in the room where de Lérins sat, and in the confusion of sound and questions de Lérins own words came to him quite clearly:

"No, sirs, there is no way of escape by that casement, as I would have told any felon who asked it of me."

A moment later, the window was again pushed open. The heads that were thrust out were so close to him that he could hear their heavy breathing, but no-one else attempted an exit on to that narrow ledge. After a moment they withdrew and the window was slammed closed again.

For a long time Rory remained in his cramped hiding place, growing more cold and more stiff as time went on. Far down below him he could see the courtyard and from time to time small figures coming and going, and at length the main body of the Highland chiefs being escorted out. He craned his neck, but could not tell whether Kintail was with them or no. Hoping that when all was safe de Lérins might call him in, he remained still, listening.

But at last, cramp entered his limbs to such an extent that he began to feel he would not be able to straighten himself if he did not move now. He raised himself slowly and, with great caution, edged his way back again and, fumbled at the casement and pulled it open. There was no light in the room, save the fire, which glowed dully and by which he ascertained there was no-one there. He clambered in, closed the window and crossed to the fireplace and stood there warming his chilled limbs by the little glow and deliberating in himself what he should do.

A few moments later the door was opened quietly and de Lérins entered, bearing a glass carafe of wine and bread and meat on a plate. Rory had started nervously at the sound of his footsteps. He looked at the minstrel uncertainly, still not knowing whether he was a friend or not. De Lérins closed the door behind him with his foot, placed the food and wine on the table and said:

"Well, you are not frozen stiff or turned into a fossil out there in the wind. I have brought food and drink to warm you and I have enquired, myself, about what has occurred this afternoon."

Rory accepted the wine but waved away the food.

"I must beg you to find me a manner to escape this place when night falls," he requested.

"Well, sir, I can do so, but I am persuaded you have little chance to leave the city for His Grace has sent out word that roads be guarded and all exits manned, so that you may be brought in to him again as soon as you are apprehended."

"Does he hold my Lord of Kintail?" Rory asked apprehensively.

"No, he let him go after he begged pardon for his unruly manners in the royal presence."

"Then perhaps I too would go free if I asked mercy and begged pardon," Rory said, almost against his will. He turned and looked at the fire and considered. "But Kintail is a man much older, a chief of consequence with much land and power…"

"And you a beardless boy of little consequence. It is easy to see how the tables have been turned against you," de Lérins answered.

"Will he imprison me?"

"I don't know."

"I must make my get-away this night and yet, if I do, he will forever hold against MacLeod the actions of this day and mayhap penalise my brother or appease his wrath on us in other ways."

"Yes," de Lérins answered. "You might well escape his clutches in the city but you would not escape his vengeance in the end. Already they are saying that you were the very man who said to the King 'We Island men are not barbarians but civilised folk like you yourselves at Court.' Sir, you have done your cause much harm."

Rory took up the wine glass and lowered it again, his expression agitated and troubled.

"My brother bade me guard my tongue and I pledged myself to wisdom and restraint. Ah, what folly – how can I…"

He looked about him into the corners of the darkening room and then again into the minstrel's face. De Lérins said nothing at all, neither giving advice nor expressing condemnation. At last:

"Do you think I could get into the King's presence now?" he asked. "Could you take me to him?"

De Lérins hesitated. "If it is your will, sir."

They left the room together and traversed the long passages and up and down stairways in silence. When they were nearing the great hall where the King would be at meat, Rory paused and said on a rising note of fear:

"If I am thrown into some prison cell I could lie there for years and be forgotten. It has happened often enough to other men, both here and in the Islands."

"You will not be forgotten. You have a friend at Court," the minstrel replied. He smiled for the first time, with an expression of sweetness, and gentleness on his countenance. He was an older man than Rory and much more widely travelled and experienced in the world, and in the moment of looking into his eyes Rory felt calmness and reassurance enter him and went forward purposefully into the royal apartments.

When King James learned that MacLeod had been apprehended he had him brought before him in the midst of dinner and looked at him standing there dishevelled, with his cut hand roughly bound with a kerchief and blood on his shirt.

"Ah, you are that civilised gentleman who spoke to me about barbarian habits with such knowledge." He said after a moment, between mouthfuls of roast venison.

Rory went down awkwardly on one knee and said:

"I come to beseech your Grace's mercy and pardon for my folly."

"We will not have our subjects brawling like a rabble in our presence," the King said coldly. "My Lord of Kintail is old enough to be your father and I hold him in respect."

"My Lord of Kintail insulted me most uncouthly." Rory answered sulkily, looking at the ground.

"A gentleman, such as you claim to be, knows the right time and place to avenge an insult and that is not in his sovereign's presence." The King answered.

"Sir," Rory blurted out, but already His Grace's attention had moved elsewhere. He waved to the stewards who had brought the young chief in to take him off again and as they hauled him to his feet roughly, as though he had been any malefactor and turned him about, he raised his voice and said:

"We will have you housed below ground in the Castle to cool your heels awhile and reflect upon the attribute of a Scottish gentleman."

A chill smote Rory's heart as he was hurried away, protesting at first at the violence with which he was treated and then falling into a helpless silence.

Somewhere along the corridor he saw the minstrel waiting watchfully. There was no chance to speak with him, but they exchanged a look and Rory was satisfied he would surely go with speed to Iain MacIain and bear the news of what had become of him.

The jostling journey through the streets from Holyrood House to the Castle was a nightmare of confusion and terror in his memory in after days, and when the great oak door of a prison room clanged to behind him at last and he was left in silence, he could only stand in the darkness saying desperately within his mind:

"I have a friend at Court. I am not lost for I have a friend at Court."

He could see nothing and hear nothing, and trembling and sweating, stood there until at last his legs began to buckle with fatigue and he sank down upon his knees amid dank slime. Above the beating of his heart in his ears, the faint trickling of water running somewhere down a wall and the rustle of rats unseen in a distant corner now penetrated to his listening ears and in his nostrils was the evil smell of lingering death.

Chapter Nine

THE PRISONER UNDER THE HILL

Towards the end of a winter afternoon, a year later, Iain MacIain came from Skye to Edinburgh with news that was to be conveyed – by the King's will and charity – to the prisoner who now lay in a slightly ventilated though wretched prison chamber beneath the ground level of the castle.

As he went down the stairs, treading softly behind the jailor with his jangling keys, he looked with a shudder at the damp rough walls, smelt the dank earthy smell of these underground rooms and almost feared that his master could no longer be alive down there at all, but must have perished long ago, and he would be shown a coffin, or a bag of bones and locked in with them as a macabre jest. Fear made the hair prick on his skull, and sweat start in the palms of his hands, for though he had courage enough to face the hazards of life above ground, these semi-dungeon chambers with their clanging doors, and this silent, pale-faced jailor who trod on ahead as though at home among them, seemed a species of horror such as came to a Highlander in the worst of nightmare dreams.

When the door of Rory's chamber was opened, he was seated – in a ragged unwashed shirt and stained black breeches, and unbarbed, reading a much thumbed book by the light of the narrow high-up slit of the window. He turned his head, without hope or expectancy at the sound of the opening door, surveyed the jailor's familiar countenance for a moment uninterestedly: then looked beyond, into the semi-darkness and saw the face of the tall man who stood behind.

"The Holy Saints! MacIain!"

Iain came in, looked dumbly at him for a space of time, then dropped to one knee, swallowing, and keeping his eyes down-turned.

"Well, well, get up, get up," Rory said with a touch of his old impatience, though his voice was hoarse and had lost the clear ring of youth and confidence. "What good hand guided you here? What news do you bring? What news?"

"By the King's grace, sir, I am permitted to visit you to give you news of – of the death of your brother MacLeod of MacLeod."

Rory drew in his breath. He rose slowly from the plain wooden chair, and stood with his hands hanging by his sides. His face showed lined and grim in the down-slanting rays of light, and he was so thin that his clothes hung loosely on his frame. His hair, unwashed and unkempt, his chin unbarbed, betokened the privations he had undergone this past twelve months, for the King had seemingly forgotten him long since and he had become one of many whose pleas were unheard since they never reached the royal ears.

"William – dead?" He said at last. "By the Holy Rood, MacIain, what will happen at Dunvegan? His son John, is only a child. How did MacLeod meet his death?"

"By natural means, sir, so Dr Beaton said. He had grown short of breath and carried too much weight…"

"Yes, he liked good food and wine, as my father did."

"He died in the Tower Room, breathless from climbing up the stairs. They say his heart gave out."

Rory looked about him. "What can I do – shut down here like a rat in a trap?" he asked, indicating the walls of the prison room with a helpless gesture. "Will the King now free me? How did you get in here to me?"

"Our friend, Hugh Whitby de Lérins, the minstrel. He lives here in Edinburgh still, since he could not go to Skye with you. When I went to him, he contrived to speak with the King and make a plea for you. His Grace sent word that you might go free and attend to your business, since you must surely tutor the young chief and be regent for him. But he will bind you still for he will have a hostage on your behalf and hold him here, as he has done with others of the chiefs who show themselves too independent and not to be relied upon."

Rory groaned, putting a hand across his face in an attitude of dejected thought.

"But Iain, I have no-one near of kin. Who could I send? There were only the three of us brothers, and Alexander is still hostage to Dunnyveg I suppose – though they treat him well enough, and he is not a prisoner there."

Iain nodded, and hesitated before going on, for he had taken action beyond the bounds of his true duty, risking Rory's wrath by using his own intelligence to find a way out of this cul-de-sac, wherein his master lay prisoner in Edinburgh, and the only other possible claimant to the regency quite out of reach in a like circumstance at Dunnyveg. In a diffident voice he explained at last that he and de Lérins had talked far into the previous night, and this morning, the musician had wheedled his way into the court, where he had been often enough before of an evening, with his viol or his lute. He had returned with the permission Iain had sought, to visit Rory; and the news that Alexander would be sent for from Dunnyveg and held in Rory's place, if Rory would have it so.

When he had heard MacIain out, Rory was silent. He sat down slowly, laying his hands on the arms of his chair, and beginning to slide them up and down against the smooth wood in a mechanical way. His shoulders sagged a little and he shook his head, and then said wretchedly:

"Iain, Iain, I have brought myself, and my young brother and the clan to such a pass. All in a moment I brought myself to this! All in a moment of action without thought, without attention to where it would lead. Truly if I am freed, I swear upon the Rood I'll never speak my mind again without due care. Yes, that I truly swear, upon the Holy Rood."

Iain gazed at him, his face gentle and compassionate. His knowledge of Rory and his deep regard for him took him beyond the moment's words, and he saw that many, many times in these long, empty months the young chieftain had sat thus, in just such an attitude repeating again and again: "Upon the Rood, if I am ever freed, I swear it."

"Yes, sir, if you are freed to do so, you will rule the clan with a wise intelligence," Iain said, softly, after a little while.

Rory turned his head slowly and regarded him.

"And my young brother? What am I to do? Alexander has had no pleasure in his life, for my father *would* send him to Duart to be fostered, and that old rascal handed him over without a murmur when Dunnyveg demanded a hostage of him for a token that they would live in peace as neighbours. He was to marry Duart's young daughter too, but that was all put off. How will he stand this cell? True it is not a dungeon – they put me in a worse place at first and this seemed good when I was brought to it and when I still had a few coins, the jailor sometimes brought me a book. Look – Plato's Republic, to test the Latin that I learned at my grandfather's feet at Rodel. It is fortunate it is not in the original Greek language. What shall I do? Advise me Iain."

"I think you have little choice but to do as the King now bids," Iain said. "I do assure you, sir, it is not an easy thing to persuade him off his course. MacLeod sent many letters, begging your freedom and even sent word he would come himself and lay his plea before the King in person. For the most part, there was no answer. But to *that* letter, his Grace sent word he held you, not for your own misdemeanors only, but also hostage for the good behaviour of MacLeod himself, that there should be no more baiting of the foreign fishermen who have been given a charter to fish off our shores and for sundry other small affairs. Truly sir, the King has an astute and obstinate mind. If you begin a further dispute now, we shall not see you home again, nor your young brother either, and the clan will be in dreadful straits. The young chief is a sickly child, and scarcely past infancy."

At last, when all the argument had been gone over two or three times and no other way was seen, Rory looked into Iain's face, and said:

"It must be so. I see it must be so, so go and take a message to the Palace, that I will go to Skye to my duties. And Alexander must replace me here. Perhaps it will not be long, and King James will relent and set him free, if all goes well at Dunvegan and we do not irk him at all."

Rory's departure from Edinburgh was discreet and quiet, and the home-going was a sober business.

At the last moment, when horses had been brought and the small amount of baggage loaded in to pack-saddles, MacIain went to his master, who was now lodged in comparative comfort in the castle, and asked if Hugh de Lérins might accompany them.

Rory was looking harassed and distressed, for he had just seen young Alexander descend the dank staircase to the prison cells, and had scarcely had time to exchange a word with his brother before he was hurried off. His thoughts were full of his own affairs and he was weak for lack of good food and the long confinement.

He turned at last.

"Tell him he is welcome. We owe him our gratitude. He shall cheer us with a song," Rory said, but looking as though he would never be cheered again.

They left the city, with no-one to say farewell and rode all through the day, through the wild, hilly country. At night they stayed at a minister's house in the Highlands, and Rory, contrary to his former custom, went up to the disused chapel of the now empty abbey nearby and knelt there alone far into the night.

His countenance and his bearing troubled MacIain, for while he had been forever sharp-tempered, he had always had a cheerful turn of mind, and laughed easily. In the year of imprisonment he had grown so grim-faced and taciturn that there was scarcely a word to be had out of him at all, throughout the day. But when they crossed to Skye, from Glenelg over Kyle Rhea, as Iain had arranged, and found a galley awaiting them at Kylerhea, and came at length within sight of Dunvegan Castle from the sea, he braced his shoulders, and smiled a moment, briefly, and seemed a little more at ease.

He stood up, listening to the solitary piper who had begun to play a welcome from the battlements. At the sea gate a small knot of people had begun to gather, among them the little Chief, holding his mother's hand, and waiting to greet his uncle and guardian. Rory stepped from the boat and went up the steps slowly and steadily, looking upwards at the child and his widowed sister-in-law and his own stepmother, standing just behind. He saluted the boy, then laid a hand on his head, smoothing the fine, fair hair that was so like William's in colour and texture, and looking at him with a grave expression.

"Welcome, Uncle," John said politely, looking up at the lined and dark-eyed face uncertainly, seeming in awe of his grim countenance.

Then: "Welcome, brother," William's widow echoed, and offered her cheek to kiss with a formal gesture. "Indeed sir, you *are* welcome," she repeated, when he stood back, "for we have been a poor household here these last few months, with not a man of the chief's family among us. MacSweyn and MacAskill have done nobly. But we have longed for your return."

Rory turned to greet his stepmother, who being a gentle, unskilled woman, had gone into the background speedily when Tormod died, and wielded no authority.

In the banqueting hall already many people were assembled, waiting to greet him formally and to demand of him that he be the Regent Chief until young John should be of age to rule, all in accordance with the clan tradition.

When they had raised their drinking horns together he indicated that he would do his duty by his nephew, and would be "Tutor" to him, for so, by custom, he would be called.

"When all my kin and clansmen have been assembled, we will feast with all due ceremony," he said. "Are my sisters and their husbands coming? I would like Donald Gorme to witness our family tradition, for it will please him, and Torquil Dubh will be very welcome too."

Young MacAskill, who had succeeded his father as Warden of the castle, answered that messengers were on their way by sea to Duntulm and to Rodel and the Lewis, and others had gone overland to bring in all the clan to the feasting for the installation of the chief.

"Very good," Rory answered, nodding. "We will do it all correctly and with great exactitude. For though the King will surely break our power, we will not let him break our hearts as well."

He turned on his heel and strode off so abruptly that those who stood about looked after him surprised, then turned again to the great business of the preparations.

Rory went straight away towards the Fairy Tower to the room where he had always slept.

A number of changes had been made in the dwelling quarters and he had seen great piles of stone and lead tiles below for a new wing that William had intended to build. With his foot on the threshold of his room, a sudden fear struck him that there might be changes also in this chamber that he regarded as his own, and he stood with his hand on the door, not entering. It seemed to him suddenly that it would be a hard thing to bear if even the leather stool, or the chessmen, or the nurse's spinning wheel had been moved a yard from their accustomed places, so often had he dreamed of this room in the long year of his imprisonment.

At last he unlatched the door softly and went inside.

All was as it used to be, even to a freshly-hung nosegay of dried herbs suspended above the chimney piece, where Christiana always used to place one for him, to scent the air, and keep infection down.

But he could not hear the sound of the little waterfall which used to be called "Rory's Nurse", for it had lulled him to sleep as a child. The window, which had been unglazed, and stuffed with a bale of straw when needed, had been given a glass casement like Edinburgh or Stirling.

*****

In a few days time, when all the clan and many of their kindred from the other isles had reached the castle, the customary feast took place to install the young chief formally, and Rory as his guardian and regent.

Rory looked without much interest at the great dishes of venison, the sucking pigs, the caponed fowls, and the bowls of ale, which the clansmen and the dwellers in the guardroom and barrack quarters were quaffing with great gusto, amid laughter and talk. He sat back, holding a drinking horn of red wine in his hand, sipping only occasionally. Instead of whetting his appetite, the long period of semi-starvation had killed in him the desire to eat and drink, and he subsisted at present on half the rations of a normal active man.

During the meal, the musicians and bards played and sang, and Hugh de Lérins came to the fore for the first time, and seemed to please the clan with his medley of foreign songs. Although they looked askance at his garments and seemed prepared to mock him, it was a merry occasion and he was welcome enough.

When at length Rory signaled that the right moment had come, the old seanachie rose from his seat at the end of the high board. The soft accompaniment of the clarsach – the Highland harp – to all the song and laughter faded away on a last ripple of notes. De Lérins put away his lute, and the room listened in a quiet and respectful silence as the old man began to recite in slow and leisured tones, the genealogy of the clan MacLeod:

From Olave the Black, Norse King of the Isle of Man, to Leod, the Norseman to Tormod Mac-Leod and Torquil Mac-Leod the two sons, one who took the Harris and Skye, the other the Lewis, as his own…to Malcolm, son of Tormod, third chief of the Siol Tormod, who held fast to the horns of the Great Bull of Glenelg…to William of the Long Sword, who fought the great battle of Bloody Bay, where the Fairy Flag was for the first time unfurled…and on down the table of the chief's ancestry, until at last he reached the name of the little pale-faced boy, John, seated wide-eyed and silent at his uncle's side at the high board. The telling of the history took a full hour.

When all the deeds and the virtues of his father had been described, and the child John himself had been well looked over by all who were crowded into the great hall, the seanachie, having proved the boy's right to succeed, leaned forward and touched the great two-handed claymore of William Long Sword, which had lain on the table before him.

"Men of the Siol Tormod of the clan MacLeod, will you take this child, John, to be your chief?" he asked.

"We will have him. Give him the sword of his fathers!" the assembled people cried.

Ceremoniously, the old seanachie lifted the great claymore a little nearer the boy, though it was too heavy for his old hands.

John stood up, as he had been told to do, and with his small fists, grasped the great weapon that his ancestor had wielded. But it was so weighty that he could not lift it at all, and Rory leaned across his shoulder from behind and laid his own hands on his nephew's, and gently drew it from the old man's grasp, until he and the child had it. But Rory himself was still so weak he could only support it a moment, and laid it down quickly.

"Great-great-Grandfather must have been *very* strong" the little boy's voice said, echoing clearly in the hushed silence of the hall. The clansmen laughed indulgently. "Am I to give it to you now Uncle?"

Rory, smiling a little, answered:

"First present it to your men, for it is not mine, but yours."

Assisted by Rory, John lifted the sword a little again and presented it, saying in answer to Rory's prompting:

"Sirs, I do present you the sword of my ancestor, and I swear to serve and protect you with this sword, under God, all the days of my life."

There was a murmur of approval, and slowly the clansmen and the ladies rose from their benches and began in spontaneous fashion to pay their respectful acknowledgments to the young chief, some with a bow or a curtsey, others with a raised drinking horn or goblet; and all with a rising clamour of voices for a full minute.

Rory offered John the Dunvegan drinking horn and he sipped some wine from it.

"The chief must always drink from this horn, for it is the horn of the Great Bull of Glenelg which our ancestor Malcolm the third chief cut off when he vanquished the beast. And all the people shouted "hold fast McLeod!" as he fought. So our clan motto since then has always been "Hold Fast" Rory told him.

When there was quiet again at last, John turned to Rory, his small pale face raised to the dark, lined one above him, and said as he had been instructed:

"I desire my father's brother, my Uncle Roderick, to be my Tutor and the Regent Chief until I am of age to wield authority. And I require you to accept him in my stead until I am of age."

Again the people indicated their assent. The great sword was touched again, and Rory with his hand on it said to the young chief:

"With the sword of our ancestor and by God's grace, I will defend you, sir." And then turning to the people down the length of the hall, he cried: "With the sword of my ancestor, and by God's grace, I will uphold the Clan MacLeod!"

There were shouts and acclamations from all sides, for Rory was known to them all, and his ready tongue and keen eye had long been respected throughout MacLeod's lands. Besides, he had suffered imprisonment for their sakes, so they thought, and had come back, no longer an eager, sharp-tongued boy, but a man, with a lined and purposeful face who looked as though he could be trusted to know what to do, and relied upon to do it.

The claymore being too big and heavy, Rory called for and formally buckled on the sword that had belonged to the previous chief, his brother William. And then, the ceremony being at an end, signed to the bards and the minstrels to begin again, and the servants to bring on more wine and see that no guest lacked for food and drink.

Then he turned to his sister Christiana, a young mother now and rounder of face than before and asked: "Who is that maiden over there with the merry, brown eyes, and the brown curls peeping from a chignon threaded with blue?"

"Glengarry's elder daughter," she answered, "Donald MacDonald of Glengarry, who is kin to Donald Gorme. They are guests at Duntulm Castle, and came with Donald Gorme and his own party. You gave them leave to come, I think."

"What is her name?" Rory asked, smiling in the girl's direction.

"I don't know," she answered, and leaned across to Rory's stepmother, and asked:

"Do you know what Glengarry's daughter is called?"

Janet MacLeod shook her head, and asked a neighbour, who asked again, until at last the name "Isabel" was whispered somewhere down the table: And "Isabel...Isabel...Isabel..." came up from lip to lip in sibilant whispers to where Rory sat.

"Isabel of Glengarry," Rory said softly, watching her head turn at the sound of her name being said all along the table. "Is that her father? I will have him bring her to me later on. She has a pretty face and a happy laugh. I noticed her earlier. When a man has had long, solitary thoughts in a prison, he grows too melancholy, and needs to be cheered by a happy face and a mind that is innocent of sorrow." Seeing him smiling normally, his cousin Mairi known as the clan poet, sang one of her own compositions: -

> "Rory, Rory, Rory Rare one,
> Many a head would cast its snood for thee,
> Many a coif waits head for love of thee,
> Rory, Rory, Rory Rare one."

Everyone laughed and cheered that life was returning to normal at last.

*****

Little John was sent away to rest. In a room below Rory's in the Fairy Tower, a fire blazed for the chief's ladies and the children would often gather there to be away from the more raucous noise in the big

116

banquetting hall. Mairi Nighean Alasdair Ruadh, the poet, took him there.

"Oh, cousin, I am so tired," he said, dropping beside her and leaning his fair head against her shoulder. "I wish I were on my pallet in my chamber. It is very late for me to be still up."

"Can you not go to bed now, sweetheart?" Mairi asked putting an arm round him and holding him close. "Have you asked your mother?"

"Uncle Rory said I must not, yet, for I must be a man for this night, until the feasting is done, and then I may be a little boy again – for which I am very thankful. But he said I could go and sleep a little and come again later to the hall when I am rested. May I sleep here against you, cousin Mairi? Will you wake me, if I sleep too long?"

"Yes, lean against me. I will nurse you," she replied.

He wriggled down with his head in her lap, and she stroked his hair gently, now looking at his little delicate, fair-skinned face – so like William's and Alexander's had been as children – so unlike to Rory: now raising her eyes to gaze into the flames of the fire with a faraway stare. Mairi, a distant cousin and a child of Red Alasdair, had been fostered at Dunvegan and always lived there.

"Sing the Dunvegan Lullaby," John whispered, snuggling close to her, his eyes already drooping shut, on the verge of sleep.

"Are you not too old for it?"

"No, sing it," he pleaded, "sing it as you always did at my cradle, when I was a baby."

"Yes, I sang it over your cradle," she answered softly. "And over Alexander and over your Uncle Rory – though I was only a little girl myself: and doubtless later I shall sing it over Rory's children…" She sighed, and then began, in a low voice, to tell as usual the preliminary tale that the child-hearers of the lullaby always demanded: -

"It is the song the fairy-woman was singing in the Tower Room one winter night when the baby chief was left lying there alone while his nursemaid was away downstairs at the feasting to celebrate his birth, and his mother, the Lady MacLeod, was still in childbed. His mother heard the strange voice singing in her baby son's room, and the nursemaid heard it too as she came running up the stairs to fetch the baby, for the chiefs had asked for him to be shown to them. They listened outside the room, rather frightened, for they did not know what was happening in the nursery room, save that it was not of this earth. Then the Lady MacLeod opened the door, and went in. And what did she see but a wonderful fairy thing of softest silk, wrapped round her baby son. And when she touched it wonderingly, what did she hear again, but those same voices singing softly in the darkness all around her, the sweetest lullaby that ever she had heard. And since that day all chiefs of the Clan MacLeod who are born at Dunvegan, always have that song sung to them by their mothers and their nursemaids in their cradles. And the silken thing is the Fairy Flag that is here at Dunvegan still.

She began to sing, in the old island Gaelic.

> *"Sleep, my little child,*
> *Hero tenderling,*
> *Dream, my little child,*
> *Hero, gentle bred,*
> *High on mountain brows*
> *Be thy stag-tryst,*
> *Speed thy yew arrows straight antlerwards...*
>
> *Ho-ro veel-a-vok, Ho ro aily,*
> *Ho-ro veel-a-vok, Ho ro aily,*
> *Our clan galley sail*
> *To thy dreamland."*

"Is it a true story?" Came the sleepy voice of the little chief, as the young voices of other chiefs had asked the singer all through the years.

"Yes," Mairi answered.

After a while, when the boy was sleeping soundly, cradled against her, MacIain came to the door.

She raised her face, and seeing him hesitating on the threshold, bade him enter. Although he was still technically a servant, since his long sojourn in Rodel and especially since his recent expedition to Edinburgh, and all he had done there to secure Rory's release, Iain had become accepted by the family almost as though he was of their own flesh and blood. But because of his natural diffidence, he never abused the privileges of his position.

"Are you all right, Mistress Mairi?" he asked softly. "Shall I put more peats on the fire for you? Would you like me to take the young Chief to his bed?"

"No, no," she whispered. "Sit you down, Iain. The fire is hot enough. Keep me company a while, for I am low in spirits."

He drew up a three-legged stool, and sat on it on the opposite side of the fireplace, leaning with his elbows on his knees, ready to speak or be silent.

"Do you think MacLeod's two sisters are happy in their marriages?" she asked at length. "I thought Christiana seemed well enough, and proud that she is to bear another child so soon. But Margaret seemed wan and lacking in cheerfulness."

"Her sight is much worse," Iain answered, shaking his head. "I found her groping in the passage-way for a reel of silk she had dropped. It had rolled a little away from her feet, but there it was, visible enough against a chair-leg, and she groping and feeling all about for it with her hands."

"Poor child! I do not think Donald Gorme has enough patience with her. And Dr Beaton has already said he cannot save the sight of her one eye, though he is treating the other still."

"Do you think MacDonald does not care for her?" Iain asked.

"Not very deeply, it seems to me," Mairi told him. "She pleased him with her pretty face and winsome ways. But to keep her all her days if she goes blind – ah, that is a different matter."

"Well, it was only a hand-fasting and not a marriage in the church," Iain reminded her. "Doubtless he could return her here, when the year is done, though who would marry her then, with one eye gone, I do not know."

"You know Rory does not agree with hand-fasting?" Mairi remarked. "Even though it is a very old custom and much used in the Islands still, he will have it that a wedding is for life, and no man should have a right to take a maid, and make her his, and then return her in a year if she does not please him. Besides, the question of children – who are not bastards neither rightful heirs if they are born of a hand-fasting – he says also it is an abuse of the maid herself, and women should be treated with more respect."

"Did he say that?" Iain asked. "Well, if I should wed – though I shall not, I think – I would have the blessing of God on the union in church, for I think hand-fasting is a heathenish thing and should be put away when men advance in knowledge and understanding. The union of man and woman is sacred, for it symbolises higher things – things of the Spirit, where the duality of natures seeks ever to be united into one. Each soul, says Plato, cries ever for its other half, from which it was torn asunder at the first creation."

"Do you think all life is a duel of two forces?" Mairi asked, her eyes interested.

"Good and evil. Right hand and left hand. The busyness of manhood. The stillness of woman. Day and night, light and dark. The growth of all things in sunlight, the quiet out-breathing under the moon. And many more," Iain answered slowly.

"Yes, it is the true meaning of the cloven hoof, this doubleness of things," Mairi responded. "I see it that way too. But there is a third thing, surely, in the nature of all life, for if there were not, what then is the Trinity?"

"That is surely so," Iain answered. "But it is not easy to see the Trinity in life. Though if it is true God dwells in us and also that in Him we live and move and have our being, as St Paul says, it is surely true the Trinity must be in all things, if we could only see it."

"Sometimes we can," Mairi said. "The third thing is that which links the duality and has also the power to transform it in some manner. Think of man and woman: He active, she the passive one. And what makes the Trinity live in them, but love, which both joins them and recreates itself, and them, by the birth of children, from the union of their physical bodies, and the birth of their joined spirit from the union of their souls? Thus three in one."

"If they be well mated," Iain answered soberly, thinking sadly of Christiana, so happy and maternal and content, though he had once dreamed of her as his soul-mate in learning and in love.

Chapter Ten

TORQUIL THE BLACK-HAIRED

Throughout the next three years the extensions and changes to the castle that William had planned but had not had time to carry out before his sudden death, went ahead under Rory's direction.

Since the days when Alasdair Crottach had rebuilt the tower at the opposite end of the rocky outcrop from the main block of buildings, the castle as a whole had been almost in two separate halves, for the buildings linking it in the middle were only single-storey affairs of mud and heather, straw-thatched, and occupied by servants, or used for storage, and with a covered passage-way along one side of them.

Now Rory planned to demolish all that seemed outmoded in this day and age, and they were pulled down altogether, and a great new range, strongly constructed of stone, grew up, which made the castle a formidable place, larger than Duntulm for all MacDonald's pleasances.

"Yet it is small compared with the castles of the mainland," Rory declared. "I do not think we are extravagant in the way we live here." And it was true that by comparison with the royal castles at Stirling and Edinburgh and Inverness, and many of the castles of the nobility of Scotland, none of the Island strongholds were large, but rather compact and small and sturdy on their rocky promontories, where many men had crowded closely into a little space as much for safety in more lawless days as for warmth and companionship. "We have not yet the graces of Edinburgh, but we will give ourselves somewhat more space and add to our dignity of living," he said, watching the walls go up, stone upon great rough-hewed stone.

"Who will we house in these chambers, Uncle?" the young chief asked.

"Well, your father planned to have some of Master MacCrimmon's pipers here, so that they are on hand and need not be fetched from Borreraig each time we want them to play," Rory told him. "And Master de Lérins deserves a new chamber to himself, for he is accustomed to the Court. And Master MacIain shall be better housed. And when I am married with Mistress MacDonald of Glengarry, as I shall be before this year is done, we shall perhaps find more rooms still are needed. And we will have a second hall, for dining in, as they do in Edinburgh. We will withdraw to the great hall when the feast is done, and there the musicians shall be heard to better advantage than with the drinking horns and goblets and platters rattling and men eating and drinking themselves into a stupor at the tables. Those who wish to do so may have leave to remain at table, but the music will be played to those who want to hear it, in the other chamber."

"Master de Lérins will approve of your choice," MacIain remarked. "He always says 'a light song and a merry while men eat and drink, but for the music that quivers in a man's marrow bones and stirs his very soul, there must be silence'."

"Yes," Rory responded, smiling. "So we are agreed on this, Master de Lérins and I." And he went off, leaving MacIain almost sure the very idea of this new mode of living had originated with de Lérins and not with Rory himself.

In the chamber in the base of the tower Rory threw off the plaid that he had worn against the wind and drizzle of rain out on the battlements while he was inspecting the progress of the building, and seated himself before a table laden with documents.

"You'd best give me your services as scribe this morning," he said to Iain, who came after him a few minutes later, closing the outer door with difficulty against the wind. "There are several letters to be written."

"Yes, sir. There is also a letter just come from the Earl of Argyll, by a messenger who is still below," Iain told him, holding out a parchment scroll with the great seal of the house of Campbell hanging from it. Rory tore it open, and perused the small, close hand.

"Thomas Fowlis," he muttered at length. "Who in St Clement's name is Thomas Fowlis?" And then, having read on, he made an exclamation of indignation, and flung down the parchment on the littered table, where at once it rolled itself up again, and tumbled to the rush-strewn floor. "God save us from the entanglements made for us by our fathers!" he cried. "Here is my Lord of Argyll – who has had vested interest in Dunvegan and Harris since his father married off the little female heir into his own family, and thus acquired her rights – selling us lock, stock and barrel over our heads to one Thomas Fowlis, a goldsmith, and a burgess of Edinburgh, who has now become on Argyll's bond, our overlord!"

"God save us, sir! What does that mean in truth?" Iain asked, astonished.

"Nothing. Nothing. It is all only words on paper. No, wait, it could be used against us, if the King should ask for our titles and charters of possession, as he has of Donald Gorme and Lachlan MacKinnon, and some of the other chiefs," Rory said slowly, as all the complications of the document became clearer to him. "Let me see it again. Here. I have already wondered why it is that the charters of land rights of the past are not to be found in the kist among the letters and documents preserved by my brother and my father. I see now. Argyll doubtless has them all, and he is transferring them for ready cash, without a by-your-leave from us at all."

"But what then would Master Fowlis want with such documents?" Iain asked, for his mind was less ready than Rory's to understand politics and legal matters. "Does he wish to take Dunvegan from you?"

"Let him try!" Rory snorted. "The home of my ancestors given up to some city gentleman at my Lord of Argyll's whim? No, but he will claim the revenues of the land and properties on it, here in Skye and in Harris. That is where he will have us in most uncomfortable grip. But we will fight him, Iain, and pay him nothing, even if I am put to the horn for it. By the Rood!" he cried suddenly, his temper rising uncontrollably, "The machinations of these nobles almost make me vomit."

Flinging the document away from him a second time, Rory pushed back his chair, and strode out, without his plaid, on to the windswept battlements again, and went marching up and down there, with his face black as thunder. Iain watched him for a few minutes from the open doorway, and then seeing how the wind was blowing in leaves and dust and tossing the parchments and documents on the table, he closed the door and shut himself into the room again.

After a while Rory returned. Iain was tranquilly stoking the fire with his back to him, and made no comment until Rory cleared his throat loudly, and said:

"Well, I have forgotten my vow already," Iain looked over his shoulder and saw a sheepish grin on his face:

"What vow, sir?" he asked.

"Why, the vow I made to myself so earnestly in prison, that I would never more act in hot temper, or throw out ill-considered words in haste!"

Iain laughed.

"Well, sir, when an Isle-man is provoked he most often flies off in rage before he thinks. No harm is done unless he happens to have a dirk in hand and his provoker there in the same room with him!"

"Well, never the less, I am ashamed." Rory answered soberly. "I swore upon the Holy Rood, and now I see I cannot trust myself. Come, we will write to the King on this matter – but most soberly and in most temperate terms. Come, bring your quill and write:

"Most Gracious and sacred Soverane, I, Roderick MacLeod of Harris and Dunvegan, Tutor, do tender my humble duty and obedience –"

But the carefully worded letter to the king availed him little, for when an answer came at length it was to say his Grace, as superior overlord of all the Island territories, confirmed the granting to Thomas Fowlis of the whole net profits of the estate at Dunvegan after due provision had been made for the maintenance and education of the heir, and an annual payment of 160 merks during the heir's minority and a tax on his marriage, of 500 merks.

In addition, Rory was required to produce his charters to all his lands to be re-assessed for Crown rents and the teinds due to the Bishop of the Isles, as was now being done on all the main estates throughout the Hebrides.

"By St Clement, how am I to produce charters which I have not?" Rory said despairingly. "Lord Lovat has still the instrument of seisin that affects Glenelg – though he declares he has not got it, since he claims all that territory as his own. And of the other charters – most are missing. I do not doubt Argyll's father had them, but the young earl says he does not know where they are, and will not even say if he has given them to Master Fowlis with his bond, though I dare say he has."

Rory set himself to make a study of all the land rights held by Dunvegan and Harris since the beginning of the clan's history, as best he might, and wrote at length declaring, with protestations of his obedience and loyalty, that he held now only half his rightful heritage since the MacDonalds had installed themselves in Sleat and Trotternish, and had from these parts "most violently detruded my forebears." And Lord Lovat "most wrongously refused to produce the instrument of seisin to Glenelg and mayhap he hath fraudfullie put away ye same." And almost no documents proving his nephew's rights of inheritance could be found, though there was no doubt that "I and my predicessors be heritable tenants to your Majestie and your predicessors of the lands of Sleat, North Uist and utheris landis byand in the North Isles wherein we were heritable infeft by your Majestie's worthy goodsire of famous memorie."

To his long, courteously worded letter, the King vouchsafed no answer at all.

Finding King James's silence ominous, Rory took horse at length and rode to Duntulm to consult with Donald Gorme, only to find that he in like predicament had gone off to Edinburgh in hopes of seeing the King in person and explaining the situation with regard to his lands and the income from them – which was never overlarge, especially in a bad year, and could not with reason bear such heavy taxation as the King envisaged from them. Donald Gorme's return had been looked for, for some days, but only that morning news had come that he was held at Edinburgh Castle at the King's pleasure and would not be freed until a fine of £4,000 was paid, to cover arrears of crown-rents, "and to provide a fund for the reimbursement of any who might suffer loss at the hands of his clansmen," and notably the MacLeans, against whom he had been carrying on an intermittent war ever since his cousin Hugh MacGillespie had stirred up their tempers towards each other.

Poor Margaret, still childless and with the sight of her one eye gone entirely, clung to her brother Rory, crying fearfully that her husband was surely imprisoned in some dungeon or in the Tolbooth as Rory himself had been for a while. And though he was not always kind to her these days, she loved him still and greatly feared for his safety.

Rory came away from Duntulm at length as dusk was falling and began the long ride home in grim and cheerless mood. He was accompanied only by Hugh de Lérins and the two man-servants he had brought with him. They rode behind on their palfreys somewhat apprehensively through the quiet winter woods, the open stony corries and the uplands where the sharp frost made the dry bracken crackle under the horses' hooves.

As long as there was a little daylight left, Rory rode quickly, for horses stumble if ridden after dark falls. The palfreys lagged further and further back, unable to sustain the pace his own beast set.

Suddenly his horse, which had pressed on willingly under his familiar guidance, hesitated and started and shied back and reared in fright. At once Rory's hand went to his belt for his dirk. Almost on top of him, unheard because of the vagaries of the wind, three plaid-wrapped figures were tramping silently in line ahead through the heather. Their hands went to their sides with equal speed when they saw the solitary horseman outlined against the racing, moonlit clouds, and they came into a defensive huddle and stood still.

"Who crosses my land?" Rory called authoritatively.

"It is the chief," a relieved solitary voice muttered. "You frightened us, MacLeod, riding solitary like a spectre."

"Where are you going?" Rory asked, approaching. "It is late for landsmen to be abroad. What is in those bundles you are carrying?"

There was a hesitant, awkward silence, as though while not wishing to show hostility or impertinence, the three men searched their minds for a ready answer, and could find none suitable.

"Come," Rory said, sensing at once that something was going on that he knew nothing of, and sharp-witted enough to suspect it could lead to more trouble than he was already involved in. "Am I to search your bundles for myself?"

"It is only meat and bread, and some other stores for hungry men," one of the three answered, civilly enough.

"What hungry men?" Rory asked, turning to the speaker, and as he did so, in a sudden uncovering of the moon, he saw the man was wearing the tartan of MacLeod of the Lewis, unlike the other two in their local-woven plaid of his own family.

"What are you doing here?" he asked, staring at him. "I do not want men of the Lewis at this time, for I know all the Lewis is in a ferment over the inheritance, and all men taking sides against each other. What is your business?"

The Lewis man looked down at his horny feet, unshod in spite of the frozen ground, which did not seem to trouble him, though the other two had tied rags over their feet, well-padded into make-shift boots, with straw. Seeing that he would not answer unless forced, Rory moved on his horse and reached down as though to grab and cuff the words out of him. But one of the other two answered for him.

"Your kinsman Torquil Dubh sent him. His galleys are moored this night in Loch Snizort, and taking on supplies."

"What for? What for?" Rory demanded.

"Why, for a battle campaign, so he says. He is off to Kintail to harry the MacKenzies in their own territory, since he says they are always harrying him at home, with raiding parties and attacks on Stornaway, for Torquil Conanach's sake."

"Holy Jesu!" Rory breathed. "Is my kinsman there below in Snizort this very night? Why did he not come to me? I ought to have known of this."

The men laughed. "Why, men say you will have nothing to do with war, and are afraid to unsheath your sword since the King imprisoned you," he responded bluntly. "Now it is all talk and words on paper, so they say. So men of action do not wait on you. And Torquil of the Lewis does not want you standing in his way, so he gets provisions where he can – and pays in money, and does not ask your leave."

"By the Rood!" Rory cried, incensed. "Am I afraid to unsheath my sword? Well, fellows, you'd best lead me to my brother-in-law, and I'll have words with him. Yes, words! For words have their uses, whatever you may believe."

At that moment, the three palfreys came jogging up. Taking de Lérins with him, Rory sent the men home to Dunvegan on their own.

The two parties separated, and the Lewis men and the Skye cottagers padded on downhill through the heather towards the long, narrow inlet at the end of Loch Snizort between the land wings of Waternish and Trotternish.

"There, MacLeod! Do you see those lights flickering?" One of the Skye men said, after a time, coming to a standstill and pointing down towards the water, far below. "There are the three galleys. See their masts against the moonlight on the waters? Yes, those are your kinsman's ships."

"I see them," Rory answered, as he and de Lérins pulled up their horses, and looked downwards into the narrow end of the loch with its cliffy sides. They moved onwards, the horses reined in to keep pace with the men on foot, whose panting breath could be heard as they struggled beneath their heavy loads.

"We should not have to hurry so if we had not met MacLeod of MacLeod," the one grumbled to the other, as he slipped on a loose stone and recovered himself again. "It was ill luck, and who knows what Torquil of the Lewis will say when he finds who comes with us?"

Overhearing the words, Rory said to them:

"I am not the MacLeod of MacLeod, you know. It is your young chief who bears the title. I am only his Tutor until he is a man."

"The little Chief will never grow to manhood," the Skye man answered. "You are the chief. All men of Skye know that."

"How can they know any such thing?" Rory enquired curiously. "My nephew is a delicate little boy it is true, but…"

"It is known all over the island. The old women say so over the peats of a night. And the young men pray that when you are instated in your own right, you will not make them lay aside their swords for good."

"Do they?" he said softly. "How do they know whether I will be chief, or not?" But he spoke into the darkness and the wind not expecting or receiving any answer.

*****

Torquil Dubh was seated on an iron-studded chest amidships, eating an apple, with one lanky leg curled under him and a nonchalant expression on his handsome young face as he watched the loading of supplies from the two or three small curraghs which were drawn alongside.

Rory climbed over the side, helped by friendly hands, for many of the men of the Lewis knew him by sight and were pleased enough to think he might be with them on this venture. Hearing his familiar voice, Torquil turned his head enquiringly. And then stiffened with a look of alertness as he saw his brother-in-law's expression.

"Well, cousin, what brings you here?" he asked.

"I might ask that of you, sir." Rory said shortly. "Seeing you are moored in my waters and without my leave."

"Seeing this loch lies between Waternish and Trotternish, I would say that it is no more your water than that of Donald Gorme," Torquil snapped back with equal asperity. "In fact, I would say it is like the high seas – free to all men."

"However that may be, your men have been ashore on my land, robbing my foolish cottagers by taking from them their winter stores – which they need to live on – in return for gold, which will be no use at all to them when their bellies are empty. Why did you not come to me and tell me of your intended enterprise?" He demanded.

"What would you have said to me if I had done so?" Torquil asked, biting a hunk out of the apple. "You are not quick to draw your sword these days on any man's behalf – so they say."

"Do they say that?" Rory asked with ominous quiet. "You are the second man to accuse me this night of not knowing where my duty lies."

"If men drew their swords only for duty's sake, life would be tame indeed," Torquil laughed. "Was it duty made you draw yours on Kintail in Edinburgh in the presence of the King?"

There was a silence.

"Yes, I have my own quarrel with Robert MacKenzie of Kintail," Rory said grimly. "But it is not part of my concern to get your inheritance for you."

"No? Well, no-one asked you, cousin," Torquil answered. "I can deal with Kintail – and with his protégé Torquil Conanach – without your aid."

He cast the apple core overboard into the dark troubled waters that rippled beside the boats where the curraghs were unloading the last of their supplies. "Nearly finished, Jamie?" he called to a burly, bearded man with a yellow cap set rakishly on his head. "I want to be away before the moon is down. We must draw anchor before the tide begins to set against us."

"Yes, master. It is nearly done," the man answered.

He heaved up a great side of beef and stowed it away and a cog of bland - the whisked whey stored in wood until it fermented well and became a strong brew – was put down after it. "Now we shall not starve even if you keep us at sea till the moon is full again!" he laughed with satisfaction.

"Well, Rory, it is time you were off," Torquil said. "We will have a curragh take you back ashore."

"Why did you get my men to stock you?" Rory asked, on a note of disapproval. Torquil had risen to his feet and moved to the gunwale to call down to the boatmen. He also went across, but he was unwilling to take his departure, for the adventurousness of his lawless forbears moved in his blood, and the stocking of the boats, the preparation for battle, the tension and excitement that he sensed on every side got into him in spite of himself.

"The Lewis is torn with dissention since my father's death, and no man knows who he can trust and who will prove to be against him," Torquil Dubh told him. "If I had loaded up at Stornaway, I might have discovered when I got to Kintail that someone had gone before me with warning of my coming."

"Where is my sister, your wife, while you are off on this venture?" Rory asked.

"I took her down to Harris with the babes, for safety. Now cousin, away with you. I have paid your men well and robbed them of nothing. And perhaps – if the venture goes well with me – I'll bring them goods enough from Kintail's land to answer all their troubles."

"You have a fair night. The wind is with you. It will fill your sails well," Rory remarked. He moved into the stern, and standing there feet apart with his plaid wind-ruffled, his body lightly and familiarly balanced against the dip and sway of the boat as the crew moved about on her, preparing to cast off, he looked around him at the moon-touched waters, stirring constantly, darkly translucent, and at the steep mass of the distant cliffs, and at the lively sky.

"I will not act in haste," he told himself. "I will keep my vow and take no action without thought." He clenched his hand on the gunwale, and stared seaward, his back turned to Torquil, and tried by the steady pressure of his fingers on the old, salt-hardened oak, and his attention to the movement, so to awaken his consciousness that he could not afterwards feel he had behaved like a youth, impetuously and foolishly, and without the wisdom that the years should have brought to birth in him.

"He has a just cause," he thought, "for I am quite sure Torquil Conanach was sired by the Breve of the Lewis and is no son of my kinsman. He has a right cause – apart from my own grievance with MacKenzie – which I shall not at this moment think about." Excitement mounted in him. "He is my sister's husband," he thought. "Would not the Old Chief, my grandfather, have gone to war in this cause? Yes, in his young manhood he would – and I do not know what it is like to be an old man, yet, so I cannot judge how it would be later on."

He felt the blood rising in him and the deep pumping of his heart. Without thinking, he laid a hand to his belt and finding there no sword-sheath, but only the short dirk which he carried on ordinary occasions, he turned his head and said out of his own thoughts: "But I am not armed!"

Torquil Dubh looked at him steadily.

"I have a blade to spare," he remarked, his mouth twitching suddenly with a swiftly suppressed amusement. "And an extra shield."

Behind them the first of the great hempen sails was being unfurled. The ropes clattered and pulled through the rattling cleats, and the brown-speckled sail rose slowly, billowing upwards.

"Wait!" Rory cried, staring at it. Already the last curragh was pulling away from the galley's side. Hearing his voice and seeing the pale oval of his face turned landwards in the moonlight, the boatman rested on his oars, looking back enquiringly.

For a moment Rory said nothing more. He drew his breath deeply, and then called out:

"There is a fellow of mine ashore – a minstrel. Bring him over – if he will come willingly."

In a few minutes the curragh returned, bringing de Lérins, who clambered over the side of the boat with a look of enquiry on his face.

"Well, Hugh," Rory called to him from his place in the bows, "are you a willing passenger?"

"Why, yes sir," he responded, puzzled.

"Are you prepared to venture with us on the seas to bait MacKenzie in his stronghold?"

"If you are going, sir."

"Come and join me here! You shall sing for me on the voyage."

Hugh de Lérins scrambled over the sacks and bundles of provisions that lay in his way, and went up to where his master stood. Rory's face wore an expression of alertness and exhilaration. His short black hair was ruffled from the running of his hands through it in agitation. He breathed quickly, and turned and seated himself suddenly with a look of boyish confidence, high up in the bows, facing seaward.

The Frenchman moved near him, looking into his face. In all the time that he had known MacLeod, he had never seen such a look of energy and vigour and latent power as was now visible in him. His first memory of him was of the grave and serious expression he had worn during the conference at Edinburgh. And later, after his release from prison, the lined countenance and grim tension of the mouth that rarely softened into smiles or laughter.

During Rory's imprisonment, the minstrel had remained in Edinburgh, keeping his contact with the Court and the King, but certain, with a strange inward knowing, beyond the reach of the intellect, that the time would come when he would go to Skye and live beneath the protection of the Clan MacLeod.

But although he had thought of this coming event as being "like Talliessin come to Glastonbury," he had, until this moment, failed to recognize what he had sought and expected.

Now, meeting MacLeod's eyes with a surge of pleasure, he began to sing as the sail ran up behind them, not of the troubadours from the Frankish Court, but for the first time, a song of the Isles that he had learned from the bards:

> *"Thou who dwellest*
> *In the heights above,*
> *O, succour us in the depths below,*
> *Vouchsafe to us a day breeze*
> *As Thou Thyself wouldst wish,*
> *Vouchsafe to us a night-breeze,*
> *As we ourselves would choose.*
> *May the clouds hide us,*
> *May the moon shine on the foe,*
> *Be we to windward*
> *And becalmed be they."*

At the first sound of the familiar words, Rory turned his head sharply, with such an expression that, for a moment, de Lérins faltered, thinking that he had displeased him, but he gestured to him to continue, saying:

"It is the first time I have heard you sing one of our songs. The Dunvegan Sea Hymn was always more pleasing to me than all the ballads of my family, and I am pleased that you should sing it today in these circumstances!"

Softly, de Lérins continued:

> *"Oh, keep firmly tethered,*
> *All sudden blasts and accidents*
> *And leave the rest to us.*
> *And we will give the glory*
> *To the Trinity and Clement,*
> *And the Great Clerk who lives in Rodel."*

On either side of them the two other galleys, their sails fully unfurled and billowing forward, began to take the wind and move up the waterway. Behind them, the last of the hempen ropes ran clattering through the iron cleat and was secured. With a tugging and billowing of the great hempen sails, their own galley heeled and strained under way through the dark ruffled water.

"Those last are not the lines my ancestors sang," Rory said, craning forward and speaking over his shoulder. "They are MacCrimmon's words. He was my grandfather – that "Great Clerk who lives in Rodel."

"Men speak of him as though he were a saint," de Lérins answered.

"But do not sing that verse to other men," Rory told him, "for the Reformers will not have it that the saints may intercede for us. It is supposed each man must make his own connection with his Maker."

"It is perhaps a dangerous thing to imagine otherwise," de Lérins answered, "yet it seems to me there may well be minds of higher levels between my own and His almighty One."

"Who knows?" said Rory. "In these isles we often feel the seen and the unseen are all one, and we walk close to many things that other men know nothing of. Do you dislike the teaching of Calvin and of Master Knox?"

"No, sir. I think it is all the same in the end, whether men say God lives in their own hearts and they can find Him there, or whether they look for Him above and worship Him with ritual and with liturgy."

"Do you still hold to Rome, then?"

"My ancestors came from the Isle of Lérins off the coast of France, whence came many of those saints, who built the Celtic church," de Lérins told him in a rush of words.

"Ah," Rory breathed. "I had often thought you are of the same stuff as Iain MacIain. He is always full of mystical questions and theological argument. But for myself, it seems to me, if a man uses his body aright and keeps his mind keen and alert and his heart awake, then these three parts of him, in balance, will serve him well enough for this life and the next."

He turned away, leaning on the gunwale and staring forward into the grey half-light as the three galleys moved onward together where the loch widened to the open sea.

*****

Torquil Dubh's first intention had been to run around Trotternish and through the Sound of Raasay to Kintail's stronghold at Eileen Donan on the mainland. But off Rona they saw galleys lying with MacKenzie's pennant flying and therefore changed their course, sailing northward up the coast of Scotland all the next day until they reached the Summer Isles by evening.

In the morning they landed at Coigeach and went down along Loch Broom by land, burning and destroying all the cottages and terrorising MacKenzie's people, who lived in these parts. This was in the manner of all the raids the chiefs had made one upon another from time immemorial. Though Rory protested that he and Lewis had no quarrel with these people but only with MacKenzie himself, he went on with them, wielding his sword with the rest, buoyed up by the thought that sooner or later he would surely come to grips with his old enemy.

For three days they ran riot through all these lands, driving off the cattle, bearing away the household goods and stores and loading their galleys with the loot they had so easily gathered.

As they set sail on the fourth evening, thinking to make straight for Stornaway, MacKenzie's fleet appeared round Cailleach Head, with the bearded chief himself standing forward in the leading birlinn, and the two forces came to grips among the little isles and skerries off Loch Broom and Gruinard Bay.

In the gathering darkness they fought so close that men struggled in the water between the boats or were crushed against their hulls as the galleys ran one against the next, and the whipped foam at dawn was stained with the blood that had flowed freely in the hours of darkness.

They drew apart at length, exhausted, neither side victor, and Torquil MacLeod's three galleys, with sails torn and tattered by sword-thrust and arrow-head, and wounded men lying beneath the feet of the oarsmen, moved off slowly in a light wind and early mist for Stornaway and the Lewis.

In a few days, Rory and Hugh de Lérins went south again to Skye in one of Torquil's boats. Throughout the journey Rory maintained a silence that de Lérins could not penetrate with either song or word until they rounded Ardmore Point at last, and turned into the mouth of Loch Dunvegan. Then he said suddenly:

"You are a good swordsman, Hugh, but you seemed somewhat reluctant to fight, I noticed."

"There was no lack of skill – and seemingly no reluctance – in *your* sword-hand," de Lérins replied.

"Well," Rory answered him, after a moment, "since I have seen the treachery of Kings and Chiefs and men one to another, I have begun to think that the most a man can do in this life is to pursue his honest purposes with courage and conviction, do what seems right at the time and to fear no man."

"It is a fair enough thought for a man of the Western Isles," said de Lérins. "And yet I would make a guess that when your life is run, if men remember you, it will be for other matters."

They looked at one another, as though each speculated what lay in the other's mind, then turned their faces homeward.

From that time onward Rory wielded his sword and his pen with equal vigour, in his protracted correspondence with the King over his kinsmen's and his own land rights in the Hebrides.

Chapter Eleven

THE LONG SWORD

As the two landsmen had predicted, the boy chief, John did not live to wield the sword of his ancestors in battle. After five years of Rory's regency, the boy took a chill, after being caught in a squall, fishing off Sheep Island one March morning. He quickly ran a fever, and the congestion of the lungs, which he was always prone to, took hold of him. In spite of Dr Beaton's herbal poultices, the mulled wine and all the remedies that Mairi MacLeod could muster, he did not recover, and died a few days later, with his widowed mother and Mairi herself beside him.

When Rory came in and stood at the foot of the boy's bed, his kinswoman looked up with tear-stained face, and said:

"I have sung the Dunvegan Lullaby over three chiefs, and already two of them are dead!"

"Alas," he answered quietly, and then he put a hand on the shoulders of either woman, and said to them:

"The third is still alive. And Isabel and I have sons, my heartlings, who will succeed me."

He stooped and kissed his brother's widow lightly, smiled into Mairi's face, and went away.

After the burial at Rodel, Rory was installed formally as chief of the Clan MacLeod. The new wing of the castle was still not yet complete, for a shortage of lead for roofing tiles and timber for the great beams, and also the high taxation on the estate which the King was now imposing, had delayed the builders.

In these circumstances, the feast was held, not in the new great dining room that he was building, but in the old hall, where all such previous ceremonies had taken place.

Once again Rory received ceremonially the two-handed claymore of William of the Long Sword. Then raised his brother William's sword aloft, and said with confidence: "With the sword of my forebear I will defend you and uphold the Clan," as he had already said before on the little boy's behalf.

The clansmen received the declaration with strong and ready acclamation. Although there had been no major actions or battles or trials during the past five years, they had seen how willingly he unsheathed his sword in defense of the rights of his kinsmen: how readily he looked to their individual needs: how quickly he grasped the intricacies of politics, and the courage with which he dealt with the strangle-hold that the King was intent on maintaining on these island territories. They looked to him as they had towards his grandfather in his younger days – as one whose eyes could see beyond the length and breadth of their own vision, and whose sword-hand could be trusted with the best.

From his place at the high board, where he sat with his wife and two elder sons, Iain and Roderick on one hand, and his kinswoman, Mairi, on the other, Rory looked the length of the hall and surveyed his people with satisfaction.

On one side of the hall, Torquil Dubh and Christiana sat, with their own three boys; and seeing Christiana's laughing face at some jest of the minstrels, and Torquil's handsome countenance turned tenderly towards her, he smiled and thought how good an alliance this had been between the houses of Dunvegan and Harris, and of the Lewis.

But on the other side, Donald Gorme sat apart from Margaret, and, surveying him, Rory's thoughts took a sombre turn.

Donald Gorme was a big-boned man and had become red-faced and heavy-jowled now, and with small piercing eyes that looked far but not widely, in their flickering glances. Looking the length of the table at him, and seeing how he had coarsened since they had eaten the roebuck together at Duntulm years ago, Rory felt little friendship in his heart towards him. Whenever they spoke together they seemed to be in some way at loggerheads.

Besides, Margaret was a sad little figure, her almost sightless eyes downcast, her thin small hands toying nervously with a ribbon on her bodice. Her tremulous start whenever she heard her husband's boisterous voice raised above other men's, betokened the fear in which she lived at Duntulm. Though she was never treated with physical cruelty, MacDonald's harsh contempt of her infirmity had subdued and shrivelled her little spirit into nothingness.

Rory's own marriage pleased him well enough, and he turned to Isabel gladly in all his hours of ease, made her laugh, laughed with her, played light games of love and looked with pleasure on her winsome face and into her dancing eyes – still much unchanged since he had first seen her at Glengarry's side at that other feasting. His elder boy, Iain,

136

was like her – full of laughter and mischief; and the second, Roderick, showed promise to be like his father in feature. Now, with a third child on the way, he was well content that the inheritance was assured.

But it was to Mairi Nighean Alastair Ruadh – the poet – that he turned for true companionship. She had acquired so strong and clear a grasp of clan affairs during his imprisonment and had so tender a love for all their people and for the Island ways, that he brought most of his problems to her, and discussed them with her as though she had been a man.

Iain MacIain approached the high table, and, above the clamour of voices and laughter and music, leant over Rory and said to him:

"Sir, MacLeod of the Lewis would like a word with you in privacy before he takes his departure."

"Tell him to come up here then," Rory responded, and looking down to where Torquil and Christiana sat, and seeing his brother-in-law's expectant face turned towards him, he raised a hand and beckoned him.

Mairi got up at once to make a space on the long bench, and Iain bent down to her, assisted her with smiling gentleness and led her off, his hand beneath her arm, to find a seat at another table.

Rory watched them for a moment, and saw how she smiled her thanks, and then, turned to look elsewhere.

"Why do they not get married, those two?" he asked his wife.

"Iain and Mairi? They would be well suited," Isabel answered. "But she will never marry him, for she loves another man."

"Does she?" Rory said dubiously. "I know nothing of it."

"For all your lively mind and speedy thoughts, you are often very blind!" she said, half-laughing, "It is you she loves."

"No, how could she?" he answered, with real astonishment. "We are like brother and sister together, and have been all our lives. I would never have thought of making her my wife – even if you had not come to me, my darling."

Torquil Dubh came up with long easy strides, flung one lanky leg over the bench beside Rory and, sitting astride it, looked into the chief's face, and said:

"Sir, I want to ask a favour of you."

"I hope you are not going to ask me to bring out all my men again in your cause," Rory remarked, ruefully, "for we are full of wine and beer and good roast meat, and for myself, I would rather sleep a while! We have been to your aid often enough, these past five years."

"No, it is another matter," Torquil replied. "It has been said, though not yet confirmed by high authority, that the King plans to remove the

Lewis altogether from Conanach and myself – because he is tired of our wrangling over it. And that he will plant there some Lowland gentleman to farm the land, or do what they will with it."

"By St Clement, does he plan to take you over?" Rory ejaculated. "Is it certain? What are your own plans, Torquil?"

"It is in my mind that Torquil Conanach and I, whether we are half-brothers or not, must come to grips in person and fight this out in words between us," Torquil Dubh answered. "I want to ask you, Rory, to take Christiana and the boys under your protection here at Dunvegan until this trouble is concluded."

"Yes, I will willingly, if it seems to you you can bring so tangled a coil into a proper knot – or cut the string in two – in so simple a manner."

"It is not a simple matter, that I know well," Torquil said gravely. "You know Kintail holds Stornaway, now, and all the north part of the Lewis is at this moment under Conanach's sway, while my men have had to retreat almost as far as Tarbert on the borders of your land of Harris. But even now, surely all men of Harris and the Lewis would unite together against an invasion by these Lowland adventurers, which would deprive us of all our ancient rights."

"You speak wisely," Rory told him seriously, "and I will keep your family here with me until we know the outcome."

"There is one more small matter," Torquil said, after a moment's silence, looking down at the table with an expression of embarrassment. "There is at Tarbert a son of mine – Neil – for whom I have great regard. Would you take him under your guardianship if anything should go wrong?"

Rory looked at him, then suddenly gave a shout of laughter.

"A bastard brat? What will my sister Christiana say?"

"She knows about the boy," Torquil said, with a shamefaced laugh. "His mother is nothing to me – it was a youthful escapade – but I am fond of the lad and I would like to see him secure."

"Well, send him here," Rory told him. "He shall be safe enough. But do not go to Conanach with fear in your thoughts, for fear brings its own reward – disaster."

"I am not afraid," Torquil answered, looking up with his countenance tranquil and composed. "I am only planning for my household, as any wise man does. And all the more must he do so when his own stronghold is wrested from him, as mine is now."

"The blessing of our Patron Saint on your enterprise," Rory said quietly.

"May St Clement grant us grace," Torquil responded gravely.

And then, remembering the new edict of the church, that they should not invoke saints or angels, they smiled at one another.

"I often ask myself whether the Reformers of the Church of Scotland are destroying us inwardly, as the King and the Privy Council are destroying us outwardly." Torquil said suddenly, in a manner so much more grave than was his custom that Rory looked at him in surprise.

"No, no, it is beyond their reach to touch the core of the spirit of the Isles," Rory answered him. "I think it best to fulfil our obligations to the Presbyterian cause, now that it is accepted and established on the mainland. Indeed, I have brought Father O'Colgan over from Rodel to minister to us here at Dunvegan, for he has embraced the new faith and sees in it deep and simple truths that the church of Rome has long forgotten."

"Then will you close the monastery at Rodel all together?" Torquil asked. "I remember it when I was a young boy, in the old Abbot's day."

"There is no-one now to lead them, and its days are done," Rory answered. "Its life was short, but very deep and rich, like a good seam of peat that goes down very far into the depths of living things. I have brought over all the good silver things and other household objects that the monks made; and the manuscripts are in the keeping of Brother Allan of Bernera, the Scribe. There was a fine Communion cup, hand-wrought with great intricacy that MacIain brought over to us, and I have bequeathed it to the new church we are building for Duirinish, for our people's use."

"Ah," Torquil said, "indeed the times are changing."

Chapter Twelve

THE OUTLAW

On a fine afternoon in the late spring, Iain MacIain and Mairi and Rory's three sons had been spending an afternoon out on the headland above the great rocks called MacLeod's Maidens, which the cottagers believed to be Seal Women, turned to stone by a witch long ago.

On the cliff top, as the children played in the sunshine above a turquoise blue sea, with ripples of light foam splashing far below, the two old friends had discussed a prophesy which had been made by old Dun Kenneth, who had second-sight, and which was being told and re-told round the peats from house to house all over MacLeod's lands. In great detail it described the eventual downfall of the MacLeods of Dunvegan which should begin when MacLeod's Maidens were sold to a Campbell; and end with the household of the chief being so reduced, "that one small curragh would suffice to carry MacLeod and all his possessions across Loch Dunvegan."

"It will never happen!" Rory's son Ian declared, smoothing out the seabirds' feathers he had collected on the rocks. "Why, my father's lands stretch so far, you can see them in every direction, wherever you look. Even some of the Outer Isles are under him – and there they are on this clear day: North Uist, and South Uist, with all its islets and skerries. And Benbecula. And right round there is Harris, with Rodel at its tip, where great-grandfather had his monastery. And little Isle Bernera. Only the Lewis is not under his sway, or in allegiance with him. He is a very strong chief, and most clans prefer to be with him rather than against him."

"Bernera is my island, isn't it?" young Norman, the middle son asked, counting out sea shells and laying them in rows. "My father told me I should not have the big islands, because they have to go to Ian, as he is the oldest. But he won't have Roderick and William and me forgotten, so there will be 'William of Hamera,' and 'Roderick of Talisker' and I shall have Bernera, when I am a man. You can come and visit me there, if you like."

"I will indeed," Mairi answered, looking at the dark, curly head fondly, as the little boy bent again over his collection of shells. "How like Rory this one is," she thought for the hundredth time. He was the dearest to her of all her cousin's family.

"Even strong chiefs do not live for ever," Roderick, the second boy put in in a matter-of-fact voice. "Clans rise and fall – the seanachie tells us this in our history lessons. The prophecy might come true."

"Well, even if it does, it is not such a sad story," Mairi said swiftly seeing the other boys look up. "It does not end there, because Dun Kenneth says later on there will come a great chief called Ian Breac – the scarred or pock-marked one – and he will redeem the fortunes of the clan."

"Surely all things have their life-span," MacIain said. "They are born, and grow to maturity and then decline and die. I suppose the clan must die at length, like any other living thing. But not for many centuries."

"And then Ian Breac will come!" the young heir said confidently.

"Yes – as King Arthur will come to England again, so the legends say. And St Columba will return to Iona, and the monastery there will rise up again. And even as it is said the Jesus Christ Himself will come a second time. But perhaps not in time such as we know it. Not within centuries such as we understand with our small minds, but in another way."

"Perhaps, or perhaps he will really come – the scarred one. Scarred by battle or scarred inwardly by life, who knows?" Mairi suggested.

"I sometimes think you have second-sight yourself," Iain said fondly, looking at her fine-boned face turned seawards, and the far-away look in the eyes that he knew so well.

She sighed.

"Perhaps a little – because I am a minstrel – or I would have been, if I had been born a man," she responded. "Do you know what Hugh de Lérins says about minstrels and bards and story-tellers? He says they are always homeless in this life. They belong nowhere, and have no true possessions, no matter where they lodge, for their home is beyond this world."

"Come," Iain said, "there are clouds round Heleavel Mor. The Cuillins have hidden their faces in cloud. We must start for home."

Norman took Mairi's hand and swung it to and fro. Leaping and dancing beside her, he demanded:

"Tell us again the story of how my great-grandfather took King James the Fifth up to the very top of Heleavel Mor and they dined there under the stars, with great flaming torches for candles."

"Why, you know it Norman," the boy Ian said, with brotherly impatience. "You have heard it many times."

"I know, I know, but I like Mairi to tell it," Norman repeated.

"Why, it was when your great-grandfather, Alasdair the Hunchback, had dined at Holyrood with the King," Mairi said, "and someone there had said to him: 'I warrant you have not in your island fastnesses any such table as this, or such a great rich hall or such silver candlesticks!' and your great-grandfather responded: 'I have far better ones at home!'. So the King told him he would come and visit Dunvegan and dine with him and see.

"And when the King came, he had him carried right to the top of Heleavel Mor - MacLeod's Great Table, and there was a great banquet laid out on the grass and all the clansmen standing with their torches," Norman cried joyfully, skipping up and down.

"And he said to the King: 'This is my table and these are my candlesticks and all the starry sky is the ceiling of my hall!'" Mairi concluded.

The boys laughed, looking up at the cloud-wreathed hill, for the stories of great-grandfather's day never ceased to please them. They had been days of great vigour and gaiety and love of life, for all their violence.

*****

When they came up the sea stairs into the castle, they sensed at once that something had happened in their absence. There was movement and noise up above, and Rory's voice could be heard raised in anger.

Mairi sent the children to the tower nursery and she and MacIain turned together towards the great hall. But before they reached it, Christiana ran out, sobbing wildly, with her elder son white-faced behind her.

"They have killed Torquil! They have killed my husband!" Christiana cried. Flinging herself into Mairi's arms.

"It was Conanach himself," Torquil's son told them soberly. "They met at sea to discuss a partition of the Lewis. Old Hutcheon who used to be the Breve was there too. And while my father had his attention distracted, Torquil Conanach stabbed him in the shoulder blade. He fell over the galley side, and was left in the sea to drown."

142

MacIain went at once into the great hall. Rory was standing at the far end, with his back to the wide fireplace, where logs had been kindled, for the evening would be chilly. He was dressed in a crimson jerkin and kilted plaid and white lawn shirt, with wide sleeves in the fashion, and had on him a leather pistol-brace which he had seized and buckled on, more as a token of his temper than for immediate use.

"Whatever rights there are on Conanach's side – though I doubt if there are any – he shall not sit pretty and undisturbed, now he has murdered my sister's husband!" he was saying. "We have been out at half strength with Torquil Dubh three times: I could not bring myself to do more than hazard my own body, and those of the men of the clan who volunteered for such duty, before this. But now I will have every man and boy of you who can bear arms to come out with me and hunt Conanach to his death! Yes, and Kintail also, for he was there – and this foul treachery as like as not was born in his evil mind!"

"You hate MacKenzie of Kintail, don't you?" said a thin, dark youth, who was leaning propped against the wall the other side of the fireplace. "It is good to see it in you, for now I know you will surely kill my father's murderers."

"I hate no man, Neil," Rory answered shortly, glancing at him. This was Torquil Dubh's bastard son. But even as he spoke, Rory realised in his heart that it was not the scarcely-known face of Torquil Conanach, but the bearded one of MacKenzie that his mind was set upon destroying; for the old wound to his pride still rankled deeply in him.

"MacSweyn, we will send out the fiery cross through all my territories. MacAskill, have the beacons lit. Man all the galleys. And MacCrimmon, I would have your pipers pipe us into battle.

"I am very glad to hear you speak like that," Neil MacLeod said softly, so that only Rory heard. "For now that my father is dead, the Lewis belongs to my half-brothers by rights, does it not, sir?"

Rory looked at him sharply. The thin, young face was inscrutable. There was neither grief, nor a look of vengeance upon it, but a clear purpose moved behind the eyes. It seemed to Rory that he had no time in this moment to consider Neil MacLeod, but it passed through his mind fleetingly that here was a young man who must be reckoned with in the years to come.

Because of the present disposition of his fleet, while some of the galleys and birlinns set out from Loch Dunvegan, and some from Bracadale, he himself rode overland to Loch Ainort, intending to embark in a galley that was beached there. Iain MacIain and Hugh de Lérins were his chosen companions, and young Neil rode with them, a silent witness of events, while MacSweyn and two of the MacAskill s came behind. When they had crossed the island, they saw to their astonishment, a ship flying the royal pennant moving along off the coast between Scalpay and Raasay – a white-sailed vessel, seemingly a peaceful craft, though her presence could bode no good.

"What do you think that means?" Iain MacIain asked Rory dubiously.

"I don't know. I think we should do well to watch her progress," Rory answered.

He had to wait some hours for his galley, the *"Dominant"* to be equipped, and made ready for her voyage. The boat had been beached there in a storm, and her hull badly holed some weeks before, and had been laid up for repairs, which were now completed. But her crew were scattered and the tide was not right for her immediate launching. While they waited, he sent MacIain and de Lérins up along the coast towards Portree, to follow the royal vessel's progress. She turned towards the harbour there and her white sails were run down, and an anchor dropped.

"Her purpose may be peaceful," MacIain said.

"Or maybe double-edged, like the king's sword!" de Lérins reported. "Let us go down and see for ourselves." They rode together in easy friendship, for they were continually in each other's company these days, although the clansmen were never entirely at ease, or trusting, with the foreign minstrel. They enjoyed his singing, but avoided his company. "He is not one of us," they said.

Around Portree harbour a little town had begun to grow up in the past few years, and here there were a few scattered houses, two or three merchants, and a tavern at the water's edge. By the time they had made the long downhill ride and reached the enclosed inner harbour, into which the vessel could not pass, some officers in uniform, breeched and booted and with swords buckled on, had reached the quayside in a small boat and were gathered there. Among the bare-kneed and bare-footed island people, who had come out to watch, and stood arms akimbo, gaping, these Lowland troops made an incongruous sight. Though they were spurred, where in such a place would they find horses to carry them?

MacIain laughed. "His Grace's men may be a sight to make one tremble in one's belly on the mainland," he remarked, watching their awkward deliberations and attempts to make themselves understood in the Island Gaelic, "but here they are somewhat like mermen come to land, who find they cannot walk upon their tails!"

"Let us go down and see what they are about," de Lérins suggested.

There was no difficulty in discovering this, for the name "MacLeod" was on every man's lips. And when the two rode in, and their tartans proclaimed their allegiance to Dunvegan, they were hailed at once and brought before the group at the quayside.

"You are gentlemen of MacLeod of Dunvegan and Harris?" the officer in charge demanded in the English tongue.

"We are, sir," both answered together, in the same language.

"Your master is to answer to the King for certain offences against his Majesty."

"What offences?" Iain asked cautiously.

The officer gestured to his lieutenant, who produced at once documents with the Royal Seal upon them.

"For breaches of the General Band which he signed in Edinburgh eight years ago; for repeated harrying of his fellow chiefs; for raiding his neighbour's territory and for other unlawful expeditions."

Iain stretched out his hand to take the rolled parchments but the gloved fingers that held them drew them away imperiously.

"Bring horses for us and conduct us to the castle of Dunvegan," he said sharply.

MacIain and de Lérins glanced at one another.

"There are no horses here, sir, save these two unshod ponies that we ourselves are riding on," de Lérins said. "They would be terrified and bolt if you used spurs on them. And MacLeod is not at home, but on business elsewhere."

The officer looked at him with a long stare, which degenerated into a puzzled frown.

"Have I not seen you at Court?" he asked as though he could scarcely believe it. "Are you not one of the King's minstrels?"

"I am a minstrel sir, and earn bread for my body and wine for my soul's sake, wherever I may find it," de Lérins replied. "If you will give us the documents His Grace has sent, I will promise you MacLeod shall receive them, as surely as His Grace the King received music from my hands, and a song from my voice."

The officer looked him up and down as though considering further, then turned to consult his companions in a low voice. After a moment, he looked again at Iain and de Lérins, and said in a more conciliatory tone:

"Well, since it is clear there are no horses and we cannot make our way in force overland from here, I will entrust you with these documents."

They took them, and remounted.

"We have here also a writ for the Pretender to the Lewis," the officer said suddenly. "Is he under MacLeod's protection at Dunvegan?"

De Lérins turned on his horse:

"You speak of Torquil Dubh?" he asked.

"Yes, that is the soubriquet by which you Island men call him, I think."

"Why he is…" Some doubt of the wisdom of giving out the news of Torquil's death, brought him up shortly. "His family live under Dunvegan's protection. They are near of kin to MacLeod of MacLeod," he said. "If you wish, I will take the writ with me with the others."

Seemingly by now reassured, both by the courtesy and dignity of the two men's bearing and by the fact that they spoke the Lowland tongue, the officer handed over the last of the documents, and they rode off with all speed along the coast to Loch Ainort.

The "*Dominant*" was already floated with the tide, manned and ready to put to sea. Rory was watching impatiently for the two riders to return, and seeing them coming at a full gallop, he leapt up from the rock on which he was seated and hastened over the stony beach to meet them.

De Lérins leaned from the saddle with the documents.

"By the saints, what is all this?" Rory said, more with irritation than alarm. He tore the great seals impatiently, saying as he did so: "We should be at sea long since. If we do not leave within the next half hour, the tide will not run with us and we may beach, and not reach our other ships off Rona this night-fall, as I arranged with them –"

He stopped his mouth still open, his breath held still. Then:

"By the Rood!" he cried. "By the Holy Rood, the King has declared me outlawed and put to the horn and forfeit of all my estates."

He stared up at Iain and de Lérins, his face looking stricken and unbelieving. They dismounted, and stood beside him.

"By the blood of my fathers!" he cried, after a moment. "I will not accept this! I cannot! What is this other one?"

He tore open the other document, and read a formal declaration from the Council, on the King's authority, to Torquil Dubh and Torquil Conanach both, that the land of the Lewis was declared forfeit to the King and would be colonized by ten gentlemen of the King's choice, whose names were appended thereto.

His expression was such that MacIain, knowing his fiery anger of old, instinctively drew his horse back a little and looked down warily; and then across at the galley, and at the young figure of Neil MacLeod,

146

who was approaching with crunching steps over the stones towards them. But after his initial drawing in of breath, and flooding of colour to his face, Rory made no sound or movement. He stood looking at the thick black script on the new parchment, seeming not to be reading again, but to be penetrating with his eyes and mind the depth of the meaning and the purport of these new manoeuvres. Then, raising his head, he flung the documents from him with a silent rage, betokening more than the violent outbursts to which Iain had become accustomed from time to time down the years.

They fell at the feet of Neil MacLeod. Stooping, he coolly picked them up, and glancing at the title written on them each in turn, said:

"This was for my father, I think?"

"Yes, read it, read it, if you can read!" Rory told him impatiently, gesturing him away. Then, turning to MacIain:

"Has the King's ship set sail again?" he asked.

"No, sir, not when we left," Iain responded, "nor could we discover whether they would sail for the mainland now or whether to Dunvegan."

"Are they armed? I thought she was no man o' war."

"I think so, sir."

"Well, this must change my plans," Rory said, after a moment's silent consideration. "I must get home. And yet we must not leave my fleet off Rona, knowing nothing of this matter. Go in the galley, Iain, and bring the news to them, and tell them to turn for home, until we have decided what to do."

"Sir, if you will permit me, I will go with the galley," young Neil MacLeod said suddenly. He looked up, white-faced, the document of the forfeiture of the Lewis trembling in his hands.

Rory looked at him dubiously.

"You are too young to command one of my galleys," he said "and yet – well, there is MacSweyn, and the MacAskill brothers, who have experience enough -. Well, I would rather take MacIain and de Lérins with me, it is true. I will come down with you, and tell MacAskill what has occurred and instruct him to take the boat, with you aboard as bearer of the news; if you put off sharply now, you will make Rona before dark and then sail all together round the coast for home. But keep a watch for the King's vessel, in case she challenges you."

Neil MacLeod stood silently by, while Rory gave his orders to MacSweyn. Then climbed aboard and stood saluting in the stern, as the boat moved off along the waterway. Rory acknowledged the salute briefly, and then turned at once to where Iain and de Lérins had brought the other horses from the farmsteading where they had left them that morning, and mounted and urged his beast forward with a hasty violence.

"We will go to Portree," he said, "and if they are no longer there, we have still time enough to make up through the hills and overland to Dunvegan before the King's ship has rounded Trotternish and Waternish."

They rode with all speed, not speaking, drawing along with them the riderless mounts that had brought MacSweyn and the MacAskills and Neil MacLeod through the hills early that morning. Rory's face was so set and tense, that MacIain and the minstrel vouchsafed no comment as the unshod hooves clattered along a stony corrie, waded a burn, plunged up a grassy hillside and came down at length within sight of the sea again.

"She is gone," Rory said, as the empty expanse of the harbour became visible ahead and below them. "We will turn away and cut the distance short."

They rode for an hour along the steep and rocky way that led across the widest part of the island, further from the sea than any other track. Partly they went through woodland and rough forests, but in many places the land on this side was denuded of timber where MacDonald had cut liberally to build his galleys and supply his household with logs for his great fires. In these places, the thin soil that covered the rocky base of the island had eroded in wind and rain, giving the land a barren look where little but thin grass would grow.

Further on, they came into a narrow gorge where a stone-strewn burn tumbled with noisy steps downwards, and flowers and small ferns leaned their heads into the water at every little linn.

Rory urged his mount along the rough and difficult way, and when they could cross, he drove the beast up a narrow slanting shelf of a steep escarpment on to high ground again among the bracken and the heather.

They had been riding for two hours in silence and at top speed, and save for a pause down below in the corrie for the horses to drink; they had not slackened their pace at all. Here, high up, suddenly Rory drew rein and gazed about him at the great hills and the wild uninhabited country. To the East, the Black Cuillins thrust their sharp peaks heavenwards, and through a gap in the hills in the distance to the right, the opalescent seas glistened in the late afternoon sunlight. He sat his horse with a look of such stillness and tension about him, that for a moment, Iain thought he was listening for something. But there was no sound save the mountain wind and, down below, the chattering of the little burn; and nearby a small finch singing in a little bush. The horses snorted and panted from the climb that they had been forced to take so violently. At last:

"We will dismount," Rory said abruptly. He threw his reins over his horse's head, slid from the saddle and stood by its side with his hand laid on the sweat-shiny flank. Then, tossing the rein to Iain, he said briefly: "Tether them," and moved away.

For a few moments, as Iain fastened the horses one to another by the reins, and the last to a bush, Rory stood at the cliff edge of the gorge, looking downwards. Then he seated himself in the heather, where he could look into the depths where the water flowed and away also towards the distant sea, drew up his knees and took out the documents which he had thrust into his doublet, and read them through again. When he had perused each one at length, he lay on his face in the heather, still and silent. Iain picked up the scrolls as they rolled away and tucked them in a saddle bag. Then at last, Rory turned over and lay back with his hands behind his head and his eyes shut so that Iain, watching, thought that all haste had gone out of him, for he seemed as much at ease as though it had been an ordinary day, and they two riding in the hills for the pleasure of it.

Iain waited, sitting on a smooth round boulder, keeping a watch on the horses and on his master's face. But de Lérins rose after a while, and rode ahead to Dunvegan. Iain strove to remain silent. But anxiety for Rory, and the House of MacLeod, mounted in him with such pressure and urgency that he could not contain it, and at last he burst out:

"What is to become of us?"

Rory turned his head slowly and opened his eyes. His vision, lying there among the heather, was so changed that the little plants among the heather, the small bell-flowers and saxifrage, looked huge and strong as trees, and Iain MacIain on his rock seemed to leap up, demanding his attention from a great distance, and then, slowly coming into perspective as he raised himself on his elbow:

"Iain," he said, "all the wording of the King's letter so distorts my purposes that it makes me seem a miscreant which I am not, although he handled me unjustly in the past. I desire to live lawfully, and to bring us all peaceably under the guidance of the King's hand, for so I am sure we must live in the end. And yet, for all I have tried to do, I find myself an outlaw, like any villain who has meted out defiance. Was it a fault of mine I could not produce my charters on demand? No!

And it is not wrong of me to uphold my kinsman's just claims to the Lewis. That is a different matter from war for conquest, or from idle deeds of violence. It seems no matter how strong a man may be; he can control nothing, and is borne always on the wind of circumstance."

Iain smiled:

"You ride very fast into that wind, sir. You seem to me often wind-tossed and all awry," he said.

"What then would you do, my friend?" Rory asked, looking at him straightly.

"Ride with the wind of God," Iain said simply.

Rory laughed. "It is easy to say that," he answered. "But what shall I do now?" They looked at one another without speaking. Then: "No, you cannot answer. I must answer myself." He pulled himself up, sat still a moment, and then said: "Well, we will go with all the calm we can and face the clan at home. I don't know why I made you ride with such speed, for in truth there was no great haste. The haste was only in my own mind, I think. Has Hugh gone on ahead?"

They re-mounted and went on along the top of the gorge and through the break in the hills down towards Bracadale, and thence along the coast and over the River Ose.

"Why does the King concern himself with what you did in Ireland?" Iain asked, for there was a clause in the document referring to a youthful expedition Rory had made across the sea with Donald Gorme. "It is not his territory. I think he seeks all possible ways to discredit you."

"No," Rory told him. "He has his eye on the throne of England, when Queen Elizabeth dies. He is a true claimant by right of birth. It is his own credit with the English, and not mine he is thinking about."

They went on in silence. After a while, Rory said grimly:

"Besides outlawry, these documents impose a fine upon me of 10,000 merks. If I am bereft of my estate, I do not know how I shall ever raise it."

When they came at last within sight of Dunvegan Castle, its turrets rising above the belt of trees at the end of the loch, just visible still in the gathering dusk, and the waterway beyond dyed coral pink in the last rays of the sunset, Rory drew rein and brought his horse and those he was leading to a standstill.

"It can't be that all this shall be taken from us!" he cried. "Our home? Our heritage? I have a mind to go to Edinburgh myself and see the King. In his presence I could surely explain to him all our purposes so that he sees we are not ruffian bands, but loyal subjects of His Majesty."

"I beg you not to!" Iain said in alarm. "It would be a most unwise thing to do now you are outlawed."

"An outlaw – I!" Rory ejaculated, as the thought struck him anew. He urged his horse onward without further words.

In the castle all had been normal and quiet, and the women and children and few remaining men folk had been preparing for bed when de Lérins brought the news. When they heard of MacLeod's return, almost everyone was already in the hall, hurriedly dressed or wrapped in their plaids over night attire. Immediately Rory explained the purport of the writs that had been served upon him.

"Where shall we go? What shall we do?" Isabel asked, wide-eyed. She was holding her new-born baby, shawl-wrapped, against herself, and trembling with the evening chill, for she had not been long out of childbed and had not regained her usual health. Christiana too looked terrified. Drawing her youngest son against her skirts, she said:

"If you are outlawed, we must all take to the hills, and every man's hand will be against us. Can such a thing be?"

Mairi's face looked sternly composed. She folded her arms and looked at the floor and said nothing.

"We are in no immediate peril," Rory told them, "but we must be prepared for what may come."

"We cannot garrison the castle, since all the men are at sea," Mairi said quietly.

"We can keep watch," Rory told her, looking into her face, "and while we watch, we will think what we may do if the King's men come."

She raised her eyes and looked straightly at him, but neither of them voiced the thought that lay at the back of their minds.

151

Chapter Thirteen

THE BASTARD CLAIMANT

At midday the following day, the galleys began to return, drifting in, strung out one behind the other with their sails flapping loose, for there was little wind. Rory watched their progress from the tower. The last was the *"Sea Avenger"*, but there was no sign of the *"Dominant"*, the vessel he had sent up from Ainort with the news. As the boats came in, running close below the castle, for the tide was high; he went down to the sea gate himself to greet them there.

"What has happened to the *"Dominant"* that she lags so far behind?" he asked the men of the leading birlinn. They looked at one another awkwardly, and did not answer. The *"Sea Avenger"* came in close alongside at this moment, and to his astonishment he saw old Torquil MacSweyn clamber over her side and come ashore, his round face creased with anxiety and his clothes bedraggled and wet.

"What has happened?" Rory shouted to him. The old man came up over the stones with all the haste he could, slipping and stumbling, and kneeled at MacLeod's feet.

"Sir, I have lost my ship," he said, his voice tremulous with fright and emotion.

"How is that?" Rory demanded.

"Sir, young Neil MacLeod took command of her," MacSweyn told him, still kneeling there on the wet, stony shore. "He was determined from the moment that we sailed to go in pursuit of Torquil Conanach, no matter what your instructions were. The men would have none of him at first, but Murdo MacAskill spoke on his behalf, and said it was useless now to bring the ship back here to Dunvegan, since MacLeod was outlawed, and had lost his rights, and they should go off to the Lewis about Torquil Dubh's affairs as his son wished; and the men were persuaded by those two agile tongues to go. When we encountered the fleet off Rona we passed the news to them, and for myself, since I would not agree to disobey you, sir, I was thrown overboard," he finished miserably. "The *"Sea Avenger"* got me out of the water and here I am, with this ill news to add to your great troubles, sir."

"By St Clement, this is beyond belief," Rory said, almost beneath his breath, staring down at his old warden, kneeling there shivering with cold and shame and distress. "Well, get up and go inside and change your clothes. You did your best."

Though he had not summoned them, by common and unspoken accord, almost all the men who had come in, assembled in the great hall as soon as they had left the boats. When he had finished his discussions with MacSweyn and the other captains of craft, Rory went up to the hall and entered, and looked at their faces, but at first said nothing. He crossed to the great fireplace where he habitually stood with his back to the blaze and feet astride, when he intended to address them. But there, toying with the hasp of a sword scabbard, he still did not speak. After a moment, the murmur of angry and indignant voices died away in face of his silence, and in the eventual quiet, one man was heard to say:

"It will be a mighty strong band will roam the hills of Skye, if MacLeod is truly put to the horn, for every man and woman will go with you."

"Shall we take to the hills?" another asked.

"Shall we not garrison the castle and hold it against the King?"

"It is wicked that such a thing should come to pass. Whether we stay or are driven out we stand by you, sir," said a fourth.

"Well, fellows, now I know your minds," Rory said steadily, looking up at length, "and I will tell you what to do. We will man the castle at full strength and all our fleet shall lie ready within full sight of any ships that may come down the sea loch. But you will loose no bowshot, and unsheath no sword until I give you orders. Go now and refresh yourselves, and then take your watches in your accustomed order with all vigilance."

"Will you defy the King?" Isabel asked in terror, when she heard what orders the chief had given. He kissed her cheek, touched the small baby that lay cradled against her and made no answer.

For seven days the watch was kept with all alertness. Men slept little and there was an air of tension throughout the whole demesne. But the eighth day came and still no sign of the King's men or of any authority sent to enforce His Grace's and the Council's decrees. There came a gradual flagging of tension. Men yawned and scratched themselves at their posts, and thought of their bellies, and their wives; and those who lived outside the castle precincts, and tilled the land, turned their minds to the growing crops, and the young lambs untended, and wished they might go home.

On the tenth day of the vigil, Hugh de Lérins, wandering on his own down to a neighbouring turf-roofed cottage, encountered there a fisherman who had come round from Portree, and who had talked with the crew of the King's vessel, before she sailed for the Kyle of Lochalsh and the mainland.

"Why, there is nothing to fear from her, sir," the man said, learning that MacLeod had garrisoned the castle at full strength. "She made off at full speed as though she was glad enough to get away out of these wild waters!" He laughed. "I think the King has bitten off a bigger morsel than he can swallow, by all accounts," he said. "The sailors told us they had been from isle to isle throughout the Hebrides, serving writs on many of the chiefs. Since they have proved so intractable his Grace thinks to outlaw all the strongest of them, and develop the Hebrides himself, and take a profit for the nation's sake. But I would guess he does not know MacLeod as well as the rest of us know him hereabouts. He will not be put in a panic by a few words on paper, I reckon."

"I dare say he will not," the minstrel answered, and rode off to tell Rory what he had learned.

MacLeod looked at de Lérins with astonishment and seemed at first as though he could not believe that nothing whatsoever would come of his outlawry, the forfeiture of his estates and all the dire threats that had been meted out. But when he had enquired further he was at last assured that the royal vessel had turned for home, leaving no-one ashore and with no message about the garrisoning of the island.

He listened intently to the messenger. Then burst into a great shout of laugher, and slapped his thigh and called for liquor to celebrate the news.

"Tell them out on the battlements!" he ordered, "And let them all have ale to drink and a good meal tonight. By Heaven, we have overrated the King this time!" He threw back his head and laughed again, and the great hall echoed with the joyous and relieved laughter of the household.

Over their meat and ale that night, the watchmen on the battlements said to one another with irony and scorn: "To be put to the horn these days means no more than a toot on the royal trumpet. We need not fear the King. Let us pursue our own affairs." And they drank deeply and set off about their family concerns.

Rory, as soon as the morning came, resolved that he would not pay the fine of 10,000 merks, unless His Grace's men came in person and wrested it from him, and when he was convinced that the King's men were not coming to the Isles, he resolved to go off after Neil MacLeod and bring the *"Dominant"* home again.

Taking one galley, manned by his most tried and faithful crew, Rory ran among the skerries and the islets of the Lewis, seeking the truant everywhere until eventually he had news of him. Several of Conanach's vessels, and those of Kintail with them, patrolled this coast consistently these days, and the old *"Dominant"* had been in an encounter with one of them and had taken refuge after the battle in Loch Ouirn, so said a Lewis fisherman whom they questioned, as he brought in his lobster baskets early one morning.

They rounded Cabog Head and spied her lying well up the small inlet, and running down their sail, went in under oar and came alongside.

Her crew looked both mutinous and scared when they saw MacLeod. He unsheathed his sword and boarded her at once.

"By the Rood!" he roared at Neil, who rose from the stern and looked at him defiantly. "If you had been of any clan but that of my kinsman of the Lewis, I would have made short work of you!"

"I owe greater allegiance to the Lewis than to Dunvegan," Neil answered him back. "And you are outlawed, sir. It is no greater loss to you if I take your galley than if the King removed it from you."

"Is it not?" Rory said angrily. "It is as though my own son had thieved it from me! You are no son of mine, but since you are fatherless, and have not grown to man's maturity, you shall be dealt with as an honest man would deal with his own son."

He gestured to his men to seize the lad, and at his orders, they took him aft, struggling vigorously, and, stripping him of his single garment, whipped him severely with their leather belts.

Meanwhile, ignoring Neil's cries behind him, Rory faced his erring crew, and lashed them as violently with his tongue as his young kinsman was being lashed with the leather.

Later, Rory sent half the sulky clansmen aboard the other galley, and Iain MacIain with them, and so disposed both crews that he was certain of no further truancy among them.

For several days the two galleys together cruised up and down the sea ways of the Lewis, taking a measure of the condition of that island, until, by questioning of landsmen and fishermen and by his own observations, Rory realised that the place was too well garrisoned, both by land and sea, to be re-taken, save by his whole fleet together.

The Lowland gentlemen appointed by the King to take possession of the land and develop its resources had sailed in to Stornaway, escorted by a man o' war a few days past. Already there had been skirmishes throughout the Eye Peninsula, and a battle in Stornaway itself between the Royal troops and Torquil Conanach's men, and Stornaway Castle had suffered from bombardment. Lying overnight in Loch Leurbost, Rory learned from Lewis men there more details about the "Adventurers from Fife" as they were already called, with mighty scorn.

"There is in charge the Duke of Lennox, sir, and one Patrick, Commendator of Lindores, and a bearded gentleman named William of Pittenweem," an old man of MacLeod's own family told him. "And Sir James Anstruther, and Sir James Sandlands of Slamono, and a captain whose name is Murray and several more besides whose names I have not learnt. There are ten in all, besides their own attendant gentlemen, and we have learned they have the King's authority to divide the Lewis and develop it as best they may, and other lands besides, if they are able to succeed in this."

"And will they succeed, do you think?" Rory asked.

The old man and his sons laughed heartily. "It would be very unlike us islanders to permit it, unless we are forced to assist them, by great weight of arms," the old man said.

"I think you have right on your side," Rory answered gravely. "I shall concern myself more with Torquil Conanach and the Chief of Kintail, and we will let these Fife Adventurers alone to make out as best they may in this hostile island."

He began to sail southward, challenging and fighting every vessel that he encountered with Conanach's or Kintail's flags on their masts, until the crews of his own two boats were weakened by fatigue and wounds. Then, he sailed slowly down to the shelter of Rodel Harbour. Once there, he sent word across to Dunvegan that the castle should be left lightly garrisoned, and the rest of his fleet should join him for a running fight with the usurper and his men, until eventual defeat of one side or the other.

After their few days' rest, the *"Dominant"* and the *"Sea Adventurer"* set off again at the head of all the others, in high spirits, and confident that their own strength matched MacKenzie's. To their pleasure and their scorn, Kintail would not face a running fight with the whole fleet, and turned back at sight of them off the Eye Peninsula. The

MacLeods yelled their derision after the retreating vessels. Then, taking advantage of their temporary absence, Rory impulsively ran his own galleys straight on, into the outer harbour of Stornaway under full sail.

The Royal vessel that had escorted the Lowland Adventurers some weeks before had put out to sea and left them to their fate, but the Duke of Lennox and Sir James Anstruther had since mustered a fair fleet of their own – some of them small boats manned by Lewis men who had been paid in gold for their loyalty to the Lowlanders.

Rory ran in flushed with confidence, not knowing the strength of the band which lay well hidden from the open sea in the inner harbour. With the old war cries and the war pipes playing, the men of Dunvegan went to encounter them. They had the advantage of surprise and were able to come right up under the lea of the castle and round the bend where the smaller vessels were moored.

Confident of victory, for there was no-one nowadays who seriously challenged the strength of Dunvegan at sea, Rory ordered his bowmen to stand, and loose their arrows into the apparently defenceless vessels, and towards the tree-lined shore, where a few uniformed figures could be seen mustering themselves and moving hastily in bunches along the water's edge.

"Fire now, lads!" he called. "Be ready with your swords," he shouted a moment later, as the leading galley moved close in among the vessels moored bow to stern along the waterway. "We will board these fellows' ships before they have time to get their wits about them."

He himself stood well forward. As the galley drifted close in, and lurched gently against the timbers of a high-prowed, white-painted vessel with an unfamiliar pennant on her masthead, he unsheathed his sword, and lightly leapt aboard, followed by a shouting hoard of his men. The other ships were boarded likewise, as the *"Sea Avenger"*, and the *"Pride of Lochlann"* and the *"Sea Sprite"* ran in behind.

In a moment, chaos was loosed throughout the harbour. With yells and cries, men leapt from boat to boat. The short, one-edged knives of the Highlanders cut away canvas sails and halyards, slashed rapidly and surely into stores and provisions and gear and were thrust with equal speed and readiness into the throats and bellies of the Lowlanders who ran to defend their property.

Leaping rapidly from vessel to vessel, Rory called orders to his men to deal with the seamen as speedily as they could, and turn their attention beyond, to the grey walls of Stornaway Castle itself.

Suddenly, behind him, with a wild rush of sound, a great sheet of flame shot up, from the decks of the tall, white ship. He paused, one foot upon the quayside and turned his head to look. Then leapt back in amazement and sudden fear as a great thundering roar burst overhead, and reverberated across the harbour and along the waterway.

"St Clement, what was that?" MacSweyn shouted as MacLeod turned. For a moment Rory made no answer. His face, which had been all alight with the wild joy of righteous purpose in battle, changed in expression. He stood back, swaying with the rocking of the small quayside boat into which he had jumped and looked upwards at the impregnable-looking granite walls.

High up, where the narrow bow-slits were just visible, something ominous and menacing was happening. A long and pointed snout was protruding, and being slowly manoeuvred so that it was aimed towards the quay. Suddenly, the great thundering roar burst forth again, and fire and smoke shot up from the *"Sea Avenger's"* deck.

"In Heaven's name!" Rory ejaculated. "These Lowlanders have gunpowder, and the new firearms that the King's soldiers use abroad." He stared, immobile, robbed temporarily of his air of authority by the sight and the sound of the booming cannon, and the sheer horror of the sight of the great metal balls that were being launched mechanically far beyond the reach of a man's sword-hand, and with far greater effect than a whole rain of arrows. This was a new experience in the Isles – and even in the first moments of alarm and consternation the far distant implications of these new weapons registered itself in his mind. Then:

"To our boats!" her called, turning swiftly. "Make off now, with all speed, and head for Harris."

Though the *"Sea Avenger"* had been hit, the hole in her side was above the water-line, and she was still sea-worthy. The *"Dominant" had* suffered minor damage amidships, but because of the brevity of the encounter, and the speed of Rory's withdrawal, all his vessels were able to make their get away, though with a number of wounded and one dying man aboard. With more haste than dignity, the crews hauled up the sails again, manned oars, and sped out into the open sea, one after the other in a straggling line. Agitated talk broke out among them as they went, for to have had a cannon firing at them was an unheard of experience, entirely different from the hand-to-hand warfare they were accustomed to.

"A barbarous thing – this new invention," they said, as they saw the number of their wounded, and the extent of the damage.

Some days before, two vessels manned by Lewis men, but with no gentlemen to lead them, had joined themselves to Rory's fleet, asking his protection and leadership now that Torquil Dubh and his seven captains were all dead. And on this day, as they ran out to sea, they found more boats lying off-shore, flying the colours of MacLeod of Lewis, waiting to join them, and sail with them down to Harris.

In spite of the presence of these fresh crews, Rory dared not risk a further encounter with either of the usurpers to the Lewis, until his men had had a little respite, and the seriously wounded had been put ashore. And he himself felt great need to pause and think, for he realised now how rash he had been to challenge the Adventurers themselves at Stornaway. So he took the whole fleet down the wild coast line again, past Tarbert, which divides Harris from the Lewis, and into the sheltered harbour at Rodel. That night all men who wished might come ashore and stretch their legs on land, and sleep at ease upon the heather, and talk as much as they wished about their experiences. But Rory himself looked in no mood to relax or be at peaceful ease.

He and Iain MacIain, with Torquil MacSweyn and the other captains of craft went into the building of the now disused monastery, which was guarded and kept in order by the aged sacristan, who lived alone there. All Harris and the Lewis knew of MacLeod's efforts on his kinsmen's behalf, and almost before the fleet had dropped their anchors and stowed their sails and come ashore, there were great joints of meat roasting on the fore-shore for the men, and a meal laid out in greater comfort in the old monastic hostelry, for the chiefs. But Rory ate sparingly for his mind was full of the gravity of the implication of the bringing of firearms to the Hebrides.

In the morning Rory sent word to Dunvegan and asked for news from home. On his return, the messenger brought a long document, which Hugh de Lérins had written at Mairi's behest, explaining that an urgent plea for help had come from Rory's mother's kin, the MacLeans of Duart, who were once again harried by MacDonald of Dunnyveg and turned out of the long disputed land in Islay.

"Sir James MacDonald of Dunnyveg has trounced your mother's kin at Loch Gruinart," Mairi wrote, "and now he begs for the aid of his loyal friend of Dunvegan and Harris, and asks you to join him and Lochiel and MacNeil and MacKinnon of Strath, and try to come to battle with Dunnyveg at Bern Bige or somewhere in those parts."

Rory considered this further demand upon his loyalty with a troubled face. There had always been a most strong bond between Hector MacLean and himself, but he had his hands full, with the Lewis, and was loath to leave. He rose from the table at length and went out on to the hillside, and up to the now empty church of the monastery, thinking to pray for guidance, though, unlike Iain MacIain, he rarely went upon his knees except in times of trouble. As he was about to lay his hand on the heavy oaken door and push it open, he heard a step behind him in the darkness and turned his head, with his hand upon his sword-sheath. Young Neil MacLeod stood there, a few feet from him, having followed him in silence from the table.

"Well?" Rory asked when the lad remained wordless and motionless.

"Sir," Neil answered, coming up to him, "I flouted your orders ungraciously when once you trusted me, but I took my punishment, and I have served you since with loyalty and without complaint. May I ask a favour?"

"Well?" Rory said again, without hostility but without friendship in his voice, for though it was true that Neil had shown himself a moderate swordsman, and had given no further trouble, he was never sure now how far he could trust him.

"Sir, if you go to aid your kin at Duart, as you have been discussing at table, there will be no-one to fight our cause for us here in the Lewis," Neil said.

Rory peered at the strained young face in the faint light.

"What do you want me to do?" he asked. "I can't be in two places. And you have seen for yourself how the King has an advantage over us at Stornaway."

"If you would trust me, sir, I declare upon my drawn sword and in St Columba's name, that I will not defy you again on any count, or in any way," Neil said with urgency in his voice. "I beg you to give me command of those vessels that are manned by my father's men."

Rory stared at him a long while in silence.

"Well," he said at length, "am I to trust you with the lives of those good men of your father's who have put themselves under the protection of Dunvegan and Harris? You have little knowledge of warfare yet. You are too young. And the odds are overwhelmingly against you."

"Sir," Neil cried, going down suddenly on one knee before the chief, "I will defend them with my life blood for our heritage and for my half-brothers' sake. And I bind myself, from this day forward, in obedience to you."

Rory looked at the bent head in silence, weighing up his sincerity.

"Would you take the guidance of your elders and betters among the captains of those crews," he asked, "if I should put them under you?"

"I would sir," the lad answered fervently.

160

"I can't order them to be led by you," Rory warned him, "but we will ask them if they will have you lead them."

"I thank you with my whole heart," Neil cried, looking up with such an expression of purpose and determination in his face that Rory thought again, as he had when he had first noticed the boy on the day of Torquil's death, that this was a young lad to be reckoned with.

"You had best ask God's blessing on your enterprise," he said shortly, "as I shall do on my behalf and yours. You are taking on a very dangerous mission."

He laid hold of the iron latch and opened the great creaking door and entered the dark church. Just inside, a cruisie lamp filled with whale oil was fixed on a bracket, and flint and tinder near. Rory ignited it and, carrying it shoulder high, walked on the echoing paving stones the length of the building to the now denuded altar. He raised his hand and crossed himself; then turned to the great carved tomb where the remains of his grandfather, his father, his brother and his brother's son lay now together. He stared at it, remembering the boyhood day when he and Iain had first examined it. It had been empty then. Forgetting the watchful eyes behind him for a moment, he laid a hand upon the little carved figure of the angel with its sweeping wing tip tilting the scales of good and evil in Alasdair Crottach's favour. Then with a sigh, turned his head to the other tomb, where the standard bearers lay, and touched that also. He sighed again. Then, conscious once more of the lad standing silent behind him, he slowly knelt down facing the eastern window and bowed his head to pray. Behind him, he heard Neil go down upon his knees, his sword scabbard clattering against the stone floor; and after ten minutes heard again the scraping clatter as he rose and left the building swiftly, and went out into the darkness of the open hillside by himself.

In the morning, Rory consulted the men of the Lewis boats, and found that, although they were somewhat reluctant to put themselves under young Neil's command, knowing him to be almost untried in battle, and in any case, not a true claimant to their territory, being a bastard, they nevertheless preferred his leadership to none at all. Overnight, Rory had decided that if they would accept the lad's authority, he would go down to Islay straight away, and deal with matters there; and he therefore set sail at midday with the rest of his fleet for Dunvegan.

He knew little of Neil's potential strength and courage, but he was glad enough to see that a number of small craft of all kinds, manned by the clansmen of MacLeod of the Lewis, had come into the harbour and joined themselves with harrying Kintail's men, until he could return to their aid. But by the look in their eyes he felt almost certain that they would soon put their heads into the lion's mouth again, as he himself had rashly and impulsively done.

On the way home, Iain MacIain was very quiet. Rory was so lost in thoughts about his own affairs, that at first he noticed nothing unusual about his friend's bearing. But towards the end of the journey, as they passed into Loch Dunvegan, and the pitching and tossing of the galley on the open seas quietened to a smooth gliding into the long loch, he noticed Iain's unhappy expression.

"What is the matter, my friend?" he asked.

Iain was standing looking forward into the wind to where the great Piping College of Borreraig rose up on its cliff top, and along past the islets where the seals foregathered every spring, and away to the further extreme of the long inlet where the castle itself rose, solid and impregnable, on its rocky table at the water's edge. He did not answer at once, but after a moment, turning his head, he said:

"Sir, when you go to Islay about your kinsmen's business there, leave me behind at the castle."

"In St Clement's name, why?" Rory demanded, with a touch of his old impatience. "I have need of all my good men with me! You have a strong sword arm and can be relied upon. Are you deserting me in an hour of need?"

"Sir, I would never desert MacLeod in an hour of need," Iain answered soberly. "I have fought with you loyally in battles for your causes this long time, but I think often that it is not God's Will that I should unsheath my sword in battle for any cause, save only to defend my chief's own person or his family. Let me serve you with my pen, and my prayers."

"Your prayers will not avail me much if my fleet is under-manned and I lack good swordsmen," Rory answered with some asperity.

"Will they not?" Iain said shortly, and repeated: "Will they not?"

Rory glanced at him, looking for a moment almost surly.

"I don't know," he muttered; and then, regarding him more openly, he added: "I sometimes think that your mind touches worlds unknown to me."

"Sir, my mind cannot attain the speed or depth of yours in any way," MacIain answered humbly, "but I will do what I can to serve your House."

When he saw that Iain was resolved beyond all persuading not to fight again, Rory reluctantly granted his request that he remain at home.

As though taking courage from Iain MacIain's action, Hugh de Lérins went to Rory with the same plea the following day at Dunvegan.

"Why, Hugh," Rory said exasperatedly, "you are a most skilled swordsman, with all the tricks of the trade which you have learned at the Frankish Court. Am I to lose you too? I have often noticed that you are reluctant in battle, for all your aptitude."

"I only learned these matters for my own defence. I have been in many outlandish places, and I would not be alive now if I had not acquired some skill and power in my right arm," de Lérins answered. "But I am a music-maker and a teller of tales – and perhaps a dreamer of dreams. I too serve MacLeod as loyally as our friend MacIain. But I would serve you with music."

"He with prayers and you with music!" Rory said, ruefully. "What is becoming of my men?" but he granted his permission, nevertheless.

In a few days, Rory left, taking with him most of his fleet and sailing on the long journey past Mull and Iona to Isle Islay. On his orders MacIain took charge of the business affairs of the castle answering the letters and dealing with the various documents that had accumulated during their absence. As de Lérins had anticipated, nothing further was heard from the King on the matter of the chief's banishment, and in a little while correspondence with the Privy Council was resumed again on a number of counts, as though indeed such writs had never been served at all.

*****

At length one day, a letter arrived, with the Earl of Argyll's seal on it, which gave great pleasure to the household, for it proclaimed that Rory's younger brother, Alexander, had at last been released from prison into Argyll 's custody. In all the time since he had been himself released from Edinburgh Castle, Rory had never ceased to write letters pleading for his brother to be freed, but they had been of no avail.

Learning of his release, Iain wrote at once at Mairi's instigation, to the Castle of Lorne where the Earl of Argyll was living, pleading that the chief's young brother should be returned to the care of his own family when he was strong enough to travel. It seemed he was very feeble in his health, and almost likely to die. Evidently not wanting to be encumbered with the invalid longer than necessary, or to risk having his death on his hands, Argyll acceded to the request.

Alexander was brought in on a vessel flying the Campbell colours. He had to be carried ashore, for he could scarcely walk. His once flaxen hair was white, and the fair skin was drawn so tightly over his prominent cheek bones that there seemed no flesh at all beneath it. His body was thin and bloodless and he trembled and shivered at every draught of wind, and sweated as though with a fever when he was brought before the heat of the great log fire.

When he had eaten a little, and consumed some wine, Iain asked him:

"Will you take command here, sir, in MacLeod's absence?"

"No, no, as yet I am scarcely in command of myself," Alexander answered. His eyes filled suddenly with tears. "I could not command a castle. Let me rest a while until I have recovered."

He lay back, looking at the leaping flames of the fire and gazed at the wine goblet trembling in his hand; and then, seeing how many people were gathered about him, looking down at him, he smiled uncertainly and bewilderedly as though he could scarcely believe that he was truly home again.

One day, as Iain was working in the lower room of the tower, which Rory had always used as an office for his letters and documents, Father O'Colgan came in about some matter concerning the new church that Rory was building for the growing settlement outside the castle walls, where already services were held according to the Calvinistic faith. Such churches as had previously existed in the small townships of the Isles had been abandoned at the Reformers' behest, and Rory had seen to it that in his own lands, in Bracadale and Lyndale, Duirinish and Waternish, new churches were built.

"It is a fine wee place and yet people do not come as willingly as they did of old," the one-time Catholic priest, who was now turned Presbyterian minister, remarked regretfully. "There is apathy, I do not know why. The Holy Spirit moved most strongly at Rodel, as it did at Mellifont in Ireland, where I came from. But here it is a feeble thing, half asleep, like a small bird in an egg not yet hatched out, for all my preaching."

"It will take more time," Iain said composedly. "The Islanders believed most strongly in the mystical teachings of the old faith. Now that they may not go to Mass, or smell incense burn, and it is said there is no transubstantiation at the Communion table, and the doctrines of the Holy Mother, and the intervention of the saints are Popish inventions, they are robbed of some of the bulwarks of the faith. They must change the direction of their understanding."

"These are long words," the simple Irish priest said, shaking his head. "I hear the Old Abbot speak in you. He knew about such things.

164

But for myself, I tell the folk that Jesus Christ dwells in any heart that opens willingly to Him. And indeed, it is so," he added confidently. "I do not know why they seem to feel so little of these truths."

Hugh de Lérins was leaning over a table, re-stringing his lute. He twanged a few notes on it, and looking up, said:

"When I was in London I encountered there a strange new movement which called itself by a Latin name – the "Devotio Moderno". Have you heard of it?"

Iain and the priest both shook their heads.

"No, it would not have penetrated to these islands," de Lérins said. "It was an almost secret hidden thing, among a few serious men of the Court, and other gentlemen of good estate, and learned clerks at the seats of Oxford and Cambridge." He adjusted the lute strings, running his delicate hands along them with an air of concentration. Then he seated himself with his hands clasped between his knees, and told them:

"The purpose of these devotions was so to exercise the spirit of man that he might grow a strong and intimate link with the Holy Spirit from on high. It seems to me that when sincere and learned men attempt such exercises, they draw upon themselves a great ray of the strength of God, and His power and His help."

"But the strength of God and His power and help are available free at any time to any man," Father O'Colgan said immediately.

"Yes," de Lérins answered, "they are free for all who want such things with all their hearts. But do we always? The need for God is strongly felt for a while, and the way to Him is glimpsed – then lost, as man's desire fades. Again it comes, again it fades and is lost, for our wills are weak, and do not reach out towards the Spirit with sufficient strength and purpose." He rose and took his lute upon his shoulder and turned as though to leave the room. Then paused and said:

"MacLeod does not pray with all his heart."

"Indeed he does," MacIain protested at once.

"I have seen him on his knees," de Lérins said. "He prays with his intelligence, which is great. But true prayer, like music and all true art, must spring not only from the brain of man, but from his very marrow bones."

Iain looked at the floor. "Yes," he said softly. "That is true."

"When the time comes that MacLeod prays like that, your little bird within its egg will hatch into a great eagle, I think," de Lérins told the priest. "Do not despair, but wait. It is a time of change and of transition – but the Spirit will come to birth again in Skye.

*****

Iain and Hugh de Lérins were much alone these days and in the long evenings or the peaceful afternoons they talked of the teachings of the old Celtic church in which Iain was so well versed, and of the Druids that came before Christ, and of whose ancient learnings and old disciplines Hugh had a great deal of knowledge.

One evening by the fireside, Hugh said:

"Kenneth the Seer speaks of a woman warrior called *Scathach*, who once lived in the Cuillins. Have you heard tell of her, Iain?"

"Yes. A myth, no doubt. They say she taught the young chieftains their swordsmanship. Nowadays most clans have a master to teach the young boys their swordplay. But I had to make do with what little my father could instill into me. Where did you learn, Hugh? I noticed you were very quick and skilful, with exactly the same strokes and possible reposts that we all make."

Lérins regarded him thoughtfully. "Maybe I learned from the same source," he said. "*Scathach* could well have had secret knowledge brought from far away. In the Far East, all the battle arts are very ancient skills, taught by wise men, for the survival of mankind, and for growth of knowledge about ourselves, and the underlying universal laws of movement and action. I learned from an old school in Florence, long ago. I learned that there are certain sequences of swordplay that need to be mastered. Like the game of chess, which is very old, there are only certain possibilities. The most skilled and swift in any circumstances wins the day."

"And *Scathach* may have had this knowledge? So perhaps she really *did* exist!" Iain said excitedly, his eyes alight with interest.

"Very likely."

One day, out walking, they paused by a solitary old oak tree, one of the few trees still standing, for many had been cut for boat building or fires. De Lérins told him:

"The Druids are said to have carved three names on oak trees such as these. 'BEL, TARAN, HESUS.'"

"But it was before the time of our Lord"

"It was before, yet they seem to have known the name – or something like it. The Earth God – Bel – whose feast was at Beltane. Taran was Taranis, God of Thunder. And Hesus, 'He who should come'."

"May be on a tree like this," Iain said, touching the old gnarled bark. "Hugh, I learn so much from you! I learn something new every day. You are the dearest, truest friend I have ever had!" To his surprise, he heard a catch in his own voice and felt emotion rise in him as he realised the depth of feeling there was between himself and the Frankish minstrel. To his discomfiture, Hugh put his arms round him, drew his head down, looked in his eyes and seemed as though he would have kissed him had Iain not drawn back. He had always lived in monkish celibacy, and in any case, physical intimacy with another man had never entered his thoughts. There was no man-with-man culture among the island men, and he had attributed Hugh's slightly feminine side to his foreign background. The clansmen had never accepted the minstrel with warmth, and now the little incident made a slight, embarrassed coolness between the two of them.

*****

For some months Rory was away on one affair or another, fighting at times for MacLean of Duart against MacDonald of Dunnyveg and at times taking himself up again to lend what help he could in the disputed land of the Lewis. His ships were interchanged continually with those at home so that his crews might rest and the craft be repaired and re-stocked, but he himself remained away. At last, one morning in September, his own galley the *"Pride of Lochlann"* was seen approaching with her pennant flying and he was home again.

For several days the clan feasted, and Mairi invented a new song. It began:

"You who have been to minstrels as their homecoming"

Lérins sang it with a warm look towards the chief, and all the musicians cheered loudly, accepting the theme if not the singer.

Alexander, much recovered, but still a very quiet addition to the household, with little confidence or purpose in him, sat by his brother's side at the high board.

One day, young Neil came down with his own crews, having heard that MacLeod of MacLeod was back at Dunvegan. He marched in swiftly, bringing with him as a gift a great old cup of dark carved bog oak embossed with silver and some ancient Celtic words carved upon it, and laid it before Rory on the table, with an air of triumph.

"Where did you get this?" Rory asked, taking it in his hands and turning it curiously. He saw that it was a thing so ancient and so worn with much polishing, that it must have been treasured somewhere, and would not have been lightly given. It might have been Irish, he thought. He hoped the boy had not stolen it, but Neil passed off his question lightly, saying:

"You ought not to question me, as though I were still that boy whom you whipped for disobedience! I bring a gift to MacLeod of MacLeod, which I was at great pains to get for you. And now I beg you, drink to the Lewis in it and let us be merry!"

But in spite of his bravado, Rory knew well that the hopes of retaining the Lewis for the Siol Torquil of the Clan MacLeod were less with each passing month, for the Gentlemen Adventurers had been reinforced by royal troops, and what land they themselves did not control, Kintail had taken with arms and made his own.

"In truth, I do not know if I shall ever win my father's heritage again," Neil said in much less jubilant tones later that evening, when he and Rory and a few of the chief men of the clan were gathered in that small room where Mairi had held the little boy, John, in her arms on the night of his instatement as chief.

Looking at the strong-chinned, cold-eyed young face by the leaping firelight, Rory wondered as he had several times in the last year, how far this boy of Torquil Dubh's could be trusted, and if indeed the Lewis would ever be reclaimed.

"It will be a sad day for your young brothers if we must tell them at length their territory is gone for ever," Rory said, watching him. Neil's eyes flickered.

"Yes," he answered, "it will be sad for them."

And Rory thought again that it was surely himself and not his half brothers whom he desired to see installed at Stornaway.

As conversation flowed back and forth on many matters of politics and clan affairs, the door was opened suddenly and one of Rory's men came in with a wide-eyed look and his mouth agape with news that he could scarcely contain.

"MacLeod!" he cried, "Master Morrison has come on foot from the township, all breathless, to say they have seen on the hillside bound this way a lady in black, riding a palfrey and weeping, and a boy all blood-bespattered, walking with her."

Rory asked sharply. "What lady? What boy?" For all the people in these parts were known by sight, each to the other. But the man shook his head. Iain got up at once, to go and see. He mounted the battlement and looked out over the landward side of the castle where several of the men indicated, and sure enough, almost immediately, there merged along the way through the woods a most strange cavalcade. At its head, a young boy in a ragged plaid came stumbling, one hand holding a blood-spattered cloth to his face. Tied by a long chain attached to his wrist was an ancient brindled hound, which by the manner of its blundering walk seemed to be almost sightless; and behind, a halt old palfrey bore upon it the bowed figure of a woman, whom Iain recognised at once.

"By Colum Cille! It is Mistress Margaret, Donald Gorme Mor's wife," he ejaculated.

"No, surely not – in the black weeds of widowhood?" a bystander queried. "And on so aged a beast, and unescorted?"

"And yet I know it is," Iain answered immediately, and turning, ran swiftly down the stone stairs and across the court-yard and down to the gate, and round to the landward side just as the little group drew up beneath the castle walls.

"Why, Madam!" he cried, approaching them. "What does this mean? What has happened at Duntulm?"

"MacDonald has turned her out, and I was sent to bring her home to Dunvegan," the boy said in a faint voice. He stumbled and seemed as though he would fall. Seeing his exhaustion, Iain put out a hand to steady him, at the same time asking:

"Are you wounded?"

Dumbly, the boy removed the bloody cloth from his face, and Iain saw with horror that his eye had been gouged out, by a spear or dirk.

"By our Lady!" he said, drawing in his breath. "Did Donald Gorme do this to you?"

But having reached his destination somehow the boy drooped suddenly as exhaustion overcame him, in spite of his will, and he made no answer. Supporting him with one arm, Iain took the bridle of the palfrey. The beast jerked its head, as though startled by the unexpected touch of another hand than the rider's and glancing at it, Iain saw that it was also blind in one eye, which was filmed over and white. His own eyes travelled upwards to the silent cloaked figure on the horse's back. Though Margaret's face was turned towards him, he saw that she could not see him. Her expression was empty. She no longer wept, but tears had dried in long soiled runnels on her cheeks.

"It is I – Iain MacIain, Madam," he said gently.

"Ah, Iain MacIain," she repeated expressionlessly, nodding her head as though it meant nothing to her. And then, after a moment, "Will MacLeod take me in?" she asked, in an uncertain way.

"Indeed he will – his own sister!" Iain answered immediately. "But how can such a thing be – that you are sent to us, in a manner so insulting to MacLeod and to your goodself?"

"Indeed, it was not my husband's desire that this should come about," she answered in a trembling voice. "He just told me to go home. Alas, he has no use for a one-eyed wife, whose other eye is also nearly sightless. And a barren woman too, when he needs sons. He has wearied of me long since. But he would not have sent me in this company. It was his clansmen who did this thing, to make a laughing stock of us."

"A one-eyed horse, a blind old dog – " Iain ejaculated on a note of revulsion.

"It was the beast they could best spare, they said, for he is old and lame. And when they noticed how he, like the rider, had one eye alone with which to see the homeward way, they thought it amusing to add the old, blind dog as well. and since they had no one-eyed boy to lead us, they – they – "

"Holy saints!" Iain said, almost to himself. "I dare not think what MacLeod will do when he learns of this barbarity. It is worse than all our ancestors used to do in the old lawless days. Violence for violence's sake, and no Christian charity. But come, Mistress Margaret, I will lead you in."

He passed the fainting boy to one of the group of clansmen who had followed him, and bade them bring him in. Then turned to Margaret, and lifted her gently from the horse.

When they re-entered the castle, the boy was carried off at once to have the blood staunched from his wound, while a messenger went overland for Dr Beaton, to come and tend him. Iain escorted Margaret slowly up the long flight of stairs and along the corridor of Rory's new wing to the small room with the great fireplace where he was sitting with Alexander and Neil and the captains of the clan, in conversation. All the way, at every few steps she paused, delayed and faltered, saying:

"How shall I face MacLeod, my brother? What shall I say to him? Will he have me here, disgraced and blind, a burden on his household?"

"He will, he will, indeed he will," Iain assured her, leading her carefully onward. His arm about her felt the thinness of her small frame, and horror smote him anew at her timidity and feebleness. He remembered well the day she had walked the battlements with Donald Gorme before they were betrothed, her pale blue eyes upturned to his, her expression of admiration and tender love. And anger and pity smouldered in him together, so that his own body trembled to match the shivering of hers.

When she was brought into Rory's presence and he had heard the story of her coming and the manner of it, he emitted a single, violent oath as he had been used to do in his younger days. Then the discipline that he had imposed upon his tongue and on his actions, in all the years since his imprisonment, commanded him again, and instead of bursting forth with further words, he drew her to him and held her close. In spite of the firmness of his hold upon her, she did not lean against her brother, but still held off, her head tilted back, peering anxiously from the one feeble sighted eye into his down-turned face.

"May I live here with you until I am a little recovered from this day?" she asked. "And then – I have been thinking on the way – I will go to a nunnery, if there are any left in these strange days of reforms, and there I can live in quietness and safety."

"You will stay here with me, sister, under my roof. That is your right, and my duty to you," Rory answered firmly.

He kissed her lightly on the forehead, and, turning, bade Iain MacIain take her to Mairi, who was, as was usual, singing to the younger children in the tower nursery at bed time.

When Iain had delivered her safely into those compassionate hands, he began at once to return down the long passage through the new wing to the room where Rory was. But on the way, anger flooded into him anew at the thought of Margaret's sufferings. He paused in a window embrasure, and plucked the casement open and leant his head and face out into the night.

"Even now, after this monstrous thing, she excuses her husband of it and will not have him blamed," he muttered to himself; and leaning there he pondered long on the love of women, its irrational nature, and illogicality, and strength beyond a man's deserts. At length, remembering his duty, he withdrew his head and slammed the casement closed and went on his way again.

When he re-entered it, the small chamber was crowded to over-flowing, for every man who had heard the news had come hot-foot to hear what MacLeod would do in face of this great insult to his sister and the Clan.

"Surely no man at Duntulm or Dunscaith shall live to see another spring after this foul deed!" they said to one another. And: "Shall we not man the galleys this very night?" And yet again: "Will you have us light the beacons, MacLeod? Shall we send out word through all the estates that we are at war with MacDonald, for your one-eyed sister's sake?" So great was the noise that Iain hesitated in the doorway, listening. He could not see Rory at all: and then, after a moment, he discovered that he was not standing, but was seated in the great leather chair by the blazing fire, where he had been reclining comfortably, and drinking wine from Neil's cup, before the little party had arrived. He was leaning forward now, his hands clasped round his knees, staring into the flames in silence, seeming almost unaware of the clamour and commotion going on about him.

Seeing his countenance by the leaping light of great fresh logs, newly kindled, Iain thought how greatly it had changed in this last year. It was most deeply lined, and the closed mouth was turned somewhat down at the corners. The beard which he had grown on his campaigns was already touched with grey and his hair receding a little at his temples. Only the eyes, when he turned his head, had the same look of deep attention and intelligence, and a fire in them which could kindle as swiftly in laughter as in anger, and was rarely totally extinguished.

He moved towards Rory's side, wondering for a moment if he was so beside himself with inward rage that he could indeed not hear his clansmen clamouring for his leadership. But when he had lowered himself on to a small stool near his master's chair, so that he looked upwards and sideways into Rory's face, he remembered that other time when Rory had remained silent in the presence of his clan, on the day of the serving of the King's writs; and how he had delayed all speech until he knew their minds.

But this time, the silence was very long. After a while, seeing that he did not answer them, the captains and the clansmen began to speak one to another of old treachery and ancient deeds that they had always held against MacDonald of Clanranald; for memories of the long, long feuds of past generations moved still in the hot blood in their veins, in spite of all Rory himself had done to encourage friendship between MacDonald and MacLeod. Now, suddenly, men of MacLeod who had loosed their arrows with MacDonald's clansmen at the butts on festive days, and raised wine horns with them, and competed with them in wrestling and jumping, remembered every one of them, some private episode that had stirred them to wrath, and whipped themselves and each other into a passion of hatred of Donald Gorme Mor and his men.

Rory's elder son, Ian, and Torquil Dubh's eldest boy, had both come in in the last few moments and pressed through the throng to be near Rory's side.

"Are we going to battle, Father?" young Ian asked. Slowly Rory shook his head; and at last said in a low voice that only the boys and Alexander and Iain MacIain could hear:

"How can I bring the clan out again so soon? And for a private insult? And with the King's men so watchful? Have we not fought this year long for my kinsmen's purposes? At every turn I seek a way to bring purposeless violence to an end. If we do not, we shall destroy ourselves within this generation. For now – there are these firearms to be had."

"But Father, we must fight for honour's sake!" his son said. "Must we not, Master MacIain?"

Iain looked at Rory.

"You must act, sir," he urged him. "You must speak. Hear how the men's tempers rise. If you do not lead them, they may become a rabble out of hand. Who slights you, slights the clan. Was it not always so?"

Slowly Rory raised his head and looked towards his men gathered close about him. He raised himself to his feet with a weary look, gazing from face to face. The reluctance of his expression was not lost on them. Their eagerness began to die in them and resentfulness and surly looks began to take its place.

Behind him, Iain MacIain also rose to his feet. Feeling the tension of the atmosphere in the room, and the subtle change in its nature, fear began to rise in him that if Rory did not lead them immediately, with the full strength and vigour of his anger, for his honour's sake, they would remember their traditional privileges. They might choose a new chief from among themselves, and in a moment, their allegiance to Rory would die in them. That such a thing might even be possible was so startling and fearful a thought that he drew in his breath, staring from one man to another in agitation and anxiety, realising as he had done first long ago in the battles with Kintail that men moving together have a far lower level of their understanding than each one individually might have.

But while Iain faced and pondered these fears, Rory's own quicker-witted mind had seen and summed up the situation and had made a decision. He straightened his shoulders. Then:

"Angus of the Red Coat," he said, turning to that old warrior, "Go over to Duntulm with a message for Donald Gorme Mor."

"At your bidding, sir," Angus answered promptly, and pushing his way forward, awaited his instructions.

"Tell him," Rory said slowly, weighing his words, and holding in the emotion that trembled in him, "that I regret we had no bonfires to celebrate his hand fasting with my sister Margaret. But I declare to him that there shall be as mighty a conflagration as ever Skye has seen, to mark the dissolution of the contract."

At his words a great exultant roar went up from the assembled men. Rory stared at them a long moment, grave-faced.

Torquil Dubh and Christiana's boy, looking up into the chief's eyes, asked him:

"Macleod, may I go with you into battle? I warrant I am old enough."

Rory looked down into the eager young face, soft-featured still, untried, untouched by pain; and by a turning of the memory, recalled how he himself at that same age had heard the tales of the unfurling of the Fairy Flag at Trumpan and listened eagerly to the glorious battle legends. He turned away, not answering. But the boy seized his arm, and cried excitedly:

"Sir, I need to learn to handle my sword in battle – and fire a pistol, too! My half-brother Neil fights for my rights in the Lewis now, but one day I myself must take command for my clan's sake, must I not?"

"Yes," Rory said, and abruptly drew his arm away and turned his back. With his hand resting against the mantel over the fireplace and his face averted, he said across his shoulder:

"Get you all to your pallets now, and rise before the sun, so that we may make ready and set forth on our campaign."

When the room had emptied, the men clattering out one after another, full of boisterous talk and anger and reminiscences, only Rory and Iain, and the boys and the frail figure of Alexander, remained alone by the great fire.

"Well, Iain, I do not ride into the wind so fast these days," Rory said, looking at his friend. "Did you see how the wind was blowing in this room tonight? I ride with it, as you told me to; but I doubt if it is the wind of God which blows the clan."

"Indeed, sir, I know not," Iain said in a troubled voice. "For such a cause as this I would even unsheath my own sword again, for Mistress Margaret's sake and for our own."

Rory jerked his head round.

"You also? Even you?" He asked, with an expression of his face so torn and so complex that Iain could not interpret it at all. "I have chided you in the past for wanting to pray, when action was required, and now you wish to act when, in truth, I think you would do well to pray. It is certain Donald Gorme will get firearms. Already they have them in Islay and the Lewis. Men get them by barter, on the mainland and sell them to each other. Now that guns and modern weapons have come, if we do not find a way to terminate these feuds between the clans, we shall destroy ourselves, and all the Western Isles will become a wilderness."

"Still, you have no choice, brother," the quiet voice of Alexander put in suddenly. "You must calm yourself. We have faced worse things than this in our clan history." And both boys put in eagerly:

"We have no choice but to fight! It is honourable and right to go to battle with MacDonald."

Rory shook his head; and then, rising, turned to leave the room. Automatically, Iain followed, but Rory gestured him away and went out, closing the door.

In the long corridor, all was silent, for the men had gone away to their own quarters, whence came a distant murmur of voices, and the ladies of the household had retired to their chambers. A cruisie lamp flickering in a little draught of wind was all the light in that long tunnel-like way. He strode swiftly past the window embrasures, against which wind and a light rain pattered, and climbed the stone stairs to his own room in the tower. For a few moments he stood still there, breathing deeply; then turned again and, taking a taper lit it from the fire and shielded it with his hand from the draught. He opened the door to the spiral staircase and ascended into the small low room under the roof where all the old charters and deeds were kept in their boxes, and many things were stored. By the little flickering light, he crossed to the place where lay the iron kist that housed the Fairy Flag. For a moment he stood still in front of it. There was dust on the lid, for it had not been touched for many a year. He laid his hand upon the lock, but it was fastened, and realising that the key was not here, but down below, he remained still, just touching the lock, with his head bent in front of it.

"I do not know what deeps and narrows, what whirlpools and what fearful currents we shall encounter in these coming days," he said beneath his breath. "Preserve us in this hour."

Chapter Fourteen

THE WAR OF THE ONE-EYED WOMAN.

When a man is so wearied in body and in such distress of mind that he is unable to relax his limbs and loosen the tension of his muscles and sinews, sleep will not come to him no matter how he may woo it – and in such a condition even the springy heather tops beneath a summer sky make a poor cradle for a Highlander.

Iain MacIain stretched his lean and bony frame this way and that, sighing, and stifling his sighs and his inward groaning, for his companions' sakes, for a few of the ragged fellows were sleeping peacefully enough, for all their cares. The War of the One-Eyed Woman, as men were already calling it, had continued for two long years, spreading wider and wider among the clans of the Western Isles as more and more old enmities became rekindled and the complications of it became greater and greater. But, of the clansmen lying nearby, he reflected, turning his head once again and gazing towards the humped forms among the curling, stalky fronds, they have no responsibility. They complain, sharp and bitter, of their sufferings and deprivations. But it is their chiefs who lie wakeful, while they snore away the night hours like children.

He raised himself on one skinny elbow and gazed about him in the warm, half-darkness. They lay on a small heather upland hidden away at the end of a narrow winding corry of the Black Cuillins – a place among sharp, low foothills, where the way had been so rough and stony and forbidding that none had thought to follow their little fugitive band, as they scrambled and ran and stumbled into the mountain fastnesses.

"Let them go! It is an ill enough place to seek shelter – there beneath old Blavaan, where all men know the evil spirits dwell!" One of MacDonald's leaders had called to his men. "Back, I say, and take up the spoil and away now to the ships, while the tide runs high."

"St Clement be thanked for his mercy," Iain had half-sobbed under his breath, and with a wave of his sword arm, he had urged his ragged crew forwards and upwards, blindly, without any forethought or logical plan in his exhausted mind save only the putting of distance between themselves and that bloodthirsty band down below, where the corry opened out into the flat rye fields, and the meandering track to Loch Eynort and the sea.

"We are beaten," he had thought, letting the words into the conscious forefront of his mind for the first time in all the wretched months that had preceded this last dreadful day of slaughter.

And now, though the almost windless air of the June night was mild enough, he shivered suddenly and uncontrollably, and at the same moment drew his body upright in an almost involuntary reaction to his own weakness.

Sitting there with his stained and tattered plaid drawn close about him, he turned his gaunt features and gazed with the wild brilliance of eyes too rarely closed in sleep for many weeks, down the narrow inlet which had so unexpectedly and so mercifully led up to this dry and sheltered spot.

"We are beaten," he said again, mouthing the words in silence, and running his tongue over his dry lips. "And yet – there was the Fairy Flag and all men crying for the unfurling of it! Ah, why was it not unfurled? Twice in one century though? Would that be too much to ask of it? And yet, if MacLeod himself had been with us, he would surely have ordered it. It is true it was always said none but the chief himself might order the unfurling – but Alexander of Minginish is his brother's deputy in Rory's absence. He surely had the right and the authority?"

In his wearied brain, the long train of events that had led up to this hour ran back and forth, now in true sequence, now in reverse order, now in mere meaningless and nonsensical jumble. But always, in each sudden jarring cessation of thought that seized him he saw again the frail, thin figure of Alexander, clad in the heavy, clumsy armour that had fitted Tormod, his father, and that no-one had since donned, standing with his sword down-drooping from a bloodied hand, and his white head exposed, helmetless to the enemy.

At the full tide of battle, when all the men of the clan MacLeod who still lived and could be mustered had poured down through the wild hills of Glen Brittle to encounter the Clanranald once again and block their retreat along the Cuillin foothills to their moored galleys, a spark of hope had kindled in Iain's heart. The MacLeods were clearly outnumbered from the start but they had the advantage of surprise. And the invaders were weighed down and encumbered with the booty they had collected in the corry in the previous day's marauding. Cattle and sheep, petrified into complete witlessness, had stampeded here and there, uttering loud bellows and baas of panic, and impeding their captors' passage. Great sacks of grain, barrels of bland, salt sides of beef and household goods and chattels, piled in the narrow corry for safety and easy transportation to the boats, had proved an encumbrance, and almost, at some points, hemmed the marauders in, where otherwise a path would have been clear for them to emerge into the open cornfields and make full use of their superior numbers.

But though MacLeod's men pressed their small advantage to the uttermost, pushing inwards into the corry, thrusting, stabbing, crying the old war cries with a wild ferocity, harrying every group that sought to emerge into the open, and even slaying their own cattle where necessary to prevent the beasts being driven further seaward, yet as the hours of daylight passed the greater weight of MacDonald's force gained its inevitable ascendancy.

Looking back over the course of the battle, it seemed to Iain now, that even from the start the day had been doomed for the islanders were tired to the point of exhaustion.

The fruitless, bitter wrangling had continued all the two whole years starting over the insult to MacLeod's blind sister. It had worn them all out, and reduced the Hebrides to the verge of starvation. Rory himself was fighting at sea off North Uist at present and everywhere throughout his land and the Clanranald's. Alexander of Minginish, as his brother was now styled by virtue of the chief's bestowal of property upon him, was in charge at Dunvegan. But he was at best a broken reed since his long imprisonment.

"You must call the standard bearer before all else, Uncle," Rory's eldest son had urged. "For if MacLeod himself is absent, we have greater need than ever to take the Flag with us!"

But Alexander, too agitated and alarmed by the authority and responsibility that the day had brought, had scarcely heeded the boy and somehow, unaccountably, the clan went off without the precious Flag.

When the Lady Isabel heard from her children that the clan had gone standardless into battle, she herself had brought it after them. She had run up the spiral staircase to the tower room, taking with her Rory's keys, and unlocked the iron box that it lay in. There was no time to look for the staff for it, and anyway it would encumber her, so she went without it, riding full tilt with plaid skirts flying, and the precious silk clutched at her bosom, lest it stream outward, against all custom, into the wind, without the chief's command. Though Iain had been too harassed and occupied to pay much heed at the moment of its arrival, the muttering and the turned heads all about him had drawn his eyes suddenly to the armed figure of their leader, and the Lady MacLeod leaning downwards from the black stallion, that pranced and snorted beneath her, pleading in agitation and dismay.

"Unfurl it, sir, or we are lost!" A bearded, barefoot clansman had shouted. And the cry had gone up on all sides from the lips of the wounded and the dying, as well as from those who struggled still to stem the ever out-flowing tide of MacDonalds from the corry:

"Unfurl the Fairy Flag, Minginish, as your grandfather did at the Battle of Trumpan, on the day of the Broken Wall!"

"No, no, I dare not!" Alexander had cried. "It is the chief alone who may order its unfurling, and today we have not even our rightful standard bearer." He added with a look of agitation on his face: "And the Fairy Flag has been brought to the field of battle by a woman, which is against all custom."

The Lady of MacLeod drew in her breath.

"By St Clement, sir – it is better that a woman should bear it than none at all. If you will not order its unfurling – let us at least put it upon a sword tip and raise it as a rallying point, as was your clan custom in the former days."

Hearing the spirit in her voice, and thinking suddenly that if she were not prevented, she might even loose the silken bonds herself, Alexander reached up and took it from her. And then, as the soft folds of it ran through his hands, a feeling of awe and fear such as he had never known before, ran through his frame so that he trembled and shook as though with an ague, staring at it.

He doffed his helmet and stood bareheaded.

"I cannot. Our tradition forbids me – and besides the legend says the clan may only use the Flag three times, and twice already we have called down its aid in time of need. Not mine to be the last authority."

And turning to a young lad who was employed about the stables at Dunvegan and who had run up to hold the stallion's head, he cried:

"Hold this! Guard it well."

"Alexander! No!" Isabel had ejaculated. But an obscure terror was in him lest his own neglectfulness before the outset, and the bringing of the Flag to the field of battle by a woman's hand, would together merit disaster, and he thrust the ancient silk into the lad's hands and sent him off the field with it in haste.

"By Colum Cille, that was our final undoing," MacIain thought, recalling the lad's startled face, and the bewildered silence that had followed the deputy leader's command. "From that moment the tide was all against us."

He dragged himself to his feet, and stared about him. On all sides the wearied clansmen lay sprawled in a variety of attitudes of abandonment and exhaustion.

Two years ago, how strange a body this would have seemed to bear the name of MacLeod and fight at the chief's right hand. Not one now whose tartan was distinguishable from any other, for all their garments were bloodied and dirty, and rent and tattered by sword thrusts, and jagged rocks or the cutting wind. On many expeditions, their plaids had streamed out scarecrow-wise when they ran, revealing limbs from which all surplus flesh had vanished, leaving them spare and sinewy and gaunt.

So ferocious had been MacLeod's first onslaught on Duntulm, with his men all taut with their individual hatreds and bitternesses, that Donald Gorme Mor had had to call on his uncle down at Dunscaith in Sleat to help him garrison what remained of his property in Trotternish when MacLeod withdrew. Within a week all those outlying branches of the Clanranald who bore allegiance to MacDonald of Duntulm had mustered and invaded Waternish, and Rory's losses in men and cattle were heavy. From that time onwards the clans had fought, not only in Skye itself, but on the high seas and in the sea lochs of the Isles of North and South Uist, Canna, Eigg, Rum, Raasay and all the smaller islets where by custom MacLeod or MacDonald held sway over the small communities.

Unlike old days, when one clan had generally dominated over the other by weight of numbers and good leadership, MacDonald and MacLeod, with their allies, were evenly matched and each under a leader with strength and determination.

Back and forth the battles had raged by water and by land, growing in bitterness: and the struggle for some kind of decisive victory became more fruitless and hopeless as time went on. Those who by tradition tilled the land and did not bear arms for the chiefs, suffered as continually as the warriors, for time and again their crops were destroyed, their food stocks raided and cattle driven off and slaughtered and left lying among the hills and corries.

So little was left to feed the populations of the war-torn islands that spring, that in Waternish the peasants ate their cats and dogs for meat; and haggard women clutched spindly children to their milkless breasts, and rocked them helplessly when they could not sleep for hunger.

Though the women and the old men of both sides had pleaded, off and on, round the peat fires at night, that this senseless slaughter should be made an end of, there was no controlling its machine-like churning, now in one quarter, now another. For by now, the clans MacLean and MacKintosh and other old allies were in the fray on MacLeod's behalf, and MacDonald of Islay and a score of other chiefs had risen in defence of Donald Gorme. Each fresh defeat brought with it its own impulse to revenge, by those who had suffered it. Each vengeful rising meant attack and slaughter in some new quarter - more blood, more fury, more outraged pride and sense of injustice and abuse.

*****

"God's mercy!" Iain said to himself, pacing the hillside in the early dawn. "Rory must have foreseen all this on the night of our decision, when I myself was blind with indignation on Mistress Margaret's behalf. I remember well the way he turned his face from us, and how bewildered I was to see him look so afraid…and yet, we surely had no choice but to defend her honour. For if we were without chivalry and honour, we should be lost."

He turned about on the heather, looking this way and that – now at the heavy grey mass of Blavaan rising bleakly to the right, now away to distant peaks just faintly visible in the growing light, now down the stony cleft up which they had scrambled to their safety. And then again, at the plaid-wrap forms that lay unstirring on the ground.

"In truth," he muttered to himself, "if a man could see into the future, I think may be he could still do nothing to change it. And those who try, perhaps only suffer more. Yes, I remember well the look in MacLeod's eyes that night."

When the sun was almost up and the little wind of dawn stirred the sleepers, lifting unkempt hair from sweat-stained foreheads and ragged plaids from bruised or wounded limbs, so that they moaned restlessly in their sleep, Iain went to them one by one, and with a touch of his hand, wakened them.

"Ah, it is a braw day," one man said grumblingly, with a shiver as he felt the dew on his plaid.

"I could do right well with a bite to eat," sighed another, "but we'll get nothing this day, I warrant."

"Come, rouse yourselves," Iain said briskly when he had watched them yawning and scratching themselves for a moment or two. "Away down to the burn, and wash the sleep from your eyes, and wet your tongues before we make for home."

Here at the foot of the Cuillins, they were almost thirty miles from Dunvegan, but they had been driven that distance by the course of the fighting these last few days.

The clansmen looked at him sulkily, but they scrambled to their feet nonetheless, and went slithering and struggling down into the narrow cleft and stony bed, on its way down from the mountain peaks to the sea.

Not for the first time it occurred to Iain how strange a change of circumstances had come upon him, who had reached Dunvegan as a homeless wanderer from a broken clan in his boyhood; and now fought with, and helped to command these men of a clan who it seemed fortune was about to break in the same manner as the MacIains of Ardnamurchan had been broken long ago.

He went down and splashed the ice-cold water on his own face and hands and drank deeply, cupping his fingers under a little tinkling fall and drawing it into his throat in great gulps.

"Sir, do you think the deputy chief and the lady made a safe escape?" a thin-faced, pock-marked youngster asked him, as he stood back from the water, and wiped his face with the end of his soiled plaid. "We saw Minginish mount the stallion, and ride away holding the Lady Isabel before him."

"God save us all, if they did not," Iain muttered, drying his cheeks and neck. Aloud he said quietly:

"Yes, for the way up Glen Brittle was clear enough at the end and the chief's strong mount could well bear the two of them. It was a ragged flight we all made, there is no denying. But up that way went the Fairy Flag and the chief's brother, and that gallant lady. We shall find them safe at Dunvegan when we reach there."

"Well, the Fairy Flag will not have saved them, do not count on that," a roughly-bearded fellow remarked with a contemptuous laugh. "I warrant it has lost its power now."

"No, no. It was not unfurled, so who can tell?"

"If the seanachie tells the truth, in the old times it was enough that it should be among us, for its very presence brought us fairy aid!"

"Fairy aid!" a grim-faced fellow snorted, twisting his lips into a sneer. "It is not the fairies, but a cannon and muskets such as the King's troops get, that we are in need of now. We have not enough fire-arms for one tenth of our men as yet, as modern soldiers ought to have."

"MacLeod does his best. But guns cost money and goods, and his estates are forfeit," a spirited boy put in. "Our captains are well equipped, but now the slaughter is so much greater than in other days, and we do lack men."

"Yes, while an arrow kills one, a cannon kills ten. It is well enough if you have the cannon on your side, but evil if it falls to the enemy." The oldest of the warriors murmured, shaking his head. "I mind well the old days, when, before a battle, men prayed for heavenly aid and then went forward with their swords and bows and the Fairy Standard in their midst and feared no man. These weapons of fire are a most devilish thing. Who knows if even the Flag can triumph over fire misused?"

When the sun was up high enough for the mist to have lifted in the corries and from the foothills, so that their way was clear, Iain led his men downwards, and across the wide floor of the valley, where the tall rye lay flattened and blood-soaked, concealing only partially the bodies of horses, sheep and men spread-eagled among the stalks. Above them, the ravens and the carrion crows were already busy, wheeling and swooping, feasting on the dead flesh. They rose with hoarse cries as the little ragged band came stumbling along, and settled again behind them. Iain urged the men forward, not permitting any pause to search for pickings on the field of battle, and they went past in a stony silence.

At one place, a sack of porridge oats – part of MacDonald's spoil, had fallen and lay neglected, spilling its contents, and here, by contrast with the great black birds of prey working on already eyeless corpses, small finches and a linnet feasted themselves in the morning sunlight.

Seeing them fluttering inoffensively above the crushed kernels that spilled out onto the ground, Iain paused and stared with a sense of mingled amazement and sorrow at the innocence and normality of their action. Then, he advanced and waved them off, and signalled to the men to pick up the sack and carry it on with them.

There was no sign of life anywhere in the valley, or up into the hills behind, or away along Glen Brittle as far as the eyes could see. And the sunlit sea in the distance was empty and as calm as the little reed-fringed linns, and not a sail or a curragh in sight.

They came presently to a little lochan, already warmed by the sun, and though they had not walked for more than an hour, Iain halted by it, and bade the men sit down.

Taking the sack, he gave each man a share of oats into his cupped hands, and watched them stir it up as best they could, with cold water, into brochan, and swallow it down. While he waited, having eaten little himself, for his heart was too heavy he stared back to the empty battle field.

"Except for what lies among the corn, where the battle-birds are wheeling, one might say that yesterday had never been," he reflected; warm sunlight touched his shoulders and his face, but he closed his eyes against it, the muscles of his jaw and mouth drawn tense, for there was no pleasure in the summer morning.

When the men had refreshed themselves, he ordered them forward again. Their pace was made slow by fatigue for they had not the stamina of fresh young soldiers, and several were wounded. Towards the end of the day each fit man was helping a comrade or two, and one young stalwart had his old father on his back and was staggering under his weight. By nightfall on the third day, after walking and resting by turns, they came within sight of the castle walls, and saw with thankfulness the pennant of the chief flying from the tower.

"MacLeod is home," the Highlanders said, one to another, with satisfaction in their voices. And drawing up the last few drams of their energy, they pressed onward.

Iain saw his small band safely in, and made sure that the barrack quarters were not entirely void of men. Almost all the properly equipped and trained men had been with Rory in Uist, and they and the galley crews had suffered losses in a battle there against Donald Gorme's kinsman, Donald MacIain 'ic Sheamuis, who farmed the island of Eriskay. But the slaughter they had faced and inflicted against MacDonald of Eriskay, had been trivial compared with the Battle of the Corry of the Spoil, when the landsmen and the remnants of the clan under Alexander of Minginish had been so bitterly defeated.

When he had heard the news, and ascertained that Rory and his brother and the Lady Isabel were all safe back, Iain enquired about the Flag. Isabel had leaned down and taken it back from the stable-lad and had carried it in her own bosom. He left the barrack quarters and went upstairs towards his own room in the tower.

Because of his fatigue and despondency his steps on the stone staircase were slow and heavy. A great draught blew down from above, and he noticed anew how cheerless the castle had become. In most rooms the arras had been stripped from the walls, and the upholstery of the furniture was shabby and unclean, for none of the household had time or heart for the niceties of living that Rory had introduced in other years. The few valuables he had accumulated had been sold piece by piece, on the mainland, to raise money for the arms they so desperately needed. The new wing had been roofed over, but the money to pay for the lead tiles was still owed. There was no feasting now, but frugal meals at table, and no music served, as of old, with every dish, to lighten hearts and aid digestion. Even de Lérins' lute was rarely heard, save sometimes softly, of an evening in the woods below the castle, or quietly on the battlements, where he sat alone and played to himself, and stared seaward, with a long-sighted gaze.

Iain went up to the great hall, but finding it empty, and the fire not kindled and no sign of a meal to be had, he turned away towards his own quarters with a sigh. On the way he encountered James Hotfoot, a young lieutenant to whom Rory had given authority, and bade him briefly: "Tell MacLeod I am home with what remains of the men I took out." The young man nodded and went off.

In the little room where he had slept for many a year, the pallet that he had quitted in such haste when the alarm was given, lay still with a jumble of bedding on it, for there was no serving man to tidy it. He lay down on it stiffly, pillowing his head on his arm and closing his eyes.

"If I could only pray," he thought, "as I always did of old." But no prayer was in him, and he lay, tense-faced, remembering as in a dream the days when he had knelt in this small room in the night hours with his head bent: or with his face and his hands uplifted into the darkness, and prayer in his mind and on his lips, like a song of the Isles – wild and sweet and heart-warming and full of an assurance of God's loving mercy towards all mankind. Now all was blankness and darkness.

"I did declare before God and all the saints I would not take up arms again for any cause, save only in defence of the chief's own person," he thought. "And yet, I could not help myself when the hour came, for they were in such sore need of leaders and of men – and Alexander is by no means a warrior. And MacLeod away from home."

He sighed and turned on his side. Once again, as in the heather on the previous night, he tried to sleep, and could not. At last seeking at least to put an end to the turmoil of his thoughts, if he could not oust them in the oblivion of sleep, he rose and struck the flint and lit the cruisie. By its light he opened the wooden chest where he kept his clothes and few possessions and rummaged there for his most precious things – the handwritten manuscripts and the few printed books that the Deputy Abbot had given him for keeps when he had left the monastery at Rodel and returned to Dunvegan to serve MacLeod again.

He turned over the much-thumbed manuscript of the psalms which the old chief had himself used for his translation: scanned the pages of the Catalogue of Saints: looked again at the Litany of Oengus the culdee: and pored for a while over Sulpicius Severus's Life of St Martin, which he knew almost by heart. But the comfort he had found in the Holy Scriptures in former years did not visit him.

Sitting on the floor, his shoulder against the chest, and the cruisie above him on its closed lid, he started to read aloud the Altus Prosator of St Columba of the Isles, straining his eyes to the words on the page by the flickering light, even though his mind had long been familiar with them all, and hoping by this small discipline to bring himself again into a state of tranquillity

> *"Altus Prosator vestustus,*
> *Dierum et Ingenitus*
> *Erat absque origine*
> *Primordio et crepidine…"*

The grandeur of the saintly Colum Cille's profession of faith, the strength and the passion and the eloquence of the long poem had, in his young days at Rodel, moved him to tears, for in it he seemed to see all the vision and the depth and the wisdom of the Isles, and of the Norse and the Celtic ancestry close-mingled, generations back.

But now tears of another nature began to run slowly down his cheeks and fall upon the worn pages, onto the fading parchment, and onto his hands. After a while his head drooped sideways against the kist, and he fell asleep.

*****

"Tears…" whispered a voice, now distant and now so close that the breath of the words was upon his cheek. "Your face is wet with them."

"No, I am not weeping," he answered and stirred and opened his eyes again, blinking against the light that was being held close to him. He sat up stiffly against the kist and began to rub his face with his hand.

Mairi MacLeod was bending over him, her expression troubled by the tear-stained face, and the awkward, uncomfortable attitude in which he had been sleeping. She stretched down a hand as though to help him to rise. He began to scramble up.

"No, no, you are fatigued," she said. "Ah, have a care, you have forgotten the book you had upon your knee."

He grasped the book of the Altus Prosator as it slipped off, and placed it with the others in a pile.

"They will be doubly precious now," Mairi remarked, following the movement of his hand towards the books, "for all the rest are lost, alas."

"Are they?" He asked dismayed. "The books from Rodel – lost? Are they not safe on Bernera?"

"No, they are lost, and all the treasures too. Brother Allan of Bernera, to whom MacLeod entrusted them, had to flee from MacDonald of Eriskay and his men. He enshipped them, thinking to bring them to safety at Dunvegan, but he was attacked, and his boat, and he himself, and all the books are gone. MacLeod brought back this news among much else."

"Ah, no!" Iain cried in a voice of distress. "And our Abbot's translation of the psalms? Even that?"

"I suppose so," she answered sadly. But her sorrow was no more than a weak echo compared with Iain MacIain's, for she had never applied herself to learn to read, being content with song and music and poetry recited aloud, and retained in the memory like the bards of old. Not for her the candlelit studying of the Scriptures.

"So now there will be nothing left of the monastery of Rodel for posterity," he murmured. "Save only a tomb in an empty church on the hillside.

"And our clan memory," she answered softly. And then in a different voice: "If you are not too exhausted Iain, Rory wants you to come."

"Yes, I will come", he answered, but he remained standing there, swaying a little on his feet, staring into the distance, absently.

"Are you sick?" she asked in a troubled voice, peering at his grey face and unkempt hair.

"No, I will wash myself, and then I will come. I have not eaten," he added as an afterthought. "I shall be recovered when my belly is not so empty." He pressed his hand to his stomach, and brought a smile to his lips.

"I will get some food laid for you at table," she answered at once, and turned to go.

In a little while, when he had washed and put on his old, worn monk's habit, and made himself ready, Iain left his room and went along the passages and down the stairway to the hall. A meal of bread and cheese and a little salt beef had been set for him, and an empty beaker stood beside the platter, with a pitcher of water from the well next to it. He seated himself in solitude at the end of the table and began to eat. Though he had slept so short a time, in some way he felt refreshed. He filled the beaker and broke the bread.

In a moment soft footsteps sounded on the stone stairs that led up from the kitchen directly into the hall, and with his mouth full, he turned his head, expecting Mairi. But instead, Mistress Margaret entered, groping her way carefully lest she spill the jug of wine she carried, or drop the two green apples she held in her other hand.

She moved towards the table. And then, hearing Iain's breathing, and the sudden scraping back of the stool as he rose, she stood still, her wide pale blue eyes turned sightlessly towards the sound.

"Master MacIain?" she asked nervously. "Is it you sir?"

"It is I, Madam," he answered, moving to relieve her of the jug.

"My cousin says you are to eat well," she said and gave a little nervous laugh. "There is a little wine here, and see – " she held out the two apples. "Mairi says you look half starved and likely to pine away."

"Indeed, Madam, I shall not!" he answered. But he took the wine gratefully and placed the apples beside his platter. Then, seeing her still standing there, her hands folded tightly together and a half-smile on her face, he asked:

"Will you not share the wine with me?"

"Is there enough?" she asked, anxiously.

"Indeed there is. But we have only one beaker…"

"It does not matter," she answered, and groping forward felt for the bench at the side of the table near him, and seated herself. "I will take a sip from yours." And then she flushed suddenly, fearing that she was being presumptuous, and lest he should not care to drink from the same vessel with her, she rose again, and said:

"Or perhaps I should go down the stairs and fetch another?"

"As you will," he answered. She still hesitated, and suddenly understanding that she was actuated only by her excessive humility, he bade her share the wine with him from the same beaker. He passed it into her hands.

She drank a little, closing her eyes the while, as though in a close concentration on the pleasure of the moment, though open or closed she could see nothing now, and could barely tell the night from day.

Since she did not speak further, he turned again to his meal and ate with relish, feeling the strength flowing back into him as his digestion worked upon the meat and bread.

"My cousin Mairi is tending the wounded," Margaret remarked after a few moments. "I wish I could help her but I can do nothing but tear up cloth strips for bandages. It makes me feel most useless, so I don't go into the barrack quarters now. I am afraid of being in the way, for though they are polite to me if I go down, I know they are too busy to watch where I am stepping, and so they wish me gone. I tear the linen up here and roll it up and Mairi and the other ladies take it away when it is needed. I would do more, if I were able."

"No, be thankful you are spared the sight of wounds gone bad and other horrid things," Iain answered, taking a bite from one of the apples.

"But others have to see these things. You have to…"

"I am a man," he answered quickly. "And you have enough to bear."

"I have enough to bear?" she repeated slowly, turning her wide blind eyes towards him with a strange expression. "I, who am the cause of all this devastation of the Isles?"

He stopped eating and stared at her.

"Indeed Mistress Margaret, it is no fault of yours," he said. "There is no fault in you to merit blame."

She shook her head, smiling her diffident and nervous smile. Then in a moment, she rose from the table and turned to take her leave of him, but paused.

"It would do no good to anyone if I died now," she blurted out suddenly, "and so I live and make the most of what God has given me – shelter with my brother and you all here in my father's house. But if I had died before I had ever left Duntulm – or become that One-Eyed Woman, as the people call the war – and you would all – "

Iain threw down his knife and rising swiftly, took her by the hands.

"Don't say that. Don't speak in that way," he urged her in earnest tones. "No man can tell if by his own actions anything of consequence would be changed. No, do not cry," he added, as he saw her face begin to pucker.

"You are so kind," she cried. "So good!" And turning from him, she went her groping way by wall and table, to the door and left him.

When he turned to sit down again in a few seconds, he found the Lady Isabel MacLeod at the entrance that led from the barrack quarters directly into the hall, bearing a pail of bloody cloths, and with her skirts tucked up like a serving wench.

"Why do you not wed that poor soul, and give her better things to think on," she remarked with a wry look as she passed through. "No, don't rise again – the pail is not heavy, and I can well carry it. Finish your meal. MacLeod will be here soon. Margaret dotes on you," she threw over her shoulder as she reached the kitchen stair. With one foot on the step she turned her head again and finished: "A man needs a wife, Iain MacIain. I tell you that for sure. Do think of Blind Margaret. She has pretty ways, though she is sightless, and she was never wed to Donald Gorme by the church's rites, so she is free. I know she is not a young girl and not a maiden either. But neither are you young these days, my friend. You waste your years of manhood."

Without waiting for his embarrassed answer, she set off down stairs.

"Doubtless she could not give him children," she thought, as she padded downward, but who knows? They say Donald Gorme's new wife is childless still.

But Iain, finishing his meal, remembered Christiana, now homely and maternal, and heavier in weight, with the wish for learning forgotten long ago. He craved no-one, but his ancient dream. I am a celibate, like Hugh de Lérins, he told himself.

Presently, Rory came up the stairway from the barrack quarters, in his shirt-sleeves and unbarbed, for he had no sooner reached the castle late that day than he had gone down to see the stragglers from the battle of the corry as they came in and to hear all their first-hand accounts of the defeat.

"Iain," he said, "You are unwounded? And you have eaten? Mairi said you were hungry. Come down and speak with me below."

He led the way along a passage and down into that small room with the fireplace where he had been on the night his sister Margaret came home. Here Hugh de Lérins was sitting with one leg up under him, on the low window sill, his face turned seaward, and his hands idle in his lap. And Alexander was reclining almost full-length on a settle before a small fire of peats, for there was no-one to cut timber. His eyes were half-closed and his face had again the pallor and transparency that it had worn after his long imprisonment. He turned his head when Rory and Iain entered, but his expression was sleepy and his eyes slid away from them again without much interest.

Rory drew a chair to a table and seated himself and bade Iain do likewise.

"I want to hear what further account you can give me – now that the men have eased their minds by ranting at me and blaming my brother," he said.

Iain glanced sharply at him. He knew so well the different expressions of Rory's face and the various intonations of his voice that it was clear to him at once that the chief was in the same state of mind that he had been in himself a few hours back – but with him, tears rarely flowed, and fiery anger would burst forth instead after an hour of stress.

"Well, sir," Iain began, choosing his words carefully, not to arouse him more than necessary. "We were outnumbered from the start. The men fought strongly and held to your brother as they should, but…"

"But their force and courage left them when they saw the Fairy Standard go from the field – is that it?" Rory interrupted.

Iain looked quickly at Alexander and then again towards Rory. He sensed that the brothers had upbraided one another – the one for his chief's absence at a crucial time, the other for his deputy's lack of foresight and insight into the clansmen's mentality. Clearly by his dejected attitude, Alexander had had by far the worse of the dispute, as indeed did most men who dared to dispute with Rory.

"As to that, I don't know for sure what they thought," Iain said uneasily. "We were greatly outnumbered, sir, and lacked the best men, and yourself, and…"

"Ah, yes. And doubtless I should have known of what would happen in my absence and left my best men home, and fought young Eriskay alone, or with a handful of weaklings to my aid," Rory said in chilly tones.

"I only said we were greatly outnumbered, and we did our best," Iain replied unhappily. "Minginish, your brother – and your gallant lady…"

"…who mounted that powerful stallion and had to gallop – nearly thirty miles – and she with child again – to mind Minginish of his duty," Rory snapped as though Alexander of Minginish were not there at all.

"By our Lady!" Iain ejaculated. He had not known that the Lady Isabel was again in early pregnancy, but in a moment, remembering her easy gait with the pail of cloths, and the quick tongue with its unwanted advice to himself, he realised she had come to no harm, and that it was not fear for her health but a multitude of other things that had brought Rory to this sharp-tongued state. "She did a most courageous act, and was not harmed by it," he said. Perhaps she was even protected by bearing the Flag, he thought to himself.

"She should not have brought the Flag," Alexander muttered suddenly, shaking his head feebly from side to side almost like an old man.

"In St Clement's name, why not?" Rory roared at him. "The men believe in it -"

All three of them turned their faces and looked at him.

"And you, sir?" Iain almost muttered. "Do you not believe in it?" But Rory's look was such that he dared not speak.

"I don't know what to think," Alexander said unhappily. He rolled over on his side, pillowing his head on his hand, his eyes turned downward towards the small fire in the grate, his lips drooping like a boy rebuked. "Something said to me in the moment of its coming that a good magic may turn evil when a woman unlawfully…"

"Hah!" Rory spat out contemptuously. "I have never heard it said a woman may not handle the Flag. Witchcraft – black magic – all such superstition is fostered and fed by weak men. You had not your wits about you – that is the length and the breadth of it."

"Indeed, Rory, I…" Alexander said painfully, looking up. "I held it in my hands. I…I *touched* it Rory! Have you ever touched it I wonder? You would speak differently if you had."

"I have not," Rory said briefly. His eyelids flickered, remembering how once, long ago, he had slept with his head upon it, and another time in a moment of alertness and foresight, and fear, he had gone up into the tower and laid his hand upon the iron box and spoken aloud in the darkness of the empty room. "Now it is locked away again, by my lady's hand, as I instructed her," he said. "Would you have me get the seer to bless it? Or the priest – the minister – to exorcise it since her touch?" he added sarcastically.

Alexander drooped his head again, closing his eyes, and lay still with a tired expression and wrinkled forehead.

At the window de Lérins stirred and sighed and looked across at Iain with a smile

"The chief believes that women are equal with men, and there is therefore nothing they can't do," he said. "When we have all given our lives for your causes, will you have the ladies in armour and beside you on the field, sir?" He looked at Rory's flushed and angry face with laughter playing round his mouth, and his eyes so gentle and affectionate that the impertinent words lost much of their sting.

"God's blood!" Rory shouted and leapt from his chair in a threatening way. But at the sound of the oath on his own lips, he stopped, remembering how once he had remarked that the uttering of the old and barbarous oaths bred violence in men, for any cause for which they were uttered, be it good or bad. He held his tongue, and his eyes met de Lérins' gently mocking ones.

"Don't make fun of me," he said, but in spite of himself he began to smile at the thought of all the ladies of the castle with their petticoats tucked up, and steel helmets over their coifs, heaving and tugging the heavy swords along with their small hands.

"No, but there are things beside this which a woman may not do," Hugh de Lérins said in a soft voice, "for though they may serve God as nuns, it is unlawful for them to be priests. And even if they are deaconesses – as was once permitted in the Celtic church, it is forbidden for them to administer the Cup. Though Our Lady is known as Queen of Heaven, it is said in some old songs and carols that she is also Queen of Hell."

"That is no more than a corruption, born of man's fear of his own weakness towards woman," Rory answered in a voice more normal and controlled than he had used throughout the evening.

"No, sir," the minstrel said, gently, shaking his head. And:

"It is a much deeper thing, I believe, sir." MacIain put in diffidently. "Even in the world of saints – and of the fairies – there are both male and female things, each with their own parts to play in life. Of this duality, and its nature, the philosophers of old used to speak. The writers in Greek. And the Desert Fathers of Old Egypt, with whom the founders of the Celtic Church corresponded."

For the first time, Alexander opened his eyes fully and looked across at the others with a wide awake expression.

"I felt in my bones many things I had not known before, when I was holding it," he said. "I was mistaken to leave Dunvegan without young Vic Mhuirichie to bear it. But afterwards, I could do nothing but what I did."

Both Iain MacIain and Hugh de Lérins nodded as though in acknowledgement and agreement.

Rory looked from one to another of them, nonplussed – as he had been that day long ago in his grandfather's room at Rodel when Iain and the old Abbot had been speaking together and seeming to understand one another so deeply; and as he had been, passingly, on other occasions in the presence of Iain MacIain and the minstrel, when they had embarked on philosophical and religious discussions in a vein quite foreign to the line of his own clear and logical intelligence.

"So," he said after a few moments, in a voice that showed the anger had gone out of him, and he was in command of himself once more. "We will leave all that. What is done is done, and there's no changing it by words."

And Iain, recollecting the voice of one of the warriors at The Corry of the Spoil that wretched morning, put in:

"The use of explosive missiles in war is perhaps a misuse of natural forces on a new level beyond what men have done before. Perhaps the Fairy Flag has no power over them at present."

Rory rose from his seat and took a turn about the room.

"I know nothing of fairy powers," he said. "I often think there is more superstition in you two gentlemen than even in my men. There is only one power I know of, and that is the door of the intelligence – for through that door, a man treads his way with knowledge, and surely knowledge is what we need to govern our lives? Not fairy lore." But he spoke without the certainty and arrogance that had often characterised his conversations in the past. Watching his manner of walking, with his arms folded on his chest, and his head thrust forward, Iain thought he had less confidence in his own judgement than of old, and that his mind admitted of many things beyond the realms of his own intellect, these days, though he was wary still of superstition and of anything his keen mind could not quickly grasp.

"Yes, knowledge goes a long way," Hugh de Lérins answered. "Even to the grave. I remember an old morality play called "Everyman" that the townsmen of England perform to teach the people to lead their lives aright. When all his other attributes forsake him – good "Fellowship," "Discretion", "Beauty" and his own kindred and sundry other personalities, "Everyman" journeys towards his grave alone with "Knowledge" and his few "Good Deeds". But at the last, even "Knowledge" leaves his company."

Rory came to the fireplace, and putting his foot upon the hearth, stood with bent head before it in silence. After a pause he drew a long sigh.

"Yes," he said. "Each man is alone. And long before the grave, I truly think."

"Not if he loves God – for if he prays, he is not long in solitude," said Iain.

Rory sighed again, and made no response.

*****

Presently Torquil Dubh's widow, Christiana, came in bringing with her a pewter jug with a hot drink in it, at Mairi's suggestion, for the ladies had all remarked how tired both MacLeod himself and all the clan leaders seemed, and how dispirited, and in need of rest and food and proper sleep.

"We brewed this for you, your lady and I," she said to her brother with a smile. "It will make you all rest and sleep soundly and forget your troubles for a space."

"Not too soundly, I hope," Rory smiled, "in case enemies come on us once again."

"We have not given it to the guards," she answered, laughing. "No, it is only mulled elderberry wine, well spiced. It will comfort you, but it will not make you tipsy." She fetched goblets from a cupboard, and began to pour it out, but paused suddenly to remark:

"Oh, brother, I have forgotten a matter of great importance. Oh, sir. The tidings you all brought clean drove from my mind that there was yesterday a message from our kinsman Neil, of the Lewis."

"Ah, what has he to say?" Rory asked sharply. "I tried to reach him at Birsay ten days ago, but I could not, and all I learnt was a rumour that Torquil Conanach is dead, and the Fife Adventurers have sold off their rights to Kintail. No-one knew anything of young Neil's whereabouts."

"Yes, so we heard," Christiana told him. "Conanach died of a festered wound. And the Gentlemen Adventurers have given up their claims, for they have squandered all their own resources in the Lewis, and still for all they can do, the whole isle is so stubbornly hostile to them that they confess they cannot till an unciate of land and plant a crop, but someone will come by night and destroy the day's work. They go in fear of their very lives. So my Lord of Kintail has brought them out for a handsome price, and now lays claim to all the Lewis."

There was a heavy silence in the room, for though it might be in some way a matter of pride and even of laughter that the upstart Adventurers had been so put out, yet the thought of the Lewis in MacKenzie's hands was not a pretty one.

"And what of young Neil?" Rory asked at last.

"He has been holding out on the Isle of Birsay many weeks against the clan MacKenzie," Christiana told him, "but his word was that seeing his resources are all but gone, and you have not come to his aid, he thinks now to go in person to my lord of Argyll and bid him press his claim before His Majesty."

"Sister, I have done all I could do," Rory replied. "You do not think I would have left the lad to fight for the Lewis alone if I could avoid it? I have been pressed on all sides, as you know – "

"Indeed, Rory, no man blames you," Christiana answered, shaking her head. "You have done your best." She took a goblet with some mulled wine, across to where he had seated himself, and after giving it to him, stooped and touched his forehead with her lips. He took her hand as she would have turned to go.

"Your sons have lost their heritage, with the loss of the Lewis," he said, in a troubled voice.

"Yes, I am afraid it is true. But while they dwell with you, they are at least as safe as any man is, these troubled days," she answered, trying to smile.

"At least sir, now the Adventurers are beaten, we shall not need to fear their presence in Waternish or here," Iain put in. "If they had taken up the claims the King granted them two years ago in Skye itself, we should have had a greater burden still to bear."

Rory said nothing. He still held his sister's hand, absentmindedly stroking the fingers as he sipped his wine.

"I've a mind to go to Argyll myself," he said suddenly. "For if we don't seek aid soon we shall be all destroyed beyond recovery."

"But, Rory – to seek aid from the House of Campbell?" Christiana asked dubiously.

"Are they not kin to us, through our father's second wife?"

"Yes – but it is no blood relationship, Rory, and besides – "

"Ah, Christiana," he sighed, releasing her hand suddenly. "I shall go not from choice but from necessity." He put his freed hand across his eyes, resting his elbow on his knee, and sat still. Without looking up he told them: "In North Uist I heard a story that MacDonald has called on the Earl of Huntley to send aid to the Clanranald, for the sake of their old friendship. If this is so, we shall have more than ever a need to ask those above us to look kindly on our causes."

Christiana put a hand on her brother's greying hair, and smoothed it back from the creased brow.

"We shall support you, whatever you do," she said softly. "Shall we not friends?"

The others nodded, silently accepting that the fate of all of them lay in the Chief's hands.

Chapter Fifteen

THE SOJOURN IN IONA

In spite of his words that night, Rory was so reluctant to go and seek aid from his overlord, the Earl of Argyll, that he delayed his departure again and again, on one pretext or another. He said repeatedly "There must be no more great clan battles. The battle of The Corry of the Spoil is to be the last, the very last of such events, no matter what happens." But in spite of his vehemence he knew well enough it would take two to make a peace as it had taken two men's contrary actions to make the war, and Donald Gorme, far from seeking to end hostilities, was using his victory at the corry as a spur to his men to lead them on to a conquest of Dunvegan itself.

In these days the castle was guarded and garrisoned full strength, night and day, and as many as possible of the clansmen who could be accommodated had been brought to dwell, either inside the curtain wall or in the little settlement just outside, from whence they could be taken in to safety when necessity arose.

He rode through the devastated countryside by day and saw the untilled fields, the deserted turf-roofed cottages, the sparseness of the stock where once many sheep and the small black cattle of the Isles had pulled the thin grasses in safety and contentment. He took his turn on the battlements at night, where he was a familiar figure at the watchman's side.

At last, when the first snows were on the hills, and all the islands lay silent and seeming deserted beneath their humped coverlets of white, his mind was made up for him by young Neil, who arrived by sea. His galley, battered and holed in many places by war, and sorely in need of fresh paint, and new hemp for the much patched sails, crunched through the thin ice that lay on the water at the end of the loch, at dawn, and he came ashore and into the hall as the household were breakfasting.

The family all greeted him with cordiality, and led him to the fire, which was newly kindled, and shared with him the salt pork and the ale and oaten cakes that were laid out somewhat sparingly for themselves.

He seated himself with scant thanks opposite MacLeod, and stretched out an unwashed hand for the bread. He had a long jagged scar, from a sword cut, badly healed, running from eye to chin, and so evil a gleam of hatred for all men in his eyes, that Christiana and Isabel looked at him askance; and even Mairi with her more tolerant eye, drew back a little from him, after a while.

"Well," he said to Rory, "for good companionship's sake, you will no doubt be pleased to learn I too am now of the growing band of outlaws from his Majesty's domain!"

"Is that so?" Rory enquired, looking him up and down. "You have asked for aid and been refused?"

"Yes. How else would it be? I might have known," Neil said bitterly. "I asked for an audience of my Lord of Argyll and of the King himself, and – the upshot of my entreaty is – I may not show my face in Edinburgh on pain of forfeit of my life."

"Did you see the King?" Rory enquired.

Neil took his knife from his belt and sliced at the meat as though he had never eaten at table before, but only on the battlefield, or had long forgotten the niceties or living.

"Yes, in a manner," he answered with an evasive look. And though Rory questioned him further, he could not get from him with any clarity what had happened that should in particular weaken his cause, beyond the old preference that his Majesty had shown for Kintail and, his protégé Conanach.

In spite of his bitter and sarcastic tongue, the young man was full of plans for further attempts to change the course of events, and since his line of thought on the need for getting help, ran easily with Rory's own, it was only a matter of time before the two of them together agreed upon a journey to the mainland.

Rory did not risk taking a ship, for the old *"Dominant"* had been sunk off Benbecula that summer, and there was now such a scarcity of timber in all the isles that he could not replace her, or the other galleys he had lost in the sea battles.

He and Neil, with James Hotfoot and two men, went overland on horseback down to Sleat and crossed to Mallaig in one of MacKinnon's boats, and began the long ride down the broken coastline to the south. Rory had previously ascertained that Argyll was residing at Dunstaffnage Castle, a little above Oban. But when at length they reached there, to their disappointment, they learned the Earl and his lady and a number of his household were in Glasgow for some affair at the University there, of which he was patron.

To reach him there meant another journey almost as far again, and Rory's fatigue was so great that he hesitated. But young Neil, determined not to be thwarted in his intentions, urged him on.

"It will be no easy matter for outlaws like us to get near him in a great city," Rory suggested. "Here at Dunstaffnage we are safe enough, but -"

"Well, don't accompany me, if you are so nervous," Neil said contemptuously. "I will go on alone."

"No, no," Rory answered. "We will go together."

To his surprise and relief, the young Earl of Argyll seemed a cheerful fellow, full of talk and a sense of his own well-being, and not unwilling to see any who sought an audience with him.

He received the two Islanders in the sumptuous apartments he had furnished for himself for his occasional visits to the University and sat with his hands clasping his knee, listening amiably while Rory explained the purpose of his visit.

"It seems you are indeed in need of help, sir," he put in, when Rory had drawn a picture of the devastated island territories. "And now that you have spoken, I shall tell you, with the same openness that you have shown me, that I have here a great missive from the King, bidding me do exactly what you yourself request."

"Bidding you intercede for me?" Rory asked incredulously.

"Yes, something of that nature," the young nobleman answered, rising to bring the parchment letter he spoke of from the chest where it lay. "Now let me know more about this dispute you have with MacDonald – of its nature and its origins."

By his questions, Rory soon discovered that the young man's knowledge of the island territories from which he drew much of his great income, was all second-hand, gleaned from his father, and laced with the old Earl's opinions and prejudices. He spoke with levity of many things that were not matters for laughter to the islanders, and seemed to treat the warfare rather as a man speaks of the squabbles of two schoolboys.

But none the less, he listened to the MacLeods and heard them out, stroking his chin and hiding the foolish, boyish laughter that bubbled in him at the tale of the one-eyed woman on the one-eyed horse.

"Well, then," he said at length, when Rory had finished speaking. "If we can turn MacDonald's mind to sheath his sword and come to table, we will mediate between you."

"Mediate?" Rory asked doubtfully, thinking that a young nobleman whose knowledge of the Hebrides was as light-hearted and inaccurate as he had shown it to be in his conversation, was no fit mediator between grown men filled with anger and bitterness. "I had thought, my lord, to plead with you for arms, and men –"

"No, that I will not," Argyll answered smiling. "Besides, the King bade me mediate, for he says MacDonald has enlisted the Earl of Huntley to his aid, and His Grace will not have Huntley and his Popish followers run throughout the island territories, undoing all the good work done there by the Reformers."

"My lord -" Rory began. But unwilling to be talked out of his intentions, Argyll interrupted.

"We will mediate between you, my lord of Huntley and I. We will not lend you arms. Indeed, we have both a stake in your territories. Why should we assist you to destroy them? Is it not time to make an end?"

"It is so," Rory answered, for he had thought this himself many times. But he had not visualised such an end as this, with a boy almost young enough to be his son to speak on his behalf, teasingly and with laughter, on matters of gravity.

Seeing the reluctance of his expression, the young nobleman smiled suddenly again, and slapped his leg, and said:

"Then let us make an end! Indeed, sir, I can't help laughing, for if there is one thing I do know that men say of MacLeod of MacLeod it is that he cries always 'Peace! Let no man draw his sword, but talk and parley and settle his disputes by mediation.' And yet in truth he is the very first to draw his sword, and last to sheath it, on many an occasion."

Rory lowered his eyes, swallowing the injured pride the young taunting voice was causing him.

"If it is so – and I hope it is not – I am sorry that men should speak so of me," he said in a low voice. "I have never unsheathed my sword save in an honourable cause."

"Well, we will do our best for you so that your 'honourable causes' are not turned against you," Argyll said still with a cheerful laugh. "Will you sit down at table with MacDonald of Clanranald? Shall we tell him so?"

"Yes, I suppose so," Rory replied reluctantly. He added with a bitter cynicism: "You may tell him, if he will honour us at Dunvegan, we will feast him there in like manner as he feasted me and my men at Duntulm, long ago. Yes, tell him that."

Argyll looked at the older man's expression, and straightened his face as he promised to do what he could. Indeed, though the King had clipped his father's wings somewhat, his monetary interests in the Isles were so considerable that he certainly would do all he could to keep the territories of which he was overlord, out of Huntley's grasp.

On the following two or three days, Argyll listened to young Neil's story, as well as having further talk with Rory himself. Now that he had grasped, by this first-hand contact, that there was much more to be known about the problems of the Hebrides than his father would have had him believe, he discussed, willingly enough, the fishing rights, and stock-breeding and the raising of crops and many ways in which greater prosperity might be brought to the islands.

"I know well the King has in his head the thought that these are all fertile and valuable lands going to waste in the hands of barbarians," Rory told him on the second or third occasion. "But in truth, they are very rocky and windswept, and no man can raise the full amount of the taxes and rents imposed on us these past years."

"Have you not yourselves destroyed their fertility by felling trees in great number, for your galleys, so that the soil erodes away and the bare rock is exposed?" Argyll asked. "So I have heard said."

"Yes, in some measure," Rory had to admit. "For myself I would replant for posterity, if I had means and a space of peace, in which to do it."

When they left at last, Rory felt satisfied with all that had passed, and even relieved that he had sought Argyll out in Glasgow and not waited to be summoned as a result of the King's command. But Neil MacLeod had a countenance dark as thunder, for he had made no headway whatsoever, and had made an enemy where Rory, with his restraint, felt he had made a friend.

"Ah, Neil, I would have done more to aid you, if I had been able to," Rory sighed, as they rode away towards their lodgings. "I did my best – but you were very ill-mannered and unaccommodating in your words."

"He supported those upstarts the Gentlemen Adventurers!" Neil ejaculated, as though the bitterness of that discovery was still half-choking him.

"He only said he was a loyal subject of King James and could not go against his purposes," Rory said mildly. "He was not very set in his opinion. You could well have turned him, with patience and well-chosen words, to see your case in different light."

"Patience! Ha! I am a man of few words and those plain and straightforward ones," Neil answered in a contemptuous voice. "I come here thinking to find a man – not a silky, smug-faced young gentleman, with a "by-your-leave" and "may-it-please-you", and "we-await-your-pleasure"."

He mimicked Argyll's accent with scorn, and then fell into a gloomy silence.

Rory made no further comment. He had spurred himself to the utmost to make this journey, and had used every effort to keep his mind attentive and clear throughout the interviews. But now that they were over, he was conscious of something more than the fatigue that dogged him these many weeks past. It seemed every bone in his body ached, and a hard, dry cough that he had ever since the first snows fell and the frosty autumn mornings started, seemed suddenly so much worse that he could hardly bear the racking of it in the night. His brow felt hot and fevered, and yet he shivered as he rode. He thought how young Neil had alienated the Earl from the start, by his arrogant contempt for courtesy and decency of behaviour. How he had argued and even shouted the young nobleman down on one occasion, and given offence by uncouth behaviour in the dignified dwelling.

How different was this boy from his elegant young father, Torquil Dubh, whose death Rory so regretted.

Rory sagged in the saddle, troubled that he could not at least say at home that all possible effort had been made for MacLeod of the Lewis.

At the house where they lodged, Rory made efforts to cheer the young man, but with no result, for he only scowled and sulked and would not eat. At last, since he also had no desire for food, Rory rose and left the table and lay down on the bed, with his eyes closed. As soon as his limbs relaxed from the tension of the day, his thoughts began to whirl and churn in him in an uncontrollable maze and confusion, and he started to tremble and shiver. Drawing the coverlet over himself, he tried to sleep, but almost at once he began to cough and to clutch his chest which was contracted with pain. He drew his breath with difficulty, audibly and shallowly. Fearing that he might fall into a delirium, so extremely ill did he feel, he began to call Neil's name, but in a voice so strangled and painful that it did not penetrate to the next room. After a while he desisted and lay back. And then he heard Neil's footsteps cross the room and go out of the other door, and down the stairs. He tried to rise, thinking he ought not to let his young kinsman out of sight, to roam the streets in so belligerent a state of mind, but as soon as his feet touched the floor, his legs buckled under him and he pitched forward in a faint.

For some days, Rory lay in so serious a state of fever that young James Hotfoot and the two serving men were filled with dread that he would die. He recognised no-one, and rambled in a maze of incoherent talk that none of them could understand. Here was no kind-faced familiar Dr Beaton and his son to tend the chief. And in the lodgings, none but hostile faces, for the islanders were strangers to the host and his family – and clearly they wished them gone.

Neil swore at them for their unhelpful manner and unfriendly faces, but went himself in search of a physician. When one was found he expressed so much inquisitive interest in his patient and the party of islanders, that Neil said curtly:

"Yes, we be not only Hebrideans and foreigners, but outlaws from the King's domain, to boot. Will you tend him or not? If he is good enough to sup at my lord of Argyll's table, I warrant he is high-born enough for *you* to handle without questioning. But have your way."

The doctor looked affronted. He answered in an offended way that he did not request to know a man's antecedents in order to save his life, and had only enquired from civility and common courtesy. But: -

"Two outlawed gentlemen, at the Earl of Argyll's table?" he said to himself. "How is that, and for what purpose?"

In a matter of days, as a result of this exchange, many men knew the name of the man who lay so sick, and wandering in his wits, and knew his business – and that young Argyll, too inexperienced to be prudent, had received him and seemed to enjoy his company. There was a sudden spate of talk and rumours that the whole party would be arrested by the King's men, and those who had befriended them might be tried for treason.

Neil found himself avoided on the stairs of the lodgings, and drinking alone in the ale houses he frequented in the evenings. For lack of company, he drank too much, and shouted and cursed as he reeled his way home again.

When Argyll heard what was happening, his amiable face took on a look of sharp wariness that made him very like his father.

"I received MacLeod of Dunvegan on the King's business," he said, "but now I would as soon see the back of him. I'll have no truck with the pretender to the Lewis – it seems he is as troublesome a fellow about the city as I found him in my own house."

He frowned, and decided it were best to watch the course of events without becoming personally involved, for he did not doubt there would be more to come if Neil MacLeod could not hold his liquor or his tongue. And in due course, he was not surprised to receive a message from the Privy Council, that the Islanders were to be arrested and taken to Edinburgh to account for their unauthorised journey to the mainland, and other matters.

Argyll's face took on the prim, chill look of his fathers, as he pondered the document. Then, thinking to play this matter out to the best advantage, not alienating either side overmuch, he called for men, and went himself to see the MacLeods, since Rory was too ill to come to him.

Rory was still far away from the things of this world, and though he opened his eyes briefly and stared into the young nobleman's face as he bent over him, it was clear that he did not hear or understand the urgent words that were being poured into his ears.

Argyll stood back nonplussed, stroking his chin in thought.

At last, he signalled to his men to take young Neil, whom they had already pinioned by the arms, fearing the murderous look in his eyes.

He turned away from the bed and went slowly down the stairs, while Neil was dragged, kicking and cursing, after him.

James Hotfoot stood with sword half out of his scabbard, and his mouth open, not knowing whether to attempt to defend his master's kinsman or not. Fearing to oppose the King's authority, he delayed and did nothing to help Neil, and at length he sheathed his sword reluctantly and let the party go.

That evening, Argyll wrote a letter to the Privy Council, justifying Rory's presence in Glasgow, "for had he not come to me, I should have had need to summon him for our noble sovereign hath enjoined me to enquire in my own person on certain matters that concern the Western Isles." He added that MacLeod was sick, and that he would have him taken back to the island territories as speedily as his health permitted.

When the letter was ready, it went by messenger to Edinburgh. And Neil MacLeod, in bonds, was taken too.

As soon as Rory could be moved, Argyll planned to get him off his hands. He was nervous at having defied the Privy Council even though he could reasonably justify his action to the King. Realising that it would be a long time before MacLeod could ride his horse; he planned to move him by sea to whichever of his kindred in the isles should prove to be more accessible. His enquiries soon established that MacLean, at Duart Castle in the isle of Mull was a near kinsman, and thence he resolved to send him with his serving men.

*****

Winter was far advanced and the rocky Isle of Mull fast bound by ice and snow when Rory at last came to himself sufficiently to understand where he was and what had happened to him.

The long, cold journey in the open boat, well-wrapped in plaids as he had been, had set him back so far that by its end he was barely conscious of his whereabouts. He had been lifted, unresistant, into the boat from a horse litter, and out of it again into the island fortress. And for a long period after, he had seemed indifferent to or unaware of his surroundings. But at last he was strong enough to raise himself a little on his pillows, and demand to know on whose authority he had come to this place, and where young Neil had gone.

James Hotfoot, to whom he addressed his first question, prevaricated nervously. But bluff old Hector MacLean had no such fear of plain words. He answered bluntly:

"By the orders of the Privy Council Neil MacLeod was hanged at Edinburgh some three weeks gone."

The little colour that had come to Rory's cheeks when he asked his questions, drained from them again, leaving him with a mask-like pallor, and a drawn countenance. He lay back slowly and shut his eyes. After a moment, tears forced themselves beneath his closed lids. He did not speak. Old Hector cleared his throat in embarrassment.

"It cannot be helped at all," he said. "You did your best for him and when all is said, he was a bastard, and no true chief of the Lewis."

Rory opened his eyes.

"So ends the Siol Torquil of the Clan MacLeod," he whispered. "If it were not certain before, I warrant now the Lewis will be in alien hands from this day forth for ever. So shall we all be robbed at length of our true heritage in this new age, if we cannot find a way to become masters of our own fate."

"No, your nephews will grow up, and press their claim," Hector MacLean answered cheerfully. "And you will feel courage again when you are recovered from your illness."

But Rory only shook his head. Suddenly, he covered his face with his hands, and began to sob weakly, turning his head this way and that upon the pillow, and drawing gasping, croaking breaths, that he could not control.

MacLean laid his hand with rough affection on the sick man's shoulder, but looking nonplussed, for in all the years in which he had known MacLeod, he had never seen the smallest sign of womanish weakness or lack of courage and purpose. Rory hauled himself feebly over on to his other side, so that the old man's hand was shaken off, and there, with his face to the wall, continued to cry in an abandoned, despairing manner, unaware of anyone, lost in the web of his own grief for himself and all his kindred, and the people of the Isles of the Hebrides.

As soon as he had strength to raise himself up fully in his bed, and could eat solid food again, Rory demanded of his host that he should be allowed to leave Castle Duart and set out by sea again.

"It is a long way from Mull to Skye," his old kinsman answered dubiously. "You have little strength in your limbs. Wait here a while, my friend. You are always welcome in my household."

Rory shook his head.

"I want to go to Iona," he answered, in a weak voice. "If you give me leave, cousin? The Sacred Isle is now your own territory, I think?"

"It was," MacLean told him laughing a little ruefully. "But the House of Campbell has acquired it without a by your leave from me! Argyll gave me token payment, and turned my few clansmen out."

"He'll have paid you as little as your father gave the old monks at the monastery, I warrant, after the Dissolution," Rory whispered. "Do you think Argyll would give me leave to land there?"

"I don't suppose he will know or care," Duart answered. "There is nothing there now but ruins, and the ancient tombs. Why do you want to go there?"

"I don't know," MacLeod replied in the same uncertain voice. "But the name 'Iona' keeps sounding in my heart like a bell, continuously,"

Though MacLean tried to delay him, Rory persisted, until even before he could walk properly or even stand and dress himself without assistance, a horse litter was brought and a boat was prepared, and he was helped into it, to make the journey on which he was determined. Having sent messages both to Argyll and Dunvegan, and bade his host farewell, he set his face seaward, with an empty look, that Duart found strange and perturbing.

Only a few shepherds and fishermen dwelt now on the small island of Iona that had once maintained a great community of monks. The Abbey buildings were already falling down from disuse, and lack of maintenance against the winter snows and violent winds. Everything of value had been removed years ago, and the great church and cloistered walks were filled with sand and leaves and debris brought by the winter storms.

Rory had himself carried up to them, and climbing from the litter, stood leaning with an expressionless face against the great west door, which had come half off its hinges, and gaped wide. He looked in on the abandoned church – so much greater and more dignified and ancient than his grandfather's small edifice at Rodel – but like that small one, empty of all human life, and filled only with the sea sound from the sandy shore behind.

Young James went off to see the lodging in a shepherd's cottage which was all the hospitality he could get for his chief; and to unload foodstuffs, and warm bedding from the boat and see them taken up there. Since one of Rory's servants had been sent off home to Skye with letters, and the other back with a message to Argyll, no-one else save a deaf and dumb fellow of MacLean's remained with him on the Sacred Isle.

Having occupied the small turf-roofed cottage, he left Hotfoot to make what arrangements he might, and the dumb fellow to dig peat and carry water and stir the porridge pot in the mornings. And while they occupied themselves with the domestic tasks, he sat, empty-handed, by the peat fire or walked out, a few, slow steps, leaning on a shepherd's cromach, but never far from the door.

As the snows abated, his steps lengthened. He would go, by morning the little distance to Queen Margaret's Nunnery, and enter the wild, cloistered gardens, where little but weeds and sea thrift grew now that there were no women's hands to tend it. When he had rested a little while on the mossy seat in the pale sunlight, he would wander out along the foreshore, crunching on the wet green and brown pebbles and the white cowrie shells, and looking ever and again inland to the low green hill of Dun-I, where legend says St Bride of the Isles saw the Druids make the sacrificial fire one midsummer morning.

Sometimes he walked among the grass-grown graves of the kings and chiefs in the Reilig Odhrain – peering intently at the faint names engraved upon them; or stood gazing upwards at the great stone cross of St John outside the Abbey, with its Celtic interlaced design and its symbolic figures from the Christian mysteries: or at the other crosses that wind and storms had broken and that lay now by the wayside or in the turf, or half hidden under heather – lost relics of the early days when the Abbey community had held to the Celtic church and to Irish ways and Irish symbolism in their lives and worship.

James Hotfoot saw that his master was gaining strength, and his stamina was greater. But he could make out nothing of his thoughts, as he kept his solitary vigil by wayside cross, or empty church, or long abandoned culdee cell in the wild country inland from the Abbey.

After some weeks, a curragh came over from Fionnport in Mull to the small harbour, with letters from Castle Duart and from Dunvegan.

Young Hotfoot took them eagerly, glad to think that the long sojourn in this wild and empty place might now end, and Rory would set out for home. He found him where he was sitting, as he often did, on the great flat stone that the islanders called St Columba's Table. But though Rory broke the seals, he penned no answer.

That night, by cruisie light and the peat fire, Hotfoot looked into MacLeod's face and said with awkward diffidence:

"Sir, shall we not return home soon? The messenger says that the war is all ended, God be praised."

"I know it is ended," Rory answered.

"And sir, it is said a great feast is to be given at Dunvegan. It is said, by your orders, sir."

"Yes," Rory replied.

"And, further, that MacDonald of Clanranald is coming, to sign a pact of friendship with you, by arrangement with the Earl of Argyll and the Earl of Huntley."

"That is so," Rory said.

"Then, sir," the young man burst out, leaning forward into he firelight "shall we not start for home?"

"Not yet," MacLeod responded, staring into the red glow of the peats, and falling again into silent thought, his face looking sad and melancholy.

After a while Hotfoot spoke again:

"Are you still sick, then, MacLeod?"

"No, but I seem to be driven to a place where I can go no longer forward, neither can I go backward," Rory said in a despairing way. "So I must pause a while, and see if there is another way. Not forward and not backwards. But – in some manner – inwards into life. I do not know. I understand very little of the nature of life and man, and of God's purposes."

"Say you so?" the young man answered, but seemingly without understanding. "And is this why you remain alone, in this desolate place, without company and friends?"

"It is where I happen to find myself," MacLeod replied. "Here is no – music. And no fire. And nothing but silence, and emptiness, and snow, and the sea wind on the shore. And yet… The whole Isle is full of voices. What is required of me? What is required of the clan?"

In the morning, Rory bade MacLean's messenger take back the news that he was well and would come again to his island "with the coming of the seals, in the spring". But James Hotfoot added his own message, bidding all men at home pray most earnestly for MacLeod, for he was sick in the mind and very strange in manner.

Iain MacIain was the recipient of the verbal messages, which MacLean's men brought at length to Skye from Mull.

He was sitting at the table in the office room in the tower at Dunvegan, trying with furrowed brow to sort out unaided many matters that required the chief's own guidance and direction. He made the messenger repeat his words twice but could make out little save that "MacLeod dwelt with the seal people, and would come back in the spring, if the clan prayed for him."

"What do you say?" Iain asked a third time, seeking some sense behind the strange, improbable words. But the man shook his head stupidly, and could only repeat parrot-fashion what he had said before.

All the family looked grave and troubled when they heard this garbled version of what Rory and James Hotfoot had said.

At last Mairi rose from her chair and went to the casement window, and looked out along the loch, where the soft light of a spring morning touched the rocky shore and the green islands.

"Well," she said over her shoulder. "I think we shall not wait long for the seals to come – so let us take the fellow at his word, and pray that MacLeod may come soon."

"Indeed, indeed, I do pray, day and night," Lady Isabel sighed. "And our sons entreat the Lord that their father may be safe and well."

"Then let us all join prayers for him," Christiana cried. "Let us send for Father O'Colgan that he may direct our efforts."

In the sharp light wind of the April day, Hugh de Lérins took his lute out on to the battlements, and sitting there with one foot under him, began to sing and play softly a song of the troubadours, while the prayers went on indoors.

"Have they finished?" he asked when MacIain appeared at length and stood beside him. Iain nodded. After a moment:

"Hugh, do you recall how you once said MacLeod did not pray aright?" he asked.

"Yes," the minstrel answered. "I remember well. Perhaps this is now the time when that feeble chick the good minister is hatching will show itself in its great eagle strength."

"Then – for Jesu's sake, Hugh, pray also for MacLeod!"

"I do so in my fashion," the minstrel answered touching the lute strings, and turning to the sea. "But we can do little but think of him there on the Sacred Isle, and wait patiently for his return."

"What thoughts can be in his mind?" Iain muttered to himself, sitting beside de Lérins on the battlements, with his face also turned outwards into the sharp sea breeze. "What is he doing there? What questions does he ask himself?"

And suddenly, with a strange lurch of his heart, he remembered how the old Abbot at Rodel had talked of King Arthur of England, and of the question no knight ever asked. For lack of it, the Holy Grail departed from their midst, and King Pelleas was left suffering.

He turned the memory in his mind, but some inner meaning that seemed to tremble on the verge of his consciousness, eluded him. A wave of compassion towards Rory filled him. He looked at de Lérins and the minstrel's eyes met his own in silence. Then:

"Think of him with love," de Lérins said. "For love is a powerfully strong force, and the love of friends can help a man, I warrant. We all need love." He stretched out a hand, towards Iain, but he was looking in the other direction.

"I do," MacIain answered. "But there is so much we do not understand. I shall be very glad to see him home again, and under our own roof, here at Dunvegan."

Chapter Sixteen

RETURN TO DUNVEGAN

Late in the month, and as it happened, within a day or two of the morning when the first seals came swimming into Loch Dunvegan from the northern lands, to take up their summer quarters on the islets, Rory MacLeod returned home.

Though there had been no forewarning of his coming, some instinct in the clan had caused many a man to look from window or battlemented walk off and on through the preceding hours. And when at last MacLean's galley appeared, pennant flying, and a piper standing forward beginning to play him in, the word went throughout the castle and the precincts in the twinkling of an eye, and every look-out point was filled with women and children waving kerchiefs and men shouting their greeting.

Young Padruig MacCrimmon was at the sea gate with his pipes before it could be opened, and old Padruig Mor, his father, and the old, old grandfather Donald Mor, and a dozen students from Borreraig were all in the courtyard above the sea stairs with their bagpipes too, and the mild air of the late spring morning was soon filled with the great notes of "MacLeod's Homecoming". Rory was standing in the bows smiling, and saluting upwards to his wife and children who had hastened to a window overlooking the waterway.

To the relief of every man, he looked well recovered from his illness, composed, and clear-eyed as of old. But, strangely, with a less bitter set to his mouth than the clan had grown familiar with in the past year.

When he had disembarked, he greeted the captains and his kindred at the gates, and walked up the sea stairs at once to find Isabel and embrace the boys.

"Welcome, husband! And are you well again? May Colum Cille be thanked," his wife exclaimed, as he took her hands in his, kissed them and smiled into her face.

"Yes, blessed be that name St Columba of the Isle," he answered.

She looked at him in surprise, for the tone of his voice had seemed in some way strange. But then he smiled again, and took his youngest son in his arms and kissed the child's cheek. Carrying him, and holding his little daughter by the hand, he went on again with all his family, and greeted everyone by turn in the great hall.

When they had seen his face close to, Iain Maclain and Hugh de Lérins glanced at one another, and held each other's eye with a long look. Mairi, half-laughing said: "Well, it was well that we prayed the "seal people" that they send him home to us! He has gained somewhat by his visiting, don't you think?" She gave her swift smile, looking up at Iain; and because he knew her face so deeply and so well, he read much more than laughter in her warm eyes, and the soft curve of her mouth.

Late in the evening, Rory went out and stood above the little waterfall beside the tower that had been known since his childhood as "Rory's Nurse".

Moonlight slanting through the trees touched and dappled the water with silver and dark shadows, and the tranquil, familiar sound of its little, stepping fall warmed his heart with recognition of home.

Yet still, it seemed to him, half of his mind and heart dwelt in Iona, where the bones of his ancestors lay in the peaty earth. And the great crosses stood, arms outstretched, against the evening sky.

He stared downwards into the moving water, and seemed in imagination to be again in the ruined beehive cell on the hillside where St Columba had once prayed; and later his grandfather had made his solitary vow; and where he himself had gone one night at midnight all alone. He remembered, as though it were again upon him, the desolate emptiness of his mind and heart, the helplessness of his small will, against the great wills of the many living, moving forces, that he seemed to feel controlling the air, and the earth life, and the waters; and the complex deeds and confused activities of men.

He remembered how the sweat had stood upon his brow, and heard again the sound of his own breathing, each expiration like a groan of anguish and despair, uttered into the night.

And then, the slow and indeterminate turning, upon the darkened grass slopes of Dun-I. The long, dragging walk across the stony raised way called the Abbot's Causeway, which led down into the open forecourt of the Abbey church.

Fatigue of the body had filled him so that his shoulders ached, and his arms and hands felt heavy and his legs moved stiffly, for he was still weakened from illness.

Outside the great door with its one hinged side creaking and swinging in the wind, he had sunk down, as often in past days, on the stone step at the base of the great cross, and leaned his head back against it with closed eyes.

He saw now, that for all his efforts and his vigorous activity, the life of his clan and of his island and of all the Western Isles was still fraught with the killing violence of its own spirit, and headed swiftly downward to destruction. He felt no hope of any change. No hope of any help for those fiery Hebridean hearts, at the mercy of the winds of time. What is required of me? He had asked before, but there had been no answer. Now all his despairs had culminated in a total emptiness of hope or of desire.

Then suddenly, it seemed to him, the cold stone beneath his cheek had warmth in it. Through his bemused, uncomprehending brain, there ran the strange notion that the stone on which he leant his head was a living thing, with power pulsating in it, and a greater energy and steadiness, and purpose than any he had felt in his own hot blood and rapid run of thought.

He had raised himself, bewildered, and looking up, seen the great carved pillar standing above him against swift-moving clouds in moonlight; and the two arms running horizontally; and the huge circle that the ancients carved on the Celtic crosses, light-touched like a halo; or the great ring of eternity; or the circle of the sun.

He had looked up. And then as his fumbling thoughts took new and unfamiliar shapes, he turned his head and looked into that low doorway nearby that led into the cell-like chapel where it was said St Columba's bones once lay.

Although he had been often enough into the Abbey church, and the small church of St Oran, where the last Druidic rites had been performed when Christianity grafted new knowledge onto the old earth magic, he had never stooped his head through Colum Cille's small doorway till this hour.

He stumbled in, groping in the darkness, and because of its low ceiling and his own fatigue, went more by chance than by intention abruptly to his knees.

"And even now, I do not really know what happened there, or who visited me, or what it was about," he thought to himself, stooping over the waterfall back at Dunvegan. But I know that great strength and great arms upheld me for a while. And I, who was always alone, in all my life, saw suddenly that I was one with all of life on earth. And what I could not of my own strength and will, and for my own small purposes ever fashion or accomplish, could by another means and for a greater Will be done. And so I pray my own will may not separately exist, from this time onward, till I end my days, but I abide in that higher Will, that greater understanding. "But whether it was my saintly grandfather; or St Clement; or Colum Cille; or Jesus Christ Himself who stooped above me there," he thought, "I cannot tell."

*****

Though MacDonald and MacLeod both felt their pride affronted by the plans made by Huntley and Argyll on their behalf, they met as they were instructed, and feasted as well as they could, in a land bereft of goods, and set their hands to the bond of friendship drawn up by two notaries on their behalf.

Argyll, filled with the innocent self-importance of the young, had thought at first to come himself to Dunvegan, and bestow upon his underlings there the honour of his noble presence. But the affair of Neil MacLeod, together with Rory's sudden departure caused him to ponder longer on the advisability of pressing his authority too far, and he had stayed away.

He sent a gift of French wine, by sea, to the feasting. But at the same time, realising on second thoughts that the Islanders were not easy men to handle, he impressed anew upon the King that they were most strong and proud and stubborn, and not to be relied upon at all.

His young countenance, as he knelt before King James, assumed the tight and careful look of his forebears, and the haughty arrogance of his father was audible already in the prepared speech, which struck a note completely at variance with his impulsive boyishness when first he received the two MacLeods and learnt about conditions in the islands. Already he was learning to play his traditional role.

*****

Across the long table in the new dining room, that was to be taken into use at last, now that normal life was resumed in Skye, Rory and Donald Gorme clasped each others hands, and listened gravely to the wording of their Bond:

"The said parties, being certainly persuadit of their dread Soverane his Majestis clemencie and mercie towards them, and willing of their reformation and their living together in peace as His Hynesses gude modest and peaceable subjects, and considering the Godless and

214

unhappie turns done by each of them to other, which from heir hairtis each repentis, thairfor ilk ane of them freely remittis, dischargis, and forgives each of them the other for all murderis, slaughteris, hairdships, spulzis of goodis, and raising of fire committit by each of them against other..."

They took quill in hand and signed their names in silence.

"Well, now let us look to the future," Rory said, when the formalities were done. "Firstly it seems to me we should do best to begin to repair our homes and lands, and set our people to plant new crops, with assurance that they need not fear the raising of any man's hand against them at their task."

He looked into MacDonald's eyes for affirmation or reassurance, but could see little there save the dull look of fatigue that was the aftermath of war, and a sulky depression at the turn events had taken.

Duntulm Castle had been much damaged in the war, and the pleasaunces, once so well laid out and trim, had run to weeds and were filled with household rubbish. The whole place had by now an air of desolation and neglect, and in addition to the ravages of war, the continuing childlessness of the chief troubled men's hearts.

It was even said that Donald Gorme might put away his second wife soon, as he had done blind Margaret, and take another woman in marriage. But some, recalling how drear the place looked these days, and how strange, ghostly cries were heard about the walks and towers at night, declared Duntulm to be haunted, and thought MacDonald of Duntulm would never thrive beyond this time.

Looking at the depressed faces of the Clanranald stretched either side of his table, Rory thought that the only life among them lay in young Donald MacIain 'ic Sheamuis Eriskay, who had fought so boldly against him in North Uist. He, a farmer by nature, had a plan to breed the small black cattle of the isles, and take them over to the mainland in large numbers, and there sell them for good money. He was also growing the new vegetable the potato, which was said to be very good and to fill a man's stomach well.

"It is not goods for barter that we need now, so much as gold, to bring us up to the times!" he was saying to MacLeod of Gesto and his daughter who sat opposite. "I warrant it is in trade with the mainland that our future lies. We must not hold ourselves aloof, or feel shamed to trade with the lowlanders, for the time is gone when the Isles can support themselves without assistance."

"Yes, that is a right reasonable notion," Rory said to himself, nodding his head. And raising his voice he called:

"I have a mind to help you in that matter, Eriskay. Though we are old combatants in war, I dare say we can pull the same way together now in peace."

During the next months, as the islanders began to repair the ravages that the long period of warfare had brought, a change in the leadership of Skye began to be apparent.

Though neither MacLeod nor MacDonald had been victor in the long drawn-out campaign, and each side had suffered deeply, in the peace it became clear that MacDonald was in some manner inwardly defeated. His once great vigorous body sagged, his face became puffy with too much liquor and he was more morose than ever in his ways. Little was done to repair the castle of Duntulm, and lacking direction, the landsmen did nothing to improve the demesnes, but contented themselves with replanting their small patches of ground round their own cottages, and raising just enough food to keep starvation away.

Rory replanted vigorously – trees and crops alike, and turfed and rebuilt his houses and his clansmen's cottages through his lands in Skye and Harris and Glenelg, which he had at last wrested from Lord Lovat's grip.

He was up at dawn most days, and about his estates on horse or on foot, or crossing the lochs by boat on one affair or another, until dusk or later. Isabel, knowing how he drove himself, sleeping little and continually working, writing, seeing his people who came for his advice, dictating letters to MacIain in his office, pleaded with him to rest and take leisure and to play the pipes, as he had done of old in days of peace: or listen, of an evening, to the clarsach, the Highland harp, and the bards and de Lérins with his lute. But as though he worked against time, he went on without slackening his pace, and seemed to have the energy of a much younger man.

"There is much we must do during this next year," he said, when his wife protested. "The King is only withholding his hand, because he does not want to give too great a power to either of those two noblemen who hold sway over us. But he has not forgotten his "rebel subjects" as he calls us – of that I am sure. It needs only a new trouble to start up somewhere in the Western Isles, and he will have us in a tighter net. I was most fortunate to escape the Council, when young Neil was taken. When next the Royal Countenance is turned towards us, we will have nothing disorderly, nothing misplaced, but all the estates in good trim and our people law-abiding."

"Do you trust the King then, Father?" his son young Roderick of Talisker asked him. "Did he not imprison you, long ago? I thought we could not trust him."

"We can never judge the future," Rory replied. "But it is good sense and wisdom to put our house in order, don't you think?" He looked down on the thin, dark-eyed little face, so like his own in childhood and smiled.

MacIain'ic Sheamuis of Eriskay, finding Rory co-operative, while his own chief was indifferent, moved himself over to Bracadale, and began there to build up a great herd of cattle. The following year, with a bold self-confidence, he took them by land and sea on the long journey to the mainland, and sold them in the market at Glasgow without any difficulty, and came back cock-a-hoop that his plan was successful. Rory applauded his efforts and had him to dine at Dunvegan on his return.

One day, as Rory crossed the courtyard with his swift stride, and a preoccupied expression on his face, he heard the unfamiliar sound of his sister, Margaret, laughing, and turning his head, was surprised to see her being led along by Iain MacIain by the courtyard well.

Seeing the chief pause, Iain took the opportunity he had been seeking, and bringing Margaret forward, asked in diffident tone if MacLeod would permit that they two should marry.

"Why surely – if it is the desire of both of you?" Rory answered slowly, looking from one face to the other, with an expression of surprise.

"I have neither land nor property to offer your sister," Iain said, "but my heart is kind towards her."

"And you, Margaret?" Rory asked.

"Oh, Rory!" Margaret said, feeling again for Iain's hand and turning her happy face towards his, with eyes closed, as was her custom now. "How fortunate I am that such a man should want me, and with my deformity. Now all the black things of the past are gone, and I shall not think further of my early failures."

Rory gave a kind look to both of them and said they should have his blessing. It did not occur to him that MacIain might have been pressurised a little, and was, as always, doing what he felt to be his duty.

A few minutes later, as he turned on the steps, he looked down and saw Christiana in the courtyard below, with an arisaid over her head against the wind, and her skirt held up, and a bowl of soup in her hand, going swiftly down to the gate, to feed some poor cottager, or an ailing child, whose need had touched her maternal heart. Rory looked down and then back. Above him, Iain with Margaret on his arm, was looking downwards too, his eyes following Christiana's quick and light step. But in a moment, he turned away again, as though he too had learned to accept the inevitable in life and in his fellows, and no longer broke his heart for what was beyond his reach.

Iain and Margaret were married in the little church outside the castle walls, which the Reverend Allen O'Colgan administered according to the simple rites of the reformed church. The Highland hand-fasting she had gone through before, was no barrier to this true marriage.

Iain escorted her with gentle courtesy, using his own eyes for her, to give her pleasure in the day. And took her, after the feasting, to the chambers in the new wing of the castle that Rory had set aside for them.

"I fear I may be a clumsy lover," he told her diffidently, leaning above the bed that night. "For many years I had only one thought in my foolish head, and latterly I had never thought to marry. I never did more than kiss a woman's hand till you gave me your lips, a few weeks ago."

"Now I give you more than my lips, dear love, and that most joyously," she answered, reaching out from the darkness in which she lived to draw him into her arms. In this matter at least, she had more experience than he. "Ah, you are trembling like a boy."

"Alas, I am no boy," he told her. "But I will serve you truly as your husband should."

"What one thought was it you held in your head these many years, heartling?" she asked him later as she lay close-cradled in his arms. "Was it of Mairi, or of a monk's cell? Or the duties of the church?"

"Young men think foolish thoughts – of how they must give all, or give nothing at all," he answered slowly. And then, lest she should be disturbed at his evasiveness, he added: "I warrant I can serve God as a married man, don't you think so?"

"So will we serve Him together," she whispered, holding him.

After she had fallen asleep, Iain lay long with his eyes open staring at the grey square of the window, and hearing the slight rain beating against the pane. But at last he too slept.

Chapter Seventeen

THE ROYAL COMMISSIONERS

As Rory had foreseen, King James' interest in the Western Isles lapsed for a time while the matter of his accession to the throne of England was in the balance. Even up to the very hour of Queen Elizabeth's death, no Scotsman knew for sure whether the two kingdoms would be joined together under a Scottish King or not, and while such great matters were in the forefront of minds at Edinburgh, the lesser problems of the realm were almost forgotten.

Tidings trickled through slowly to Skye: of the great funeral of the English queen at Westminster: the many consultations between the peers of both realms; and at last, the news that the invitation had been sent to King James VI, who was nearest living claimant, to become also King James I of England. The slow triumphant journey from Edinburgh to London had begun.

"So the House of Stuart reigns at Westminster, and the Border is no more a frontier," Allen O'Colgan the minister, announced to his assembled congregation on the Sabbath Day. "May the good Lord so dispose of all barriers between His peoples that we live united in Him. God save King James, the First of England and Sixth of Scotland!"

"What do you think? Is it a good thing or a bad, Rory?" Christiana asked the Chief as the family strolled back along the loch side from the small church to the castle. "Shall we all be Anglicised now, and made to follow the customs of London Town?"

"It is a good thing for all men that there should be unity, where formerly was division," Rory answered confidently. He caught the skirt of his young daughter as she darted away and drew her back, protesting. "No, no, it is dinner time, sweetheart. You shall play after."

"Can man ever live in unity?" Isabel asked. "They have never done so for long in the Western Isles."

"But now we do," Ian Mor, the tall young lad who was Rory's heir and would succeed him, put in tranquilly. "I warrant there will be no more war when I am chief!"

MacLeod turned his head and looked into the calm, clear eyes in the face that was already higher up than his own. It seemed to him that if any man could keep the peace this lad would, for unlike Rory himself, his temper was rarely ruffled, and he had a kindly toleration towards all men.

He laid a hand on his eldest son's shoulder. Then glanced about him at the whole cavalcade of his family, who walked together, this little, peaceful distance from castle to church and back again each Sunday morning, along the water's edge, without fear, nowadays, of molestation by anyone.

His wife and the younger boys, Christiana and her two tall sons, young men already, and dignified of bearing, though they had no inheritance. Margaret and her husband, Iain, hand in hand. Mairi, her head shawl-covered, pausing to ask news of an old cottager who had been hurt in a fall. Hugh de Lérins, scuffling the stones under his feet like a schoolboy, and whistling a new tune beneath his breath. Alexander of Minginish, with Fiona MacAskill on his arm, and Padruig Mor MacCrimmon walking composedly beside them. And a number of the captains of the clan who dwelt inside or in the precincts of the castle, strung out along the road.

A sense of thankfulness and of achievement filled him, on this peaceful morning, with sunlight on the treetops, and the blue waters ruffled, and all his kindred safe about him.

"On such a day a man could die happy," he thought.

But almost at once, his face took on again its purposeful concentration as he pondered the immediate future. More and more now, he felt that time was short and there was much still to be done, though what its nature was he could not surely tell. Unlike Iain, he did not pray for guidance or for help on all occasions before he acted, but in all the time since he had returned from Iona, he had carried in him a sense of the closeness of things unseen, and a certainty that he lived voluntarily beneath a power beyond his own strength and understanding. His insight was deepening as his impatient determination lessened, and wisdom had begun to grow, where before had been only the keenness of his intellect.

In a few months, and before the year was out, a noisy dispute between Sir James MacDonald of Islay in the Southern Hebrides and his neighbouring chiefs over land in Jura and Islay, drew the King's attention back again to the islanders. From London there came almost at once an edict requiring all island clans to send their chief or his representative to meet Lord Ochiltree and the Bishop of the Isles, who

220

would together convey to them the orders of their sovereign as to their future behaviour.

"It is not my lord of Argyll, nor yet the Earl of Huntley this time?" Iain MacIain remarked when he had read the document aloud.

"No, this time the trap is baited somewhat differently," Alexander of Minginish responded with a wry smile. "No doubt His Majesty will appeal to all our consciences through the Bishop, and he shows how altruistic is this approach by sending as negotiator a nobleman who makes no claim upon our island properties."

"But it does not say where this meeting shall take place," Rory interrupted with a frown. "Are we to go to Jura then? So far South?"

"Why not ask them here to Skye, and have them at Dunvegan?" Mairi suggested in a lively voice. "It would be a friendly thing to do, and stand all of us in good stead with the king – since we must needs obey him."

"I don't know. I don't think it would be wise to draw attention to all we have accomplished here – lest there are covetous eyes among the parties who come," Rory said slowly. He thought for a space of time and then said:

"I will suggest the Isle of Iona as a meeting place."

MacLeod's suggestion was acceded to without demur. And thither the chiefs, with their leaders and right-hand men and heirs and deputies, repaired by sea, or overland from Mull, to hear their orders.

Already a thin coating of ice touched the light surf in the Sound of Mull, as the great galleys sailed in peacefully and moored in the shallow water off Iona's shores.

Flags flew from the ruined Abbey buildings, which had had their gaping doors and windows shuttered with wooden boards to keep out the cold. Carpets brought from Edinburgh had been laid on the stone floors, and arras had been hung, and great fires lit in the refectory and the dormitory and the Abbot's private chamber.

All about the island, officials in the King's uniform hustled and talked, turning out cottagers from their own beds to make room for Lord Ochiltree's retainers, and commandeering food and peats and firewood for the Abbey.

Rory's lips pursed in disapproval, and disappointment filled him because these busy, harassed men had taken hasty charge of Iona, and had not therefore allowed Iona to take a hold on their own hearts and minds. It did not augur well, he thought, for the days of conference. But he had learnt to hold his tongue, and did so now.

Bishop Andrew Knox was already installed in the Abbot's quarters, to which he felt assured of rightly occupancy, the more so as he was nominally president of the royal commissioners. He was glad to see the place had been made habitable with creature comforts – for in this wild and comfortless isle he had supposed he might suffer cold and other inconveniences. He stood before the great fire, running his hands up and down the fur-lined gown that he had, with foresight, acquired in Edinburgh before commencing this mission to his island Bishopric. But in spite of the blazing logs, the handsome furs, and the wine that he had been offered and readily consumed on arrival, he shivered still, and gazed morosely about him, as he waited for Lord Ochiltree to disembark from the man o' war called the *"Moon"* that the king had put at the commission's disposal. He felt little liking for this errand, for all his dealings with the islanders since they had been brought forcibly under the Episcopalian bishopric, after the old Roman Catholic Bishop of Dunkeld had been displaced, had served to convince him that the "wicked blood of the Isles" still flowed too strongly, for all his attempts to alter events in the Hebrides.

"If we are to be dispossessed of the old church, we'll be done with bishops altogether, and appoint our own presbyters from among ourselves," one of his constituent chiefs had told him, in response to his oft-repeated demand for payment of the church's dues.

"We would as soon look to our own spiritual affairs and make our own terms with the Lord," another had said brusquely. "Now the King has taken from us all our old heritage of worship, he must leave us to find our own way. We have no need of bishops now I say!"

Because of his growing unease, Bishop Knox had kept to the mainland these last few years, and had tried to excuse himself altogether from this business, by begging the king to substitute someone else as president of the commissioners, "since I fear my credit with the islands is gone of late." But the King had responded by bidding him anew meet the chiefs and "tame their wild blood", and he had seen no way to evade the repeated command.

Lord Ochiltree came in at length, briskly rubbing his ringed hands together and smiling with great amiability on everyone.

"Well, well, we have all your little flock most neatly drawn up for our inspection," he said gaily. "We will see the foremost of them – that is Sir Robert MacKenzie of Kintail and Sir James MacDonald of Islay and such as are recognised by His Majesty and acknowledged by him – say old MacLean from Duart in Mull, for example, and a few others. We will have them ashore to dine with us this evening, and fill their stomachs and look into their minds the while, and see what goes on in their shaggy heads, and what makes their hearts beat, eh?"

"As your lordship pleases," the Bishop answered glumly.

"No, no, it shall all be as my lord Bishop pleases. That is as it ought to be. That is how the King would wish it, eh?" Ochiltree said, glancing about him with jaunty satisfaction. "We will dine here in your chamber, shall we not, my lord Bishop? It is too cold in the great hall below, and we must sit there long enough I warrant in the morning when all your flock assembles there to hear us. But for this evening, just a pleasant, small assembly, hm? The elite, eh? Just such as may have a little brain that works, inside their scarred old heads!"

Rory MacLeod found himself included in the small dinner party, not by virtue of any title, or any credit he might hold with the King, for he had none. But because the official delegated by Ochiltree and the Bishop to invite "a few suitable parties" chose the leaders of the principal Island clans whose names happened to be familiar to him, and sent out word to them.

They seated themselves round the table that had been brought, with much of the other furnishings and hangings, from Castle Aros in Mull for the occasion.

Ochiltree's genial mood all but eclipsed the Bishop's uncertain and unwilling looks, and when roast venison had been consumed, and wine had flowed liberally, and a good crowdie cheese tasted, and all topped off with sugared apricots and dainties to fill any empty spaces in the guests' full stomachs, tongues began to wag freely enough in the congenial atmosphere.

"If the King feeds all his subjects so, I'd gladly serve nearer to his heart," said one to another.

"I grant you, I came most unwillingly to this place, seeing I have a dozen pressing duties at home, but in truth, I feel a deal more satisfied than I have done since the war," exclaimed another, patting his waistline appreciatively.

"It is well, gentlemen, that we are all in good and jovial mood, and merry friends too." Lord Ochiltree said. "For we shall know one another better when we all sit down below in the great hall with your fellows and your followers tomorrow. Eh? Now, let my lord Bishop hear how we are all faring and what we are doing to carry out His Majesty's instructions to improve conditions in the Western Isles. Sir Robert MacKenzie, now, has much to tell us of the Isle of Lewis, I know. And Sir James MacDonald, sir - you have settled matters in your own estates to the satisfaction of yourself and your good neighbours, I am sure!"

Disarmed by the commissioner's easy friendliness and apparent approval of all that they had done, or were doing, the chiefs on the whole talked freely and openly – both of their own affairs and of their neighbours who had not been invited to be present at the dining table.

Rory for the most part did not speak, contenting himself with turning a wine goblet about between his fingers and listening to what was being said so readily on all sides.

"And the Isle of Skye? How fares it with the great Isle of Skye?" Ochiltree enquired presently, looking from one to another. "We have heard much of the smaller isles. Who speaks for Skye?"

"Why, Rory Mor MacLeod of Dunvegan is here. He is almost overlord of Skye and Harris," someone said. Rory did not at once speak. Faces turned towards him, and he looked from one to another of them and answered evenly:

"I claim no overlordship, sirs. We are repairing our lands as best we can, and we are seeking to trade somewhat in cattle and goods with the people of the mainland. There is little of importance to tell my lord Bishop – save only that we are law-abiding, and we do progress."

"And that is very well said. And so may it be with all of us," Ochiltree beamed. "We are law-abiding, and we do progress. It is well reported and will please His Majesty."

The party disbanded cheerfully in the early hours, some of the chiefs to go back aboard their ships to sleep, others to the quarters that had been allotted them in the Abbey buildings. Old Hector MacLean took Rory by the arm as they passed through the chill and echoing cloisters in the half-darkness and said lightly:

"This matter will be quite simply and easily accomplished, don't you think so? These fellows will ask our names on further documents to bind us to the King, as they have warned us, but it will amount to nothing of any consequence."

"I am not sure, cousin," Rory answered doubtfully. "I don't like the expression in my Lord Ochiltree's eyes, for all his smiling, and I never felt much reliance on a man who rubs his hands together so repeatedly."

Early in the morning, while the frost was still on the short grasses and the air chill, the chiefs and their representatives and heirs and deputies began coming ashore in number from the galleys lying mist-shrouded in the Sound of Mull. Their cheerful voices echoed lightly across the water, amid the dip and splash of oars and soon the great refectory hall with its fires newly kindled and chairs and stools laid out in readiness, was full of their noisy and confident presence.

Rory had stayed with the cottager who had so amiably accommodated him on his previous visit, and he walked the familiar path down to the Abbey. The mist had begun to lift from the water, and a pale sun pierced the clouds, making a pleasant spectacle of the assembled ships, their hulls ghost-like and their masts and rigging delicate as wraiths, rising towards the clearing sky. The royal vessel, the *"Moon"* lay somewhat apart, a formidable-looking ship, fully armed as though for war, her cannons gleaming, her quietly disciplined crew much in evidence on morning duties, cleaning and swabbing her white decks. Rory looked at her as he strode along.

As soon as the morning's talk and discussions were under way, the result of the dinner party in the Abbot's chambers made itself felt. Those few chiefs who had been invited to it clearly felt themselves to be in a position of special privilege, following the intimate evening table talk. The majority, by contrast, felt obliged to argue, contradict and oppose at every turn the advice put forward in heavy tones by the Bishop, and elaborated smilingly by Lord Ochiltree.

By mid-morning, smiles were somewhat strained and hot tempers quivering on the edge of eruption, and the chiefs were noticeably divided among themselves on every matter – from the question of compulsory church tithes, to the control and marketing of crops, the harbouring of sorners and the regulations to restrict the use of firearms in the islands.

Watching their faces with his sharply smiling eyes, Ochiltree played off one against another, standing himself as friend to every man, seeming in deepest personal sympathy with each, against his neighbour.

At midday, they disbanded, all at sixes and sevens, and none sure of anything, save that the Bishop seemed to be just a pawn, and Ochiltree a man of wit and speedy thought, bent on a clear purpose on the King's behalf.

In the few hours of leisure, old quarrels were revived among the chiefs and their clansmen and retainers, reawakened by the irritability caused by the affairs of the morning. The commissioners, strolling with apparent unconcern about the cloisters and the half-ruined courtyards where the islanders sat or walked or stood in groups conversing heatedly, took the measure of their minds and reported back to Ochiltree and the Bishop in the early evening.

"It is still as fiery and quarrelsome a lot as ever drew sword in olden days, eh?" his Lordship said, nodding and smiling, when he had heard what his followers had to tell him of all they had overhead. "It is much as I thought last evening – a veneer of gentleness, and ruffian minds beneath. They will never live at peace and develop these isles for the profit of the State, unless their wings are clipped a good deal shorter than the General Band decrees. We will see them set their hands to something more binding to them, eh, my lord Bishop? I have already drafted out for you, new statutes and regulations in some detail, based on all the details of the island clans that we received from the Council in advance. We'll have them sign their bond, eh? Hm?"

"Yes, if you can persuade them, my lord," the bishop replied "when they have dined tonight."

When the islanders filed into the great refectory that evening they found a meal laid out for all, but on a less luxurious scale than the smaller party had consumed the night before. Their liquor, too, was somewhat severely rationed, "that your minds may be clear, gentlemen, for our parleys after we have satisfied our hunger", Lord Ochiltree remarked, still smiling. "And in deference also to our gracious Bishop," he added with a slight bow to the unresponsive president.

When all the food had been consumed, and the tables cleared, and the hum of conversation had died away somewhat, in anticipation of the evening's work, Bishop Knox rose ponderously to his feet, and in a voice both sonorous and doleful, as though he spoke of an impending doom, addressed the assembled company.

He spoke of the need of Christian brotherhood and love and trust and kindness between neighbours and near kindred – "for we are mindful that all of you are closely related, one to another, throughout these territories…of all men's duty to Our Lord.…Of the virtues of humility and submissiveness." And a great deal more in like vein, running on as long as a Sabbath sermon, until some of the chiefs dozed, heads on their chests, and others spoke in whispers among themselves, and a host more let their attention wander about the room and towards the serving hatch to the kitchen, whence the platters had been removed – perhaps for a later replenishing?

"Dear Jesu, he runs on like a widow-woman at a funeral," Donald Gorme muttered to MacKintosh of Dunachton, who sat next to him. "When will he lose his breath, and stop, and let us set our hands to this document they speak of, and get off to bed?"

When at length the Bishop resumed his seat and Ochiltree took his turn, all men were fidgeting and yawning. But he started off, regardless, smiling blandly, to recall the ancient history of the island territories, and praise their rich heritage of courage and of valour; of

226

encouragement of the arts of singing and playing of the harp and story-telling, "ever since the far off days of the Kingdom of Sodor and Man, when all of you southern islanders admitted fealty to the Norse monarch of the Isle of Man".

"Come, come, we know all this. When do we finish with the rind and get to the pith of it?" Hector MacLean muttered irritably to MacLeod.

But Lord Ochiltree was not to be hurried. His face, though amiable still, had upon it a somewhat different expression than in the preliminary discussions, and when he spoke of fealty and obedience and bondage to a monarch "and the willing submission of all man's private purpose for the furtherance of the will of their dread sovereign," his eyes were sharply attentive to his audience and his voice authoritative and strong.

Hearing the change of tone, first one and then another of the chiefs opened his eyes and turned his head, and looked and listened.

"...wherefore his Majesty, King James, requires of you certain assurances and somewhat of action also, in token of your goodwill and respect towards his most gracious Majesty..." Lord Ochiltree was saying. "We present to you, therefore, in our sovereign's name, and in the name of the Privy Council of the United Kingdom of England and Scotland, these Regulations for the chiefs of the Western Isles, embodied in a form henceforth to be known as "The Statutes of Iona."

He signed to a junior member of the commission to rise; the young man unrolled the lengthy parchment and began to read:

"All chiefs of the island clans shall be required to find security for the payment of his Majesty's rents...All chiefs and vassals shall most strictly observe all laws of the realm...All garrisoned houses shall be surrendered to the king..."

"What do you say? No, sir! Certainly not!" Sir James MacDonald exclaimed.

All the chiefs looked up sharply.

"They shall renounce the heritable jurisdiction and submit to sheriffs appointed by the crown..." the commissioner went on unheeding. "All galleys, save such as be used for conveyance to the mainland and between the islands of the crown rents, in kind, shall be burned..."

"No, no! Why should we burn our ships? It is monstrous to demand that!" young Islay cried and others joined in with angry negatives.

"...All children above the age of nine years shall be sent to school in the Lowlands, to learn the English tongue, and the use of the barbarous tongue of the Isles shall be discouraged…The use of all claymores, guns, and bows and arrows is prohibited…"

"God's truth, I'll sign no document like this," MacKinnon shouted wrathfully. "What do you say, fellows?"

"All chieftains shall present themselves in person annually before the Privy Council…No chief shall maintain more than one birlinn. No chief shall maintain in his household more that the statutory number of gentlemen permitted him, viz, in the Isle of Skye: Roderick, known as Rory Mor MacLeod of Dunvegan, six gentlemen. Donald MacDonald, known as Donald Gorme Mor of Duntulm, six gentlemen. Lachlan MacKinnon of Strath, three gentlemen…"

The confident, impersonal young voice ran on, enumerating and detailing one matter after the next until he came finally to even more intimate household matters: "There shall be no excessive drinking among the commons and the tenants, as heretofore led to barbarous acts and inhumanities. Henceforth the drinking of wine shall be restricted thus: MacLeod of Dunvegan and his household: four tuns of wine per annum…MacKinnon: one tun of wine per annum…MacLean…"

"By Our Lady, I'll not stand for this!" Dunachton roared, leaping to his feet. "What do you say, sirs?"

"Nor I. That last surpasses all!" another chief exclaimed bitterly. "We'll never lay our hands to such a bond –"

In a moment so much noise and disorderly talking and shouting started that no man could hear his neighbour clearly, let alone attend to the commissioner's voice, which petered out defeated.

Lord Ochiltree rose to his feet.

"Now, gentlemen, do not lose your dignity, and your wits as well," he said soothingly as soon as he could make himself heard. "These statutes are just a guidance to your good selves. Come, I am persuaded of you goodwill and your intelligence, eh? But I see we are much fatigued with too much talk. Let us adjourn until the morrow then."

The voices subsided grumblingly, to silence.

"We cannot meet tomorrow," someone said at length, "for it is the Sabbath."

"Ah, yes, indeed," Lord Ochiltree said cheerfully. "We shall have the pleasure and the edification of a sermon by our Lord Bishop, hm? And in token of our goodwill and mutual trust and understanding, we extend to all clan chiefs a cordial invitation to visit us aboard his Majesty's vessel, which lies close offshore. Let us attend our morning service there, together, and hear our Bishop, and then dine all together in amity and friendship aboard the ship."

The chiefs went out, in so sulky and depressed a state of mind, that for once they were all but wordless as they made their way to the sea shore and the curraghs drawn up to take them to the galleys.

"It is beyond all credence that such demands are made in the King's name," one said to another. "Our fathers would turn in their graves in the Reilig Odhrain, if they could hear it."

But the times had changed since their fathers' day. And though one or two spoke of drawing anchor and going home without more ado, or even of challenging the commissioners privately to fight with arms, none thought seriously that there was any choice for them but to stay and see the matter out.

The morning, therefore found the galleys still at anchor off the shore.

Rory had walked about during much of the night, turning his thoughts this way and that and so in the morning he slept late in the cottager's bed. He rose in haste at Iain's gentle touch, consumed a mouthful of porridge and an oatcake as he pulled his breeches on – for he had taken pains to dress formally for the conference. When he was dressed, he went out at once to walk to the small quay to the curragh that waited to convey him to the King's vessel for the service at the stated time.

Already he saw that most of the small boats that had lain alongside the quay during the night had pulled away, and few people were about. He did not want to give offence by arriving late, perhaps after the service had already started, and causing a commotion by having to scramble up the rope ladder on to the ship after everyone had fallen into silence, and prayers were being said. He glanced out towards the Sound, but there was no movement among the mist-shrouded vessels, and the *"Moon"* herself was barely visible at all, for she lay far enough off-shore to be almost hidden in the fog that lay across the open sea that morning.

"I have a good mind not to go at this late hour," he muttered to himself, hesitating on the stony path. "I am in no right mind to listen to another sermon. It would be no loss to anyone if I remained ashore, and said my own prayers in the Abbey here – for even though it is disused, it is for sure a holier place than an armed vessel commanded by the Bishop of the Isles."

He dawdled, almost stopping, then going on a step or two, and stopping finally by the wayside near the still new-looking tall cross that Hector MacLean had had erected a few years back to proclaim his overlordship of the island. Rory glanced at it, remembering again that strange night when he had sat at the foot of the other far, far older cross outside the door of St Columba's cell, in such a mood of anguish and despair.

Now there was in his mind, not despair, but the angry conflict of thought which comes when a man wishes to do well, and right, and justly by his fellows, and does not know how to act or what attitude to maintain.

He had spoken very little at the conferences, not, nowadays, from fear of speaking rashly and unwisely, but from a sense that if he held in reserve his own clear powers of brain, they might be of service to his fellow chiefs when Lord Ochiltree and the Bishop had fully displayed the hand they held, and what their powers were. To this end he had sorted and analysed in his mind all the matters of dispute, and considered arguments that might lead to modification of the proposed new statutes, whole not leading fruitlessly to their total and violent rejection. The armed vessel lying out there in the fog was token enough of the folly of any vigorous refusal – and his swift mind foresaw that in any such event, anarchy and lawlessness would run rife throughout the isles – and the eventual destruction of all the Hebridean clans by government troops would follow, as inevitably as the night follows the day.

"We must seek to compromise," he thought. "I will not go aboard, this morning. But-" He still stood, irresolute, by MacLean's cross. Then sighed, and moved on a few yards more, past the ruined nunnery wall, where a bantam cock that was scratching the frosty ground hopefully, squawked suddenly at his approach and ran off, neck extended in a fright. And slowly down the little slope to the place where his own man was standing, holding the curragh by the hempen painter, and watching his irresolute approach with a puzzled look.

"By Colum Cille, why am I so reluctant this morning?" he asked himself irritably. "In truth, it will do me no harm to go aboard, and I need cause no disturbance, for I can climb up softly. And no man yet died of a dull sermon!" Yet he still did not advance purposefully. Before he had time to think further, he found himself looking down into the boatman's face and saying, as calmly as though the words were the result of careful decision:

"I shall not go over, Tom. I have a mind to stay ashore. Go over to our galley and get your porridge."

The man touched his forelock respectfully, and climbed back into his little boat, and pulled away.

In a restless manner, Rory wandered about the precincts of the Abbey for an hour or more, entering one by one the tumbled-down small chapels – seven of them – that had at one time surrounded the great mother church.

Not far from St Columba's cell there stood still the broken stump of a tall round tower, like the watch towers of old Ireland, that marked the ancient Celtic settlements. Men said they were only watch towers built against the Norse invaders. But Rory's grandfather, Alasdair Crottach, who had studied the Druidic teachings, had believed that they were first built in pre-Christian times for other purposes. They had had wells at the bottom, and in the dark translucent waters of the wells, the heavens were reflected, and the great constellations of the stars, and the moon, even at mid-day. And the Druids knew and understood astronomy and astrology as two kindred sciences, the one linked with the other, Hugh de Lérins had told him. And they had understood an ancient geometry by which men could foretell and foresee the causes and the courses of events in the lives of men, and peoples, in this world.

Rory came to the brink of the ruined circle, and peered down into the rubble-filled interior, where once, he was sure, a clear spring of water had flowed, when Iona was the Isle of Druids, before Columba's time. There was no water now, but the stones in there were all shiny white with frost, and the morning sunlight made them glisten like quartz.

He was still looking down at them, almost absentmindedly, for many other thoughts were still upon the surface of his brain, when suddenly a shout and commotion behind him made him turn his head.

Upon the foreshore and by the quay, the several stragglers from the chiefs' parties were standing, gesticulating and running up and down in seeming agitation. He watched them, puzzled. Then, shading his eyes with his hand against the sunlight, he looked beyond them out to sea, and saw to his astonishment that the *"Moon"* had drawn up her anchor and was running up her sails, and moving out swiftly on the morning wind that was dispersing the fog, along the length of the Sound into the open sea.

Chapter Eighteen

THE VENTURE TO LONDON

After the chiefs had dispersed in anger and confusion the night before, Lord Ochiltree and Bishop Knox had sat side by side at the end of the empty table, drinking mulled wine to keep the cold out of their bones.

"Nothing that you can say will make these ruffians sign," the Bishop protested for the third or fourth time. "You don't seem to remember that I have dealt with them these five years as their bishop. They are stubborn as a pack of mules and as quick to show their teeth and claws as a mountain cat. You can't press them so far, my Lord."

"Can't I?" Ochiltree answered. "Since I have been instructed by His Majesty to tame their wild blood – tame it I will, or know some better reason why not, than any you give me, sir! Haven't we the backing of the Council and the King for all we do? I tell you, my lord Bishop – and with all respect, sir, to your own Christian charity – I will have them sign this bond even if I must hold them aboard the *"Moon"* until I force them to it."

"It was for that purpose you requested them to come aboard on the Sabbath morning, then!" the Bishop said. "I wondered you had not consulted me, before you told them I would preach a sermon."

"Now, don't take offence, good sir, I beg of you," Ochiltree replied with a mingling of amusement and exasperation in his voice. "In truth, you shall preach to them the livelong Sabbath day, if it pleases you! Or not a word at all to them, if you can't abide their mulish faces any further. But either way, when they are safe aboard, there shall they stay, in our joint custody, until they give their bond."

At first, no-one on the island could make out for sure what was happening out in the Sound. The fog was clearing patchily, and a host of smaller boats were milling and turning, out there round the King's great vessel. But as soon as her sails were fully up, and the wind took them, she outstripped all followers, and rounded the last point of land and went from sight.

Rory could not at first credit that the commissioners had been so bold as to kidnap all the island chiefs and bear them off, like so many chickens in a coop. But when the small boats came in, one and another told of having been pushed away from the vessel's side, where they had been holding on to ropes and halyards awaiting their masters' return. The King's sailors had slashed them off with scant courtesy, shouting that the commissioners had ordered them to sea forthwith, and they wanted no hangers-on.

"What about our chiefs?" the boatmen had called, in anger and astonishment and fright.

"What do you think? They are prisoners, of course. So pull away if you would not be hauled aboard and clapped in irons," the boatswain had roared back at them from the deck.

Rory stood on the quay among the shouting, frightened men, who clamoured about him, on the steps and on the jetty, or called up at him from the small, jostling curraghs in which they still sat, pushing against one another down below.

"What shall we do, MacLeod, sir?"

"Sir, there is none left aboard our galley save only us fellows…no gentlemen to direct us."

"Wait. Wait." He said to them, turning to one and then another. "Wait now, until nightfall and maybe well into the morrow, and take no action, lest the *"Moon"* returns, and no harm done. If not – then when tomorrow's tide runs high, go all aboard your own vessels and navigate towards your master's isles and territories. And there again, wait, wait. Let no man act till he has heard – from me."

"From you, sir," they repeated, nodding their heads, somewhat appeased and quietened.

"MacLeod will take charge and do his best for us," they told one another. "It is best to do what he says for we can't pursue that great ship with our galleys. We would never catch her."

"She would fire on us, if we did, and I didn't like the look of those cannons ranged along her deck," another said.

"No, there is nothing we can do, save only wait and see what tomorrow's day may bring."

"It is very fortunate MacLeod didn't go over with the rest of them," one of MacLean's men remarked as the small boats pulled away from the shore again. "We should have had no-one to turn to, to tell us what to do at all, if he had gone, for not another chief remains free, that I know of."

Iain, who had come down to the shore at the sound of the shouting, turned to Rory as soon as they were alone again and said:

"Truly, sir, I think the saints protect you! I swear this morning I came three times to waken you in good time for the service, and each time my hand was stayed – I don't know how – as I would have touched you. And but for your late rising -"

Rory said nothing, but he too thought about the strangeness of his tarrying and dawdling, filled with unwillingness to enter the curragh that would take him over to the *"Moon"*. And the final decision he had made to say his prayers alone, and not join his fellows on the ship.

But he could never bring himself to speak easily of the things he thought and believed in his heart, in the cheerful way that Iain MacIain spoke of them. He answered only: "It was very providential," and spoke of it no further, but turned at once to the matter of the kidnapping.

"If they are not freed and back with us by the morrow, what do you think I should do, Iain?" he asked. And then, as so often in his conversations, he answered his own question, with: "I will go to Argyll and plead. I will *demand* their freedom. No, I think I will go to the King. I can't believe His Majesty would permit such action in his name. It is against such very acts of violence and force that he is trying to legislate. Ochiltree has gone beyond his orders, I am sure. If the chiefs are held, and perhaps ill-treated, till they sign those monstrous bonds, his lordship will go cock-a-hoop to London and show where they have put their hands to it, and think his duty well done.

"But if they sign under duress, no sooner will he set them free than they will take up arms against the King, and blood will flow throughout the Isles again. I shall go to the King, Iain. We will put our case before him. He shall know what is done in these islands in his name."

"You will go to London, sir?" Iain asked doubtfully. "So long a journey into a foreign city? And with no papers that permit your presence there?"

"Needs must when the Devil drives," Rory answered with a sudden, swift smile. "We will send our birlinns home with the news, and take the *"Pride of Lochlann"* and trim our sails for the south.

On the following day, when the tide ran right, Rory's galley moved out of the Sound, to the accompaniment of ragged cheers and shouts of encouragement from the other vessels, and began her great journey through the unknown seas south of the Isle of Man. It had seemed clear to MacLeod that he would reach his destination quicker by this means. He would if his fortune held, run unimpeded with the wind, and could keep well outward from the shore to avoid being challenged. Besides, a ship was the easiest means of transport for his men, and cost them nothing, and all the trouble that would ensue if they went overland – the hiring of horses, the permits for Scotsmen to travel south, which were not freely given – would be avoided.

They made good speed, unmolested, putting in to shore only occasionally to bargain for food, and fill the water casks at some small fishing village, and pulling out again before there were questions asked. In a week, by use of oars and sail for as many hours of the twenty-four that the crew were able to keep awake and at their posts, they rounded St David's Head, and turned into the Estuary of the Severn.

In Bristol harbour, a fisherman off the Welsh coast told him, fishing vessels and trading ships of other lands lay always along the quay, and the presence of the Highlanders would cause no more than passing comment. They sailed in boldly, and Rory left young MacAskill and James Hotfoot in charge there, and went ashore with Iain. In the town he bargained for two horses, which he got for ten Scottish shillings, from a startled inn-keeper, who was so impressed by Rory's urgent and authoritative air and fierce expression, that he dared not point out that the beasts were worth double what he was given – and in good English money, too, not foreign coinage.

Rory and Iain rode with all speed eastward, through Trowbridge and Devizes, and by nightfall they were on the edge of the Wiltshire Downs. Thereafter they were able to avoid towns, and could seek wayside shelter wherever a hostelry would take them in, and give them food and lodging. They left behind their tired horses in return for fresh mounts, and rode on again each day at dawn, and came on the third day into the streets of London.

Rory had decided that he would go immediately to Whitehall and try by all means to get at once into the presence of the King.

Without waiting even to find lodgings, or to wash and rest and eat, Rory and Iain turned their weary beasts towards the Palace. But immediately they reached the great gates they met a setback, for their first enquiries and demands established that the King was not there, but had gone down with the Queen and the young Princes to Greenwich.

Rory reacted with characteristic impatience at this frustration of his plan.

"Must I then ride on another journey to seek an audience?" he asked.

"Yes, unless you will wait here, until it pleases His Majesty to return," the sentry at the gate answered, grinning. Rory was so mud-bespattered and begrimed that it appeared to the man a most unlikely thing that he would gain an audience of his Majesty at all. He thought the Scotsman looked a ruffianly fellow.

"When will he return?" Rory asked sharply.

"I don't know," the man shrugged. "He goes to Greenwich to hunt, and to enjoy himself away from affairs of state. He probably won't stay long. If you want to ask for an audience, you could send in your petition here, or take a chance in the press in the great Hall of Westminster, where anyone may go to him, from time to time, when he gives audiences there."

"No, no, I have no time to wait," Rory answered impatiently. "I will go to Greenwich. What is it, a hunting lodge?"

The man laughed.

"A palace."

"Nevertheless, if it is in the country, and away from affairs of state, I could probably get into his presence there with greater ease than here," Rory said reflectively.

In this he was proved right, for though at Whitehall or Westminster he must of necessity have taken his turn, and might even have been held off with excuses, and prevented from reaching the King at all, the more informal atmosphere at Greenwich made things easier. Hearing his authoritative voice, the guard gave way, and he found himself in the Palace courtyard, and then in the great entrance hall.

Here he was stopped, and asked to explain his business. But while he did so, looking all the time over the shoulder of the chamberlain who had waylaid him, he saw to his relief a familiar face among the few people moving about in an inner chamber. It was the little bow-legged figure of Robert Logan – a piper who had studied at Borreraig under old Donald MacCrimmon, and who had attended the King on certain ceremonial occasions. Rory leapt past the chamberlain and seized the startled piper by the arm, and in the Gaelic of the isles, demanded his urgent help.

"Why, sir, I would help you if I could," the little man answered with a dubious look. "But I have no authority to –"

"Well, well, tell me what you know of His Majesty's movements," Rory demanded, while the chamberlain hovered, not understanding the strange tongue. "Where does he hunt? Does he walk in the gardens? I tell you, Robert Logan, I must reach him this very day by whatever means."

"I think he is riding out across the park. If so, he will come into the stable yard, for he needs a block to mount and dismount. He will walk along the colonnaded walk to his own quarters -" Logan told him, before the chamberlain interceded once again.

Rory left his name and his urgent plea for audience, and his reason, and bowing, went off down the steps. He glanced to left and right, to see that he was unwatched. Then strode off in the direction Logan had indicated, and came at length to the place where he supposed the King would dismount, and the door by which he would enter his own quarters. Fearing that if he were seen he would be turned away – though in fact the King's person was not much guarded here – he concealed himself in a doorway, waiting.

Already the early winter afternoon was drawing into dusk. A bronze light, touched the water of the River Thames, where the grounds ran, gently sloping to the water's edge, and the last leaves floated damply from the great trees in the park to lie on the dank grasses.

Rory shivered. He realised suddenly how fatigued he was, and how hungry, and how ill-kempt and in need of clean garments. As the time passed, sleep began to creep over him, so that he was forced to move about to keep himself awake.

In the yard was a water pump that caught his eye, and seeing no-one about to stop him, he crossed to it, worked the handle and sluiced his face, and hands, and drank from it. The shock of the cold water drew him from his sleepy state back to full wakefulness, and sitting down on the mounting block nearby, in the half-dusk he started to consider what he would say to the king. Suddenly, the sound of horses' hooves moving at a steady trot on the soft grass of the park reached his ears. He raised his head and listened. In a moment, a groom appeared lantern in hand, holding it up and going out in readiness.

Rory leapt up and moved swiftly forward in the shadows of the wall, and saw the familiar though now much older figure of the King, with young Prince Henry and Prince Charles and two attendants, come up the last green ride, and clatter into the courtyard and prepare to dismount.

He nerved himself to move, but fear started up in him unexpectedly at sight of that chill countenance, seeming sharply lined and grave by the wavering lantern light. The memory of the prison room under the castle at Edinburgh rushed into his mind, and sweat started coldly on his palms and across his upper lip. He felt suddenly as though he were young again, in this august presence – a vigorous youth whose tongue outran his wits. He remembered kneeling humbly at these royal feel, with a bloodstained shirt, and a quaking heart, at Holyrood.

The King and the Princes left the horses, and began to turn away. The murmur of their voices, speaking amicably together, reached Rory's ears, as they approached the door. Drawing in his breath, he walked swiftly forward over the cobblestones, and cried:

"Your Grace! Your Majesty –" and knelt down before the King, as he turned a startled and unsmiling face.

With shouts of disapproval, the attendant noblemen moved to take hold of Rory, and the groom who had the horses by the bridle turned back with an inquisitive expression.

"Well, sir?" the King asked, as Rory was hauled up somewhat sharply to his feet.

"Your Majesty – Roderick MacLeod of Dunvegan and Harris in the Western Isles," Rory got out, shaking off the restraining hands. "Your humble servant, sir."

"Who do you say that you are?" the King asked, seeming puzzled. The lilting island voice struck on his ears with an old familiarity. He peered into MacLeod's exhausted face. "MacLeod, eh? A Scotsman – from the Hebrides? No, leave him free."

"An island chief, Your Majesty, and one who – "

"Are you not that man who insulted us at Holyrood by brawling with your kinsman in our presence years ago?" the King asked, remembering the name, and half recollecting the dark-eyed face before him.

"To my shame, sir," Rory answered instantly, and lowered his eyes.

There was a little silence. Then the King gave his sudden short laugh. "And who hid himself upon the roof of the palace among the jackdaws' nests?"

Rory looked up. "It was very uncomfortable, sir," he said, daring to let his face relax somewhat. "And foolish of me, but I was very young."

The King continued to look at him as though considering. He longed to blurt out his business, straight away, but something in the grave face quietly regarding him caused him to hesitate and wait. There was a look of pleasure and something of sorrow and gentleness in the eyes that had once seemed to Rory to have nothing in them but a cold intelligence. He realised suddenly that the King was homesick for his own country: for the minds of men of his own native stock, downright and simple and straight forward in their approach. For the easy manner of his households at Stirling and at Edinburgh. And for the soft burr of Scottish voices all about him.

He was almost a foreigner in England still, and retreated here to Greenwich to relax, the haughty manners and formalities of Whitehall thrown aside, the mask of sovereignty temporarily in abeyance.

"By Colum Cille, I am most fortunate," Rory thought. He straightened his back, and in a normal voice, looking into the King's eyes confidently, said:

"Sir, I have travelled a long and hard road these ten days, in urgent need to see my King."

"Have you, sir?" the King asked. "Yes you look almost as though you had come this moment out of the jackdaws' nest!" He smiled suddenly, "Well, let us see you in the light."

He walked to the doorway that was being held open for him, and entered, and Rory walked in behind him

"I remember your countenance – though the years have marked it somewhat," the King said when they were inside. "Well, sir, what would you ask your King, now you are come into our presence with so little ceremony? Indeed you do haunt the most strange places in our residences: the roof: the stable yard…"

"…And even the dungeons underneath," Rory finished with a bold look and a swift smile on his face.

"Were you not put to the horn, sir?" King James asked suddenly, his memory of MacLeod of Dunvegan and all his deeds and exploits growing clearer with each passing moment.

"I was, your Majesty."

"And your estate at Dunvegan declared forfeit for disobedience?"

"Yes."

"Where then do you live?"

Rory hesitated a perceptible moment before he answered. Then:

"At Dunvegan, sir," he said in the same characteristic voice, confident and without apology.

A complex expression of anger and amusement and pleasure at this honest answer came into the king's face. He stared at the Highlander and then said brusquely:

"Well, you need not tell me more. That is enough!" And gave his short laugh again. "You have ridden far and are wearied out? You shall refresh yourself and come and make your plea to us later – whatever it is." He gave a word of instruction to the gentlemen who attended him, and turned to go, but paused and looked again at Rory Mor.

"It pleases me to hear the voice of the Hebrides again," he said. "A wild part of our domains, and far from ceremony, where a man may breathe the clean air of the Scottish Highlands, and hear the great pipes playing strongly in the wind across the Western seas."

Rory was conducted to a guest chamber, and at his request Iain MacIain was brought in and the horses sent for feeding, watering and stabling. Food was set before them and they managed to borrow clean garments. When they had bathed themselves and rested, Rory awaited the King's summons, and at last was sent for to go down below.

There was no longer the atmosphere of complete informality that he had hoped for, but at least his Majesty had withdrawn himself from the great salon where he had spent the early evening with the Queen, and where a number of ladies and gentlemen still stood or moved about or talked in groups. He was in a pleasant panelled room beyond, reclining at ease by a great fireplace with no more than three or four attendants present.

Rory knelt and kissed his ringed hand, and saw again the momentary softening of his face as he was bidden to rise, and seat himself.

As soon as he received permission to speak, he began to talk, in a voice as calm and quiet as he could make it, of the reason for his journey down to London. Of all the happenings at Iona: The terms of the proposed statues and regulations for the island chiefs. The chiefs' rejection of them. And the removal of them all on the royal vessel.

"And now I don't know where they are" he ended unhappily. "But I do know it is a very dangerous thing to restrain my fellows forcefully, sir, and I dread what will come of it."

"Do you say then that you should all have again your ancient sovereign rights?" King James enquired.

"No, sir. That time is gone," Rory responded immediately. "No, but neither can we be held in bondage like slaves. There must be a middle course."

"We will ponder on it," the King said presently. "And for the present, we will find out where the chiefs are held. We will send word to Whitehall, to enquire – and if necessary we shall send to Edinburgh for news."

The following day, Rory waited impatiently to be sent for by the King again, but no word came to him. He dined, and supped, and sat alone with Iain. But the next morning, he was again sent for, and the King, after greeting him in cheerful manner, told him that the message to Edinburgh had been forestalled by the arrival the previous night of news, direct from the commissioners.

"They have your fellow chiefs at Stirling, and propose to keep them there in safety for the time, until they reach agreement on the new regulations proposed to them."

"Why, sir, that means by force – much as I said to your Majesty," Rory protested. "They will never sign, of their free wills!"

"Will they not?" the King asked. "But one of them has done so already by all accounts, for I read here, among sundry other things, that Donald Gorme MacDonald of Duntulm in Skye was put off at Blackness Castle, having declared his willingness to keep the bond, and after signing, he has been released."

Rory said nothing. He foresaw that Donald Gorme would not hold himself bound by what had been extracted from him under duress, any more than he had held himself honour-bound to pay taxes and fulfill other obligations after the King had held him at Edinburgh long ago.

He had in mind to say: "He will spit in their faces, afterwards, and hold your Majesty in contempt for it," but he thought better of it, and held his tongue. Instead he said with great earnestness:

"I do beseech you, Sir, with all my heart, to have those gentlemen released and set on their way home."

Once again, as on the previous occasion on which they had talked, the King replied:

"We will ponder on it." And in a few minutes signalled that Rory should leave.

A few days later, he was called across the gardens, where he had been walking idly under the trees, conversing with MacIain, and given a horse, and bade to get up and ride with the King for an hour in the woods.

He went eagerly, and drew his mount in among the little group of riders that pressed about His Majesty, and came up close beside him.

The King raised a welcoming hand, and as they drew a little ahead, out of earshot of others, he asked:

"Which of these statues of Iona trouble you most deeply, MacLeod?"

"Your Grace," Rory said, thinking quickly, "Perhaps above all the one that says the use of the island tongue shall be forbidden, and our children at nine years sent all to be schooled on the mainland, and taught the English tongue instead."

The King nodded gravely.

"And yet," he said, "it is in my mind that that ancient language, which you claim your own, by its very incomprehensibility to us, sets you all apart and makes you feel you are not of the realm of Scotland and of England."

"It is our heritage, sir, and a proud one," Rory answered with dignity. "As the Norsemen and the Celts are mingled in our blood, so are the old tongues mingled in the island Gaelic. It is our birthright. Didn't your Majesty's great-grandsire, King James IV, speak the island tongue himself? In the Hebrides the people tell one another this in song and fable still, with pride and pleasure. But his sons never learned it, more's the pity."

"Well, and if we should say it were not forbidden to use your native tongue, but only that your children should learn English also, would that ease the matter?" the King asked.

"Very greatly so, your Majesty," Rory responded warmly.

"We will have the children of your families schooled some little while at Edinburgh or Glasgow, so that they learn something of the Kingdom, and their knowledge is not bounded by the Hebridean Seas," the King went on. "Is this not wise in us?"

"Yes – if there is more persuasion and less compulsion in the letter of it," Rory admitted, somewhat placated.

"And of the other clauses: What troubles you most deeply?"

"Sir, we felt most outraged and affronted by your Majesty's commissioners when they sought to interfere in our domestic matters," Rory replied quickly. "For example, when they sought to tell us how much – how little – liquor ought to be consumed by us at home -."

The King gave his short, shouting laugh, and looking Rory smilingly in the eye. As they jogged on side by side beneath the trees, he said:

"Is that restriction not then needed? I fancy we have heard that fellow Robert Logan who pipes for us, sing a merry song thes bard wrote after a feast at Dunvegan. It goes, if I remember, somewhat thus: He threw back his head, and in a thin treble voice, chanted:

> *"At Dunvegan, twenty times a day were we drunken,*
> *And I warrant that Himself was no less drunk than we!"*

"That was written in my father's time," Rory told him somewhat crossly, and with a momentarily sulky look. "And at a feasting they drink heartily in any man's house, I suppose."

"We think it well you should be restricted, at least on parchment, in these matters," the King said after a moment.

"If it is only on parchment it does not matter," Rory said unwillingly. "But…"

"Well, don't make a great issue of this matter, MacLeod. Who knows what a man drinks at home?" King James asked with a twinkle in his eye. Then, with a grave face again: "So, so. What else displeases you?" he asked.

"Sir," Rory swallowed, and drew in breath to say what was in his private thoughts by far the greatest and most dreadful of all these statutes. "Sir, it is required that we burn our galleys, keeping no vessels, save one vessel for conveyance of the rents in kind. Sir, I would implore you, for all the people of the Hebrides, that our ships be not taken from us."

In his anxiety to reach the King's heart in this matter above all, he turned in his saddle, and inadvertently drew rein, so that his horse stood still at once, with its head turned towards the King's own mount. The King brought his own beast to a stop and turned so that they looked into one another's faces as they sat.

"Is this then the pith of all your bitterness?" he asked. "The disbanding of your fleet?"

To his own surprise Rory felt tears start up in him so that his throat contracted as he muttered:

"Yes."

"Why? You will not lack transport between the islands, with one birlinn each to carry you."

"It is not that! It is not just that!" he cried, and looking up, eyes smarting uncontrollably, he said:

"The ships are our pride and joy, and the sign of our noble ancestry. We are by blood sea-farers, and adventurous and strong. In the running up of the sails in the morning – in the creaking of the timbers as the tide takes them, in the movement of our lovely ships upon our seas between our island territories – in that we live and breathe and have our whole existence. In the rushing waters under the bows, and the rushing wind in our plaids, is all the song and music and life-blood of the Hebrides. My Liege, our hearts are in our ships. Do not destroy our hearts."

The King sat still, looking into Rory's face, while pale winter sunlight through the boughs touched their hands and the shining flanks of the horses, who stood placidly unmoving.

"Ah," he said at last, on a long, slow sigh, and nodded his head as though in acknowledgement. "Now we are reaching the heart of *all* these matters."

He looked long into the dark, lined face, and then at length, slowly withdrew his eyes and gathered up the reins, and touched his heels into his horse's sides, and rode ahead.

Seeing that the interview was ended, Rory let his own mount hang back and tagged along behind, looking dispiritedly at the royal back, now far ahead, in other company. But after all, the matter was not ended, for as they turned again, and rode across the park and drew towards the courtyard, he found himself again beside his King and heard him say, as though the conversation between them had never ceased:

"And yet, sir, for all this pretty picture that you paint, we think the island fleets are a direct threat to peace in the Hebrides, for they are used entirely in the service of your quarrelsome natures, for inter-island warfare. And in addition, the existence of these great private fleets constitutes danger to our shipping, and to the foreigners who fish round our shores; and threatens, even, our own sovereignty on the Western Seas."

"No, sir, your Majesty's vessels outstrip ours by far," Rory protested. But his just mind recognised the truth of the King's argument, none-the-less.

"Therefore, these fleets must go, MacLeod," the King said, but in a courteous voice in which Rory heard both sympathy and regret. "But you shall have left each and every one of you chiefs, a vessel great enough to bear you on your peaceful occasions. That we assure you, as our personal bond."

On the following day the King was to return to Whitehall. He sent for Rory just before he went, and told him that the chiefs were to be released and set on their way home. Then, he went swiftly through all the other statutes, and heard his views on them, and asked if MacLeod could speak with authority for the chiefs, and whether they would abide by him and be led by him.

"I believe so," he answered. "There is no lawful leader since the Lordship of the Isles was ended, but men do look somewhat to me, I think."

"You shall pass freely between Edinburgh and London, and mediate for them with us and for us with them," the King said. "We will give you our authority. But prepare them to be summoned again to have new statutes read to them."

When he had backed from the royal presence, a chamberlain came after him along the corridor and told him that the King bade him receive a purse of gold to set him on his way back to Bristol, where the *"Pride of Lochlann"* still lay waiting for him. And to buy what tokens he wished of his visit to London.

He took the purse and went away. In his chamber, a mood of conflicting emotions filled him, and he stood by the window looking out towards the river, considering all that had taken place in the past days, and to what extent he had influenced the fate of the Hebrides.

Suddenly, hurrying feet, and a knock on the door, caused him to turn, and he learned the King would have him go back yet again.

As though conflicting thoughts disturbed him also, King James could not entirely let the Hebridean go, for in that sturdy, fearless face, the lilting island voice, and the clear eyes that looked boldly and with dignity into his own, he was reminded of all that was best in his own ancestry, and saw all that he missed and hungered for of home. In a few hours, the ceremonies and elaborate courtesies of Whitehall and Westminster would enfold and grip him fast, and English voices that insisted on attention, would drive away the memory of Rory Mor, or make him see this interlude in a different light. But for the moment, sentiment had him in its gentle hold.

He rose slowly to his feet, as Rory entered, and asked for a ceremonial sword to be brought to him.

"You shall not go unrecompensed for all your efforts, MacLeod," he said, and bidding him kneel, dubbed him Sir Roderick MacLeod of Dunvegan and Harris, in the Western Isles.

Chapter Nineteen

THE KING'S BOUNTY

After his return to Whitehall the King kept his promise by sending word to the Privy Council in Edinburgh that Sir Rory MacLeod should henceforth pass between Scotland and England "without let or hindrance" whenever he would, and that all his former crimes were to be considered pardoned.

At the same time, having pondered on the words they had exchanged as they rode across the parkland at Greenwich that winter afternoon, and recalled how little humility there had been in the islander's bearing towards his royal self, he wrote to Argyll, a rambling unclear letter, designed to draw the young Earl's attention to MacLeod as a man of stature and strength, but neither bidding him trust him, nor distrust him. After explaining that he had honoured him with the order of Knighthood, he added that he had done so, so that "being allured by our good usage, he may in time coming be so much the more allured to manifest his good-will to our service."

His Majesty sighed as he took quill in hand to put his signature on this document that he had just dictated. He no longer felt sure that so bold a man as MacLeod could be trusted out of his sight, and he realised how far he had been moved by sentiment towards the Scots because of his ineffectiveness in many of his dealings with the English. He signed the letter and saw it rolled and sealed and sent away.

Rory and Iain left Greenwich shortly after King James departed, having now nothing further to detain them.

By turns, Rory talked merrily of their homecoming, and of the gifts they would buy with the King's bounty, and take home as proof of the success of their mission, and then sat astride his horse with head sunk almost on his chest, and did not answer a word to all Iain's talk. It was clear to him now that the Statutes of Iona would, sooner or later, be imposed, if not by persuasion, then by force on all the island territories. He could pride himself only that their harshness had been somewhat lessened as the result of his intervention with the King.

246

However, when they came into the streets of London, the more cheerful side of his mind was uppermost. He sent Iain to find lodgings for them for the night, and set out himself on a shopping expedition such as any woman might envy, with a purse full of gold tucked in his shirt, and a host of his kindred in mind to buy presents for. A length of silk and a silver-headed staff for Mairi, a set of silver dishes and a box of ribbons for Isabel, gloves of French kid for Hugh de Lérins, pretty trinkets for Christiana and Margaret, marbles of shining glass, a great case of sweetmeats for all the family, a case of French brandy for Alexander, a prie dieu for Iain himself and so many other things besides accumulated as the day wore on that he had to hire some lads to carry them all.

Iain met him by the steps of old St Paul's church and stared open-mouthed at the sight of the little procession plodding dutifully behind his horse.

"Well don't be so aghast yet, for this is not all," Rory said grinning, as they all trooped on together along the street to the lodging house. "I had a mind to buy something as a gift to myself, for all the pains I have taken on my fellows' behalf. Don't you think they would wish me to be somewhat recompensed?"

"Doubtless, sir, but…" Iain began, knowing by the look on Rory's face that he had been led away by impulse, as still happened on and off in spite of his advancing years.

"Well, here comes my own gift to myself," Rory said, as a rumbling sound of wheels and voices and laughter was borne down the narrow street between the overhanging houses.

"What is it, in St Clement's name?" Iain asked, gaping at the great rattling swaying thing that was approaching, surrounded by urchins dancing and shrieking with glee. "A bedstead? A great cupboard? A clothes chest?"

"No, it is a sideboard for the new dining hall," Rory answered grinning half-shamefacedly. "It is well-carved and exquisitely fashioned – our island carpenters shall come and see it. They will learn more of the trade of wood-carving, and it will surely be to their advantage, for in the old days we had most skilled carvers in stone, and why should we not encourage a new trade, now when the trees grow big enough?"

"But, sir," Iain protested, "how in the name of all the saints are we to carry so great a thing to Bristol?"

"We shall hire a wagon," Rory said airily, "or carry it like a wounded man in a horse litter. We will get it there some way."

After dinner, Iain went distractedly about the neighbourhood, seeking transport for all the goods and at last succeeded in hiring a horse and cart. He paid for it with what little Rory could spare from his fast emptying purse, and left instructions for an old man to bring it round at daybreak to set out ahead of them on the road, for the pace would be slow.

When he returned with news of his arrangement, Rory looked at him somewhat sheepishly.

"I suppose I am a foolish fellow at times," he said. "But it is so like the one the King had in his dining room at Greenwich, and I took a great liking to the furniture at Greenwich."

Iain laughed. Still behind the face of the stern and purposeful chief, lurked the boy who had romped in the woods at Dunvegan, seeking cob nuts or cuckoos eggs, or run barefoot along the shore to see a curlew's nest among the stones, or the first seals thrusting their sleek heads through the ruffled waters on a spring morning. They looked at one another with affection, and no more was said.

Rory had been troubled in his mind about the crew of his galley, left with little food and no money to fend for themselves at Bristol. In his haste to reach the King, he had taken MacAskill's word that they would manage alright to get employment about the docks and "earn their porridge thus", but later he had feared they would find no employment, being foreigners, and would be in dire straits before he could return. He was thankful to discover that instead, his tartan-clad clansmen had become such general favourites with their willing hands, their cheerful voices, and the playing of the Highland pipes, that they had lived off the fat of the land, and stocked the galley up against the homeward journey.

They greeted their chief with so shrill and merry a piping, and loaded his great sideboard and all his other goods with so good a will and so much laughter and singing that all work stopped in the docks while all who were employed or traded there stood gaping and grinning with astonishment and amusement. They set to sea at last low in the water and with little room to spare, but with pipes playing and joyous shouting, and cries of farewell and "good voyaging" from all who lined the quay and the riverside. Up ran the great speckled sail and everyone aboard took the oars while Rory turned his face with tranquil, happy looks, towards the waves of the Western Sea.

*****

At home there was joyous excitement and many cries of delight at the unexpected gifts bestowed on everyone.

Iain went to his chamber, and stripped off his soiled city clothes. He had his arms above his head, pulling on the old lay brother's robe from Rodel that he still donned for comfort though it was long worn out, when his door burst open without ceremony and Hugh de Lérins rushed in. He cried: "You are back at last! I thank the saints you are home, Iain! I thought you would never return again safely - -"

Iain had thought of Hugh constantly in London, missing their daily companionship and longing to point out interesting buildings, enter old churches, or make comments that Rory would not have acknowledged, so deeply was he involved in his own affairs. He missed the familiar friendship, with its barely acknowledged emotional undertones of understanding and mutual affection.

Quite unexpectedly, Hugh flung his arms round Iain's naked body. To his own astonishment, Iain found himself clutching the slight, vibrant figure in a passionate hold, realising in a flood of suddenly released emotion, how dear the French minstrel had become to him.

Contrary to their previous behaviour towards one another, they fell to the bed in a wild embrace, clutching and entwined, caressing one another with intense passion. Such excitement had never been aroused by Margaret, his gentle wife, and it was quite beyond Iain's previous experience. As Margaret had, however, guided and led him on their wedding night, so Hugh led him now, with the obvious experience born of previous relationships with other men. Iain, completely at the mercy of the situation, had no control or boundary of constraint.

Downstairs, Rory called for de Lérins, to give him his gift and hear him sing, as the harps and viols were brought out and everyone ate and drank and talked with gusto. He was not to be seen and a few clansmen ran out cheerfully, calling 'Lay Rann!' for they could never pronounce his French name. In a corner, old Kenneth, blind and sleepy, raised his head when they shook him and answered:

"He lies with a man, as was always his wont."

They stopped and stared at him. There was no tradition in the isles, save a man with a maid, a hand fasting and a man and woman wedded and childbearing. Any who had other inclinations, would find themselves essential loners, usually partnerless or outcasts, whose lives could easily be forfeit if they offended.

The men's tempers rose, and they began to say that they had never liked the foreigner anyway. He was not one of them. Did he not dress like a popinjay? Had he not been seen to fondle a servant lad once? He comes too near and breathes over us, and touches us. Did he not once touch one of them …….It is like Sodom and Gomorrah they cried one to another, having learned of the Old Testament from the priests. A sodomite. They ran on roaring: "Lay Rann! You sodomite! Where are you?"

Iain and Hugh were jerked out of their self-absorption by the clamour, raised themselves and stared at one another with fear on their faces. Iain leapt up and bolted his door, which was so often bolted against them when he was at prayer that they thought nothing of it when it did not open, and ran on shouting.

They flung on their clothes and waited a while, trembling. When all was quiet, Iain led the way down a back staircase and through to the sea stairs. By good luck there was no cockman on duty. They hastened round the castle. Iain caught one of the unshod ponies that grazed nearby, Hugh took the rope halter since they dared not delay to fetch saddle and bridle, and leapt up lightly on to the bare back.

Leaning down, he caught Iain's tall form in a grip, cradled his head close and kissed him. He glanced back at the castle, "I never touched the Flag" he said with seeming irrelevance. Then he urged the pony away through the woods and towards the uplands. If the beast did not fall in the half dark, he would be well away by morning, and would pay a fisherman somewhere to take him across to the mainland. Clearly it would never be safe for him to come to Dunvegan again. His years there were finished.

Alone, Iain turned into the woods and came quickly to a tall waterfall that tumbled in to a narrow ravine behind the castle where he would sit sometimes on warm days, reading or pondering. He was still trembling violently, shaking and crying. Suddenly he flung off his robe, plunged in to the icy waters and began to wash himself vigorously. At the same time sobs rose in him, and drowned by the sound of the waterfall, he wept aloud as he had not done since he was a little boy whose mother and siblings had been killed and his home taken away.

"Hugh! My dear, oh my dear…..Oh Hugh!"

Eventually he stood still and quieter, then clambered out, put on his robe and returned to his chamber. There he knelt at the new prie dieu weeping and begging God's forgiveness for what he had always been taught was a mortal sin. He wished there were a priest-confessor to go to, and tell of it, and receive a heavy penance. But the new church had abolished all such aids and comforts, and the thought of visiting the Minister at Duirinish was not an idea worth entertaining at all. He knelt long into the night, his tears trickling between his fingers as he called alternately upon de Lérins and the Lord.

The hue and cry over de Lérins disappearance soon died down, for many people came and went at Dunvegan. Two Irish fiddlers had arrived, and pleased the clansmen far more than the Frankish minstrel. Only Rory, looking at Iain's strained and abstracted face, wondered. But he asked no questions.

Iain had always spent more time on his knees than in his wife's bed, but had visited her chamber once or twice a week. Now, though there was no conscious moment of decision, he resumed the celibate life he had lived for many years. Though kind and attentive by day to Blind Margaret, she lay alone at night, believing humbly that she was no longer worthy of her dear husband's attentions.

Chapter Twenty

THE FIRE AND THE MUSIC

A little before dawn on a spring morning, Sir Rory Mor awakened in the half darkness of his bedroom in the Fairy Tower. He had slept deeply with the untroubled dreamlessness of age, for nowadays he no longer fretted away the hours of darkness in troubled thought.

Yet, he was no sooner fully awake than his mind and his heart stirred in sad anticipation of the hours that lay ahead; for this was no ordinary morning and all the resources that lay in his almost worn-out frame would be needed for the unwelcome duty he needs must undertake.

He lay still in his bed, his grey and bearded head turned towards the casement, which he had left open, and straining his ears, could just hear still the faint splashing of the small waterfall, over the rocks outside, in the damp greyness of the dawn.

"I don't hear it so loud as it used to sound to me," he thought, and sighed, for he was growing deaf, and stiff in his limbs, and no longer so clear-sighted as of old. But his mind was clear still, and his memory long, and well-stocked with the experience and the knowledge that the years had brought him. He sighed and smiled a little, remembering how the old woman who had had the care of him in childhood had called the little fall "Rory's Nurse", because he would always turn his head and listen to it when he was troubled or dissatisfied, as children are sometimes, without seeming to have reason for it. And its soft murmur would soothe him into quietude. The window was unglazed in those days, and only stuffed with a bale of straw in extreme cold, he remembered.

It was all so long ago, he thought, the days of the old nurse's ministrations in this room. When alone, he always preferred it to the new larger chambers. In his mind, he heard again the soft whirr of her spinning wheel beside the fire; the lively chatter of the children down below; he himself and his brother William seated by the chess board; and the echo of Mairi's voice singing the Dunvegan Lullaby to her infant charges.

*"Our clan galley sail
To thy dreamland…"*

"Ah, I am growing foolish and soft in my old age," he thought to himself, stirring against the pillow. He pulled himself upright in the bed, and sat there in his pleated linen shirt, shivering a little in the cold, trying to master the mood of melancholy that had descended on him with his first awakening. For this was the day, long postponed, long held at bay by argument and counter-argument on one pretext or another, when, in accordance with the ruling of the Statutes of Iona, the island fleets were to be burned and destroyed, in the presence of the King's commissioners.

Already out in the loch many galleys and birlinns were assembled, lying huddled close one against another, like sheep in a pen – their masts stripped, their rigging gone, their holds empty of equipment and provisions, so that they were just hollow shells, knocking and swaying against each other gently on the full tide. Silent and powerless, roped one to the next, they awaited without defences, the coming of the full day.

So that the commissioners might see at least some token that the order was being carried out in earnestness, each chief had been required to send his principal boats and present them for the burning. They had come to Dunvegan because for many years now Rory had been the acknowledged leader of the chiefs.

When they had been stripped, Rory's own men had gone with straw and bracken and brushwood and piled it in readiness in the foremost of the Dunvegan boats, so that it could be fired easily.

"But grandfather, it will surely be only a *token* burning, won't it" young Roderick, the son of Rory's heir, had asked at supper the previous night, when the many chiefs who had been sent for were silently eating their fill, with little wish for talk or laughter. The only music that night was MacCrimmon out of doors playing a lament on his old, speckled pipes.

"Master MacSweyn said it was only to satisfy the Royal commissioners that we have brought so many vessels together," the boy went on, too anxious to remember the need for discretion in his speech. "He said only some will be burned, for the officers to see we mean well by the King's command."

"All who have come here have come in good faith," Sir Rory Mor answered quietly, laying his hand on his grandson's shoulder.

Remembering his words, and the authoritative way in which he had spoken them, looking into the clear-eyed young face the while, Rory felt the muscles round his mouth contract and tremble. When my son, Tall Ian, has lived his full span and is laid in the tomb, that little lad will touch the claymore of William of the Long Sword, before asking for the sword of his father and buckling it on, he thought. And by the action of this day, I am robbing him of his heritage, which I got from my father and my grandfather: The great ships that the clan has built and maintained for their safety and deliverance from danger, and for their pride and their delight.

It seemed to him an ill wind that laid upon his own shoulders this responsibility, for ever since his strange and solitary sojourn in Iona, after his illness, he had sought always to build and to make, and to create, and never wittingly or intentionally to destroy what had been shaped and fashioned by a man's hand for his own usage. But he no longer fretted and wondered at the irony of fate, with its strange labyrinths and twisting ways, and there was no shaking his conviction that he must do what was required with dignity and inner discipline.

After a few moments, he pushed back the deerskin cover from the bed, and without calling his servants, climbed out on to the cold floor. He took his garments and pulled them on slowly one by one: lifted the heavy plaid from the bed and pinned it about his shoulders with the silver Celtic circlet studded with cairngorms which his father and his brother William had worn; took up the cromach that he leaned upon these days, and went out softly down the narrow stairway to the courtyard, and down again towards the sea gate.

Young Rabbie MacAskill – a grandson of Murdo MacAskill who had stood on guard on that other morning long ago when MacAskill and Iain MacIain went out as boys to bathe themselves – was standing propped against the door, half asleep at this low ebb of time between night and full day; and the two youngsters who were on guard with him slumbered unashamedly, heads on knees, half way down the steps by the covered well.

"Why, sir, you are about early?" MacAskill said looking upward, blinking sleepy-eyed, as the Chief descended. And seeing the expression on the tired, old face:

"Is all well?" he asked.

"Yes, all is well, lad," Rory answered softly, glancing at the sleeping boys, who had not stirred at the sound of his tread behind them. "No – don't wake them, there is no need. Unbolt the door, Rabbie. I shall go out and taste the air before men are about."

"So early, sir?" MacAskill asked, surprised and puzzled. "You also?"

Rory ran his hands up and down the stones of the door-side, deeply grooved where men of many generations had sharpened their swords before going into battle.

"Has someone else gone out?" Rory enquired, as the young man turned to draw back the bolts.

"Yes, Mistress Mairi, sir, almost half an hour ago. I would have sent a lad with her, but she would have no one accompany her," MacAskill told him. "I did say to her she should not walk out alone, at her age, on the foreshore in the dark, lest she should fall, or come into some danger –"

"Mistress Mairi has walked the shore at night since before you were born, Rabbie," MacLeod said chidingly. "It would take a stronger man than I am to restrain her. And there is no danger outside these walls nowadays. We must let her be – especially on this day."

"Yes, it is a bitter day that has come upon us all," MacAskill sighed. He pushed the door wide open and stood back from it in the narrow entrance way, watching his chief as he stepped out onto the rough-hewn steps, outside the wall, where the wind at once tore at his plaid and tugged at his grey hair and his beard.

"Sir, is there nothing we can do even now to avert what is to come?" The young man asked.

"There is nothing a man can do to change his fate," Sir Rory Mor answered over his shoulder. "That I have understood long since. But he can change his attitude towards it, and not be bitter and distraught by what must come. So is it with the clans; and with the nations; and with the world. We will not batter our heads against the granite walls of our fate."

"That is how old Master MacIain speaks. And Master Lérins, the minstrel, used to sing like that in the old songs," the young man answered. He pronounced the Frenchman's name Lay Rann as all the clansmen did. "But you have changed and shaped the very destiny of the Isles with your own hands, and men say –"

"No, no," Rory answered, cutting him short, "a man can do no more than be fate's willing instrument – without bitterness or anger in him at the course of things. Yet he may strive with his little strength towards the ideals that he glimpses in the ebb and flow of life from time to time."

He turned his old head, and smiled into the young man's eyes. Then he straightened his shoulders and stood there, feet apart, a sturdy thickset figure. Then raised his eyes in his grey old head, and looked along the inlet towards the waterway.

There were vessels lying all down the navigable channel, as far as his eyes could see. In the rising wind of dawn and the swift running of the tide, they were moving and jostling vigorously, one against the next. Now they seemed not so much like penned sheep as like tethered horses: or a great leaderless army awaiting some order by which they would know whether to retreat or to advance.

Here and there, aboard the empty boats, Rory could see, in the lightening morning, a guardian figure, moving and yawning and stretching as he rose from a night's vigil on an empty forepeak – a watchman sent by some chief who could not bring himself to abandon his vessel altogether before the appointed hour, though there was no longer anything aboard that needed guarding.

Sir Rory Mor watched the midget figures, moving back and forth on some last imaginary ministrations on the boats that they had loved and served with a good heart, through many a storm and many a battle, and many a tranquil voyage. The very presence of these humble, barefoot boatmen clambering about aboard, added in some way to the desolation of the scene, he thought. Why could they not go lightly, with courage and decision, to the shore, and to their breakfast in the castle barrack room? But they moved back and forth, calling to one another with echoing voices over the water, swabbing or cleaning, or making some last adjustment to the hawsers, delaying the hour of their final landing.

Though they were stripped and all but empty, almost all the vessels still flew the pennant of their clans. And though no orders had been given and no suggestions made about it, Sir Rory knew well that by common and unspoken consent, these tokens of ownership and pride of possession would be consigned to the flames with the vessels themselves in the conflagration that was to come, like the garments of a chieftain of old, cast on his funeral pyre. He watched the small scraps of stuff, each with its colour and marking of a friend or old foe of the clan MacLeod, tossing in lines and ranks together in the wind and the grey light – and then sunlight tipped, all in a moment, in the first rays of a clear morning. He remained standing in the wind, a long time, leaning on his cromach, staring.

Then Mairi's much lined face appeared a little way below him, looking up. She was wearing two tartan plaids, a little one round her head with the white frill of the *mutch* showing through, and a large *tonnag* draped round her shoulders and fastened by a silver circlet at her throat, above a gown of heavy grey silk. In her hand she carried the silver-headed staff that Rory had brought her from London long ago.

She came very slowly these days, and somewhat stiffly, placing her feet with care and looking where she stepped so that she did not slip on the wet seaweed on the shore or the loose stones of the path – but she was wilful still in spite of her advanced years, and scorned to be assisted.

In a moment she was beside Rory, and they looked at one another, not speaking. And then turned their faces again, and in a long silence, looked outward to the ships.

She said at length: "See how they move and dip and sway on the waters! They are alive still. But by this night they will be ashes on the tide. Has the King the right to destroy the very soul of the Hebrides - for that is what he is doing, by ordering their burning."

"Is not a soul a thing eternal, born of the Spirit?" Rory responded, wanting to comfort her, even though at this moment he could scarcely console himself, let alone reassure another.

"No, I think all things have their life-span, even the soul of a people," she answered. "What do you mean by the Spirit? The Holy Ghost?"

"Why, I mean that which moves in all men who live, and makes them conscious of themselves and desirous of life," he answered. "That which moves in a man's hands when he hews the timber and smoothes the planks and measures and nails and begins to build himself a boat. And that which moves in his mind when he considers it, and thinks how he will shape the vessel and make it seaworthy – a ship after his own heart. And that which moves in his soul when he feels the keel first slide into the water, and the water uplifts and bears his vessel, and the winds of the heavens fill her sails and carry her forwards…is this not the eternal spirit of man?"

"Perhaps it is so," she said slowly. "And yet it seems to me that all things beneath the sun have their own life-span – even the spirit of man. The Spirit of God moved upon the face of the waters long before men built their boats, and used their hands to make rigging or trim a sail to the wind. The Spirit of God alone is eternal – unchangeable. All else is transient and passing. There is nothing else but lasts its own life-span, and then comes to its own ending."

"Does that then comfort you – that sombre thought, cousin?" he asked, looking down at her. "You will be reminding me next of Dun Kenneth telling people how the Fairy Flag will one day be exposed for the last time, and after, the fortunes of the Siol Tormod of the clan

MacLeod will decline, and one small curragh will suffice to bear the chief and all his goods across Loch Dunvegan!"

Rory said the words swiftly, on a note that seemed almost jocular and mocking, as his tone had often been in his younger days when he spoke of matters near his heart and wished to hide his feelings. But in spite of himself his voice shook suddenly before he could finish and he looked into Mairi's face with an expression of fear in his eyes: and the dread, that the thought of a final extinction brings, whenever man contemplates his destiny.

"No, no, that can't be! For in the clan lies all our hope of immortality beyond our own life span," she cried, clasping her hands together on the staff she held. "No, it will not be yet, Rory, not yet. On this day if the clan dies, it is only to be born in a new age."

"Is there then re-birth before a final death?" Sir Rory Mor asked slowly, knowing how often in the past her vision had outsoared his own.

"I think surely all living things have three parts to their lives," she answered. "First youth, and then maturity and then old age. Perhaps between each one of these there is a kind of death. Perhaps death hovers close this day – but I don't believe it is the final end. Indeed, perhaps there are seven full stages that we must live through, for so it says in the old books that came from Rodel, that Iain MacIain reads. But of this I know little. Perhaps it is another matter. When we baptise a child, do we not say by custom: 'The three blessings of the priests and the seven blessings of the people be upon you'? Truly there is an ancient meaning there, that men have forgotten."

He put his hand on her shoulder.

"Come, let's go in, for now the household is awake," he said.

The Earl of Argyll, and old Lord Ochiltree and the other commissioners had exercised a tact born of caution in their dealings with the islanders these last few years. Although they had sailed up between the islands with speed and confidence in a man o' war escorted by two smaller, but fully armed vessels, they had thought best, after consultations on board among themselves, not to run into the mouth of Loch Dunvegan itself, and had anchored instead in the neighbouring Loch Pooltiel overnight.

"Although we must witness the carrying out of orders, I would as soon not sleep overnight at Dunvegan Castle among those fellows," Ochiltree had said. "I have no wish for a dirk in my chest while I slumber."

"No, we can trust Sir Rory MacLeod," Argyll answered. "But it is suitable enough we should lie off until the morning. We need not ask unwilling hospitality." So they turned in the wide entrance to Pooltiel, and moved up cautiously in the unfamiliar waters, and dropped anchor there as soon as the grappling irons would make a hold on the rocky sea bed.

If they had imagined that the three royal ships could lie there unobserved until the following morning, they soon discovered their mistake, for the sharp eyes of a cottager, tending sheep on the uninhabited uplands, spied them almost before they had turned in from the open sea. And Sir Rory Mor MacLeod had news of the commissioners' arrival in the neighbouring loch before they had even found anchorage there, for news travels swiftly and silently in the Isles.

The chief nodded with an expression of satisfaction.

"Very well," he told the messenger who came to him. "We will send greetings, and bid them come overland in the morning, for there is so much shipping in the channel of Loch Dunvegan that I had already thought they could not well approach us here by sea."

James Hotfoot had gone over in the evening to Glendale, and bade a fisherman who dwelt near the river mouth by old St Congan's church to row him out into Loch Pooltiel to the commissioners' vessel. Once on board, he delivered Rory's greetings, and his message that there would be horses sent over early to bear them to Dunvegan Castle by land on the morrow.

The Royal Commissioners consulted one another, always suspicious of being tricked by the islanders since they themselves had tricked the chiefs at Iona. But once again, Argyll, who had seen enough of Sir Rory Mor in the intervening years to have a healthy respect for him, said confidently:

"It is a reasonable suggestion and enables us to keep our own ships clear of the flames. It is only a three or four mile ride overland from here, my lords. We need not go round by sea."

When the chiefs learned that the commissioners would not be coming into Loch Dunvegan by sea, and would not therefore pass near the assembled galleys and birlinns, they looked at one another and smiled and nodded and chuckled in their beards. Then they looked at Sir Rory Mor, and nodded their heads and laughed, half-inviting him to comment on the possibility that had entered their minds, and that must have been apparent to him too. But he looked gravely back at them, as though he saw nothing of their satisfaction and heard nothing of any plotting that might be going on.

His own old galley, the *"Pride of Lochlann"* that his father had built, lay well to the forefront of the ships, and there were a number of other vessels with his pennant flying, drawn up within clear view of the castle battlements. Behind them were discernable vessels bearing the pennant of Donald Gorme MacDonald, and then MacLean, MacKinnon, MacKintosh, MacDonald of Islay and other branches of the old Clanranald with their own separate colours; an old vessel with the obsolete flag of MacLeod of the Lewis, two of MacLeod of Raasay and in the distance, barely distinguishable by shape or size or colour, a host of other flags on dimly discernable boats lying low on the water, where the loch widened towards the sea.

Voices spoke openly and sensibly of the wind and the weather, the state of the tide and the length of time it would take to burn a vessel lying on the water, until the water entered through the cracks and it would sink. But even while tongues wagged in this manner, heads were turned over shoulders, ears were stretched to listen to whispered words, footsteps hurried on battlement or loch side, down below, heads were together in sheltered hidden corners of the courtyard, discussing things not spoken of in the rooms above.

Sir Rory Mor went apparently serenely to and fro among his guests, offering wine and seeing goblets filled and platters well supplied, for on full stomachs men were less inclined for hasty or violent actions, and more peaceable in their ways: which would be just as well, he thought, with three armed vessels bearing cannons not four miles off, and a party of mighty nervous gentlemen on horseback approaching, guarded by soldiers with muskets, who would shoot on command, no doubt, and in the King's name.

Tall Ian, his son and heir, came up beside him suddenly and bent his head to whisper in the old chief's ear in urgent tones:

"Sir, they are planning – I have overheard just now –"

"How blows the wind, my son?" Sir Rory Mor enquired looking away, seeming like a very old man, inattentive, wandering of eye and slow of wits.

"Why, it blows from the south, sir, soft but steady, and will blow the flames northward and away from us, as we desired. But Father, even now, I heard someone say that since the commissioners can only see the foremost of the vessels, they will try to…"

"Blows the wind to the north, my son?" Sir Rory Mor said, cutting across Tall Ian's words as though they had not been spoken.

Tall Ian looked at his father with a puzzled frown, wondering if the events that were impending had proved too grievous for the balance of

260

the old man's mind to endure. But the old eyes seemed clear and intelligent enough, and the hand that bore a jug of wine had scarcely a tremor to it. Ian was left standing alone as his father turned away, quite clearly not wanting to be told what his son might have overheard.

At mid-morning the commissioners were seen approaching along the hillside on MacLeod's horses, with attendants and armed men running on foot beside them. There was a nervous stir among the many people gathered in the castle courtyards and the hall and all fell silent, looking to the sea stairs. Soon old Lord Ochiltree, the Earl of Argyll, looking pinched-faced and stern, and a number of younger noblemen began to come in and to ascend the stairs with cautious looks.

Sir Rory Mor received them at the doorway to the hall, bowed courteously and presented his sons, Ian Mor, Roderick of Talister, Norman of Bernera, William of Hamera and Robert of Greshornish. He had sent his young daughter Janet away with her mother the Lady Isabel until the dangers of this day would be over.

Since old Bishop Knox had died and his successor had no authority at all, in these days when Episcopacy had been swept aside in favour of the Presbyterian Church, the former religious element was missing from the commissioners' ranks, and all the officials who now presented themselves one by one at the doorway had purely secular power.

Lord Ochiltree, anxious as ever to impress his goodwill on the islanders, tut-tutted sadly when he heard the Lady Isabel was not present, shook his head to learn that Sir Rory's brother Alexander of Minginish had died in his sleep two years ago; and bowed, beaming amiably, towards the Lady Christiana and her sons who should have succeeded to the Lewis; and their own young wives and families in turn; and to the Lady Mairi, standing by MacLeod's own side. Then he moved onwards into the hall, rubbing his hands together as briskly as of old, and speaking to everyone whose face was familiar to him.

Many of the older chiefs had died since they had signed the statutes the year after their captivity, and others had become too old, and too saddened and sulky by the turn of events to attend in person on this day. Younger men, not known to him, represented a number of the clans, and bowed grave-faced before him as he enquired for their fathers and their uncles in amiable tones.

For a few moments the Earl of Argyll stood silent and neglected inside the doorway, looking sardonically about him, his hand laid lightly on his sword scabbard, and his lined and tight-lipped face glancing from one to another of the assembly.

Nearby stood a tall and almost bald old man, with a gentle unassuming face that caught his eye, because unlike the others, it seemed open and frank and childlike, concealing nothing.

He moved a step or two towards the old man, and commented:

"Well, you seem to have become a grey-bearded lot at Dunvegan in these days. Do you never die, you islanders?"

The gentle old face creased in a smile, and he answered:

"No, I warrant till Sir Rory Mor dies there are many of us who will hold on to the last threads of our old lives to keep him company! Yes, we live long in the Isles, my Lord. It has always been so."

"You are of the chief's family?" Argyll asked with a casual interest.

"No, of the Clan MacIain of Ardnamurchan, my Lord," the old man answered. "But I know no family but the Clan MacLeod."

Argyll gave him a straight and somewhat sour glance.

"The Clan MacIain was broken up long since, wasn't it?" he remarked. "What were left of them were pirates on the high seas when I was a boy. But you, sir, in that long robe of yours look more like a monk than a pirate – a simple fellow and without care." He twisted his cold face into a smile.

"Yes, very likely. I possess nothing, and inherit nothing, and neither the past nor the future has any claim on me, for I have no children and my wife is dead" Iain MacIain responded. "I serve MacLeod with an easy heart, and am beholden only to him and to God Himself. And I warrant I shall lie easy enough in my grave when the time comes."

The commissioners were offered refreshments, but Lord Ochiltree was anxious that the business should proceed, and sipped only briefly from his goblet, waving the dishes of food aside impatiently.

Sir Rory Mor escorted him to the long table where the clerks and junior officials were already seated, shuffling busily through lists of shipping and clan details and whispering together.

"Well, gentlemen," Lord Ochiltree said with his bright smile, when he was seated. "This is a sad day for us all, eh? A most sad and regrettable day, but one that you, in your good sense and loyalty, have prepared for manfully. We have seen your ships assembled, and we have here the lists of all your vessels which you now submit to our hands as being surrendered to His Majesty the King. We take it as indication of your loyal duty and your wisdom that so great – indeed, so impressive a number of vessels are assembled. And we hold you honour-bound that you retain in your island strongholds only such few small and unarmed vessels as His Majesty permits you, for your conveyance of the rents in kind between your properties, and between the Western Islands and the mainland of His Majesty's domains. And now, good sirs, we will have you, as token of your honourable word, to swear before us that you submit all your vessels this day, save only those which are especially exempt in the manner mentioned. Do you so swear, sirs? Eh? Hm?"

There was a lengthy silence from the assembled chiefs, who stood or sat about the hall on stools or tables, or leaning against the wall and in the window embrasures, with expressions inscrutable but calm.

"Come, come, sirs, move before us one by one and raise your hands and let us hear your tongues," Lord Ochiltree said after a moment with a look of nervousness and impatience on his face. He glanced at Argyll and at his fellow nobles, and then at Sir Rory Mor MacLeod.

"I will take an oath, token of all that you require of us," Rory said, after a moment. "It would take a deal too long for each one of us to make his separate oath, for while we dally, the tide will run low, and the win d may change and we shall not dare to fire the ships at all until we have a current that will carry the fire away from the castle walls. So let me swear."

"Well, well, do so then," Ochiltree agreed at once, clearly only too anxious that the burning should not have to be postponed and their visit to Skye thus prolonged.

Sir Rory Mor rose slowly to his feet. He turned his head towards the window and glanced out at the waterway. In the far distance there seemed to be a movement among the vessels that had already been inspected by the junior officials who had gone along the cliff tops above the loch, counting and checking from the shore, earlier in the morning. One would almost think, now, that the numbers out there in the distance near the bend were less than were lying there at dawn. One would almost imagine some of them out there now were not seaworthy vessels at all, so low did they lie in the water and so ancient did they seem. They might almost be old hulls and wrecks that had been dredged up from their rocky graves especially for this occasion.

But in the foreground where the ships were close to view, there was no doubt that there were the galleys and the birlinns of the Clan MacLeod.

Sir Rory Mor turned again to the commissioners and slowly raised his hand.

"I do solemnly swear that my vessels are assembled below and submitted for destruction, save only those exempted by the King," he said.

"Well spoken, well spoken, my friend," Lord Ochiltree responded beaming. "Then let us go out, eh? And with brave hearts, as in honour bound, do what must be done this day. Hm?"

When the commissioners were at their vantage point, Lord Ochiltree looked at the Earl of Argyll expectantly, and he in turn nodded his head towards Sir Rory Mor. MacLeod raised his hand slowly, looking downwards at the beach.

Below, at the edge of the little surf, there stood a small group of men with James Hotfoot's son in charge, and MacSweyn's two boys and young MacAskill and several others, beside a half dozen curraghs pulled up just out of the water. They had made a small glowing fire of brushwood and peats, there at the water's edge. When they saw his hand raised, they began a scurry of movement and activity. First it seemed the little quiet fire was growing bigger, then suddenly the men were moving back, each upright, each with his own fire – a flaring, burning torch at the end of a sturdy branch.

Young men pushed out the curraghs with all speed, and into the water plunged and ran the clansmen with the torches, shouting suddenly, whooping as though they lurched forward into an uncertain battle and must needs give themselves courage to go on. They scrambled into the little, swaying boats. As the curraghs took the water, sparks flew out from the torches and were carried off on the wind. The faint whoops and shouts of men were borne upwards to the battlements and to the people along the cliff top opposite, and they began up there a sort of sighing, an indrawn breath, like the suck of the tide over pebbles on a dark, still night.

In a moment the sound that came from the people was surmounted by a clearer, surer sound – the pipes of the MacCrimmons who filled the battlemented court above the barrack quarters. In front of them stood Padruig Og, a young, sweet piper, who was Padruig's Mor's son and would be his successor at the Piping College over at Borreraig. The old man, too feeble now to leave the college walls, had nevertheless composed his last great music, so it was 'MacCrimmon's Lament', being played for the first time by his clansmen and his pupils that filled the windswept air above Dunvegan.

As the rising notes mingled with the wind and the sea, the curraghs drew close to the first of the great empty ships, which loomed blackly above the standing torch bearers in their little swaying craft.

Torches were applied to the great heaps of bracken and brushwood in the empty hulls, and as the fire took, and flames shot upwards, the torchbearers clambered on, from ship to ship, leaping the chasms between

264

each, clinging to ladder or rope or wooden strut, touching another heap of kindling and with hoarse cries moving on and on.

In the old *"Pride of Lochlann"* and the *"Sea Avenger"* already a great crackling, roaring fire was beginning to spread rapidly from stem to stern. The people on the battlements stared as if fascinated, seeming to hold their breath, to groan almost audibly, and then to hold their breath again – looking downwards, then up at the tartan clad pipers above them, and then sombrely into each other's faces.

Soon the great flames and thick belching smoke that issued from MacLeod's own galley in the forefront obscured completely the activities further down the loch. The old timbers creaked and crackled and as the gusty wind tore across the water, the fire raged ever higher and higher, until the heat of it reached even the faces of the watchers up above. Further along, where not all the vessels had been individually fired, the sparkling, crackling wind-assisted flames carried of their own accord to many of the moored boats at the loch sides. As the mooring ropes were severed by the fire, several drifted free and shifted and turned on the water like live things, each a separate living inferno.

Everyone was surprised at the speed with which the fire had been launched and got under way. Some who had predicted it would take all day long to get those salt-caked old timbers to take fire and any heart into the blaze at all, looked on bewildered, as though they imagined privately that hands other than the human ones with the torches might be propagating it, and fancied they heard above the wind and the pipe music and the roaring flames, the banshee howl of spectral things, rising and wreathing in the spiralling smoke, released from these old man-made vessels into the freedom of the upper air.

Rory and Mairi looked into each other's fire-warmed faces, standing side by side, plaid-wrapped, and yet for some reason shivering uncontrollably.

"It is very true, death hovers near us now," Rory whispered. "If the wind should turn, in this great conflagration, even Dunvegan itself and all who live here might be themselves destroyed."

"No, no, cousin, have faith and courage," Mairi answered. "By this nightfall it will all be accomplished, and we shall still be alive, I feel very sure."

Rory found Iain MacIain at his side, and to his surprise his old friend was of a tranquil and untroubled countenance. He made as though to speak to him of what was before all their eyes, but a sudden short, sharp stirring of bitterness, drew him up, and he thought: since this monkish old man was a barefoot boy he has served us well here – but these were never his own, these burning vessels, and he doesn't understand how it tears the muscles of our hearts to watch. And Iain, who understood very well all that went on in MacLeod's old mind, also shut his mouth again, and stood beside the chief, saying nothing.

Chapter Twenty One

THE UNCHARTED SEA

The fire had been burning for a considerable time, and already many of the masts had toppled, bringing down the clan pennants and making the boats indistinguishable one from another. Rory sensed that the commissioners and officials were growing restive, and he invited them indoors again, to refresh themselves, out of the blustering wind.

The groups of people along the parapets and about the courtyard began to drift away.

The MacDonalds of Duntulm had been led by Donald Gorme's young nephew, who would in time succeed his uncle, since in three marriages, no heir, male or female, had been born to the chief. Sir Rory greeted the young man, who had arrived late, that morning, and enquired after his uncle. But the boy's eyes flickered away, as though he did not want to speak of Donald Gorme Mor. Men said he was more often drunk than sober in these days, and was no credit to that ancient clan, who once inherited the Lordship of the Isles.

Sir Rory Mor escorted the Earl of Argyll and Lord Ochiltree up to the hall again, together with the chiefs.

They were all on the move, still glancing backwards at the fires, when suddenly there was a commotion on the stairs leading up from the sea gate – shouts and oaths and protests, in a number of different voices. They turned their heads to look down again.

In a moment, young MacSweyn and two stalwarts who had been standing by the open gate below appeared, stumbling back protesting angrily, but not daring to draw their swords against the huge, shambling and dishevelled figure that was swaying and shuffling and rolling its great bulk upwards, with mouth open in his upturned face, and a ranting roar emerging from his throat.

"Where is MacLeod? I shall have him yet, the scoundrel! The treasonous, treacherous offspring of the old heathen mare! Where is he? Take me up to him, you lily-livered fellow - "

"By St Clement, it is Donald Gorme Mor," Tall Ian ejaculated, turning upon the stairs. "And very drunk, it seems. Shall I have them hold him back Father?"

Sir Rory Mor looked down at his old enemy. It seemed to him that he had nothing to fear from this shuffling, drink-sodden old chief, and the insults pouring from the slack old lips scarcely reached his ears.

"Let him come up," he commanded. "He has the same rights on this day as we have all of us."

Donald Gorme shuffled upwards, and as he came, his bloodshot eyes turned from Rory Mor to the Earl of Argyll, and then ran from one to another of the commissioners.

"Well, you have enforced your evil will upon us," he said, as though deflected from his venom against MacLeod, by the sight of the commissioners. "And now you see the outcome of your devilish interference."

He paused, and stretched out a hand towards his nephew who had moved forward, and leaned heavily upon the young shoulder, breathing loudly.

"Yes, it is a fine heritage these gentlemen have left you, nephew," he said. "All our ships gone. Nothing left. Nothing left but ruins."

"It is very true there is nothing left for the young man but ruins – for Duntulm itself is nearly fallen into ruins, MacDonald!" a voice from among the warriors down below called suddenly. "It is not Sir Rory Mor who robs your heir, but your own negligence!"

There was a ripple of laughter, quickly hushed, and faces turned again to the bulky figure swaying back and forth on the stairs.

As though he had not heard the scornful interjection, Donald Gorme turned slowly, and looked out along the waterway. Since his own ships had lain close behind MacLeod's, the flames which had begun to recede somewhat from the front ranks, were at fiercest there, where the MacDonald pennant flew.

"There goes the *"Wind of Dunscaith"*, the chief cried bitterly. "And the *"Luck of Clanranald"* is next to her – see how she takes the flames to her old heart…Your ships are all but dead, MacLeod. Now are the old enemies at death's door side by side, in a last battle – with the god of fire. You tool of the King! It is you who have led us to this shameful day!" he shouted. "I will have your blood for it – even if I too die this day, like our ships!"

With sudden and unexpected agility, as though gathering his strength for a final act of violence, and hatred, he launched himself

268

upwards towards Sir Rory Mor, drawing his short dirk from his belt as he did so.

Iain MacIain, who had been following MacLeod when Donald Gorme Mor's arrival had caused the disturbance, was now to the side of his master and friend. He thrust his arm forward hastily to stop MacDonald, and found himself, all in a moment, at grips with him. Donald Gorme seemed disconcerted by the unexpected intervention of another man between himself and MacLeod. He hesitated, his arm raised with the knife in it. Then with a roar of rage he thrust it suddenly into MacIain's body, catching him more by chance than skill, between the ribs and just below the heart.

An expression of astonishment, as yet hardly touched with pain, entered MacIain's face, as he felt the dirk thrust into his flesh. He drew a gasping breath.

"No, sir! No –" he jerked out before pain swirled about him, bemusing and bewildering, as though the great flames from down below had reached up and twined themselves about his body. He tasted blood on his tongue. Still holding MacDonald's shoulder, he turned his head and looked into the face of his chief who was descending to his side. "Sir…" he whispered, with a wild, uncomprehending look, "MacLeod…"

Blood flowed suddenly from his open mouth, and he slipped downwards, his eyes still open in an expression of astonishment and grief, and fell across MacDonald's feet. With an impatient oath, MacDonald threw the crumpling body off, tossing MacIain sideways so that he rolled over, hit the low barricade above the well on the sea stairs, and lay still.

Immediately confusion broke out on all sides, while MacSweyn's men seized MacDonald, and dragged him off, protesting and swearing at everyone. Near the top of the sea stairs was the entrance to the old, deep and stairless dungeon in which many an ancient foe of MacLeod of MacLeod had died a lingering death long ago. Someone pulled up the trapdoor. They tipped him in, yelling and screaming and slammed it shut again. Women cried and shouted, men pushed up and down the stairs, to where MacIain had fallen.

MacLeod, grey-faced and shaken, had turned down the narrow way; but before he reached the fallen crumpled body beside the well, Mairi came as swiftly and speedily as she could and pressed past to kneel beside MacIain and lift the almost bald head into her lap.

"He is dead," she whispered, looking up at Rory, her face grief-stricken and horrified. "Oh, Rory! Rory! On this day of all days. Our good friend. Our dear Iain…"

She stooped and kissed the familiar gentle face, wiped the blood from his mouth with her plaid, and holding him against her breast began to weep with so uncontrollable a sorrow that all who now came running or who stood near, were affected.

The sound of the old lady crying and the sight of her face all creased, and her little shrunken body crouched there in the narrow passage holding the dead man to her, released a great wave of emotion and sorrow that the clans had contained within themselves in stoic silence throughout the hours of the morning. Suddenly all about, women began to weep, children to sob loudly, and men to cry silently, wiping their faces, unashamedly as they stared from the Lady Mairi down below them on the sea stairs, up and outward to the burning ships, and downward again to the still figures by the well.

"Is he really dead? We have known him all our lives. He was always here, even when I was a wee lad, the monkish Master MacIain," one man said.

"Yes, it will not be the same without him, at Dunvegan."

"Well, it is an omen, that is sure," Rabbie MacAskill whispered, with a shocked, white face. "To die on this day and in defence of MacLeod's own person…"

"The little people have claimed him, I reckon," an aged greybeard from the barrack room croaked up suddenly. "Their hands, unseen, draw blood on such a day as this, in tribute to themselves."

"Hush, old Jaimie," James Hotfoot said sharply. "No more of that now. It was MacDonald's arm, and no mysterious thing, that caused his blood to flow."

But Mairi, looking into Rory's face as he bent above her, whispered:

"Cousin, we knew death hovered near – and now he claims this victim from our midst."

"But for his body between me and Donald Gorme, it would have been myself," Rory answered sombrely. "He gave his life for me, as he always said he would do."

When Iain MacIain's body had been taken up slowly and carefully covered with a plaid and borne away, the people became quiet again, and went soberly indoors.

Outside the roar of the flames could still be heard, sizzling and steaming as great planks cracked open, severed by the heat, and fell splashing to be extinguished into the water. Sometimes the gusty wind seemed temporarily to bear the flames towards the castle walls as though the fire, itself a living thing, threatened those who had misused it for destruction. But even as the watchers stared, fascinated and alarmed, the tearing rage of the fire sheered off seaward once again. Yet the reek of the smoke and the hot tar was borne upward continually and all Dunvegan Castle seemed full of it.

Sir Rory Mor was anxious that none of the vessels should be so far burned that they would sink and foul the navigable channel of the loch, and he had given orders in advance that as soon as they could be approached, the burnt-out ships should be driven seaward into the Minch. The fishing vessels and the small and unarmed boats that had lain off little Isle Isay for safety all the day, were brought round. With ropes and grappling irons, the boatmen began to hook and tow the great burnt-out shells towards the entrance to the loch. It was a long slow process, for they could not be closely approached for the fierceness of the heat that still came from them. But slowly the ocean currents took them, and bore them, sinking lower and lower into the water, towards their last horizon.

Argyll cleared his throat and looked at Lord Ochiltree. And presently, the gentlemen took their leave, and went down to the horses that had been re-saddled to take them back to Loch Pooltiel.

"Well, that ensures the end of all bloody warfare and barbarity in these isles," Lord Ochiltree said as they rode. "May Christian charity begin and rule uninterrupted in these lands henceforth. Eh? Hm?"

"What of the fate of Donald Gorme MacDonald?" the Earl of Argyll asked dubiously.

"The new justices should try him, by rights, in the name of the Privy Council," Ochiltree answered. "But I am thinking that…"

"Yes, leave it in MacLeod's hands. They have always dispensed a rough justice amongst themselves, and they will know right enough how to deal with the fellow," Argyll agreed, thinking it would be a deal less trouble in the end if nothing were said in Edinburgh or London of the old chief's drunken attack.

They jogged on over the rough ground for a while in silence. Presently, a junior member of the party who had been nursing a troubled mind throughout the day, put in timidly:

"I hope we have not been hood-winked, my lords. It was awkward to discover how many vessels each chief submitted and we had no sure count, not even any true knowledge how many galleys they all had beforehand. Some lay far out in the channel, and though they gave us horses to ride along the cliffs, we did not come really near enough. And then again, many of them moved, later in the morning…"

"Well, well, we did our best, eh? And we have burned the greater part of the Hebridean fleet, it seems, so let is be," Ochiltree answered somewhat testily. "We have clipped their wings these last years, as the King desired us to. Today we have almost broken their backs, I warrant."

At Sir Rory Mor's invitation, the chiefs were to remain overnight at Dunvegan and dine with him and with his family. This seemed to them all a wise decision, for it would give the King's commissioners a chance to leave the vicinity and make their peaceful and satisfactory journey back to the mainland, before there need be any movement of other vessels in the neighbourhood. They made their way into the dining hall, and seated themselves in an orderly way, trying to look more cheerful than they felt.

As the meal was being served, a young captain who had been away since early morning came in rubbing his hands with seeming satisfaction, and took his place at table.

"Well, that was a good day's work I am thinking," he said, looking about him.

"What do you mean, young fellow?" MacLean of Duart, who was his chief, asked sharply, glowering at him.

"Why sir, we rescued the *"Castle Aros"*, and your old galley *"Fionn's Morning"* and the birlinn the *"White Hind"*, and laid them up off Isle Isay under the screen of smoke," the young man answered, grinning.

"Did you, by Our Lady! Did you now?" MacLean cried, his scarred face lighting up. "That was most wrongful of you, but…"

"Sir -" cried a rough-voiced old veteran, bursting in and almost hurling himself upon MacKintosh of Dunachton, "Sir, I gladly tell you that *"Sea Wind"* and the *"Sea Witch"* and the *"Sea Spray"* have all escaped the burning, for we got them off before the flames could reach them, and they are lying over behind Ardmore Point."

"Why, that is the best news I heard this day," Dunachton cried, slapping his thigh, and looking at his fellows with shining eyes.

In a moment some of the young men of the Clanranald entered, with similar news. And MacLeod of Raasay's steward to say he had had to let the chief's galley go, but he had saved three other vessels. And MacKinnon's son ran in, whooping with delight, to say his clan had lost only small vessels, and some damage to their two birlinns, but their principal galley, *"Strathordell"* was out of harm's way, hidden behind Sheep Island.

The chiefs looked at one another with their expressions varying from doubt about one another's reactions to slow-spreading smiles. Then someone gave a short laugh; and another a huge guffaw, with head thrown back. And in a moment, wave upon wave of laughter echoed in a great crescendo of merriment throughout the hall.

In some cases, the chiefs themselves had known nothing, until their grinning clansmen crowded in, and told them how they had moved as many ships as possible as far as they dared, while the commissioners were holding their conference in the hall, and borne them off later under cover of the pall of smoke. In their place the old crippled ships and wrecks that the chiefs had used to pad out the mass of shipping in the loch had been brought up to fill the vacant spaces in the ranks and take much of the brunt of the fire.

Now, almost every rocky inlet round Trotternish and Waternish and the whole of Great Loch Snizort, held beached or anchored out of sight, scorched but still seaworthy vessels awaiting collection when the tide was right. Those, added to the ships that had not been brought up to Skye and presented at all, but which lay concealed in sea lochs throughout the Hebrides, meant that the islanders would not lack for transport in the coming days.

Though the fleets had been crippled, their faces had been saved.

Because they had come out of the affair so much better than they had hoped, as soon as they had wine and good meat in their bellies, the chiefs became full of talk and plans for revenge, when times changed. First one then another boasted that a great fleet would be built up in the Western Isles again. Their merry talk was subdued only slightly by the sight of Sir Rory Mor's tired and aged face at the head of the table, and the memory of the attack on him, and the loss of his old and valued friend MacIain.

They knew well enough that they had owed much to his foresight and mediation, ever since the year long ago when he had obtained their release from Stirling by his courage and the boldness of his journey to London. They had abused him and complained of him often enough to his face or behind his back, when they found how he pressed them in the King's name to submit to ever greater supervision and legislation that whittled away the freedom of their lives. But they went the way he would have them go, nonetheless, respecting his able mind, and his tenacity, and glimpsing from time to time the wisdom of his actions. And they feared and admired the sudden swift lash of his tongue.

"Well, I warrant Sir Rory Mor has done as well by us this day as any chief could have done," young MacKinnon of Strath said as they ate and drank. "He saved us from the need to take an oath we could not in honour take. And he has made a sacrifice of his own ships without sparing. All honour to him."

"Yes, that was a noble gesture," MacLean replied amiably.

"Well, I stand by Sir Rory Mor from this day forth," a third chief interjected staunchly, raising his goblet. "He stands between us and that crafty fox Argyll, who grows more like his father every day. And he has done his best for all our causes with the King, whatever men may say."

"Yes, that is so!" and:

"That is true enough," the others answered, and they began to lift their goblets or drinking horns and cry:

"MacLeod! MacLeod!" and thump the table with their fists, laughing and grinning, until he got up and spoke to them at last. He said very little, careful not to damp their spirits too greatly, and whatever he thought about the future he kept to himself that night. He re-seated himself and drank with them again.

At length Sir Rory Mor rose from the table as a sign that all might now disperse. The ladies left the dining room, but seeing that many of his guests were well content to hold on to their wine goblets a while longer, he sent the musicians in from the hall to entertain those who had settled themselves back comfortably in the old way, with arms among the débris on the table, to tell old stories, and hear the harpists and the bards.

A fresh young voice began to sing the ballad addressed to him that Mairi had composed years ago:

"*You who have been to minstrels as their homecoming.*"

He smiled and bowed then left the dining hall.

For quite a while in the background there had been screaming and shouting from the dungeon where Donald Gorme MacDonald lay, but now he noticed all was silent. He called for James Hotfoot.

"Is MacDonald still alive down below? I noticed his nephew has left us."

The clansman laughed.

"Oh yes! The men have been amusing themselves pissing and shitting on him, through the hole your forebears left for that purpose." He grinned.

Rory told him without a smile:

"Get him up, and if he can sit his horse, send him home."

"But Macleod - -"

"We cannot have the King's Commissioners finding out that we still have him in our dungeon."

"But Sir, he killed Iain MacIain and he was almost one of ourselves - -"

"They will care nothing about MacIain of Ardnamurchan. That clan was broken long ago. But we cannot hold MacDonald. Do it, James."

The clansmen fetched a rope ladder, and when they found MacDonald could not climb it, they hauled him up though he yelled that his arm was broken and his shoulder out of place. Because he swore at them as soon as he was out, they tumbled him head over heels down the sea stairs, and dragged him round to where his sturdy weight-bearing horse was still tethered.

Clearly his arm was indeed broken and his shoulder out of joint, and he could not mount. They heaved him up and he grabbed the mane with his one good hand. He was bloody and filthy and seemed by now barely conscious. But when they smacked his horse's rump and it started up briskly, he managed from long habit to grip with his knees, and though he swayed, they watched him ride off into the woods.

Beyond the treebelt, as he sagged forward in his saddle, his unguided horse would slow to a dawdle, plucking the grasses and meandering towards Duntulm. By the next day he would be back in his own lands.

*****

Although he was very tired, sleep seemed far from Rory, and he opened the door and went out onto the battlements alone.

It seemed to him strange that Iain MacIain did not step forward to raise the latch for him, or to bring a plaid and place it round his shoulders against the wind. He looked about him half-expectantly, but there was no-one there. The moon rose high over the empty waters of the loch and the wind had dropped away to nothing but a damp rain-bearing breeze.

Presently he heard laughing voices and feet clattering on the stone stairway down below, and realised that a number of his younger guests were going out, and launching themselves in the small boats below the sea stairs. He leaned on the low wall, watching; and then turned his head as old MacKinnon of Strath approached and stood beside him.

"Where are those fellows bound?" he asked.

"They are off to Borreraig, for they think that from there they will see the last of the burning ships at sea, and pipe them to their graves," MacKinnon answered. He gave a sudden wide-mouthed yawn. "The young fellows are going off, but we old ones are for our beds," he said. "We will rest our bones awhile and sleep off all the good food and wine you have given us so generously. And you, sir? You will have time to rest, now all this affair is past."

"No, not for long, for I must go to Fortrose," Rory answered. "There is business awaiting me there and I must not delay further, if I am not to incur the displeasure of our masters on the mainland. Fortrose has recently become the main administration centre for Scotland. I will see the burial of my old friend, and then…"

He let his voice peter out on a long sigh, looking down at where the young chieftains and their fellows were leaping into the boats, with rollicking shouts, tumbling one of their number out and hauling him dripping over the gunwale again, with a gale of laughter; and finally setting off with most uncertain oar strokes, splashing and zig-zagging across the loch.

"Well, I shall sleep, sir – and sleep soundly, much thanks to you," MacKinnon remarked with another yawn. "Goodnight to you."

"Goodnight, my friend," Rory answered. "Goodnight."

MacKinnon wandered off, and joined his own contemporaries, who soon went drifting off to their pallets, there to dream of great new fleets of ships, and a fair wind in their sails for a homeward journey in the morning.

Sir Rory Mor remained standing, looking up the moonlit loch towards Borreraig. He had a mind to go up there himself, but his tired frame was reluctant to move again. He had decided to abandon the idea, when he was joined by Mairi and Tall Ian, who both declared they were determined to go up there, and asked him to go with them, and see what vessels still might be visible from the loch mouth. And hear the piping that would surely continue until dawn over at the College. Tall Ian brought cloaks and they all descended and boarded the chief's own small vessel, no more than a curragh and went off through the darkness over the water.

"It seems all the clans got off lighter than they feared, except ourselves," Rory's heir said soberly as they moved steadily along. "You gave all that was our own, and left so few boats that we must surely build again as soon as we have more timber. Why did you do it, Father? It can't have been necessary."

"For honour's sake, my son; and because the King has trusted me these many years," Rory answered, gazing away over the moonlit water. And then with a sudden flash of his old island independence, he added: "And also, so that the others might save and salvage what they could, and not have all their hearts broken by the King!" He gave his sudden smile. "If need be, you can build ships again, my boy, when the young trees are grown, and give you timber. Yes, you can always build again, if times should change."

But in his mind's eye he saw already that there would be no going back to the old ways; and many a warlike ship, laid up in secrecy, with her oars shipped and her sail stowed away, in some little-known inlet from the western sea, would moulder there through the years, unclaimed, and unneeded, and at last unremembered; until the timbers fell apart and rotted there, and were carried off as driftwood on the tide.

When the small boat drew near Borreraig, standing high up on the tall cliffs near the entrance to the loch, all three fell silent, listening to the pipe music borne on the night air to them across the water.

"Shall we go up and join them there?" Tall Ian asked. "I have a mind to take old Padruig's pipes and play a while – even though the old man will growl at me, for he always said I would never make a piper."

"You go up, then, lad," Rory answered. "We will stay in the boat, and will hear you from the water."

They landed Ian Mor at the small jetty and watched him climb rapidly up the steep, short hill with his long-legged stride, his kilted plaid swinging. Then, at Sir Rory Mor's command, the small boat, with Mairi and himself seated side by side in it, pushed off again and the boatmen drew it slowly along under the dark cliffs, beneath the Piper's Walk.

From here, the wide expanse of the western sea was visible, and as they had supposed, out there, drifting at varying distances between themselves and the skyline, a number of the still glowing wrecks tossed quietly on the waves.

"They will all be gone by morning, sir," one of the boatmen remarked. "They will be no danger to anyone when they sink out there."

"We shall be a seafaring people no longer, no matter what they think," Rory muttered almost to himself. Behind him the pipe-music on the cliff top rose and fell. "We are entering a new age, and new circumstances."

"Master Lay Rann, the minstrel, used to say a long speech written by Master Shakespeare in London," one of the boatmen remarked, leaning on his oars and staring at the wrecks. "Something about how a man must live through seven ages, from the time he first pulls at his nurse's paps, till the day they lay him in his shroud. If it is so of a clan, why then, I reckon we have still a way to go."

"Whether seven ages, or only three, I do not know," Rory answered slowly. "Those are the magical divisions – three and seven - of which my grandfather used to speak, and which our folk tales and our old songs have. But I reckon I have no magic in my bones. It seems to me, if a man uses his mind to the best he can, and keeps his body healthy and his heart awake, and honours God, some power will protect him still – whatever it be."

He had no sooner spoken than he remembered the occasion long ago when, as a young man and not yet a chief, he had stood in the bow of Torquil Dubh's galley in Loch Snizort, talking with Hugh de Lérins, and expressed himself in almost the selfsame way.

"Have I learned nothing then, in all the years?" he asked himself. "That was all I knew then, and in spite of everything I have experienced, that is all I know this day."

"Listen, that is Ian Mor piping up there," Mairi said suddenly, with a rueful face. "Draw off a bit, Donnie, and we will look up and see him on the Walk."

The boatman pulled obediently away from the shore, and turned their craft so that Rory and Mairi could stare upward to the top of the great sheer cliffs, and just distinguish, faintly, the tall figure of Ian Mor, walking slowly along the cliff edge with his tartan blowing back against his bare legs.

"Yes, he is right, he will never make a good piper," the blunt old boatman said, grinning and shaking his head. "Och, Donald Mor would turn in his grave to hear him."

"He has other qualities," Sir Rory Mor replied almost sternly. "He will be a good chief."

"That is not the same as being a good piper, begging your pardon, sir," Donnie answered argumentatively. Then seeing the strange and distant look on Sir Rory's face, he closed his mouth again.

"I wish Hugh were with us still," Rory said softly, turning to look into his cousin Mairi's face. "And poor Iain. He and Iain MacIain, and you – all three sustained me, with your magical thoughts and your strange mystical understanding. And the music that was in you and Hugh, and the prayer that was in Iain, are all, I think, something of the same nature, in the end. You were the same as my old grandfather at Rodel. As though your hearts were all a part of his – cast by him into the future, for the Clan's sake, and for me. I wonder, have I fulfilled all that was required of me, and of the Clan MacLeod in this age?"

Through his fatigue a sense of strangeness filled him, as though an unused door half-opened in his being. He looked into the lined old face of Mairi and saw her smiling and nodding gravely at him. It seemed to him that if he could lengthen the moment and prolong it, he would understand the nature of all life on earth, and of himself. He struggled, but all he could see was an old, imagined picture of the Fairy Flag, streaming outward in the wind on the hilltop, and old Vic Mhurichie's face upturned in awe towards it.

In a moment as the sound of Ian Mor's unskilled piping was blended with noise and laughter up on the cliff top, and the little boat turned lightly on the current and faced the north again, the tension broke in him, and the inner door swung shut.

"Now, is that not young Padruig?" Donnie said after a moment, as a clear and long note sounded up above. "Yes, there he stands. They are all silent to hear him. Och, a sweet piper, sir, like his old father and his grandfather. Yes, that is Padruig og MacCrimmon right enough."

"But listen to what he is playing" Mairi exclaimed "No more laments. It is his father's strathspey called *I got a kiss of the King's hand*! The mood up there has changed from grief to cheerfulness already. Ah, they are young!"

Rory looked upwards at the slight figure standing there, his face turned seaward, his light hair touched by moonlight, his eyes seeming to follow the last slow passage of the burned out galleys as though he looked to the legendary Isle of Tir n'an Og, the Land of Eternal youth, far out in the Western Sea.

"I understand so little," Sir Rory Mor said very softly, against the clear and so familiar sound of the bagpipes. "I see only that we must move onwards through uncharted seas. The island clans are no longer like the wild colts in the spring grasses, young and careless and free. We too must leave behind us the wild lawlessness of youth, broken to the bridle and the bit, and move onwards into the necessary bondage of maturity."

END

HISTORICAL NOTES

Sir Rory Mor died suddenly on his business visit to Fortrose in 1626, and is buried in the now ruined Cathedral there. His brother Alexander lies beside him. A later chief is buried elsewhere in the ruins.

Mairi MacLeod the poet was the first poet to discard the traditional complicated Gaelic rhythms and was therefore the pioneer of modern Scottish poetry. She never married. She did not learn to read or write. In her old age she walked with a silver topped walking stick and became "addicted to snuff and gossip." By tradition she died at 105 years of age.

Dun Kenneth the seer seems to have lived at the same time as Rory Mor. A lengthy prediction of his about the future of the clan MacLeod came true in every detail 200 years later. However there is no evidence that he was ever in the castle itself. He lived in a cottage with his mother, clutched his black stone when looking into the future, and eventually died and was buried in a locally known grave.

The remains of the Fairy Flag, now very frail and faded, hangs in the drawing room at Dunvegan Castle. It is thought to be Oriental, but nothing is really known of its origin.

The course of events in this book is based on historical records and documents. The many legends of the clans of Skye have been taken into consideration, so that there is no contradiction with the traditional versions of characters and events. The documents and letters quoted are from the original; or where the original has been lost, I have kept to the traditional contents.

Where there are conflicting versions of events, I have chosen the one most suitable to the progress of my story. For instance, the date of the Battle of the Broken Wall and the burning of Trumpan church is variously given between 1520 and 1580. It has suited my purpose to place it in mid-century. Alasdair Crottach's tomb at Rodel is dated 1528, but local legend says he had it made thirty years before his death. Sir Rory Mor's date of birth is unknown. Legends insist that in his extreme youth he was taught by his grandfather, although this is not substantiated by documentary evidence. I have therefore assumed Alasdair Crottach's life in retirement at Rodel to have been quite lengthy, and have imagined his death somewhat later than some of the histories suggest. Mairi Nighean Alasdair Ruadh MacLeod is often spoken of as being born much later than Sir Rory Mor, but her song, "You who have been to minstrels as their homecoming" is traditionally about him; and so I have imagined that she cannot have been of a younger generation altogether. However some think her poem "Rory, Rare one" is about Rory Mor's son Roderick of Talisker. Evidence does suggest that she was younger than Sir Rory Mor, and I have therefore allowed myself a small deviation from strict truth in this one instance.

Alasdair Crottach's character seems to have been a complex one. He was known for his prowess and ferocity in battle and for feats of arms, in spite of the humped back caused by MacDonald's battle axe in his youth, and the Massacre of Eigg is historically attributed to him. In mitigation, island legend records his hours of prayer before the lighting of the fire outside the cave, and his attempts to get "a sign from God." Nothing is left of the monastery at Rodel, except the old church on the hillside, with Alasdair Crottach's tomb in it, and I found no indication of what monastic order was followed there. The idea that he might have tried to revert to the old Celtic order of St Columba is my own. No documentary evidence remains that I know of. His Gaelic translation of the psalms did not survive for posterity. The tomb is carved exactly as I have described.

Sir Rory Mor's life, his dealings with King James VI of Scotland and I[st] of England, and his efforts and activities on behalf of the Hebrides are known in some detail, and all suggest a strong and lively character with an astute mind, ahead of his time in many ways. I have adhered fairly scrupulously to the records, but it has sometimes been necessary to "telescope" events. For instance, the fracas with Sir Robert MacKenzie of Kintail in the King's presence probably did not take place on the same occasion as the signing of the General Band. Similarly, the unscrupulous kidnapping of the chiefs by the Royal Commissioners did not take place during the Iona conference, but probably was the previous year after a preliminary conference at Aros in Mull, when the Statutes were first drawn up. The hanging of Neil MacLeod also took place on a somewhat later occasion. Rory was held prisoner for twelve months for a misdemeanour but this was probably later. *Alexander was held under very harsh conditions in the Tolbooth at Edinburgh, when hostage for Rory. It seemed essential to shorten these long-drawn out events, while at the same time omitting nothing which had a bearing on the future.*

Many lesser characters in the story: such as Margaret, Sir Rory Mor's sister, who was the cause of the War of the One-Eyed Woman; Big Finlay of the White Plaid; the three chief MacCrimmon s of Borreraig College; Donald Gorme Mor, Kenneth Odhar – Dun Kenneth the seer - Torquil Dubh of the Lewis, Torquil Conanach, and a host of other historical or legendary people and details which may not be apparent to the reader, are substantiated by the records.

Sir Rory Mor's sideboard, which by tradition he brought from London – though some say from Edinburgh – is in the dining room at Dunvegan Castle to this day.

Iain MacIain and Hugh Whitby de Lérins are the only two characters who are entirely imaginary, though both have an ancestry based on known families and events.

The only major event which is imaginary is the burning of the galleys and birlinns at Dunvegan. Although the Statutes of Iona – sometimes called the Statutes of Icolmkill – required the fleets to be burned, there is no record of this being done. However, it seems clear that by the middle of the 17th century, the Hebrides had no independent fleets, and so I have allowed myself to imagine that Sir Rory Mor, who was undoubtedly the acknowledged leader of the chiefs in his later days, might have arranged affairs as I have described.

Duntulm Castle was abandoned after Donald Gorme Mor's death, and fell into ruin. His nephew and successor Donald Gorme Og, lived in Sleat.

The site of Borreraig College, where much of the great pipe music of Scotland was composed, is still paid for annually, the quit rent being "a penny and the playing of a piobroch". There is a cairn marking the site.

Dunvegan was never vacated by the MacLeods – even during the time of Sir Rory Mor's disgrace and outlawry. His direct descendant, Dame

Flora MacLeod of MacLeod, D.B.E., 28th chief, who died in 1974, was succeeded there by her grandson, John MacLeod of MacLeod 29th chief. He has a son and grandson.

The castle is open to the public.

BIBLIOGRAPHY

The MacLeods: The History of a Clan. Dr. I.F. Grant (Faber and Faber).

The MacLeods of Dunvegan. Canon R.C. MacLeod of MacLeod (The Clan MacLeod Society).

The Book of Dunvegan, (Two Vols.) (Privately printed by Third Spalding Club).

Tales of Dunvegan, Brenda MacLeod. (Eneas Mackay).
The Clan MacLeod. Dr I.F. Grant (Johnstons Clan Series).
Clan MacLeod, (Elms Publishing Company).

Official Guide to Dunvegan Castle, W. Douglas Simpson (Aberdeen University Press).

The History of Skye. Alexander Nicholson, (Maclaren).
Skye, The Island and its Legends. Otta Swire (Oxford University Press).
The Songs of Skye. B.H. Humble, (Eneas Mackay).

Seventeenth Century Skye. Brenda MacLeod. (printed by Northern Chronicle, Inverness).

The History of the Western Highlands and Isles of Scotland. Donald Gregory (Hamilton Adams).

A Description of the Western Isles of Scotland. Martin Martin. (Published 1703).

History of the Outer Hebrides. W.C. Mackenzie.
The Road to the Isles. Kenneth MacLeod. (A. and C. Black).

St Columba of Iona, Lucy Menzies. (Iona Community).
Celtic Sunrise. Diana Leathan, (Hodder and Stoughton).
Behold Iona. Edited by John Morrison. (Iona Community).
Iona Abbey (Iona Community).

Celt, Druid and Culdee. Isabel Hill Elder. (Covenant Publishing Co).
The English Religious Tradition. Normal Sykes.

Printed in the United Kingdom
by Lightning Source UK Ltd.
117524UKS00001B/38